ALL FALL DOWN

Jenny Oldfield

Thorndike Press • Chivers Press
Thorndike, Maine USA   Bath, England

This Large Print edition is published by Thorndike Press, USA and by Chivers Press, England.

Published in 1998 in the U.S. by arrangement with Macmillan Publishers Limited.

Published in 1998 in the U.K. by arrangement with Macmillan Publishers Ltd.

U.S. Hardcover   0-7862-1393-0   (Romance Series Edition)
U.K. Hardcover   0-7540-1165-8   (Windsor Large Print)
U.K. Softcover   0-7540-2120-3   (Paragon Large Print)

The text of this Large Print edition is unabridged.
Other aspects of the book may vary from the original edition.

Set in 16 pt. Plantin by Rick Gundberg.   583618

Printed in the United States on permanent paper.

British Library Cataloguing in Publication Data available

Library of Congress Cataloging in Publication Data

Oldfield, Jenny, 1949–
    All fall down / Jenny Oldfield.
      p. cm.
    ISBN 0-7862-1393-0 (lg. print : hc : alk. paper)
    1. Paradise Court (London, England : Imaginary place) — Fiction.   2. World War, 1939–1945 — England — London — Fiction.   3. Large type books.   [1. East End (London, England) — Fiction.]   I. Title.
    [PR6065.L37A79   1998]
    823'.914—dc21   98-11022

For my sister, Christine

PART ONE

Dark Days

September 1939

CHAPTER ONE

The wireless kept up its steady hum in the corner of the living room as Sadie sat in a shaft of sunlight on a perfect September morning. In her mind's eye she could see the slick crooner huddled over the microphone, oozing syrupy words to his lady love.

Sadie sighed and looked up from her mending. 'Bertie, turn that down, will you?'

'Ma!'

'Turn it down. I can't hear myself think.' She only had the wireless turned on for the Home Service News, not for the Cream in My Coffee, nor Tiptoeing Through the Tulips. She snipped her thread and examined the darned heel.

'You can't hear yourself think in any case,' came Bertie's smart reply.

'No, but you'll hear me box your ears soon enough.' She rolled the pair of grey woollen socks together and turned back one ribbed end to make a neat parcel, then she tossed it to Bertie to catch. 'Butterfingers.'

Geoff lunged across the table and grabbed the socks before his brother could. Bertie leapt to his feet. 'Give me them here.'

'Or else what?'

'Or else.'

Homework books scattered as the boys wrestled. At the opposite end of the table Meggie mustered all the dignity of her six-teen years. She wore her dark hair swept back from her forehead and hanging in a glossy roll to chin length. Her frock, printed with blue forget-me-nots and yellow daisies, with a neat white collar, was one of Sadie's more ambitious sewing efforts on a machine handed down by her sister, Hettie.

'How can I get any work done in this monkey house?'

Meggie was studying to be a telephone operator. With her nice voice and quick brain, the Post Office had taken her straight from school. Sadie had high hopes that she would one day make something of herself.

'You would if you went to your room.' Sadie held her temper.

'I don't see why I should. You could make them two shut up just as easy.'

Geoff and Bertie, faces red and shiny from their tussle, skidded the hearthrug against the polished fender.

'Here.' Walter stuck out a leg to stop them cannoning into his fireside chair. 'Good job there ain't no fire lit.' He went back to his paper, and the *Express*'s 'No War This Year Or Next' column.

Meggie closed her books and gave in with bad grace. 'You're no better than a pair of monkeys, you two.'

The boys hooted and cat-called after her. 'Miss High and Blooming Mighty, who's she think she is?'

'Vivien Leigh.'

'Deanna Durbin.'

'Dorothy Lamour.' Geoff shimmied across the room after her. Bertie pouted and made wet kissing sounds.

'Don't try coming into the kitchen, I'm going to wash my hair.' She slammed the door in their faces.

'Oo-er.'

'Friday Night is Amami Night!'

'That'll do, you two,' Sadie warned.

'Yes, let's have some hush.' Walter stood up to give the wireless a thump. The humming stopped, the valves crackled as he twiddled the tuning knob. In the short hush they realized the music had stopped, interrupted by the sonorous tones of the BBC announcer. It was just gone eleven o'clock on an unusually quiet Sunday down Paradise Court.

'What's he say?' Sadie left off darning a fresh pair of socks and let them drop in her lap. She could hope right until the last second that it wasn't what they feared, that the broadcast by the Prime Minister would bring relief from the worry about the shenanigans in Europe. She glanced at Walter for reassurance.

'Pipe down,' was all he said. He put his ear to the loudspeaker and went on twiddling the knob. 'It's Mr Chamberlain.'

Geoff and Bertie stopped fighting. The wireless whined and whistled. A thin voice came wavering over the airwaves, deadly serious. Germany had considered the British request to withdraw from Poland, but the Prime Minister confirmed the worst. 'I have to tell you that no such undertaking has been received and that consequently this country is at war with Germany.'

Amy Parsons sat in her kitchen, mouth open. 'Rob, did you hear?'

'I heard.' He pulled a hand down his face, dragging the tense skin.

'It's war after all.'

'I heard.'

'What about Bobby?'

'What about him?'

'Where is he?'

'Gone swimming with his mates.' The kids didn't stay huddled round the wireless, crisis or no crisis.

Amy started up. At just turned forty-three, she was bottle-blonde, solid and vigorous. No movement was tentative, no comment half-hearted when she was galvanized into action.

'Where you off to now?'

'To fetch him home. He never took his gas mask.' There it was hanging from its string in its cardboard box from the door hook. She flung her coat over her apron and took down the mask.

Rob flicked the butt of his cigarette into the grate. He stood up and stuck his head out of the window, checking the street below. Opposite, on the corner of the Court, stood the Duke of Wellington, doors firmly closed. No one hung about on the pavement outside Henshaws, or by the Co-op further down Duke Street. It seemed that the whole of Southwark was glued to the wireless set. In the distance he saw four or five kids come running.

'Keep your hair on, here he is now.' Rob eased back from the window ledge, satisfied that the sturdy figure to the fore was Bobby heading home hell for leather. It hadn't taken long for the news to get round. He saw with a shock which he only just managed to conceal that a barrage of air balloons was already rising silently into the clear blue sky like giant, ghostly whales.

'Oh, Rob!' Amy clutched the neck of her blouse and came to the window to watch. 'Bobby, you come up here.' Her voice broke the silence. 'Quick as you can, you hear. It's started. There's a war on. Come quick.'

Annie Parsons sat quietly with Ernie and Hettie, her grown-up stepchildren and George Mann, Hettie's husband, in an upstairs room at the Duke. She was old — 76 this year — but not daft; had been expecting this for months. None of this 'Peace in Our Time' malarky. If he'd still been alive, Duke would have agreed and said that Hitler was twisting them round his little finger. The Prime Minister with his rolled-up brolly, stepping off this aeroplane and that, never stood a chance. He sounded broken-hearted, poor man.

Now it was the turn of the King, broadcasting from Buckingham Palace, telling them what they already knew; that for the second time in the lives of most of them, Britain was at war, fighting for justice and liberty. 'For the sake of all that we ourselves hold dear and of the world's order and peace . . . high purpose . . . I ask them to stand calm, firm and united in this time of trial.

The task will be hard. There may be dark days ahead . . .'

'Ain't it horrible?' Hettie breathed.

'Well, we're ready for them.' George hid his own apprehension. The jackboot would never march across British soil as it had over half of Europe. He and Walter Davidson had already trained as air raid wardens, and though they were too old to be conscripted they were still strong and willing. The black-outs were in place, the air raid shelters built.

'Ready for what?' Hettie's eyes were wide with horror. She and George had no children to worry about, but she shook at the idea of bombs dropping on innocent heads, of all the young lives that would have to be sacrificed. Hettie was deeply religious; a sensitive, fine-looking woman of fifty, successful in her half of the dress-shop business she'd set up with her sister, Jess, always ready to count her blessings, not the least of which was steady, kind, unflappable George.

'For whatever they fling at us.' He put an arm around her shoulder.

'You watch, they'll close us down,' Annie warned. She'd read it in the newspaper; a proposed emergency measure to shut the pubs up and down the country.

'And if they do, they'll have a riot,'

George predicted. 'We'll be open again within the week.' He turned off the wireless with an abrupt twist of the wrist.

'Who'd have thought it?' Hettie felt marooned by the tide of events.

'Anyone with a grain of common sense,' Annie put in. Her pointed, lined face looked grim. 'They said the last one would end it all, but it's not in human nature.'

'And what should we do?' George tried to rouse Hettie. The first signs of total war, the barrage balloons, rose silently over the grey slate roofs. 'Let them walk all over us?'

'But are we sure he's as bad as they say?'

'Worse, I shouldn't wonder.'

'Who, Hitler?' Annie considered the rights and wrongs. 'Have you seen them Sieg Heiling?' The newsreels in the cinemas gave a graphic picture of marching armies. 'Maurice says it's very bad for the Jews.' Flickering black and white films showed a small man with a dark moustache, rousing the rabble to a frenzy of saluting and chanting. Sieg Heil, Sieg Heil.

Hettie drew a deep breath. 'What will Amy and Sadie do with the kids, do you think?'

'That's the ticket.' George knew she was pulling round if she could start to think of others. 'It'll be up to them. A lot have already been evacuated.'

'I can't think what Sadie will do without the boys.'

'Who says it'll come to that?' Annie shook herself, got up and straightened her skirt. 'You never know, now that we've stood up to him and shown him we mean business, maybe it'll knock some sense into him.' Poland was one thing; even Austria and Czechoslovakia, but Britain was another. Hitler would have to sit up and take notice now.

'And what about Meggie? Will she go too?' Over the last few days, Hettie had watched the women and children in their school gaberdines, little cardboard suitcases in hand, troop off towards the muster points, ready for shipping onto trains at Paddington. She imagined a thousand tearful farewells.

'Let's wait and see,' George advised, giving silent Ernie a cheerful pat on the shoulder.

Suddenly into the silence of Duke Street came an earsplitting wail. It rose from a deep groan, gained volume, whined overhead, penetrating the courts and alleys, putting an end to that eerie suspension of activity in the heart of London's East End.

'Air raid!' Amy, in the flat above the ironmongers' shop, shot a horrified glance at Rob. 'Shelter!' She turned to Bobby. 'Double-quick.'

Bobby looked to his father.

'You heard.' Rob limped to the door and handed him and Amy their gas masks. Once more, the whine of shells, their thud into soft earth the second before they exploded flashed through his mind.

'You and all.' As she slung the string around Bobby's neck and bundled him out of the door onto the landing, she turned back. 'Please, Rob!'

'You seen my fags?' He searched the mantelpiece and paused to rummage in a drawer.

'Rob!' The siren wailed on and on.

'Hold your horses.' People were running in the street towards the community shelter in Nelson Gardens, where a deep trench had been dug, covered with corrugated sheeting and earth, big enough to hold hundreds of people. No one round here had a garden with their own Anderson shelter; it was all tenements and courts. The nearest underground station, Borough, was too far to reach in time. 'I can't go till I got my fags.'

Amy rushed back into the room. The cigarettes were on the shelf by the wireless. 'Here.' She flung them at him.

'You go ahead.' Shoving them in his pocket, he pushed her on. Bobby was already waiting at the bottom of the stairs.

'No.'

'Yes. You know why.' He couldn't run fast with his artificial leg. He had to hobble sideways down the stairs.

'But, Rob.' Amy held onto Bobby by the arm. He resisted. Outside the door, men, women and children fled towards the shelter, hatless, without jackets or cardigans, some in their stockinged feet. The planes could come, the bombs drop any second.

'Go, will you!' He clung to the bannister and cursed.

'You'll come quick as you can?'

He nodded. 'I'll see you down there.'

Amy dragged Bobby to the street to be caught up in the rush of feet, the wail of the siren. She had never in her life felt so frightened; sick in her stomach, heart pounding as she kept her eyes to the ground and tried to close her ears to the drone of aeroplane engines, the thud and crash of German bombs in the streets she'd known and felt safe in all her life. Now a terrifying jumble of noises and the sound of panicking

19

feet echoed down Union Street under the clear blue sky.

'Well, at least we're in the final.' Tommy O'Hagan drew long and hard on one of Rob Parsons' Woodbines. In the dim light of the underground shelter watchful faces lined the benches and bunks, the men in waistcoats and caps, some in overalls, fresh from digging their allotments. Women hovered over their kids, wiped smudged faces with the corners of their aprons, smacked a bare leg, buttoned a cardigan.

'How come?' Tommy's youngest brother, Jimmie, who lived with Tommy and his wife, Dorothy, was puzzled by the sporting phrase.

'Well, Hitler knocked out the Austrians, didn't he? And the Sizzeks. Now the Poles. He beat the lot. I reckon that puts us in the final, don't it?' Tommy cut the crisis down to size. 'Did you get to the match yesterday, Rob? The real one, the one that counts.'

Rob shook his head. 'I was out earning a crust.'

That was another thing. War meant blackout. Blackout would keep people at home instead of hailing a taxi and going up the West End on a Friday night. It might even involve petrol rationing and then where would he and Walter end up? Out of business, that's where. The years of the Depression had kept their taxi business small and run on a hand-to-mouth basis. Early dreams of making good with a fleet of new cars and a team of drivers had faded. They got by, that was all. And as Rob had sunk into middle age he'd grown gaunt and sour; lost his spark was how Amy put it.

'You ain't nothing to write home about neither,' he reminded her.

'Tough, 'cos I'm all you've got.' She always held her own.

'Ted Drake scored four,' Tommy was telling him. 'There was twenty thousand through the gates. Great game.'

'Make the most of it.' Rob had heard through Walter that they planned to turn the stadium at Highbury into an ARP centre the minute war broke out and that would be the end of Saturday football for the foreseeable future. 'They say the whole team will volunteer and how many of them will come back in one piece?'

'Cheerful Charlie, ain't he?' Tommy was put off his stride. Nevertheless he winked at Jimmie.

'You'll see,' Rob warned. He wandered off to brood in a corner.

'Not in these trousiz.' Tommy shrugged.

'Archibald, certainly not!' Jimmie slung in his own wireless phrase. He shadow-boxed with his older brother. He was a skinny kid just like Tommy had been, in baggy grey flannel trousers and Fair Isle pullover, his grey shirt collar torn and frayed.

'For crying out loud,' Dorothy O'Hagan drawled. She sat, or rather perched nearby, on the ARP warden's table, legs crossed, wedge-heeled shoe dangling from her free foot. Her face, lost behind a cloud of cigarette smoke, was heavily made up. 'Can't you two put a sock in it?'

'And sit around like you with a face as long as a wet weekend?'

'Better than getting yourselves chucked out.'

'You won't chuck us out, will you, George?' Tommy offered the landlord, who was doubling as warden in his tin hat and official armband, one of his own cigarettes, a Churchmans.

'Try me.' George grinned at Jimmie. 'How do you fancy joining Walter on fire-watch up there?'

'Righto!' Jimmie would have been off like a shot if George hadn't restrained him.

Hettie raised a warning eyebrow and glanced at a worried-looking Sadie. They'd managed to get Bertie, Geoff and Meggie down the shelter without too much fuss, thanks in part to poor Ernie, who had it clearly in his head what to do if the siren went off. He was to find the boys at number 32 and march them promptly to Nelson Gardens. Though simple-minded, Ernie could be relied on to look after the boys, while Sadie and Meggie gathered clothes and blankets, turned off the gas inside the house and followed. It left Walter free to carry out his fire-watching duties and mop up stragglers or strangers caught off home turf. This was the theory and it had gone like clockwork on this fateful September midday. Still, Sadie looked worn down with anxiety.

'He'll be all right, you'll see.' Hettie went and sat with her. 'Your Walter's like a cat with nine lives.'

Sadie shivered. 'I don't know, Ett. It makes you feel like putting your head in the gas oven.'

'And what good would that do?'

'Save Hitler a job, that's all.' Annie sat nearby, green felt hat pinned firmly to her head, black jacket, bought as mourning wear for her husband, Duke, ten years before, buttoned tight under her chin. She sniffed and straightened her already straight back. 'In the last war they used to say Arthur

Ogden kept an old sword on the mantelpiece, just in case. He was going to slash any Jerry that came in.' Arthur, like Duke, was long gone, though his wife, Dolly, still soldiered on. 'Ain't that right?' Annie called across to her.

'Not a word of truth in it.' Dolly gave a hearty laugh. 'God rest his soul, he spent the whole time propping up the bar at your place, Annie, telling everyone what a hero he was.'

There was a decent pause in his memory, then George answered the ring on the telephone on his table. When he came off, it was to announce the all-clear. 'False alarm,' he told them. 'You can all go home.'

'About bleeding time.' They shuffled into the daylight, relieved and grumbling, threatening to bring their crosswords, their knitting, the latest Dashiell Hammett thriller next time.

'Let's hope there won't be one,' someone said without conviction.

'This Hitler, he was a painter and decorator wasn't he?' mused her neighbour, a heavy woman in a flowered overall. 'So's my old man . . . They're all the same . . .' Hitler, husband — what could you expect?

Hettie watched the frown ease from Sadie's face. She squeezed her hand.

'Ernie's got those boys of yours licked into shape.'

They watched as their brother, a kind of gentle giant with his stiff, forward-sloping, wide-legged walk, marched Bertie and Geoff into the fresh air. They went like lambs.

'Come on, Ma.' Meggie swished by in a flurry of forget-me-not blue, slim waist shown off by a wide white belt, slim legs and ankles seen to advantage in her soft white leather sandals. 'Else they'll shut the door and forget all about us.' She, Jimmie and Bobby went out into the autumn sunshine.

Sadie, Hettie and Annie followed more slowly. The world was the same; Nelson Gardens, Union Street, Duke Street with the new W. H. Smiths, Woolworths and Co-op. Yet it was all changed. The barrage balloons drifted overhead. A poster on a billboard told them they could be sure of Shell, next to one showing a horrible gas mask with the slogan, 'Hitler Will Send No Warning.' Three Nuns was a tobacco of curious cut, and the government drummed home their message in a picture of a smiling girl with a ribbon in her hair and a younger, gap-toothed brother, 'Mothers, Send Them out of London — Give them a chance of greater safety and health.'

Sadie stopped short beneath this poster, outside Tommy O'Hagan's smart shop selling wallpaper and household paints. The smiling girl troubled her.

'I'd rather be bombed in my own home any day than live that awful country life,' Annie said, chin up, eyes glittering. Then she relented. 'Mind, it's not the same for everyone, I grant you that.' She would sorely miss her step-grandchildren, but she would back any decision Sadie made, or Amy, for that matter. 'I'm only saying I went to Hove last Whit and I couldn't get home quick enough.'

Hettie smiled. 'Talk to Walter,' she said to Sadie. 'Between you, you'll decide what's best.'

Throughout that day, with the wireless playing solemn music, East Enders made their final preparations for war.

At The Duke, George Mann took timber and nails and made blackout frames for all the pub windows according to instructions issued by the government. He made do with brown paper pinned across the frames until they could buy up a job lot of black calico from Amy's haberdashery stall. There'd been a run on any kind of heavy material the week before. In a surge of public spiritedness Hettie posted up First Aid Briefs on the inside doors of both public and lounge bars. She read one out to Ernie, who was busy with mop and bucket on the front step.

'Got that, Ern?'

'Tell me it again.' Methodical with his mop, he went into every nook and cranny.

'It says to read the instructions carefully several times and to carry a copy in your pocket or bag.' There'd be no point in this as far as Ernie was concerned. She wanted to get it into his head and make it stick. 'You have to keep calm if you find anyone injured after one of these air raids. You've to carry clean handkerchiefs. It says to be prepared to see severe wounds.' She paused as Ernie's mop stopped short. He hated the sight of blood; always had, ever since Daisy O'Hagan's terrible murder years before. His mind would go blank and he would shut out the reality. This was one of Hettie's main worries about how the family would cope in the months to come; what if Ernie got caught in an air raid and panicked? 'Never you mind,' she said gently. 'You just get yourself to Nelson Gardens quick as you can.'

Ernie's mop began to move to and fro over the patterned tiles in the hallway. 'To the shelter with Bertie and Geoff,' he reminded himself.

'If they're still in the Court, yes. You fetch them and make sure they're safe.'

'Why, where else will they be?' He tried to cover the alarm in his voice.

'We don't know yet, Ern. Sadie and Walter might send them to the country.'

He took this in as Annie came downstairs and eyed the first aid instructions. 'Bleeding morbid!' she said through clenched teeth, though she herself had just spent half an hour packing away valuables in a tin chest that she could be sure wouldn't burn in a fire, should the worst come to the worst. On the top she'd laid a photograph of Duke in a silver frame and she'd promised his fading image that she'd do her best to keep the old place going, through thick and thin, to keep the family together and not let anyone go under; not Sadie who was filled with dread for the kiddies, nor poor Ernie, nor Rob, nor Hettie, nor Frances down in Walworth, nor Jess up in Manchester with Maurice, Grace and little Mo.

CHAPTER TWO

'The worst of it is, we don't know where they'd get sent.'

Later that evening, Walter tried to come to terms with the idea of evacuating the boys to safety. Bertie and Geoff were already in bed, while Meggie sat at the table with her books. Sadie walked restlessly from window to fireplace and back again.

'Right. We just pack them off at Paddington. They could end up anywhere.' Wearing a label; Robert Davidson, 9 years, 32 Paradise Court, Southwark. Geoffrey Davidson, 7 years. Ditto. 'They might not even get the same billet.'

'No, but Meggie could go and keep an eye on things.'

She heard her name mentioned, looked up sharply, but kept quiet.

'Yes, and she could be in Kent, and they could be in Cornwall for all we know.'

'They say it's for the best.' Walter fell silent.

The picture of their two boys, joining hundreds of thousands of other children in the exodus from London frightened them beyond words. Thousands of buses and trains crawling out of the capital to unknown destinations. Strange faces to greet them, strange bedrooms to sleep in. And what if they should never see them again?

'Maybe just for the time being?' Meggie suggested a way out. 'It doesn't have to be for long, just until we see how things work out here.' She knew of other families, friends at the post office, who'd waved their kids a cheerful farewell over these last few days. By all accounts, the young ones went off in high spirits, treating the whole thing as an adventure. 'Or maybe you could go with them, Ma?'

Sadie shook her head. 'I'm needed here.' She'd signed up for munitions work and, anyway, she wouldn't leave Walter. 'I can't be in two places at once.' She stopped by the window, looking out at an orange sky flecked with golden clouds and at the ominous, silent balloons. 'Do you think they'd actually do it?' Her voice trembled. 'Actually drop those bombs on innocent kiddies?'

Walter joined her. In the past he'd always been the one to comfort and support. He wanted to be kind, but the truth stared him in the face. 'Everyone says they will, Sadie. I don't think we can risk it.'

breasted, brown pin-stripe suit and fawn
with a snappy brim. After all, he h
image to keep up.

'Where d'you hear that one,

'On the bleeding wireless?'

"Can I do you now, sir

"I don't mind if I d

Smart responses cli

smoky atmosphere

from the bar a

served steadil

'I heard

know.'

toe. H

am

was bursting at the seams with dockers, railway workers and tradesmen each determined to show that Adolf couldn't keep a man away from his pint. Nevertheless, not one had ventured out minus his gas mask, already dubbed 'nose-bag', 'dickey-bird', or even 'Hitler'. They slung them with careless bravado across their chests, the old men in white mufflers and collarless shirts, the younger in up-to-date trilbies and flashy silk ties. Tommy fell into the fashionable category in a double-

.at
.d an

. ommy?'

?" '

.!" '

.ked to and fro in the
. Annie swiped glasses
.d wiped it clean, George
.y.
.t from our Jimmie, if you must
. ommy tapped the bar rail with his
.e'd noticed a crowd of girls come in,
.ong them a couple from his own shop.
He picked out Edie Morell, in charge of
wages and accounts. She was all dressed up,
with her honey-blonde hair piled high on
her head, her dress tight over the bodice,
falling in a bright swirl of tropical flowers
to her knees.

'You don't say,' said Charlie Ogden. He
was home for the weekend from his teaching
job in Welwyn Garden City, and miserable
as sin according to his mother, Dolly. He
and his wife of ten years had just decided
to split up, and he planned to move out of
his nice semi-detached house back into
Paradise Court to live with her.

'Get it, Charlie? Course, it's the poor old

Tommy's hand she shoves away, not the pilot's. They don't get a look-in with the RAF around.' Tommy made room for the girls at the bar. Edie had recently palled up with her old school chums, since her husband, Bill, had enlisted, and they went about pretty much as they had in the good old days. Lorna Bennett in particular was regarded as fast, in her hip-hugging slacks and tight jumpers, with a striking dark pencil outline around her eyes and a bright crimson mouth. 'What's it to be, girls?' He offered to buy them a round. 'Something strong to steady your nerves?'

Lorna and the two others made a great show of deciding what they wanted to drink, while Edie quietly accepted a pale ale.

'Whisky for me, please.' Lorna dug her friend with her elbow. 'What's up? He's made of money, ain't he?'

'More money than sense, if you ask me.' Annie came to give George a hand. She didn't approve of these good-time girls. In her day the market women would come in for a drink after work, but their old men would be snug in another corner, not away fighting a war. She thought the young ones lacked respect.

'Have one yourself, Annie.' Tommy's offer was guaranteed to shut her up. 'You're looking like a million dollars tonight, you know that?'

She grunted. She kept to the style of her youth; long hair, now pure white and lifted into a bun, nice crisp blouse with pleats and tucks, navy-blue skirt of decent length. She would sometimes add bits of costume jewellery for a touch of colour, and she was always beautifully starched and ironed. 'Flattery won't get you nowhere with me, Tommy O'Hagan. That'll be three shillings and threepence to you.'

'Two and six to anyone else.' Lorna took her drink and laughed.

Not minding a bit, Tommy bantered for a minute or two before drawing up a stool alongside Edie. 'What's new?' He leaned in close and offered her a light for her cigarette.

'A war, that's what's new.'

'Apart from that.' He was determined to stay cheerful.

'I had a letter from Bill yesterday. His ship's off to Malta.'

'But he'd get home beforehand, I expect?' Tommy knew that Bill often showed up on forty-eight-hour leave. He could always tell when it happened; Edie would come into work on a Monday quieter than usual. Apparently she missed him badly when he went back to barracks.

34

'I don't know that he will, not now.'

'Still, chin up. You know what they say, it'd all be over by Christmas.'

'Yes, Christmas 1942,' she said mournfully.

'But life goes on, don't it?' It was all very well for him to say this, he realized. At forty he was well past the age of conscription and he could expect to go on pretty much as usual, not minding too much what he read in the newspapers, Hitler-this and Hitler-that, sticking to Radio Luxembourg rather than the stuffy Home Service. He even expected to turn a fast penny because of the war, as you could when certain goods were in short supply and you were well in with the dockers and the market men. He felt sorry for Edie; her husband was of fighting age and, though they'd been married for five years, they had no children. She must be lonely in her Duke Street flat.

'You're right.' She gave him a smile, then sighed as she stubbed out her cigarette. 'I never used to smoke. I hate the smell it leaves behind, if you must know.'

'You smell fine to me.' She did; it was the scent she wore. It smelt of roses or something similar. A lot of things about Edie reminded him of sweet flowers. Even at work he found it hard to forget that she was a beautiful woman, with her clear, grey eyes, straight nose, soft skin.

Edie blushed.

'Here, Edie, it's your shout,' Lorna held up her empty glass from her table by the window. 'We'll have one more here, then what do you say we head up West to a dance hall?'

She smiled at Tommy and stood up. 'Thanks for the drink. See you tomorrow.'

'Business as usual,' he promised, narrowing his eyes as the smoke curled up from his own cigarette. 'Don't stop out too late, there's a good girl.' He overheard them discussing options; Joe Loss or Henry Hall, waltz or foxtrot, falling over themselves to be asked to dance by an RAF officer in a smart airforce-blue uniform.

As for himself, old codger that he was, it was time for an early night. He left the Duke, expecting to find only Jimmie at home above the shop. Dorothy was in the habit of going out to amuse herself at one of the more local hops, often only a pub room where the carpet was pulled back to make space for the dancers. There would be a gramophone in the corner, a jitterbug record or a soupy Bing Crosby number, and no shortage of couples crowding onto the bare boards.

He walked along the street between the new electric lamps, past the usual cars parked at the kerbside, the Baby Austins and the Morris Minors. There was a milk bar now, on the corner opposite Henshaws, all glass and chromium steel, with pink neon lights.

He caught his reflection in the window, a dapper figure with a lined and shadowed face. It was the harsh light, he told himself, flinging his cigarette stub into the gutter. It made him look mean. When he came to his own expanse of plate glass, tastefully laid out with paint and wallpaper, dotted and striped matching curtain fabric, parchment lamps for the living room, white enamel fittings for the bathroom, with its own brightly lit sign reading *Ideal Home*, he gave a cynical shrug. Turning the key in the lock of the private entrance, he slammed the door behind him and went upstairs.

To his surprise he found no sign of his kid brother, but Dorothy sitting in a chair looking out-of-sorts. She was wearing a dressing-gown pulled tight across her chest, no make-up, and her blonde hair was scraped back from her face.

'Where's Jim?' He dropped his hat on the sideboard.

'How should I know?'

37

By which she meant, why should I care? Many of their rows these days were to do with them taking in Jimmie after his mother, Mary, died six years earlier. Jimmie had been only eleven at the time. Before that, Dorothy's gripes had been all about the money he spent on keeping his mother comfortable and happy in the old tenement down the Court. Since then, the objections over Jimmie poured out almost daily.

'We need to keep an eye on him now there's a war on. We don't want him nicking off without telling us where.'

'*You'd* better keep an eye on him, you mean.' She took a cigarette from the pack on the arm of her chair and lit it with a fancy silver lighter.

'Fair enough.'

'And don't leave that jacket slung on that chair.'

'Fair enough,' he repeated nastily. It made no difference that he would find her clothes on the floor of the bedroom, her pots of make-up and lipsticks open on the dressing-table. He'd stopped arguing, but he couldn't disguise his tone of voice.

'Anyhow, I can't see how you expect Jimmie to behave himself, the way you carry on. You never tell anyone what you're up to, do you?'

'Must run in the family, then.'

'Well, do you?'

'That's 'cos I never get up to anything. I work too bleeding hard, keeping you in nylon stockings. I'm always in the bleeding shop.'

'Or at the Duke.'

'Can't a man have a drink?' He was weary, sick of it; the well-worn track of their bickering. They would soon come full circle, he knew. So he went for the whisky bottle in the sideboard, which was also part of the routine.

'One drink or ten?'

'As many as I like.'

'And treat the whole pub while you're at it.'

He shrugged, knocked back the drink and felt it burn his throat.

'I know your game. Buy a round, tell a few jokes, good old Tommy O'Hagan. Then come staggering home, fit for nothing.'

'I'm not staggering, am I? Look, can you see me stagger?' He went up close to her chair, while she made a show of shrinking back in disgust.

'No wonder I don't like to be here.' She pushed him away.

'That's right, you go off and enjoy yourself.' He walked away, keeping his back to her. 'Get your glad rags on, why don't you? You've still got time if you're quick.'

But Dorothy let the challenge drop. She sat drooped forward, lethargic and bitter. Minus her make-up and smart clothes, and without the fire of resentment fully stoked, she looked all of her forty-five years. Her eyes seemed to be growing smaller, there were lines underneath them and a downturn to her once full and attractive mouth. Her figure too was slackening, though her legs were still good. Sometimes Tommy would find her in front of the bathroom mirror, examining herself from every angle, obviously angry at what she saw. He glanced over his shoulder and felt an unexpected pang of sympathy, which he warded off by going for his jacket.

'Where are you off to now?' Involuntarily she grasped the arms of her chair.

'To fetch Jim, why?' A thought struck him. Was she scared now that it was dark? Planes could come more easily under the cover of darkness and drop their terrible cargo; it stood to reason.

'Yes, of course, to fetch Jimmie!' She made it plain that she didn't believe a word.

'Look, I am, right? I want him here to talk through what to do in one of these air raids one more time. Knowing him, he won't bother with his gas mask or nothing. He needs to get his head screwed on, so we don't have to worry.'

'That's right, worry about him, why don't you?' She threw the jibe at him, which might have been genuine jealousy once; her feeling left out because of the attention he gave to his kid brother. But now this was just another well-worn groove. Since this was a bad day, however, a day that would transform all their lives, he made an effort.

He went across again and crouched beside her. 'I worry about you as well, you know that. I don't want nothing to happen to you neither.'

She looked at him with disbelieving eyes. 'Sure?'

'Sure I'm sure.'

'Sometimes I think you want me dead and out of the way.'

'Well, I don't.' He leaned forward and kissed her on the cheek. 'All right?'

'Sometimes I think to myself I wouldn't mind if *I* was dead.' Her eyes filled up, her voice choked.

'Yes you would, Dot. You've got a lot going for you if you did but know it. Nice place to live, no money worries, freedom to come and go.' That's what she'd said she wanted when she married him.

'*We've* got a lot going for us.'

She reached out and pulled his head towards her, kissing him greedily.

After a bit, he settled her back in the chair, stroking her cheek. 'All right?'

She nodded.

'Now I gotta go and find that bleeding kid.' He stood up.

She tugged at his hand, but she knew when not to push her luck. Or maybe she didn't want him enough to protest any more. Instead she let his hand drop and went for the packet of cigarettes.

Tommy left quietly. Jimmie might be round at the Davidsons' place, chatting with Meggie, or he could be holed up somewhere less salubrious with his gang of mates, hanging round outside the skittle alley on Union Street, or in a dodgy pub. One thing he was sure of; by the time he found him and hauled him back home, Dorothy would have dragged herself off to bed and be fast asleep.

The day after war broke out, Sadie let Annie and the rest of the family know that they had decided to send the boys out of London. This coincided with many other families in the Court making the same decision, and by the day after, the Tuesday, thirteen local children were prepared, suitcases packed, gas masks at the ready, to join Operation Pied Piper.

'You know you're doing the right thing,' Hettie assured Sadie. They'd arranged a send-off from the Duke, where Annie would say goodbye to her grandchildren.

'If they were just that bit older . . .' Still Sadie agonized. 'If only I knew they could take care of themselves.'

'Then they'd want to stay, like Meggie, and you wouldn't get a say in it.' Hettie knew that Meggie had turned a deaf ear to all entreaties for her to leave town.

'Or if I could be sure they'd get somewhere nice . . .' She'd heard that some country families only offered billets for the sake of the eight and sixpence a week. Some didn't even want the kids that were landed on them.

'It ain't a holiday camp,' Annie told her. 'And beggars can't be choosers.' She'd packed two carrier bags full of bully-beef, condensed milk and biscuits, little treats they could eat on the way or hand over to their new families. 'What we can be sure of is these boys know how to behave. They won't show us up.'

She went and brushed Geoff's hair back from his forehead. He submitted, then ruffled it forward as soon as her back was turned.

'Where's Walter got to?' Sadie stood in her fawn coat, a nicely patterned rayon scarf tied at her throat, her dark hair fashionably pinned back. She wanted the boys to be proud of their mother as she stood in the crowd on the station platform waving them off.

'It's too early.' Hettie went and looked down the street. She spied an upright, spruce figure heading their way, crossing the street from the pillar box opposite. 'Here's Frances come to say goodbye.'

Their oldest sister had promised to take the morning off from her work dispensing prescriptions at the chemist. The whole family wanted to back Sadie's difficult choice; after all, the government, the newspapers, everyone, was telling mothers to be brave and self-sacrificing.

As she'd made her way by bus from Walworth to Southwark, Frances saw how many families had taken the advice to heart. Hundreds of small children sat trussed up in as many clothes as they could get on their backs, nursing their suitcases, looking expectantly down from the top decks for the first sight of trains that would carry them far away. She came in now, brisk but kind, with gifts of chocolate and comics.

Geoff rushed to rip open the silver paper of his chocolate bar and cram the contents into his mouth.

'Save it for later,' Frances told him, slipping it quietly into his carrier bag. She was his godmother, not nearly so stern with him as might have been expected of a childless woman in her fifties. In fact, she spoiled him. Annie said so, 'Frances is going soft in her old age.' A charge that she was sure could never be levelled against his grandma.

'I just saw Rob's taxi at the top of Duke Street.' Frances unbuttoned the jacket of her tailored two-piece suit. It was grey and trimmed with rich brown fur. 'He said to say cheerio from him, Amy and Bobby, and to give the boys half a crown apiece.' She gave the coins to Sadie to hand on, then she turned her attention back to her nephews. 'Now, Bertie, you're to look after Geoff and make sure he doesn't get lost. And you're to write to your ma and pa the minute you get safely stowed.'

Bertie took his responsibility gravely.

'Do you have pen and paper?'

He nodded.

'Well, here's half a dozen first-class stamps. Make sure Geoff writes what he can as well. We'll all be waiting to hear how you settle in.' She tucked the stamps into an envelope and slid it into his gaberdine pocket. 'And remember, work hard and do well at school.'

'School?' Geoff echoed, standing beside his big brother.

'Yes, there'd be a school in your new village, didn't you know?'

He shook his head.

'Well, there will be. And you must be a good boy, Geoff.'

'With a new teacher?'

'A new teacher and a new classroom. Everything will be new.'

'What'll happen to my old school?'

'They'd close that down, I expect. Just for a bit, till the war ends. Don't you worry, you can come back home and go to the same school again just as soon as it's safe.' She squeezed his shoulder and smiled at him.

But Geoff's fancy took an unexpected turn. 'If I stayed here and they closed my school, that means I needn't go no more!' The idea appealed. He began to rev his lips, like an engine starting, then spread his arms like aeroplane wings. 'No school, nee-yah!' He swooped across the room. 'Nee-yah, nee-yah, pow! I'm the RAF!' He banked and curved back towards Frances.

'And I'm your commanding officer.' She put out an arm to ground him. 'And I say it's a new school for you, Corporal Davidson. The RAF doesn't take boys who can't read and write, you know.'

Reluctantly he agreed for his wings to be temporarily clipped as Walter came racing upstairs two at a time.

'The cab's outside, I left the engine running,' he told them. 'Give me the cases, Bertie, there's a good boy. Come on, Sadie.' He didn't want them to linger over fond goodbyes.

Frances gave each boy one last hug and handed them on to Hettie, who pushed them finally into Annie's arms. The ordeal over, Bertie and Geoff shot downstairs.

'You sure you got everything?' Annie dashed away a tear. Sadie nodded. 'Off you go then. And don't make a meal of it when you get them on that train. You mind you see them off nice and bright.' She sent them on their way, then joined Frances and Hettie at the window.

Walter's black cab drew away from the kerb and joined the flow of traffic heading north, across Blackfriars Bridge, along the Embankment, cutting across the top of St James's Park towards Paddington.

CHAPTER THREE

As the Indian summer gave way to October winds that stripped the park trees bare, Dorothy O'Hagan was among the many women who got over their initial fright on the day war broke out and soon resumed their everyday concerns. For some it was coping with increasing food shortages as the flow of goods through the docks dried up. Housewives ran out of sugar and had to beg or borrow, giving rough treatment to the women in fur coats who drove over from the West End with their chauffeurs to buy up remaining stocks. They sent them packing, with fleas in their ears, as they themselves joined the lengthening queues for butter and eggs.

For Dorothy, however, protected from hardship by Tommy's good connections in the docks, her preoccupation was what to wear at night, in case the sirens should sound and they were to find themselves over in Nelson Gardens for the duration. She took to going to bed in her underthings, wearing her best rayon slip, with dress, coat and shoes at the ready. Her bag was packed with comb, lipstick and vanity mirror, where others might take a torch and the latest issue of *Woman's Weekly*. During her daytime routine of occasionally serving in the shop or, more likely, flitting round to her friends' houses to listen to gramophone records and discuss the latest Fred Astaire film, she would wear a chic little black saucer-shaped hat with a small veil, a deep purple two-piece in soft wool, nipped in at the waist, black fishnet cotton gloves and a pair of high, shiny, open-toed shoes.

Barrage balloons looming overhead could soon be ignored and even the wail of the siren came to hold less of a threat, as time after time the warning proved to be a false alarm. It was a case of crying wolf too often for people to take much notice, even of the shout of, 'Put that light out!' from an irate warden, or of the fifty-pound fine threatened against careless talk. Cartoons of Hitler with his little toothbrush 'tache and slicked-back hair further boosted their confidence. That they would soon be hanging out their washing on the Siegfried Line, as the song boasted, no one doubted.

By November, Tommy was beginning to suspect that Dot was actually thriving on wartime conditions. She'd fallen for the line that life, what there was left of it, was for the living. She went out to the proper dance-halls once Lorna Bennett had cottoned onto the fact that she could easily be persuaded to stand the younger women their entrance money to the Paramount, or even the Windmill. She came home long after the official eleven o'clock closure time, humming a Mantovani waltz or, more irritatingly, a sentimental number by Gracie Fields about sending a letter to Santa Claus, 'to send back my Daddy to me.' In reality, she never took a blind bit of notice of the people suffering around her, or of him and Jimmie under her nose.

One night Jimmie came home from a day's casual work on the docks and proudly dumped his gas mask on the kitchen table.

'What's this?' Dorothy frowned and poked at it with her long fingernail.

'Open it and see.'

'What would I want with your horrible nose-bag?' Still, she lifted the lid in case the contents were worth having.

'Go on, lift it out.' Jimmie winked at Tommy.

She hooked her finger round the rubber strap, slowly drawing it out. The mask held something slimy and heavy. Blood dripped from the glass eye sockets. Dorothy screamed and dropped it. 'What the hell's that?'

'Frozen pigs' hearts. I smuggled them through. Make a tasty supper with them, you can.'

'Dirty beast. Dirty, filthy little animal!' She turned on Tommy. 'See what he's done?' Blood trickled onto the tablecloth. 'He's done it on purpose.'

'For God's sake,' Tommy muttered at her and swept the meat away. He chucked it straight in the bin.

'What the — ? Other people would give their eye-teeth for that.' Jimmie genuinely hadn't reckoned on her reaction.

'Well, I wouldn't. And don't you never do nothing like that to me again, you hear?'

'Why, what did I do?'

She ignored the question. 'You'll be out on your ear if you do. You ain't fit to live in a decent house.' Her face grew savage and contorted.

At last Jimmie took offense. 'You can stick your decent house,' he shouted back and swiped the gas mask onto the floor. The glass splintered as it spun against her feet. He seized his work jacket and pulled it roughly back on.

'Where you off to now?' Tommy tried to stand in his way, half thinking it was best to let Jimmie go and give him a chance to cool down.

'Out.' He shoved past. 'And you can ask her what she thinks she's doing in a decent house herself. From what I heard, she don't belong in one neither!'

Slamming the door, he left Tommy face to face with Dorothy and raced off to Bobby Parsons' place to see if he would help drag Meggie away from her telephonist books up to the Astoria, where they could forget their cares amidst the lush carpets and padded seats, to the strains of the Wurlitzer, into a silver-screen world of white tie and tails.

Clark Gable had done his bit with 'Frankly, my dear . . .' and reduced Scarlett O'Hara to pouting silence for once, when the sirens started up and the manager quickly appeared on-stage. He apologized for the interruption. 'Please feel free to come back afterwards,' he said cheerfully, 'once we get the all-clear.'

There was no panic as the audience filed out, Meggie, Jimmie and Bobby among them. They made for the nearest shelter at Tottenham Court Road, crowding down the escalators onto the platforms; the first time that the three had sought refuge in an Underground station.

'Here, no need to shove,' Bobby protested, knocked aside in the race for a comfortable bunk. Built in his father's mould, with a boxer's physique, but with his mother's light blonde hair, he grabbed hold of the culprit; a dirty tramp wrapped in a grey blanket, unshaven and probably riddled with lice. Squeamishly Bobby backed off. The tramp spat and climbed up to a top bunk.

'Leave him be,' Meggie said uneasily, suddenly aware of the sprinkling of down-and-outs amongst the theatre-goers and the more well-to-do.

'You're right, he ain't worth bothering with.' Bobby affected nonchalance, hands in pockets. 'Might catch something off him if you go too near.'

'It ain't that.' The surge of the crowd carried them on. They left the spitting tramp behind, but had to step over two more already asleep on the floor. Instinctively Meggie held her breath.

'What you looking at?' One of the tramps opened his eyes a fraction and snarled at her.

Hurriedly she turned and caught up with the others.

'You all right? You ain't shaking, are you?' Jimmie waited. 'What did he say?'

Beside the heavyweight Bobby, Jimmie was something of a flyweight. His readiness to square up to the half asleep bag of bones made her smile. 'He ain't said nothing, Jimmie. It's just me.'

They found an unoccupied corner at the far end of the platform. A train rattled by as the boys took off their jackets and spread them on the floor. 'You scared?' Bobby, too, was surprised by Meggie's reaction. She sat down with her knees hunched to her chest, arms wrapped round her legs.

'No, I ain't,' she flashed back.

'That's more like it. Fancy a fag?' He handed round his packet of five.

As Jimmie and Bobby played the big men, their faces hidden behind a screen of smoke, mouths puckered, eyes narrowed, Meggie took another cautious look round. A second train flashed by, rolling on the tracks, its lighted windows flickering, clickety-clack. For a moment she wanted to confess what had startled her; it was the tramp on the bunk, the wasted old man in the blanket, staring out of a once handsome face. Behind the stubble, beneath the gray-white skin, she glimpsed a young man, perhaps once well set-up with wife and family, now a hollow shell, a husk. There was something in his eyes as they

rested momentarily on her, in acknowl-
edgement of her tall, slender figure, her rich
auburn hair; a reflection of his own eyes in
her deep brown ones.

But then a train stopped at the platform,
people got on and off. When she looked
again for the tramp, the bunk was empty.
Someone else climbed into the space. The
train set off, the moment was lost.

Bertie and Geoff had ended up in a
butcher's house in a small Lancashire village
called Rendal. To Sadie it seemed the end
of the earth. Men in white armbands had
ushered them off the train, Bertie said in
his first letter home. It was written in blunt
pencil. He said he'd lost his pen on his first
day at school.

'The first place we went was the village
hall. We had to stay there all night till a
family came and chose us. Me and Geoff
waited until last, but we got a house together.'

'Thank heavens for that.' Sadie looked up
at Walter with a sigh of relief.

'We had to promise we never stole or wet
the bed, stuff like that. Mrs Whittaker
("Whittaker" was crossed out and changed
twice from "Witiker" to "Wittaker" before
he got it right) said she wanted a girl and

a boy, but Mr Whittaker wanted two boys to help in the shop and the fields at the back. He got his way in the end. We sleep in the same room. They can't put a girl in with a boy anyhow.'

'They'll get plenty to eat at any rate.' Walter folded his newspaper. 'What else does he say?'

'He says they went into the fields next day to help dig up potatoes. That's slave labour, ain't it? Making boys their age dig the fields.'

'They gotta do their bit. Does Bertie say how they got on?'

'He says Geoff didn't have a clue. When he saw the other boys digging up the spuds, he turns to Mr Whittaker and asks why he hid them in the first place.' She smiled, her eyes damp. 'Bertie says they met one nice lady. She said she belonged to the WVS and took them to see the Home Guard doing rifle drill. She said they were the LDV. She sees Bertie looking puzzled by all the letters. "Local Defence Volunteers," she explains, "otherwise known as Look, Duck and Vanish".'

Walter nodded. 'He put that in his letter?'

'Yes, it's a nice long one. Here.' She relinquished it at last, having taken in every smudge and contrary scrawl.

'It sounds like they're both managing all right.'

'I think so. I hope so. Oh, Walter!' Sadie pulled her apron up to her face and sobbed. Being brave when you saw them off on the train was one thing; learning to live without them, hanging on for every post, dreaming about them all night was another.

Walter held up over the boys' absence better than Sadie. He missed them, but he told himself they were safe and well housed. Expecting them to be happy in their new place on top of that was too much to hope for.

For years he'd lived his life within realistic horizons. When the taxi business he ran with Rob merely crawled through the Depression, he counted himself lucky that he could still turn an honest penny and look after his family. When the semi-detached house in the suburbs failed to materialize, he didn't spend time on envy or regret; anyway, he liked the Court, he said. The new estates were soulless by comparison.

Only once in his life had he gone out on a limb; he'd made his bid for Sadie when Meggie was a baby and Richie Palmer had left them in the lurch. He stood by her and she by him when he'd had his accident. He put his feelings on the line, hoped against the odds that she would settle for him. She was young, spirited, clever and beautiful. When she said she would marry him, his life's dream came true. Lucky man, he said to himself; blessed twice over when Sadie fell pregnant and the boys came along. A tall, strong man, grey haired since his mid-thirties, but still in good shape, he was a stalwart of the neighbourhood, an automatic choice when the time came to train wardens for the ARP. His readiness to serve paid off when what had started on a voluntary basis became paid work once the war had started.

Not that everyone liked him in his new role. Dolly Ogden, for instance, bristled whenever she saw him in his armband and tin hat. 'Nosey parker,' was her verdict when he came checking up on the blackout arrangements down the Court. 'Have you seen him driving that taxi of his long after we're holed up inside? What's good for the goose is good for the gander, ain't it?' The trouble was, she remembered Walter Davidson in short trousers, well before the last war, hanging about under the gas-lamp outside the Duke with the other peaky blinders; him and Rob Parsons and young Tommy O'Hagan.

'Doing your bit, Dolly?' Walter called out to her one December afternoon when he spotted her and Ernie Parsons hard at work on her Meredith Court allotment. 'I'd have thought it was time to hang up your spade by now.'

'Watch it, I ain't too old to put my back into it.' She shoved the spade into the black earth to take a rest. 'You're not saying no different, are you, Walter?'

'I never meant that and you know it.' He peered through the iron railings to scan the rows of winter cabbage and brussels sprouts. 'What I meant was, it's a bit late in the year for gardening.'

'We had to wait for the frost to break up the soil, didn't we, Ern? And the sprouts taste better if you let the frost nip them.' Over the years she'd become an authority. In fact, her allotment, taken over from poor Arthur because of his bad back, had become a profitable little venture. On a good year she could feed herself, her daughter Amy's whole family and still have produce left over to sell to the market stallholders. Now she was digging for victory and offering her neighbours the vegetables free of charge. Nevertheless, they usually managed to scrape the bottom of their purses for a few coppers in payment.

'You'll take Sadie a pound of them sprouts then?' He fished in his pocket for a sixpence, but found only two pennies. 'Here's a down payment.'

Dolly sent Ernie up to the railings to collect the money. 'Whoever heard of buying sprouts on the never-never? Do you want a cabbage to keep them company?'

'Might as well. What we need is carrots to help us see in the dark.'

'If you believe that you'll believe anything.' Dolly rolled down her sleeves, ready to pack up for the day. Ernie, willing as ever, was busy nipping sprouts off the stalks and collecting them in his cap. She trudged along the border of her neatly dug patch, boots caked with mud, face glowing. 'How are them two boys of yours? Fat as butchers' dogs, I hope, least they should be with a billet like that.'

'They're getting along fine so far as we know. Sadie would like a few more letters, but you know how it is.' He began to walk with her up the row of terraced houses towards the main street.

'She always was a worrier. Not like Amy. Amy don't let nothing bother her.' Dolly saw a certain rivalry there. Amy's Bobby and Sadie's Meggie were of an age, but the two mothers had entirely different ways of

60

bringing up kids. Dolly felt there was an edge to Sadie, who didn't seem able to get things in the right perspective. According to her, Meggie was the prettiest, the best behaved, the healthiest baby who ever lived. Then came the boys; Bertie was a genius by the age of three and Geoff could run like the wind. She talked them up to the skies. Dolly thought this was a dangerous tendency. 'You tell Sadie to count her blessings. Get her to talk to Amy, Amy'll soon put her straight.' They stopped on the corner of Duke Street. 'Your Sadie should get herself a job, keep busy. She's got too much time on her hands, what with Meggie out at work all day.'

'She already has, Dolly, you're behind the times. She started in the munitions factory last week.'

She sniffed. 'She ain't making them Lewisite bombs, is she?'

'I can't say. Careless talk cost lives. You know what they tell us.'

'I know, I know, keep it under your hat.' Even Dolly had tried to curb her love of gossip. She took the rebuff in good part. 'Is she on shift work?'

He nodded. 'That's another thing; it leaves Meggie at a loose end some evenings. Sadie's worried to death about that and all.'

'What for? She's old enough to look after herself, ain't she?'

'Sadie says she goes out too much. She never used to.' He felt disloyal confessing as much, but it was something on his mind too. Meggie had taken to ignoring the black-out to go off and see friends, she said. Not friends from the Court, but girls she'd met at work. Sometimes he and Sadie didn't have a clue where she was for hours on end.

Dolly eyed him closely. 'I'll get Bobby to keep an eye on her for you if you like.'

'You won't let on?'

'Would I?' She threatened to take offense. 'No, but Bobby will tip the wink to Jimmie O'Hagan. Meggie's very thick with him these days. Between them they ought to be able to find out what she's up to.'

'It's probably nothing.'

'Just in case.'

He nodded and then they parted; Walter to check in at the ARP centre set up at the primary school, Dolly to organize her spies.

'Hang on a tick.' Jimmie was finishing a spell serving at the petrol pump outside Powells' ironmongers on Duke Street when he spied Meggie, all dressed up in a white mac with a red beret set at a jaunty angle on her shiny brown hair. He took the three bob from the customer and whisked a washleather over the windscreen of the Ford Eight. 'I'm knocking off here. Do you fancy a game of skittles?'

'Some other time, Jimmie.'

He went in and flicked the coins through the air at the girl behind the counter. Then he ran to catch up with Meggie. There was a dismal drizzle falling and very little Christmas cheer in the shops this year. Traffic rattled and bumped over the tram tracks, cyclists swerved to avoid the puddles.

'I'm busy, didn't you hear?'

'Come again. I think I've got a bit deaf.' His confidence was undented by the brush-off. It was a Friday evening, he was dressed up to the nines in a soft green polo-neck sweater and corduroy jacket. He copied his style from the American films, casual yet sophisticated.

'I said I can't come to the skittle alley.'

'Why not?' He skipped around a lamp-post and stepped off the kerb ahead of her. Then he turned to walk backwards, hands in pockets. 'What did I do?'

'Nothing.' She was busy watching the traffic, stopping to cross at the Belisha beacon.

'It's Friday, ain't it? We always go down the alley. Bobby's gonna be there.'

'You go then.' She strode out, heels tapping, belt tied tight around her waist, collar up.

'You hurt my feelings, Meggie Davidson, you know that?' Still he wove in and out of the cars and pedestrians, bobbing ahead of her.

'You ain't got no feelings, Jimmie.' She was heading for a tube station to go up to Tottenham Court Road, but she didn't want Jimmie tagging along.

'No and it's a good job I ain't. If I had feelings you'd be mangling them good and proper.'

Grinning at last, she stopped in her tracks. 'I can't go bowling with you, Jim, honest. I got something important on my plate.'

'What?'

'Just . . . something.' She pulled him into a shop doorway out of the rain. 'It's family. I can't say what exactly, not yet. I ain't even told Ma.'

'What family?' He wasn't used to Meggie keeping secrets, or looking this good, even in the rain. The drizzle had made a network of tiny, shining droplets in her hair, her skin was moist, the collar of the white mac framed her face. 'Righto, you can't say that neither. I get you.' He took her elbow. 'Look, let's go into the milk bar till the rain

64

goes off. You're gonna get soaked.'

Thinking that ten minutes would make no difference, she agreed. They crossed back over the street into the bar and perched on the high, shiny stools at the chromium counter.

'It must be my birthday,' she said, taking a creamy-pink drink from him.

'You mean, ta for the milk shake, Jimmie. You're a real pal.'

'That's what I mean, yeah.' She looked at him over the top of her glass.

'Families, they're more trouble than they're worth,' he said.

Life above the Ideal Home shop was far from perfect. Dorothy was out on the town more often than not and Tommy either stayed in and got drunk, or went down the Duke and did the same. Jimmie told Meggie he thought the marriage was on the rocks.

'What'll Tommy do?' She thought of him first, rather than Dorothy.

'Get himself another girl if he's got any sense.'

'Jimmie!' She was conventional, having been brought up by Sadie to regard marriage as a lifetime commitment.

'I mean it. That'd teach her.'

Meggie stared down at the counter where

she could see her own distorted reflection. 'It's that bad?'

'You should try living there,' he said quietly. For a moment, the cheeky, chirpy image slipped.

She glanced up as she saw what he was going through, caught in no man's land between a bored and dissatisfied Dorothy and a disillusioned Tommy.

'Come on,' she said suddenly, 'you can come up Tottenham Court Road with me.'

They walked, instead of using the Underground, over the river which slid by, black and greasy, along the Embankment to Charing Cross and the sleazy haunts of the prostitutes who signalled their trade with small flashes of torchlight on the pavements, their pale faces illuminated from an ugly angle, their customers unable to see the bargain they'd made. Jimmie put his arm around Meggie's shoulder and they hurried on.

'Where we off to?'

'I told you, Tottenham Court Road.'

'What for?'

'You won't say nothing?'

'Cross my heart.'

'And you won't think I'm round the twist?'

'That depends — no, honest I won't.'

'Well, you know Walter ain't my real pa?' Her voice faltered, her pace slowed. Cars and buses swept along the pitch-dark street, bathing it in beams of yellow light. 'I ain't never known my real one. He left Ma and me in the lurch, and she won't never talk about him, not really. She says it ain't fair on Walter to drag up the past, but I think it's because she don't want to think about it, like my pa was a monster or something.'

'What's this got to do with tonight?' Jimmie struggled to make the connection.

'Hang on, I'm getting there. Sometimes, when I was little, I used to think he was dead and buried. I tried to draw a picture of him inside my head, but it was hard to know what he looked like. I heard once through Dolly that he was no good.'

'Did she tell you?'

'No, Bobby let it slip. We was just kids, but he let it out; he said no one in the Court would have anything to do with Richie Palmer — that's his name. Bobby's ma said it was good riddance when he scarpered, otherwise they'd all have grabbed him and strung him up from a lamppost.'

'Charming.' He walked close to her, one arm round her waist, letting her talk. It was the first time they'd shared anything important. She was letting him into the secret of how she felt and he was having to absorb this, as well as the fact that she was letting him get within arm's length and that he could smell her perfume, feel the sway of her slim hips as they walked.

'After that, the picture I got was more like a devil with horns sticking out of his head. I had a devil for a pa!'

'Families,' he said again.

'You try and put it out of your mind. You tell yourself it don't make no difference really. Only, I did wonder what he was like. And lately, with the war starting, I thought what if he's not dead after all? What if he's alive?' She stopped outside one of the big cinemas, its foyer dim, shadowy figures at the box office staring out. 'And then I just *knew* he was alive!'

'How?'

'I just knew. He ain't dead and I want to find him, Jimmie. I can't tell Ma, I can't tell no one except you. I want to find him just in case — in case we all get blown to pieces, you know.'

'Don't talk that way. We ain't gonna get blown to pieces.'

'No, but if we do? Or if he does? And I never knew him. And maybe, just maybe, he wants to know about me as much as I want to know about him. And we could both die, not knowing. That's a terrible thing, ain't it?'

He nodded. He couldn't break it to her that if this Richie Palmer had made no effort to stay in touch for sixteen whole years, the chances were that he didn't want to know.

'So where we going?' he asked quietly.

'To the tube station. You know that night, when we went to the Astoria, you, me and Bobby, and we had to go down the shelter? I had another of them feelings that he was alive, and it came over me really strong. I knew if I looked hard enough, I'd find him.'

'You and your feelings.' He was beginning to wish it wasn't so dark in the blackout, that they weren't so far from home. 'You're not saying you actually think you saw him?'

She waited a long time before she answered. They walked slowly on. 'I don't know, Jimmie. I've been coming back here as often as I can ever since. If I spot him again, I can be sure, can't I? If I see him looking at me like he knows me, I'll be right, won't I?'

'What the hell are you talking about, Meggie? See who looking at you?'

'The tramp with the blanket,' she explained. 'The one who spat at Bobby. I

69

think that was Richie Palmer. In fact, I know it in my bones. And here —' She struck her chest. 'In my heart, I know that was my pa.'

CHAPTER FOUR

'There's a bleeding queue every way you turn.' Dolly Ogden was on the warpath. Annie had just refused her a second pint of beer due to the rationing.

'It's the sugar. The brewers can't get it for love nor money.' Annie was glad at least that the threatened closure of the pubs hadn't happened. Their doors stayed open, even if supplies were strictly limited.

Dolly leaned confidentially across the bar. 'Come on, Annie, you know me. I won't say nothing if you bend the rules.' She'd spent the afternoon at Amy's flat, looking after things while her daughter waited her turn in the rain outside the Co-op. Amy had come back with her twelve ounces of butter and her pitiful portion of bacon to last the three of them a full week.

'You might not, Dolly, but every other thirsty blighter in the place would!' Annie stuck to her guns. It seemed hard, but there it was. These days, the darkest of the year, when Christmas had come and gone and January crawled to a close, you had to put up with worse things than not being able to drink yourself into a stupor at the drop of a hat.

'I thought they reckoned Guinness was good for you.' Dolly stared miserably into her empty glass. She wore a headscarf, tied turban-style around her head, still in her overall after a session pickling beetroot for Amy. 'How are we supposed to know if it's good for you if we can't get hold of it no more?' She didn't mind making do and mend, she didn't mind saving paper, metal, even bones, for the war effort and, when they came the other day and took the iron railings from the allotment, she'd watched without a murmur, as was her patriotic duty. But when they cut off her supply of alcohol it dug deep. 'I'll give them "Up, Housewives and At 'Em!"' she grumbled.

She needed something to take her mind off her privations, and it came in the shape of Dorothy O'Hagan, dressed up to the nines as usual, but in unexpected company. Her own Charlie stood there holding the door open, large as life, acting the gent, turning on the man-of-the-world charm in his dark slacks, yellow cravat and blazer. Dorothy should see him in the mornings, Dolly thought, unshaven and bleary-eyed, not a pretty sight since he'd come back to live with his mother.

'What'll it be?' Charlie guided Tommy's wife to the bar.

'A pint of Guinness, please.' Dolly tapped her glass too obviously on the polished bar top.

He ignored her and asked George for two shorts, then escorted Dorothy to a quiet corner.

'God knows what she'll do when her clothes coupons run out,' Annie observed, her differences with Dolly immediately forgotten. The two old women chewed over the morals of the younger generation.

'Trouble is, Charlie's on the rebound,' Dolly confided. 'He wouldn't thank me for saying this, but he'd take up with anyone now that his divorce is going through. If you ask me, he's getting his own back.'

'Well, Dorothy ain't no oil painting,' Annie agreed. 'Or if she is, I'd say the cracks are beginning to show.'

Charlie Ogden found himself at a low ebb. His school had been closed down for the duration, and though many evacuated children were beginning to trickle back into the streets and parks of London, the school doors were still barred to them. They took their lessons in a half-hearted way in their own homes, taught by conchies and women.

He was at a loose end and, when he looked at it from a distance, he saw that teaching was not the noble calling he'd once imagined. He'd gone into it after a false start with his job with Maurice Leigh in the early days of the cinema, thinking that all kids would share his own love of learning given half the chance, only to find that young minds were not blank pages to be filled with interesting facts and respectful attitudes. Instead, they were wilful wayward forces that ganged up in groups of thirty or forty to outwit anyone foolish enough to imagine they could be tamed. Put another way, every day in Charlie's working life there was at least one grubby, mendacious youngster, minus homework, looking devil-may-care and glowering down at him from six feet of adolescent muscle and swagger. Disillusioned yet dogged, Charlie kept at it until the war intervened and his marriage collapsed. Now he was back at home, forty-ish and nowhere.

'Ta for the drink, Charlie.' Dorothy raised her glass between bright red fingernails. She was enjoying the fact that all eyes were on them. 'It's more than I can get out of my old man these days.'

'We're all in the same boat.' He realized she was on the make but he didn't care. They'd bumped into one another on the doorstep, but she was trying to make it look like a set up thing, flaunting them as a couple to raise eyebrows.

Automatically she took out a cigarette then looked helpless.

'Light?' He leaned across. She held his hand steady as she drew in the flame.

'Ta, Charlie. You on your way somewhere nice?'

'Maybe.'

'Friday night; you should be.'

'But I hate this blackout, don't you? It don't feel like you can enjoy yourself the same.'

'Don't you believe it.' She described the dance halls that were humming with navy and RAF types.

'Bit on the young side for you, Dot.'

'Ta very much,' she pouted. 'I bet I could still show you a thing or two, though.'

He grinned in spite of himself. Dorothy wasn't his type, but she was nothing if not obvious.

'Why not come up the West End with me?' she asked.

'You'll show me a good time?'

'I mean it. Ain't no use nagging Tommy

75

to come with me. He can't stick this modern dancing.'

Charlie considered the offer; not one that he would normally have touched with a bargepole. Dorothy was dressed to kill in an expensive maroon coat with a black fur collar draped around her shoulders, over a short black dress with a low neckline. A string of artificial pearls had caught in her ample cleavage.

'Come on, Charlie, what you worried about? Not your reputation, surely.' She kidded him along, a mixture of toughness and good humour. 'Do you good to get out once in a while from what I hear.'

He felt manoeuvred into a position where he could hardly turn her down without making himself look soft and narrow-minded. And maybe she was right; it was time for him to break out and enjoy himself. It didn't mean anything, it wasn't as if they were underhand. Just the opposite; everyone and his bleeding aunt was watching.

'You hear wrong, Dot. I get out plenty.'

'Well then?'

'Righto. Finish your drink.' He stood up ready to go.

Slowly she smiled and stubbed out her cigarette, uncrossed her legs and collected her bag from under the table. He pulled back her chair and she stood up, slotting her arm into his as they crossed the room.

Dolly looked daggers at them.

'Ain't nothing you can do,' Annie sympathized, as the couple left the pub. 'They're both grown-ups, even if they are acting like little kids.'

'I could knock their heads together, I could. And him so high and mighty when he wants to be. I've a good mind to drop him in it with Tommy, even if I am his ma, worse luck.'

Annie kept her talking. She even slipped her a drink on the sly. If Dolly went and upset the applecart, things could turn messy. They all needed to pull together these days. Dorothy would have her fling with Charlie and it would all be over in a week, no harm done. She believed in common sense; Tommy himself was no angel, if it came to that.

'What's up, Meggie? You missing those two brothers of yours?' Hettie was upstairs in the living room over the pub, browsing through magazines for the latest fashion trends.

'Not likely.' She slung her gas mask over a chair and unbuttoned her mac.

'What do you think of this?' Hettie

showed her a picture of an afternoon dress, ruched on the bodice and sleeves. The model wore a hat which framed her face Anne Boleyn-style, with a little veil.

'Not bad.'

She looked up. 'Cat got your tongue, has it?'

'Sorry.' She was feeling down and she'd come to her aunt to ask for help. Now that it came to it, she was lost for words.

'Nothing wrong at home, is there?' Hettie knew they were bothered about the company Meggie seemed to be keeping. She never brought her friends home, Sadie complained, yet she was never in. That must mean she was ashamed of something; either the plainness of her home circumstances or the friends themselves. At any rate she was leading two separate lives.

Meggie shook her head.

'Is it the war? Is it starting to get on your nerves?' The endless false alarms weren't doing anyone any good; nights were interrupted and conditions in the shelters primitive, all for nothing. People were calling it the phoney war, yet still they waited in dread for the real thing to start.

'A bit.' She slumped into a chair, turning words this way and that inside her head. It was no good. She would have to come out with it. 'Auntie Ett, you knew my pa, didn't you? My real pa.'

Hattie closed the magazine. In a way, though the question came out of the blue, she wasn't surprised. 'Is that what all this is about?'

'All what?'

'You going narky on your ma. I knew it wasn't like you.'

'Who says I'm narky?' Meggie's dark eyes flashed.

'I do. That's it, isn't it? You're on your pa's trail and you don't want to let on.'

'I wish I was.'

'What?'

'On his trail. I've been up Tottenham Court Road more times than I can count.' She explained her conviction that she'd once set eyes on Richie Palmer in the Underground shelter. 'I've been back ever so many times, Auntie Ett.'

'By yourself?'

'Not always. Sometimes Jimmie O'Hagan comes along.'

'Good, I wouldn't want you up Soho on your own.' Hettie knew from her time in the Sally Army that the streets could be grim. 'And you've seen this tramp only the once?'

'Yes. There are hundreds of them everywhere you look, huddled up in the bunks, or just drifting along the platforms. Every time I see one I think, this is him! Then he turns around with his horrible old face and his stinking breath and it isn't the same one after all. He gives me a mouthful for getting in his way and off he goes.'

Hettie leaned forward to take her hands. 'It won't do you no good.'

'Why? He ain't dead, is he?'

'Not as far as we know.'

'Do you know how I could find him?' She appealed from the bottom of her heart. Her lip trembled, she sounded desperate.

'I don't, darling.' Hettie stroked her hair. It was natural for the poor girl to be curious, but she feared she would be in for a terrible shock. She didn't think for a second that the man Meggie had glimpsed could be Richie Palmer, but the truth could be equally bad. Last heard of, Richie was drinking himself to death in the back streets of Stepney, lying low from the police. 'And even if I did, don't you think it should be your ma you were asking?'

Meggie turned her head away sharply. 'I can't do that.'

'Why not? You've always been close, you two. Sometimes I think you're more like sisters than mother and daughter.'

'That's why. I know Ma too well; she ain't coping right now. She misses the boys. I can't go adding to her troubles, can I?'

Hettie thought this through. 'You're a good girl, Meggie. But truth is always better than lies.'

'I ain't telling lies!'

She meant the lie of omission. 'But you ain't telling her what you're up to, see, and she's worried sick about you. Come to that, it might be a relief for her to hear what all this is about.'

'I can't. I can't tell her.' Since she was small Meggie had been used to shielding her mother, who seemed somehow to live life on top of some sleeping volcano. There were times when she 'wasn't herself', or 'her nerves were bad'. Times when Meggie took charge of the boys and let her ma rest, not often, but the sense of Sadie's fragility was strong in the house.

Hettie sighed. Meggie was doing all the wrong things for the right reasons. 'And I can't tell you about Richie Palmer without going to Sadie and asking her first. That wouldn't be right, see?' She was scrupulous. She saw rumour and gossip as dangerous weapons.

Meggie bit her lip. 'I might as well ask her straight out myself.'

'You might,' her aunt said gently, insistently.

'If you ask me she's round the bleeding twist.' Rob switched off the radio with a violent snap. These days he and Walter had to hang around a lot in their Meredith Court depot, waiting for the phone to ring. Walter had just dropped the bombshell news that Sadie was out with Meggie, combing the streets to find Richie Palmer.

'What can I do?'

'Put your foot down, that's what.' He wouldn't have stood any such nonsense from Amy.

'It ain't that easy, Rob.' Walter was on his way to check the sandbagging around the entrance to the Nelson Gardens shelter. He reached for his tin hat and got ready to go.

Rob flicked his cigarette to the floor and ground it underfoot. 'You mean to say they're out looking for him right this minute?' For a second he was speechless. 'And you let them? I don't know why you didn't just take your taxi and drive them round, get it over and done with.'

'Look, I ain't saying I like what's going on —'

'Like it? I should bleeding well hope not.'

He worked himself up. 'And what's gonna happen if they do find him?'

'They won't, don't you worry.' Walter tightened his helmet strap under his chin, ready to step out into the raw, cold night.

'Says you. If you ask me, we should've nailed him before now, right at the start when we found out his little game.'

'Don't drag it up, Rob. It won't do no good.' He felt suddenly weary.

'It ain't me dragging it up. It's Meggie, ain't it? And Sadie. She's gone soft in the head if she thinks Palmer will welcome his kid with open arms.'

Walter shrugged. 'No need to rub it in.'

'Sorry. But that's what I mean, she ain't taken you into account, has she?' Rob's old hatred of Richie Palmer had risen up and grabbed him by the throat. 'After what he tried to do to you.'

'She does think of me. She don't sleep at night for thinking of me, and Meggie, and the boys. She's worn to a shadow thinking of others. Don't suppose it's easy for Sadie; it ain't.' She'd agonized for weeks after Meggie had come in one night and announced that she wanted to find her real pa. 'Coping with the war's bad enough, without any of this on top.'

'And didn't Meggie think of that before she opened her big mouth?'

Walter sighed. 'Don't go on, Rob. I just mentioned it in case they do manage to track him down. I didn't want it dropping on you out of the blue.' The truth was, he'd happened to be in the wrong place at the wrong time when the so-called accident happened fifteen years earlier. Richie had messed about with the taxi's brakes in an effort to get back at Rob, not him. If Walter hadn't taken the cab out on the off-chance, it would have been Rob who'd ended up under the wheels of the tram. 'Meggie don't know every little thing that went on. Sadie's kept it quiet all these years. All she knows is, her pa ran off. Now she says she wants to meet up with him before it's too late.'

'Too late for what? Maybe someone should tell the kid the whole truth.' Rob lit up another cigarette.

'No.' Walter stopped in the doorway. 'Don't do that.'

'Why not?'

'Sadie still don't want her to know.' It wasn't nice to find out your pa had tried to kill your uncle and got your stepdad by mistake.

Rob shook his head, diving for the ringing

phone across the cluttered desk. 'Bleeding mad.'

He sat shrouded by smoke, cigarette dangling from his mouth as he took down details of the job. By the time he'd finished, Walter had buttoned up his heavy jacket and was gone.

Walter didn't like any aspect of the current search for Richie Palmer any better than Rob. He had plenty of time to think of it as he paced the dark streets, finding his way by the white bands painted around the tree trunks at the edge of Nelson Gardens. For a kick-off, he didn't like to think of Sadie and Meggie out by themselves on these dark nights. After five months of waiting on tenterhooks for the German threat to materialize — for the gas rattles to sound, the fire bombs to land — it wasn't so much that he thought any longer that they'd get caught in an air raid. By now everyone was jaded, irritable, even let-down, but certainly not afraid that Jerry would suddenly arrive out of the sky in a storm of gas clouds and a burst of flames.

No, it was the blackout and what went on under cover of darkness. There were areas where it wasn't safe to walk, yet Meggie insisted that Soho was the area to search.

She'd got it into her head that her father had moved on from the East End, north of the river to the richer pickings of the theatre and club area. Reluctantly, after much soul-searching, Sadie had agreed they should look together.

'What if she's right?' Walter had wanted to know. 'What if Richie does turn up?'

Sadie had stared back at him from hollow eyes, red-rimmed with sleeplessness. 'He won't,' she assured him. 'You know Richie; when he wants to vanish he does it good and proper.'

'Well then?' He wanted to hold her close so as not to see her fears.

'Well then, let her look, get it out of her system. Where's the harm in that? But I'd rather she had me with her, and I'm glad we know what she's up to, at any rate.'

'Righto, and what if Richie don't turn up, like you say?'

'Then at least she tried. And she won't be so hard on herself after.'

'Meggie? What's she got to feel bad about?'

Sadie had sighed and turned over in bed, her face away from him. Now Walter shone his torch over the wall of sandbags at the shelter entrance. He heard her reply loud and clear as if she stood next to him.

'Meggie's got it into her head that it was her fault Richie ran off in the first place. No, it ain't sensible, I know, but that's what she thinks; that there was something the matter with her that made her pa leave us in the lurch.'

His duty done, Walter switched off his torch and headed for home. Absent-mindedly he checked the blackout as he went along Union Street and on to Duke Street. The odd car crept by, headlights hooded and dimmed. Gas mask posters hung in tatters from an old billboard, some wag had scratched a Hitler moustache onto the face of the blonde socialite beauty who bore the message, 'Keep Mum, She's Not So Dumb'. The Duke was already closed up for the night, Paradise Court was silent and empty.

At Number 32 he turned the key and opened the door into the dark, cold house. Sadie and Meggie weren't back, though it was half past eleven on the mantelpiece clock. He turned on the radio. 'Jairmany calling, Jairmany calling.' The jackass tones of Lord Haw-Haw droned over the airwaves as Walter went through to the kitchen to boil the kettle and wait.

'You ain't carrying your gas mask.' Edie

looked up from her desk. Tommy was setting off for the bank to fetch the wages. She tut-tutted in a maternal fashion.

He hitched up his jacket collar. 'It ain't me you're worried about, Edie Morell, it's your blessed pay packet.' Teasing her was one of life's few remaining pleasures.

'How did you guess?'

' 'Cos I know you women, you're all the same. You're only ever after a bloke's money.'

She smiled. 'Anyhow you should take your mask.' She went to the filing cabinet to fetch it for him. He ducked sideways as she tried to sling it around his neck.

There was something about her that knocked him off balance; not physically, though he pretended to stagger across the room. Well, yes, it was physical; her slim figure and wavy golden hair sent him reeling in earnest. He felt again that one of these days he would let this reaction slip, when he should do his best to conceal it. They could all do without that sort of complication in their lives.

'Righto then, it's your neck you're risking.' She hung the mask from the door hook and went back to work at her desk, totting up hours for Lorna Bennett who'd recently stepped into Dorothy's shoes behind the furnishing fabric counter. Tommy's wife now refused to serve in the shop; she preferred to spend her days dolling herself up ready for her nights out.

'If I'm not back in an hour send out reinforcements,' Tommy joked. He set his hat at an angle, one foot on the bottom step of the basement office. *'If you want a sack of flour send out three and fourpence.'*

'Come again?' She glanced up, trying not to laugh. It only encouraged him.

'Chinese whispers.'

'I'll whisper you,' she warned.

'Is that a threat or a promise?' He'd pushed his luck. He saw her blush and pointedly ignore him, so he took the stairs two at a time, whistling his way past Lorna, who arched her already arched and pencilled eyebrows and wriggled her skirt smooth over her hips.

'Remember my bonus, Mister O'Hagan,' she called out over the head of Dolly Ogden, in to price up net curtain material for Charlie's room. Lorna had all the cheek Edie lacked.

'What bonus is that, Lorna?'

'Danger money, for staying open like the Windmill Theatre. You know, "We never close!" ' She'd taken to ignoring the warning sirens, like many of her friends. And now she resented all the business with identity and ration cards. It made everything so drab. She was even having to consider using curtain fabric from the shop to make herself a new dress.

'Pigs might fly.' Tommy sniffed and went out. His trip to the bank might take in the market at the back of the cathedral, where he would see what he could pick up on the sly. He didn't mind doing his best for the girls who worked for him; they, at least, would appreciate his efforts.

He came back with the wages and a pair of nylon stockings each for Lorna and Edie.

'You'd never guess what I heard,' he told Jimmie, just come into the shop from his job serving petrol outside Powells. His kid brother hung around luscious Lorna like a bee round a honeypot. 'They say in the market that the whole of the cathedral crypt is stacked high with empty coffins, just in case. You can't move for the bleeding things, thousands of them, horrible boxes made of plywood.'

'Cheerful, ain't we?' Lorna took her nylons and stuffed them into her bag.

'No point hiding your head in the sand, that's what I say.'

'Well they got it wrong, ain't they?' She

tilted her head defiantly. 'Might as well chop them all up for firewood, all the use they're gonna be.'

'Touch wood.' Jimmie tapped the counter. 'See, wood — coffins — touch wood. See?'

'Yeah, yeah.' Lorna screwed up her red mouth and told him to shove off. Meanwhile Tommy went down to deliver the wages to Edie.

He caught her off-guard, reading a letter which she hastily pushed into a drawer as he came in.

'Gotcha!' He flung his hat onto the filing cabinet and dumped the wages bag on her desk. 'You heard from Bill, I take it?'

Edie nodded. 'At last.'

Winter was already almost over.

'Not bad news, I hope?'

'No, he's due a bit of leave. He missed out at Christmas, like the rest of us, really, 'cos he was off in North Africa somewhere. Malta, as it happens. They're on their way back to Portsmouth. He'll get seventy-two hours, he thinks.'

'That's good ain't it?' He couldn't work out why she still seemed flustered.

'Yes, but reading between the lines he's been having it rough. He can't say in his letter, of course, but he's been drafted onto a minesweeper, I know that much.'

Tommy nodded, at a loss over what to say. To his surprise, tears welled up in Edie's eyes. Normally a cheerful and practical sort, she seemed to be letting the worry get on top of her. 'Here.' He pushed a clean, folded hankie towards her and tactfully turned his back.

After a pause she began to explain. 'It's not what you're thinking.'

He turned again. She was staring at her hands, twisting a corner of the handkerchief. 'Look, there ain't no need . . .'

She glanced up, eyes still moist. 'I'm such a fool.'

'No.' He went and sat on the edge of the desk, facing her.

'You think I'd be glad to see him.'

'And ain't you?'

She shook her head.

This startled him. As far as he knew, Edie was happily married. She'd always behaved that way, like a respectable married woman. She was the sort other girls turned to when their own relationships hit difficulties, knowing they could rely on her common sense and kindness. But she always kept her distance; she didn't seem to gossip like the rest. Come to think of it, he knew practically nothing about her situation at home.

'It's the letter; it's knocked me sideways. When he didn't get leave at Christmas I thought that was it, that they'd hang onto him till the end of the war.'

'And now that could be longer than we thought,' he warned.

'I know. Giving him leave before he's drafted to another ship means they must think it's going to drag on, don't it?' She looked up again.

'Could do. Is that what's eating you?'

'No. The thing is, I ain't gonna be glad to see him and that's the truth.'

Tommy felt he was getting in deep. The next thing was to ask her why not. Why was the prospect of three days of married bliss making her cry?

But Edie felt she'd gone far enough. 'Don't mind me.' She took a deep breath. To reach the wages she had to stretch her arm across him.

The action did for him. He held onto her wrist, she looked up in surprise. He stooped to kiss her before she could pull back.

'Tommy, don't.'

He sprang to his feet. 'Forget I did that, will you? I don't know what came over me.'

She'd gone pale. Her complexion was the sort that showed her shifting emotions. 'My fault,' she whispered, 'crying all over you.'

Tommy stood by the door, tense and silent. He could hear footsteps coming downstairs. It seemed an age before Lorna swept in, brushing past him in her tight blue jumper.

'Edie, are your rayons the right size for you?' she demanded, ignoring him and going right up to the desk.

'What rayons?'

'These.' He pulled them abruptly out of his inside jacket pocket, the cellophane crinkling as he went and put them on the edge of her desk. Edie blushed fiercely. 'I picked them up in the market.'

'You're smaller than me, aren't you?' Lorna seized them. 'These ones are my size. Fancy doing a swap?'

He left them to it and gave himself a good talking to. If he was going to start any funny business and get his own back for the way Dorothy was carrying on, it had better not be with someone like Edie. She was too good for him; he wouldn't want her getting hurt. Calling in at the Duke for a quick pint, he tried to put her firmly out of his mind.

CHAPTER FIVE

'Conchie!' Dolly found the word chalked roughly on her front doorstep one morning early in April. It meant Charlie had been sounding off in the pub again. He would go ahead and argue, that was his problem. If Rob Parsons got up on his hind legs to say the only good German was a dead one, Charlie couldn't help answering back. He reckoned that Hitler wasn't the only guilty party, that Churchill wasn't all that he was cracked up to be. Charlie's idea was that they'd been conned into fighting again, and all because the politicians had got it wrong after the last big do. 'You won't win no popularity contests round here if you go on like that,' she would warn.

Now she went inside for a bucket of hot, soapy water and a scrubbing-brush before he crawled out of bed and spotted the offensive slogan. No point tackling him about it. No point talking to him about anything these days. Grimly she got down on her hands and knees and began to scrub.

'Your Charlie in?' a woman's voice asked.

95

Dolly glanced over her shoulder at a pair of shapely legs in black high-heeled shoes. Dorothy O'Hagan had come calling. 'He's in, but not up.'

Dorothy fished in her handbag for a bunch of keys which she dangled from her finger. 'I came by to give him these. He left them at my place.'

Dolly stood up. 'You're sure they're his?'

'Who else's?' She didn't care about Dolly's insinuation; they could say what they liked. If she and Charlie wanted to see each other, what business was it of theirs? 'Tell him I popped by with them, will you?'

She was about to slip them back into her bag, but Dolly held out a hand to intercept her. 'You can give them to me. I'll see he gets them.'

Outstared by a determined opponent, Dorothy gave in. She handed the keys to Dolly, who watched her go, trip-tripping up the pavement in her shiny shoes. With a shrug of disgust Dolly took up the bucket of dirty water and swilled it into the gutter after her. Then she pocketed the keys and went inside.

By now Charlie had roused himself and come down into the kitchen, still in rumpled pyjamas, with two days' growth of stubble on his chin.

'Who was that?'

'Wouldn't you like to know?' She rattled the enamel bucket into position under the sink and began to hum loudly.

'Cut it out, Ma.'

She chose the tune, 'There'll Always Be An England', expressly to annoy him.

Charlie glowered at his shapeless, worn out mother, wrapped in her floral pinny, headscarf around her curlers, scrawny legs poking into fleece-edged slippers.

'Give me the keys.'

'I thought you never knew who came calling.' She took the broom and began to sweep around him.

'Well, I heard, as a matter of fact, so just hand them over.' He had to step smartly out of the way to save his bare feet.

Dolly hummed on. 'I expect you didn't want her ladyship to catch sight of you, the state you're in.' She refused to give him the keys until she'd had her say. 'I'll say one thing for her, Dorothy O'Hagan must be an early riser.'

'How come?' Resigned to a ticking off, Charlie reached for a packet of cigarettes on the window sill.

'I reckon it must take her a good couple of hours to get herself dolled up like that.' Dorothy had appeared at the door in an immaculate and fashionable spring outfit; a two-piece in fine lilac wool, her blonde hair set in perfect waves, a mannish hat of black velvet framing the curls and the carefully painted face.

'Ha, ha, very funny.' He ran a hand through his hair. It felt lank and greasy. 'Cut it out, Ma, will you.'

Dolly's broom came to rest. She leaned on it.

'You're showing me up, Charlie, you know that?' She couldn't help remembering her son's early promise. The boy had been bright at school, won a scholarship, thought of himself as a cut above the rest. Now look at him.

Charlie bridled. 'Look who's talking.' Immediately he regretted the insult.

But Dolly wasn't one to back off, even though she felt his scorn like a sharp stab under her ribs. 'Since we're calling a spade a spade, you'd better sit down.' She pulled out a chair at the kitchen table. 'Charlie!'

He did as he was told, pretending to retreat behind the morning newspaper, angry with himself. His ma had had it hard all her life, scrimping and saving. Half his childhood had been spent down the pawnshop with her, taking in stuff on a Monday that they would aim to redeem at the weekend, in time to scramble together a decent outfit for church. She'd always done her best.

Dolly sat heavily opposite. 'I look at you now, Charlie, and you know who I see?'

He shook his head.

'Your pa.'

'That ain't fair.'

'I ain't saying nothing against him, don't get me wrong. But he weren't the world's best at getting up in the morning. And look at you. You know it's half past nine? And your pa had times when he was out of work, lots of them. We all did. It got to him just like it's getting to you.'

'What do you want me to do, start up my own bleeding school?' The idea that he'd fallen into the indolent, head-in-the-clouds ways of his own father got right under Charlie's skin.

'Don't be daft. But there's other things besides teaching. Look at Walter Davidson; he's on fire watch every other night, doing his bit, and getting paid for it.'

Charlie's silence spoke volumes.

'And he's not playing about with other men's wives neither.' As she came to the nub, she held firmly onto the edge of the table, watching his reaction.

'That's 'cos he's happily married, ain't it?' Once, in what seemed like another lifetime,

Sadie Davidson had been sweet on Charlie himself.

'You missed your chance there,' Dolly said, unrelenting.

He sniffed. 'Lay off, will you.' He took a long drag on his cigarette. 'Look, Ma, things ain't the same.' He felt he had to explain in simple terms. 'We got more freedom to do as we like than you had in your day, especially now the war's on. It's turned everything upside down.'

'Yes, and look at the mess you're making.'

He denied it. 'Me and Dorothy are having a fling, that's all. Where's the harm in that?'

Dolly sighed. 'You ask Tommy O'Hagan where's the harm in that; he'll soon tell you.'

'Tommy don't come into it.'

'Tell him that,' she insisted. 'I take it he still don't know?'

'Not unless you gone and opened your big mouth, Ma.' He stood up to cut the conversation short. He didn't feel brilliant about it, as a matter of fact. Dorothy was the hard-boiled one, not giving a damn whether or not her husband knew about the affair. She said it was months since they'd opened their mouths to each other, except to hurl insults.

'What about me, then?' She made a direct appeal. 'I can hardly hold my head up at the Duke, with you and her carrying on like this.'

He stood in the doorway and shrugged.

'And you. Ain't you got no self-respect? That Dorothy O'Hagan, she's got the worst name in Duke Street, if you must know. Even before you came along and fell hook, line and sinker.'

'I never fell, Ma. I can get out any time I like.'

She thought he looked miserable, standing in the cold corridor. 'Well then, I should think about doing just that if I was you.' She sighed as he went upstairs. Stubborn, wrong-headed, so sharp he cut himself. Her son.

'Ernie, cop hold of this, there's a good chap.'

Walter Davidson and George Mann had decided to line part of the cellar at the Duke with a reinforced fabric called Zylex. Amy had got hold of the roll for fifteen bob, and reckoned it was waterproof and untearable. She agreed with Annie, Hettie and Sadie that the barrel-vaulted cellar of the pub was as safe as any shelter in Nelson Gardens, should the worst eventually happen. There was a general feeling growing against the public shelters and, despite the lack of gardens in the terraces and tenements of Southwark, many families had begun to make their own arrangements.

Ernie held the sheeting in position at one end while Walter hammered it into place.

Annie had come down to supervise proceedings, and now took it upon herself to explain to her stepson the new plan. 'Nice and snug, eh, Ern?'

He looked up and nodded. With only the foggiest notion of the reality of war, which existed for him merely as a wail of sirens and the fear of bombs dropping from the sky, but without any grasp of the devastation they would cause, he still did as he was told.

'This is going to be our shelter now, Ernie. It's handier than the Gardens, see? We won't have to run there with all our belongings. What we do when the siren starts is just dive down here into the cellar.'

'What about the others?'

'Rob and Amy and Bobby? They know to head here too. There's plenty of room.'

'And Sadie?'

'Yes. And Walter and Meggie.'

'And the boys?'

'No, Bertie and Geoff are safe in the country, remember.'

Ernie frowned and nodded. 'Not the boys.'

'You got it. When the siren goes, you head straight here. Don't worry about no one else.' Not for the first time, Annie wondered if it might have been kinder to evacuate Ernie along with Sadie's boys. In a way, he hardly understood any more than seven-year-old Geoff. She pictured what the long wait, the stale boredom of the phoney war must be doing to him. Sometimes she thought she saw a haunted look, as if Ernie was playing and replaying some horrid scene inside his head. She resolved to keep an extra special eye on him, knowing that was what Duke would have done.

For instance, when Ernie asked to be allowed to go out with Sadie and Meggie in their so-far fruitless search for Richie Palmer, Annie had put her foot down. 'No, Ern, you stay and help look after things here. What would I do without you, now that George has to go out on patrol?'

That made him happy, thinking he couldn't be spared at the pub. He would queue with the ration book, to save Annie or Hettie the trouble. He would wash glasses and clean floors. He knew where he was at the Duke.

'Righto, Ern? You dive down the cellar from now on, no messing.' They were making a good job of damp-proofing the arch where they stored the barrels of bitter and mild on the long wooden gantries. Now if the water mains burst up above, or if they had to stay down for any length of time, they would be dry and safe.

Ernie stood up straight and stepped back to look at their handiwork.

'Here, take this and hammer down the bit above the door.' Walter handed him the tool. 'Nice and straight now, Ern, that's perfect.' He winked at Annie. 'What do you think?'

'I think poor little Hitler don't know what he's up against.' She winked back. 'Fancy him thinking that dropping a couple of bombs on our heads will be the end of us!'

It wasn't long before Meggie and Sadie decided it was safer to go out looking for the tramp from Tottenham Court Road during daylight hours. This became easier as spring took hold and evenings lengthened, the light sky opening up possibilities. They took to catching the tube, walking the length of Tottenham Court Road, on to Charing Cross and into Trafalgar Square, sometimes forgetting, if only for a moment, the tawdry task that faced them. Nelson's lions sat huge and powerful at the base of the towering column. Red buses circled beneath a comforting array of adverts for Bovril, Capstan and Hovis.

One Sunday morning in late April, footsore after a slog around the Sally Army hostels and along the Strand, they sat for a while in the pale sunshine beside the fountains in the square.

'I bet them pigeons don't know there's a war on,' Sadie sighed, easing her feet out of her shoes. Gone were the days when she would have flung caution to the winds and dipped them, hot and aching, into the refreshing fountain. Once she would have, before she met Richie and fell pregnant with Meggie.

The roar of a passing wagon full of soldiers peering out from under the khaki canopy made the flock of birds rise in a clatter of wings. They swept skywards and circled, settling on the column and on the nearby gallery.

'Don't you wonder what it's all for?' Meggie felt her life was stalled; the false alarms, the drab, endless queues, the blackout were all stealing her youth.

Sadie misunderstood. 'You mean, you're tired of looking?' For her part, she would give up the search the moment Meggie gave the signal.

'No, I mean the fighting. Aren't you sick of it?'

'No, I ain't.' Sadie went tight-lipped. 'And you shouldn't talk that way neither. You could get yourself locked up if you're not careful.'

Meggie laughed. In spite of everything she managed to look radiant in the morning sun. Her wavy dark brown hair glowed. It fell down her back in bright disarray now that she'd taken off her beret and teased it free in the breeze. 'No, but when you think of it, if the war goes on much longer, it'll be Bobby and Jimmy in the thick of it. What then?'

Sadie trailed a hand in the clear water. 'Don't.' She shuddered. She didn't want to think. Part of the reason she'd agreed to tramp the streets looking for Richie was to keep her mind off such things. If she was practical, helping Meggie or handling the cold steel of the shells on the assembly line, she could numb her mind, cut out the pictures of little Bertie and Geoff stranded in a strange county. Only at night, in her dreams, she would see their faces staring out at her from between sides of bloody beef. She heard the butcher's cleaver and woke up wet with irrational tears and sweat.

'Ready?' Meggie seemed to tune into her

thoughts. She stood up and held out her hand. 'Don't take no notice of me. They say things are going our way. The Jerries haven't managed to drop their bombs on us yet, have they?' Sliding her mother's arm through her own, they walked on.

Little by little, Meggie was convinced they were getting somewhere after all the weeks of searching. It was like the needle in the haystack, but they'd picked up the trail at Hettie's old mission in Bear Lane, where Richie Palmer had actually been seen some years earlier. By then he'd hit rock bottom and Meggie had had to face the fact that her father had gone wrong on women and booze, scrounging off the first to pay for the second. The Salvation Army had him down as homeless and awkward, never grateful for shelter and often abusing the charity on offer. By the end of the twenties he'd dropped out of sight again and, as the Depression swelled the ranks of those who fell on the Army for support, there was no further mention of a Richie Palmer on their books.

'What would happen to him then?' Meggie had asked in trepidation. She knew of tramps who starved or froze to death, who sank too low ever to resurface on the respectable streets.

The Sally Army sergeant remembered Hettie. He saw the Parsons spirit in the niece, and the same spark in her dark brown eyes. He would have been glad to help.

'Who knows? Maybe he moved out into the country, to the hop fields. How old was he?'

Meggie turned to her mother.

'In 1930? He'd be over thirty-five.'

'Then it's not likely he'd get work. Men like this tend to wear out quick. But you could still try the docks.'

So they'd gone on from the mission to the warehouses and wharves, where drifters clung to the riverside in their rags and filth like flotsam washed up on the tide. They muttered and swore at the two women, or ranted out loud to an invisible audience. Occasionally there was a word or two of sense. One tramp recalled an ex-mechanic who hung out when he could in the pubs around The Elephant. The Crown was his regular. No, he wasn't sure where it was, only that it was this side of the river, and come to think of it, the mechanic's name was Fynn, he was Irish, and definitely not the man they were after. Meggie's hopes were dashed.

All along the south bank Meggie and Sadie had dropped Richie's name. The walls of the half-empty warehouses towered over the mean streets, young sailors spilled ashore on leave, dashing in uniform, kitbags stuffed with cigarettes, chocolate and rum. Their high spirits made it impossible for the two women to continue their search and they often went home disheartened.

Still, they usually managed to leave word in the pubs and eating-houses; if anyone knew anything of Richie Palmer, one time of Paradise Court, Southwark, would they please telephone the Duke of Wellington public house on Duke Street?

Meggie and Sadie's brief rest by the fountain took place on the same weekend Bill Morell finally got his shore leave.

Edie had been quiet all week, building up to it, and Tommy had kept his distance. He only picked up the news through Lorna, who invited Edie out on the town with herself and Dorothy. He heard the subdued reply, 'Bill's got his leave through at long last. He'll want me at home.'

Tommy had paid the wages that Friday and ran the shop pretty well single-handed on the Saturday; easy enough since no one's mind was on home decorating these days. He swung through the double doors of the pub that evening determined to get blotto.

He grimaced at the advert above the doorway: 'Come to the pub tonight and talk things over. Beer is Best!'

'What's it to be, Tommy?' George Mann stood ready with a sparkling, empty glass.

'The usual and ten Woodbines.'

He slapped the money on the bar and was halfway down his pint of bitter, head tilted back, feeling the froth swim against his lips, when he caught sight of Edie sitting across a table from her husband. Tommy only knew Bill Morell by sight; an upright, beefy sort who used to work out at the gym before he joined up and began his training down at Hayling Island. Now, by all accounts, he was a petty officer on a DEMS gunner, plying the Med. He certainly looked the business in his naval jacket with the braid and buttons, the blancoed cap. Unreasonably, Tommy caught himself disliking the square set of the man's shoulders, the bristling, bull-like neck. He had his back to Tommy and Edie caught her employer's eye over her husband's shoulder. She gave him a brief smile.

Straight away Bill turned and beckoned him across. 'What'll you have?'

Tommy raised his glass. 'I'm OK, ta.'

'No, what'll you have?' The sailor swaggered over. 'From what I hear, I owe you one.' He insisted on filling Tommy's glass and taking him to their table. 'Edie's been telling me what you can get hold of under the counter.' He winked. 'Keep the girls happy, eh?'

Tommy shifted uncomfortably on his stool.

'First thing I noticed when I got home. Two brand new pairs of nylons in her drawer. You can't get them for love nor money unless you're in the know.' He pulled a flat bottle of rum from his inside pocket and offered it to Tommy. 'Here, one good turn deserves another.'

Tommy pulled hard at the bottle. He avoided looking at Edie and soon got Bill talking about the action he'd seen.

'I take it you don't mean the "Up Spirits" kind of action?'

He shook his head.

'It's heating up in the Med if you must know.' Bill didn't mind blowing his own trumpet. Once the rum had loosened his tongue he spouted for all he was worth about his last merchant ship which was carrying aviation fuel to Malta. 'Right in the Eyetie line of fire.'

'But you made it?'

'We did. Chaps beside us weren't so lucky. You should've seen the action stations; klaxons, men running for the life-boats, straight into this sheet of flame. Blew up like a matchbox right in their faces. Down she goes, stern first, bodies every-where. We have to drop the scrambling nets down our side. Up they come, only a couple of dozen of them. Name and number we yell as we heave them on deck. Some poor buggers couldn't even remember. You could see them in the water everywhere, burned to blazes. We had to leave them to it.'

Edie's eyes closed during this robust ac-count. Bill's ship had eventually managed to dock in Malta with the score of survivors from her sister ship. They'd all lived in caves until repairs were finished.

'No kidding, in holes in the rock, like a bleeding rabbit warren. Mind you, it's the safest place, what with Rommel's Heinkels buzzing round day and night.' Bill enjoyed the impact of his story; all neighbouring eyes and ears were glued to him. No one felt inclined to steal his glory.

'Where to next?' Tommy put in.

'Training ship, Inverary.'

'Bit of peace and quiet?'

'Who knows? Jerry's up there with his U-boats, so they say.' Without looking at Edie he got to his feet and scraped his stool back from the table. He was tall; over six foot, and aggressively handsome. He made a great show of shaking Tommy's hand. 'Thanks for keeping an eye on things on the Home Front.'

Tommy couldn't read what was going on. Was he being got at? He felt Edie stand reluctantly to button her jacket. The buzz of conversation and criss-crossing of customers to and from the bar swallowed her and Bill as they headed for the door. He spotted Dorothy sitting alone on a bar stool, taking in all that had gone on. Soon she swung off the stool and headed towards him.

'You seen Lorna anywhere?' she snapped, demanding a cigarette and a light. 'She said she'd be here.' It was clear that Dorothy had taken pleasure in seeing Tommy fail to measure up against the strapping sailor. He'd never been what you'd call well-built, and at under five-ten he'd looked weedy by comparison. 'It's all right for some,' she ruminated behind a cloud of blue smoke, watching the door swing shut.

'Meaning?' He knew very well what she meant. Bill Morell had all the requisite features of the perfect husband.

'Nothing. Here's Lorna, about bleeding time.' She sloped off, coat slung around her shoulders, and before long the two of them had set off on their West End trawl.

Dorothy came home in the early hours, alone and three-quarters drunk. She woke him to pour scorn over him for what she called his fling with that tart, Edie Morell.

Tommy felt a blank wall of anger rise up between them.

'Ain't no use denying it. Lorna says she caught you at it. Well, I'd just watch it if I was you. That husband of hers is a big boy; I wouldn't want to be in your shoes when he finds out.'

Next Monday, in the office, Edie was reaching for some catalogues on bathroom fittings from a high shelf. Her sleeve fell back. She had a row of blue-black bruises from elbow to shoulder. When she caught Tommy's eye and the look on his face, she burst into tears.

CHAPTER SIX

Tommy locked the office door. He watched Edie struggle to master her tears, his own emotions in turmoil. He was sure of one thing though, Bill Morell was the guilty party as far as those bruises were concerned.

'Sorry.' She shook her head.

'Don't be.'

'It's just that things have been getting me down. It ain't like me.' She regained control with a sharp intake of breath. 'Sorry.'

'Edie —'

'No, it ain't what you think.' Pressing her lips tightly together, she put the catalogue flat on the desk and began to thumb through it.

'No need to pretend,' he said gently. The sight of her tears had beaten down his own defences.

Her head went down again and she hid her face. 'Don't be nice to me, Tommy, I can't bear it.'

'I'll knock his block off for you if you like,' he said, matter-of-fact. 'And don't tell me you walked into no bleeding lamp-post to get them bruises, all right?'

She nodded. 'We had a bit of a tiff, that's all.'

'About them pairs of nylons?'

'He's bound to feel a bit jealous, ain't he? Him being away at sea.'

Tommy imagined the scene at the Morells' flat; Bill taking the stupid stockings out of the drawer and tearing them up out of spite, rounding on Edie and blaming her for taking presents off another man.

'Better not give you any more then.'

'Better not.'

'Still, it don't mean to say he's got any right to bash you about.'

She sighed. 'Forget it. Don't tell no one, will you?'

'Has he gone back to his ship?'

'Yes. Last night. Took the Glasgow train, the sleeper.'

There was a long pause. 'Good riddance.' Tommy paced the floor on the far side of the desk from Edie. 'It looks like I ruined your weekend good and proper.'

'Not you. If it hadn't been the nylons it would've been something else.'

Tommy stopped. 'He done it before?'

She looked at him without answering directly. 'Men like Bill get jealous. There don't have to be a reason.'

'And do you have to put up with it?'

Tommy's anger rose as he realized the sort of life she led. In his book, though the East End streets were tough and family life often hard — wives scraping by, husbands resenting the fact that their hard-earned wages were all spoken for in food, rent and clothing — still a man should never hit a woman whatever the provocation. And in Edie's case, he couldn't see why Bill shouldn't just count his blessings and take the best possible care of her.

'I'm married to him, ain't I? For better, or worse.'

'Not if he knocks you about, for God's sake!'

For her part Edie didn't want this question opened up. Once married, always married; it was simplest. And so far she'd never been tempted.

'I could ask you the same thing: why do you stay married? You ain't happy.'

'Happy's one thing. Bruises all over is another. Where else did he catch you?'

'Nowhere much. Apart from my arm, where he grabbed it.'

'The truth, Edie. Door's locked. Ain't no one coming in if you want to tell me all about it.'

She half smiled. 'Here's me trying to be

brave, chin up. I ain't used to sympathy.'

'So why not tell me?' He sat at a safe distance.

'What's to tell? We got home from the Duke on Saturday night. You saw what he was like, pretending to be all chummy with you over the nylons but course when we get back he wants to know what I've done to deserve them, looking at me all snidey, with this smile on his face.'

'Did you tell him I get them for all the girls in the shop whenever I lay my hands on a consignment coming off the dock?' He lit a cigarette to steady his nerves, blaming his own carelessness for part of it.

She nodded. 'But he don't want to know. By this time he's worked himself up, swearing and shouting. I have to lock myself in the bathroom, but that makes him worse. I'm inside, and he's outside on the landing, livid with me.' She closed her eyes. 'Next thing, he's put his fist through the glass panel in the door.'

'Bastard.' Tommy stood up.

Edie went to calm him. 'See, what good's it do to tell you?'

'No, go on. I want to know.' He held her gently by the shoulders. 'Tell me the rest.'

'Broken glass. That's what sticks in my

mind. The glass smashing and flying through the air. I don't take it lying down, though. He's managed to unlock the door and I'm trapped in a corner, but I stand up to him. He can do what he likes, but I won't show him I'm scared. I won't give him the satisfaction.'

Tommy wrapped her in his arms and held her.

'Anyhow, I know it'll stop. He never takes it too far. I just get knocked about a bit, then he stops, no real damage.'

'Next off, you'll be saying how lucky you are to have such an understanding bloke!' The feeling of holding her close nearly drove him mad. He had to make a feeble joke to steady himself.

'Oh.' She began to sob in earnest. 'What am I gonna do, Tommy? What am I gonna do?'

Sadie had bought Bertie some new wellington boots from Woolworths, packed them in a neat parcel and sent them off to Lancashire. 'Give your old ones to Geoff,' she instructed in her letter, 'and have Mrs Whittaker hand on Geoff's old ones to a small child who needs them. I've written your name in big letters inside the top rims so you can see at a glance they belong to you.' Bertie's possessions had a mysterious way of disappearing, apparently. She waited several weeks for a reply, fretting all the while that the parcel had been lost in the post, that Bertie must be ill, or that he'd already forgotten all about his real family in Southwark.

At last the long-awaited letter came, crumpled and smudged.

'Looks as if the dog got hold of that,' Walter commented as he separated it from the rest of the morning's mail and handed it over to Sadie.

Eagerly she tore it open, but she hardly got beyond the first sentence before she let it drop in dismay.

'What's wrong? What's he say?' Walter looked up from his pile of bills.

'Geoff's poorly.'

'What's wrong with him?'

'They can't make it out. Bertie says there's something wrong with his tummy. He ain't eating properly.'

'Not eating? He eats like a horse, don't he?'

She nodded. 'It ain't like him, certainly. Hold on.' She read the letter. 'He says he wrote this in bed. Geoff's poorly and he has to stay off school to look after him. They still have to earn their keep, though, running errands for Mr Whittaker.'

'Earn their keep? Whittaker gets plenty from the government to cover the cost of the billet.' Walter was slower to take alarm, but he was beginning not to like the sound of it. 'Why's he writing his letter in bed, does he say?'

'He don't. Hang on.' Sadie's hand shook. 'He wants to know why we haven't written since February.'

'Since when?'

'Since February, only he spelt it wrong.' She held up her hand. 'Listen. He hopes we haven't forgotten about him and Geoff.' Her heart was squeezed tight, she had to hand over the letter for Walter to finish.

He scanned it. 'Oh, this ain't right, Sadie. He's writing in secret because Mrs Whittaker said not to let us know poor Geoff's ill. She thinks we'll only worry.'

'Too right we will.' Sadie stood up, ready to go for her hat and coat then and there. 'That settles it.' Her mind flew over the things she would have to arrange; leave of absence from the factory, train tickets, an explanation for Annie so that she could keep an eye on Walter and Meggie.

'What you up to now?'

'I'm gonna bring them back home, no messing.'

'Wait. We aren't one hundred per cent sure yet, are we?' He couldn't help thinking of the toll on everyone's nerves; the day-in, day-out worrying about what Hitler was up to. In Walter's opinion it was a matter of when, not if, he would strike.

'Sure of what?'

'Sure it's the right thing.'

She frowned with the effort of giving him a hearing. 'I know one thing, Walt, it ain't right where they are now.'

She'd spent the winter in an agony of doubt, veering between hoping for the best; trusting human nature and the will of God and fearing the worst: that the Whittakers were the sort who might exploit evacuees, and what this might entail for her two boys. She also had the evidence before her eyes of other mothers, worried sick about their absent children, taking all means to get them back home, travelling by bus or by truck, even hitching a ride into the country to fetch them.

'I don't think it's safe to have them back,' Walter insisted quietly.

'Oh,' she cried, 'says you! What about the others who think it is perfectly safe? Why do you think we've got shelters and sand-bags and sirens and klaxons? So we don't all get blown to bits, that's why!'

'But if Jerry does start in on us —'

'If, if, if! It's been "if" for more than six months, and nothing but false alarms and rumours.' She argued as if her life depended on it.

Upstairs in her room, Meggie heard the raised voices and came down.

Walter tried to think straight. It was true, many families had taken the risk of being back together. He'd also heard some horror stories of children being abominably treated in their billets; worked to the bone, half starved even beaten. Now the letter from Bertie made it likely that their own sons had been far from kindly received.

'He ain't mentioned his new wellingtons,' Sadie said with a choking sob. 'What happened to that parcel, Walter?'

'Right.' He nodded as if this tipped the balance. 'Pack your bag.'

Sadie gasped with relief. 'I can go and fetch them?'

In the doorway, Meggie stood hugging her dressing gown to her chest. She knew this would put her own increasingly desperate search for her father well down the list of Sadie's priorities. However, she could hardly object.

'Meggie, fetch the brown suitcase from the attic, then run up to the Duke and ask your gran to come down, quick as you can. You can tell her I'm going to fetch the boys back home.' It was as if the weight of the world had lifted from Sadie's shoulders. 'Oh, Walter, I'm sure this is the best thing. It feels right. I want the boys with us, whatever happens.'

Meggie went on her errand, while Walter followed Sadie round their bedroom as she began to pack. 'Do you want me to come?'

She straightened up in the midst of folding a navy blue and white spotted blouse. 'If you want.'

'I want what you want. And what's best for the boys. And Meggie.' He left the choice to her.

'Then I think I should go. You stay and take care of things here. I have this idea to go on the train to Manchester, to Jess's house. She'll put me up for the night and, if all goes well, she'll be able to drive me over to the boys in Rendal, collect them with me, and drive us back to her place. That way we won't need to rely on buses.' She continued packing her things.

'Shall I ring Jess from the depot to tell her?'

'Please.'

'And shall you warn the Whittakers?'

She paused again, resting a half-folded skirt over one arm. 'I don't think so, do you?'

He agreed. 'We don't want to give them a chance to go covering things up before you get there.'

'And it'll be a surprise for Bertie and Geoff. We'll arrive there out of the blue and straighten everything out for them. Before they know it, we'll have them safe back home.' Now that she had a plan she grew methodical, asking Walter to check the times of the Manchester trains, leaving instructions with Annie on what meals to prepare while she was away. It was Friday; she expected to get to Jess by evening. In the morning they would set off for Rendal; by tomorrow afternoon she would see her beloved boys.

'Is Your Journey Really Necessary?' Rob Parsons scowled at the poster as his taxicab stood idling outside the Windmill Theatre, waiting for Dorothy O'Hagan and her cronies to emerge. Sleek young men with slicked-back hairdos and wide flannel trousers strolled by, their arms around girls' slim waists, parading their night's conquests. As for the girls, they seemed wickedly available in their short skirts and sleeveless tops, while

Rob, by virtue of his age and job, was relegated to the role of mere spectator.

'C'mon!' He tapped the steering wheel, looking out for familiar faces; a fellow taxi driver, or even Bobby, Jimmie O'Hagan and Meggie who were out making a night of it, while Sadie travelled north to fetch the boys. But the streets were crowded and dim and he spotted no one he knew. He wanted to be home and in bed. In his resentment he was angered by the notion that none of these good-timers even seemed to be aware that there was a war on.

At last Dorothy, Lorna Bennett and two other women in their early twenties teetered out of the theatre and headed tipsily for the cab. What did they think they looked like, he wondered, as Lorna missed her footing and had to be helped up. Dorothy piled into the back of the taxi after her, showing practically everything — stocking-tops, suspenders, the lot — while the other two young ones giggled and smirked at a couple of passing sailors.

'Home, James!' Lorna waved him on.

The two sailors stopped to leer.

'No, wait. Want a lift?' The girl in the wrap-around red dress held the door open.

'Don't you just love them tiddly suits?'

her flame-haired friend cooed. 'All that gold braid.'

'Don't just stand there, hop in!'

But the sailors felt themselves outnumbered. 'Sorry, girls, some other time.' They winked at Rob, implying that he had his hands full, then strolled on.

'Aah!' They leaned out of the window as the cab left the kerb. 'Ta-ta, boys, you don't know what you're missing!'

As they settled into their seats, pulling the window shut, Rob could smell their heavy perfume infiltrating the glass partition. In his overhead mirror, he saw the back of Lorna's head, and the pale blotch of Dorothy's face caught off-guard, mouth set in a hard red line, eyes narrowed and shadowy behind a furl of blue smoke.

'Thanks for the memory,' the two youngest girls sang. 'Da — di-di-di-di — dee . . . Oh, thanks for the memory . . .' The motion of the cab as it swerved around a corner onto Shaftesbury Avenue sent them off-key and into another fit of giggles.

Bed, Rob thought. A whisky from the corner cupboard, and bed. Oblivion. Already he was half asleep. The street was dark, his lamps hooded. Only the road immediately in front of his wheels was visible, though shapes of pedestrians might loom out from the pavement and he would jolt upright, his attention sharpened for a few seconds before it lapsed again.

'Thanks for the memory, Ba-bu-bu-bu-bu — boom.'

Rob found his way without having to think, along the Embankment in its dull wartime guise of blacked-out Ministry buildings, shadowy archways and the black mass of the river shifting silently under Waterloo Bridge.

Suddenly he slammed on his brakes. The women in the back lurched and squealed, the cab slewed sideways.

'Bleeding idiot!' Rob fought for control. The road was greasy, he wouldn't be able to stop. A man was there, caught in his headlights. Someone else tried to grab him and pull him out of the way. Just in time, the swaying figure veered sideways, forearm up to shield him from the impact, torn coat flying open in the wind.

'Christ!' Rob's wheels locked and squealed. For a second he thought he must have hit him. The women were deadly quiet. As they skidded to a halt and the engine cut out, he swung open his door and stepped out. A second tramp was hauling the inert body of the first clear of the road. 'Did I catch him?'

'Just clipped him, I think.' His job done, the rescuer wanted to shuffle out of the limelight.

'Is he dead?' Lorna recovered first and came to stand by Rob.

'Dead drunk more like.' Getting over the shock, Rob was more annoyed than anything. 'Leave him be.' Lorna was trying to turn the unconscious tramp face-up and loosen his filthy woollen scarf. Rob turned to get some sense out of his companion. 'Where does he live?'

A shrug, a noncommittal shrug.

'Nowhere.' Rob's hands were deep in his jacket pocket. 'Marvellous, ain't it?' He was all for leaving him where he was, there on the pavement.

But the two young girls in his cab had turned into would-be Florence Nightingales, along with Lorna. They piled out onto the pavement. 'Poor old thing, look at the state of him. Ain't there nowhere we can take him?' they appealed to the hero of the moment. Meanwhile Rob looked on, while Lorna tried to right the victim and Dorothy sat scornfully by, her lip curled, a fresh cigarette between her fingers.

'Dunno. You can leave him there if you want.'

'But you know him, don't you? There

must be somewhere we can drop him off.'

'Me? No, I was just passing.' Perhaps it struck the second tramp there was something in this new role of hero, however, for he stopped making as if to wander off into the night and thought again. 'I don't really, what you might call, know him. Not by name or nothing.'

By now the inert victim was stirring. Lorna succeeded in tipping him onto his back. His cap fell forward over his face.

'Mind you, I do know there's someone in Bernhardt Court what keeps an eye on him if he's in a real bad way.'

'Who?' The girl in the red dress seized on this.

Rob turned impatiently and walked back to the cab.

'Someone in a pub up there.' Their informant struggled to remember. 'No, it's gone. But it's definitely Bernhardt Court, a pub somewhere there.'

'Let's take him up there. We can't leave him in this state.'

'Who's paying?' Rob wanted to know.

Dorothy met his gaze. 'Don't look at me. I'm like you, I want my bed.'

The girls wailed in protest, then turned to the coherent vagrant. 'You could take him!'

'Not me. I ain't got two brass farthings.'

But there was no stopping them in their mission of mercy. The flame-haired girl hailed another cab, then Red Dress opened her purse. 'Here's two bob.' She handed a florin to the tramp. 'We'll put him in this taxi and you make sure he gets up to Bernhardt Court, OK?'

He took it with a stupefied look. Dorothy raised an eyebrow at Rob.

'Here, give us a hand.' Lorna gave up the unequal struggle to get the semi-conscious man to his feet. The new cabbie leaned out, obviously wondering what he'd got himself into.

In the end Rob saw it as the quickest way out of the difficulty. 'Get in,' he barked at the bemused hero, indicating the back of the new taxi. Then he turned to help the girls. They got the tramp upright, leaning against Rob's chest. Lorna pulled the cap back from the grime-lined, sagging, ruined face. A blast of stinking breath hit Rob full force. He staggered. By the time they'd got him safely stowed, Rob was white and breathing hard.

A door slammed and the second cab set off with the tramps inside, back over the river onto the Embankment. Once out of sight, the hero rapped hard on the cabby's partition. 'This'll do!'

The cab stopped and disgorged its cargo. The drunken victim fell flat on the pavement. The other tossed the cabbie a couple of coppers and went on his way, his florin intact.

Sick to his stomach, Rob dropped his own passengers one by one along Duke Street, then made his way to Walter's house. He had to tell someone what had just taken place or he would choke on it. The downstairs light was still on at number 32.

'Walt?' He knocked quietly on the door and spoke through the letter-box. 'It's me, Rob.'

Walter was late going to bed; he hated the house without Sadie in it, especially the empty bedroom. Meggie had recently come home and was upstairs in her own bed. 'Rob, you look done in.' He held the door and let him in. 'Here.' He went straight to the front room and pulled out the whisky bottle for him. 'Have a swig. Tell me what's going on for God's sake.'

Rob gulped the drink. 'Christ Almighty, Walt, you ain't gonna believe what I just did.'

'Has there been an accident?' Walter feared the worst. Rob was white as a sheet, breathing fast, the sweat standing out on his forehead. 'You ain't gone and knocked some poor blighter over?'

'I wish I bleeding well had!' He was in agony. He clenched his teeth as the whisky hit the back of his throat. Then he took another gulp. 'I wish I'd bleeding killed him!'

'Who? What is this? Come on, Rob, spit it out.' They had both raised their voices, Walter had to restrain Rob from crashing furniture about the place.

'I didn't run him over, did I? I wish I had.' He imagined the satisfaction he would have had. 'Bleeding fool stepped right in front of me, drunk as a lord. I slammed on the brakes, bleeding well missed him!'

'Who? *Who?*' Walter shook him by the shoulder.

'Richie Palmer, that's who. I just gone and saved his life.'

CHAPTER SEVEN

'You cast-iron, copper-bottom certain?'

'I'd know him a mile off.' Rob gave Walter the whole story, blow by blow. 'The girls get this idea to send him up Shaftesbury Avenue in another cab, to Bernhardt Court, so I'm lending a hand to get him back on his feet and that's when I get a look at him, close as this.' Rob held the flat of his hand against his nose. 'The man's a wreck, but I still know him and, what's more, he knows me.'

Walter took this in. 'Give me that,' he said, grabbing the whisky bottle from Rob and taking a drink. 'You all right?'

'Tip-top.'

'It's a good job Sadie ain't here to hear this.'

Rob felt the tension begin to fade. 'Would you believe it. He was there, right there under the wheels, as near as dammit.'

Walter recognized how he must feel. Even he felt a pang of regret. 'I suppose he was bound to turn up sooner or later.' He didn't relish the idea of what Sadie and Meggie would want to do next, if they did get to hear.

'But I had him, Walt, honest to God.'

'Shh, keep your voice down. I reckon it's for the best.'

'Not likely. If I'd finished him off there and then, that would've been it. A score settled, an end to your problems.' Knowing Walter as he did, Rob guessed that he would in the end want to go and blab to Sadie. Now he regretted following this urge to tell him all about it. This way, the whole thing would be sure to end in tears. He sat down to try and talk sense into his over-scrupulous partner. 'Now look, Walt . . .'

'I know what you're gonna say next, Rob.' Walter rocked back on his chair, rolling the newspaper he'd been reading into a thin column and tapping it against his knee.

'Will you have to bring this up with Sadie?'

'Who said I would?'

'No, but you will, though.' Once more Rob swiped the bottle from the table and took a long drink. 'Let's get this straight. I nearly run over the geezer what tried to do me in in the first place by cutting them brake rods, only he gets you by mistake. Then he ditches my sister, your missus, and the kid.'

'I know, I know. Keep your voice down for God's sake.'

'No, listen here. You're too soft by half, that's your trouble. All these years on, I miss my chance to pay him back. Who'd have been any the wiser? A tramp, dead drunk, walks under the wheels of my cab. Good riddance.'

'Well, it ain't happened like that, Rob.'

'Worse luck!' He worked himself up. 'But I'm stupid, I am. I have to come and tell you all about it. And now you'll go blabbing to Sadie and Meggie, and that'll send them off up Shaftesbury Avenue to Bernhardt Court and they'll be able to track him down. And what'll you do then?'

Walter hung his head. 'I don't know.'

'And what'll *they* do? You know Sadie. She ain't gonna be able to take this in her stride, is she?'

She had a lot to cope with these days. She could still be strong and determined, but the worry was definitely undermining her health. Walter would often find her in bed with a terrible headache, or so silent in her routine chores that it was like being in the house with a ghost, a hollow shell, when she turned in on herself and refused to let him come near. 'But what about Meggie?

Don't she have a right to find out about her own pa?'

Rob didn't answer at once. He'd had this argument before, at home with Amy. He saw it as a practical issue: if Meggie succeeded in her hunt for Palmer it would only cause more problems. Amy argued for allowing Meggie to go on looking for him. If she found him, they would clear the air and she would know the truth about her lousy father. Then she wouldn't have to spend her whole life caught on the hook of 'if only'.

Outside the door, sitting barefoot on the bottom stair, Meggie pulled her dressing gown around her. She'd been awake from the first knock, when her stepfather opened the door to her uncle. Their raised voices had brought her downstairs.

'For God's sake, Walt, keep this under your hat. Ain't we got enough to worry about?'

Meggie held her breath. She was on the point of standing up, opening the door and saying, 'It don't make no difference, I already heard every word.' But something made her stay put. Perhaps she wanted to test Walter's loyalties. Maybe her own mind was so shocked and confused that she lacked the presence of mind to act. So she sat and

137

shivered in the dark.

Walter rapped the newspaper on the edge of the table. 'Have another drink, Rob. And stop going on about it, will you?' Never, not once in their married life, had he kept anything from Sadie. He sighed and shook his head.

'I will if you promise you'll keep stumm.'

Meggie heard Walter stand and walk across the stone-flagged floor. She shot upstairs like a scared rabbit, too quick and sudden to hear his final answer:

'Have it your way, Rob. I won't say nothing to Sadie. Let's keep this between you and me, eh?'

All week Tommy had laid off the drink and given Edie his sober, undivided attention. Instead of repairing to the Duke in the evening, he stayed late in the office, letting her know that he was there, a shoulder to cry on if she should need it. It was the most private and most neutral place he could think of.

To look at her from the outside, coming into work each day in a smart dress, her hair pinned up at the back but falling over to one side of her face in a gentle, shiny wave of honey-gold, always with a cheery word and an instant answer to queries about stock, hours worked, wages, no one would have guessed that she had troubles of her own. Edie had pulled herself together and out of his arms on Monday evening. He was left with the memory of her burying her beautiful face against his shoulder, as if the imprint of her slight figure had left an indelible impression. At night in bed, he would turn half-expecting it to be Edie there beside him, finding only an unresponsive Dorothy, lately in from her gallivanting.

'Everything all right?' he asked again on Friday, after Edie had dealt as usual with the wages. He'd told Lorna and the others to go on home. He would lock up and finish things off.

Lorna made no bones about wanting to be off.

'You coming, Edie?' She shouted down the stairs.

'No. I've to finish cashing up.'

'Ta-ta, see you later, then.'

They'd arranged to meet to go to the cinema. 'Half seven at the bus stop.' Edie heard the shop bell ring and the door slam. She looked up as Tommy came down.

'Everything all right?'

'Fine, ta.' She piled the sixpences into silver columns next to the chunky threepenny bits.

He stood looking at her, hands in pockets. 'Sure? You don't want to go to pieces all over again?'

She laughed. 'Don't you wish?'

'As a matter of fact I do.' He walked a fine line between joking and meaning what he said. 'I like it when you go to pieces.'

Since Monday's confession, Edie had been deliberately brisk with Tommy. Not another soul knew about her row with Bill. Edie's mother was dead, her father lived up in Shoreditch with his spinster sister. They weren't close and, as an only child, she'd grown up used to living an independent emotional life. What others might have called lonely, she thought of as normal. It still wasn't her habit to go sharing her troubles; it altered people's opinion of you too much and, generally, there was little they could do.

'I hope you don't think I was leading you on?' She left off from her counting, frowning up at him.

He bit his lip. 'Silly joke. Sorry.' He'd risked the rebuff, but still it knocked him back.

Edie stood up. 'No, I'm the one that's sorry. You were good to me, Tommy. I was very grateful.'

He felt them drifting, all at sea, her flying

the flag of politeness, him making all the wrong semaphore signals in his confusion. There was a knot of tension gathering under his rib cage. 'I meant what I said; you ought to think why you stay with that old man of yours. But then, I ain't the one to be doling out advice, am I?'

She knew that he meant he had a vested interest. She wanted to be straight with him. She liked her boss. The way he handled himself by joking his way through difficulties, but never at another's expense, and how the tough shell disguised kindness. He looked after Jimmie, didn't he? And his generosity over the little gifts and bonuses was done to please, not out of ulterior motives. This week she'd even begun comparing him with Bill; the solid muscularity of her husband, set against Tommy's wiry, lithe stance.

'I got to finish this.' She gestured towards the heap of uncounted coins on her desk, blushed and turned away.

'Leave it.' He caught hold of her wrist, bent forward and kissed her.

She took half a step back then stopped. She wanted him to kiss her again, she realized.

Her tilted face was all he saw, all he thought about; her clear grey eyes, the curling lashes, the open mouth. He pressed his own lips against hers, saw her close her eyes, felt her arms slide around him. He was kissing her again and again.

'Tommy, stop!' She struggled to bring her arms up to his chest, to push him away. 'No, don't stop.' Changing her mind as she opened her eyes and saw his face so close. Her arms went up and around his neck.

They melted together, the kisses grew less urgent, more tender. Edie tilted her head back as he brushed her neck with his lips. 'Tommy, what are we gonna do?'

'You said that before.' He was breathing in her perfume, not wanting to talk.

'No, what I said then was, what am *I* gonna do? Now it's *we*. That's different.'

'You sure?'

She nodded.

'I ain't just a shoulder to cry on?'

This time it was a shake of the head. 'I ought not to be saying this, ought I?'

'Me neither.' He wouldn't let her go, though. He drew her close and swayed with her.

'I want you, Edie. I want another chance.' He rested his chin on her shoulder, she felt warm and soft.

Again she nodded. The vital move had been made: the first kiss and her decision to respond. From now on some things were relatively straightforward. 'Will you come to my place?'

He held on more tightly. 'Sure?'

'About that, yes.'

'When?'

'Soon. Let me telephone Lorna to tell her I can't meet her. You lock up here.'

'We could go along together.' He feared she would change her mind.

'Better not.'

'Half an hour, then?'

She leaned back and looked earnestly at him. 'Be careful, won't you?' She lived above the post office, near the railway bridge that ran across the top end of Duke Street.

'Leave the door open, all right? I'll slip in quietly and lock it behind me.'

They made their arrangements, still without quite believing that their tryst would take place. In a fumble back towards normality, Tommy swept the uncounted cash into a cloth bag and stashed it in a drawer, promising to deal with it in the morning. Saturday was Edie's day off, in any case. She took her cream-coloured jacket from the stand by the door and put it on over her pink flowered dress. She came to kiss him on the cheek, then slipped away, her footsteps light and quick on the stairs.

Meanwhile, early that same evening, Sadie had stepped off the train in Manchester Piccadilly. The steam from the engine swirled along the dirty roofs of the carriages and engulfed the alighting passengers in an acrid, damp cloud. She shook herself alert after the seemingly endless journey and walked determinedly along the platform under the giant glass arch towards the barrier where Jess would be waiting.

The sisters spied each other at the same moment. Sadie passed through the barrier, put down her case and embraced Jess, too moved to speak. Only after they'd wiped their eyes and picked up the luggage again did they begin to exchange the latest news. Grace, Jess's twenty-five-year-old daughter, was waiting for them at home. Mo, her son, was at work in the office of his father's cinema business. Like all young men in their early twenties, he was nervously waiting to be called up. Jess dreaded him having to go.

'It doesn't seem five minutes since I was sending him off to school with a clean hankie and his dinner wrapped up in a napkin,' she sighed. 'And now look at him, old enough to get himself shot.'

'Don't.' Sadie stowed her case in the back

of Jess's Austin. At nearly fifty, Jess had, like all the Parsons sisters, kept her slim figure and remarkably good features, her brown eyes still large and vital, her dark hair with hardly a hint of grey. She wore it fashionably long and wavy, with just enough make-up, and a modern style of dress. This evening, to meet Sadie, she had on a pair of high-waisted navy blue slacks and a tailored white top, one of her own outfits from the city centre shop. 'You look lovely, as per usual,' Sadie said, half envious.

'And you look worn out,' came the frank reply. They slammed the car doors shut and Jess started the engine. 'Let's get you home. First thing you have is a nice long soak in the bath. Then tell me all about what's going on.'

Things had worked out differently for Sadie, you only had to look. Jess, too, had had an illegitimate child, the result of a violent attack by her one-time employer's son. But her family had stood by her and she and Hettie had set up in the rag trade, in a very small way at first. Then Maurice had come along and claimed her and, eventually, whisked the family up here to Manchester, to develop his chain of cinemas. He had succeeded but she had missed her sisters sorely. Gradually she'd built up a new business, a new life. Sadie meanwhile, the youngest and in some ways the most reckless of the girls, had echoed her own misfortune. Meggie was also illegitimate, only Sadie had made it much harder for herself and the child, running away with Richie Palmer and cutting herself off from the family, until the inevitable had happened and Palmer had brought them all to the brink of tragedy, with Walter in hospital at death's door.

They motored out of the grimy city up a main road, past the redbrick university buildings. Jess and Maurice lived beyond the university in a gracious house set well back from the road, screened by trees and a high wall. Though not modern, it was well proportioned, with wide steps to a double doorway surrounded by leaded glass, leading into a square entrance hall where a long staircase window shed plenty of light. Jess had kept the furnishings simple but good, while Maurice had insisted on many of the latest design improvements, including the Ascot water heater from which Sadie filled a luxurious, deep bath.

She soon came down refreshed, having changed into a tailored powder-blue dress with padded shoulders and a neat buckled belt.

'Better?' Jess was ready with a light teatime snack, served by Grace, a shy, smiling young woman who might easily have stepped from the pages of a fashion magazine, with her beautifully made grey two-piece, a feminine touch of white silk at the collar, showing long, slim legs encased in a good pair of seamed nylon stockings.

'Much.' Sadie took her niece's hand and gave it a squeeze. 'You look just like your ma.'

Grace handed her a cup of tea. 'People say we look like sisters.'

'The same with you and Meggie, I expect.' Jess didn't want Sadie to think that the house, the car, all the new gadgets put a barrier between them. 'Now go ahead and tell us what all this is about. I could hardly make you out on the telephone.'

Sadie gave them the full story of Bertie's secretly written letter and their recently aroused suspicions about the Whittakers. Jess and Grace listened attentively, their foreheads furrowed. They wished that Manchester had been free of the threat of air raids so that they could have taken the boys themselves. Both agreed they must go to Rendal with Sadie the following morning.

Jess's soft heart melted. If only she'd known, she would have driven over to see for herself how they were treated. 'I know you and your pride, Sadie, but you should have said instead of having all this heartache.'

Sadie blew her nose into her handkerchief. 'I wanted to give them time to settle in. And we ain't sure yet. Bertie and Geoff might be right as rain for all we know.'

She found herself adopting Walter's cautious role. 'I've just come up to make sure.'

She went early to bed, with loving hugs and kisses from both Jess and Grace, in a guest room overlooking the back lawn, edged with white and purple lilac trees just coming into blossom. Her bed was wide, the linen smooth and crisp. Yet she couldn't sleep; she wondered how Walter and Meggie were managing, of the surprise that lay in store for Bertie and Geoff. Half of her hoped that they would arrive at Rendal and the decision would be a simple one. The boys' obvious misery would remove any doubts. On the other hand, how could she possibly hope that her own sons had in fact been badly treated?

Jess seemed to know what she must be going through. As she passed the door on her own way to bed, she looked in on her sister. 'You awake?'

'Wide awake.'

She came in, hair freshly brushed, in a

148

white satin dressing gown, and sat on the edge of Sadie's bed. They talked until the early hours about family, about the war. Sadie realized that just at the point when she hoped soon to have her two boys safely back home, Jess must expect to lose her only son to the glamorous uniform and the dangerous missions of the RAF, Mo's chosen branch of the armed forces. It made her cry all over again that families should suffer such grief, that young lives should be put at risk and their very futures clouded over by the immense shadows of war.

'I brought this.' Tommy pulled a half-bottle of whisky from his pocket and put it by the parchment lamp on Edie's living-room table. Half an hour was long enough for her to have had second, third and fourth thoughts. 'Dutch courage.'

'Who for? You or me?' She'd heard him come upstairs, tried to look busy by drawing the curtains and turning on the table lamp.

'Both. Got any glasses?' He looked round the room. She'd done it out in striped green wallpaper from the shop, with plenty of shiny bronze and chrome finishes on the fender, the mirror frames, the low table for the gramophone.

She watched him size up her home.

'Who did the wallpapering?'

'Me.'

'Not your old man?'

'He ain't interested. That's fine by me; it means I get to do the choosing.'

'And the paying?'

She shrugged, handing him two small glasses. She'd changed out of her frock into slacks and a short-sleeved jumper, and let her hair fall loose.

Tommy caught sight of the fading bruises on her upper arm. Somehow it made him want to go very gently. 'Anyhow, you got a nice place.'

'Ta.' She offered him a seat beside her on the fawn moquette sofa. They sat like two acquaintances on a works outing, glasses in hand. What had they rushed into, back there at the office?

'What did you tell Lorna?'

'Not much. I just said something came up.'

'Well, she won't be stuck.' He drank and clenched his teeth.

'No. She said she'd ask Dorothy instead.' Damn. She bit her tongue and glanced away.

'Well, she'll be game for anything. I'd have thought the pictures a bit tame for her though. What were you going to see?'

'George Formby in *Trouble Brewing*.'

He looked at her with a grin. 'Never.'

'Yes.' She thought about it. 'Oh, I see, trouble brewing. Yes, I suppose there is.'

There was a silence. 'Edie —'

'We could —'

'What?'

'No, after you.'

'There you go again.'

'What?'

'You're always so bleeding polite!'

'Am I?' She blushed. 'I was going to say we could listen to some music if you liked.'

He breathed a sigh of relief, nodded and watched her as she bent to choose a record and placed the needle carefully on the black disc. It scratched and fuzzed along the outside grooves. 'Electric?'

'We're up-to-date, you know. At least electricity isn't on ration yet.'

The music began, a Jack Payne number with the full big-band sound.

'Do you want to roll back the carpet and dance?' He stood up. 'Ain't that what he says on the wireless?'

'I don't mind.' She stood hesitating by the sofa.

'Let's dance then.' He went and took hold of her. 'Never mind the carpet, eh?' Once he had an arm around her waist and she rested her hand lightly on his shoulder, he seemed to calm down. 'You know what I thought you was about to say?'

She listened above the soaring note of the clarinets. 'No, when?'

'I thought you was about to give me my marching orders.'

'What, when I said we could listen to some music?'

'Yep. I'm glad you didn't, though.' He was more like his old self, chirpy and confident, as he swung her round and they neatly sidestepped a big armchair.

'Me too.'

'Sure?' His grip round her waist tightened.

'Sure I'm sure.' She was blushing and laughing at him.

'Sure you're sure you're sure?'

'Tommy O'Hagan!'

'Edie Morell.' He murmured her name. This time she kissed him.

Her bedroom led off from the living room. As the record finished and the needle ground its way towards the middle in a mush of static sound, they steered through the open door. Tommy hugged her to him and leaned on the door to close it. Together they almost overbalanced.

'Oops.' Upright and separate, she held

him at arm's length, running her fingertips down his cheek. 'What about you? You ain't gonna regret this?'

For answer he closed the gap between them. 'You're my perfect girl, you know that?' Her smile glowed back at him. 'You're beautiful, but it ain't that.'

Edie put her arms around his neck. 'Don't go making me bigheaded, Tommy.'

'Ain't nobody told you you're beautiful lately?'

'Oh, yes, I walk down the street and everyone and his aunt stops me to tell me that. What do you think I am?' She began to tease him back.

'Perfect.' He ran his hands over her back, enjoying the suppleness of her body as she rested her weight against his arms. 'Anyhow, like I said, being nice looking ain't it. Nice looking girls come ten a penny.'

'What then?' She kissed him and pulled his tie loose, unfastening the top shirt button.

He studied her face. 'You mean what you say. You don't play games.'

These sudden shifts of mood took her by surprise. She saw a backlog of mistrust and bitter experience behind his serious words.

And then neither wanted to hesitate any longer. Tommy slid onto the bed with her, following his desire, amazed by how much she wanted him. Soon she lay without clothes, hair like gold spun out on the pillow, gazing up at him. He touched her shoulder where there was still a faint bruise, then kissed it and stroked her, felt her hands along his back, pulling him towards her. She sank under his weight, then she arched her back as he ran his hands over her breasts, both quickly aroused, seeking and giving pleasure.

'See?' he said afterwards. 'I said you were my perfect girl.' All energy spent, he lay on his front, face turned towards her as she lay on her back.

She gazed at the ceiling. 'You're not so bad yourself.'

'Do you love me?'

'Now you want me to make *you* bigheaded.' She turned on to her side, her face close to his, noses touching. 'Yes I do. I love you.'

'Good.' He closed his eyes. 'It's a bleeding good job you said that, Edie. I'd've gone home and slit my throat if you'd said no.'

'It's not as bad as that, surely?' She whispered softly, her mouth covering his face in kisses.

'It ain't, because you said yes you do.' Through half closed eyes he saw the blur of her features, smelt her skin, reached across and touched her hair.

'But where does it leave us?' she wanted to know.

'On top of the world. That's where I am right this minute.'

'And me.'

They embraced. Tomorrow they would try to work things out, plan and negotiate and see what could be done. Tonight they were oblivious in each other's arms.

CHAPTER EIGHT

Sadie, Jess and Grace set off for Rendal at dawn. Jess had used up all her petrol ration for the month ahead to drive them on the two-hour journey out of the city along a sequence of ever narrower and bumpier country roads. Wartime restrictions meant there were no signposts to help them find their way, and it was only by Grace's careful study of a road map that they wound their way eastwards into the Pennines, towards the Lancashire-Yorkshire border.

'Fancy living here.' Sadie stared out at the bleak moorland hills. Even in spring they looked gloomy. Jess had tried to keep her amused with a famous local legend about witches being burned on a nearby summit; one of the last such occasions in England.

'It's only a story,' she reassured her.

'It ain't true, then?'

'Who knows? But it was a long time ago in any case.' She stopped to ask directions from an old man pushing a bike up the hill. He told them that Rendal was the next village coming up.

'You can't miss it. You come to the Methodist chapel just past Slingsby Farm, then you're in Rendal. Just one row of houses, mind. Don't blink, or you'll pass straight through it.' He could see they were city types from the way they dressed, but his curiosity was mainly directed at Jess's smart new car. He leaned on his bike, watching enviously as it disappeared round the bend.

'Nearly there, Auntie Sadie.' Grace bent forward, resting her folded arms along the back of the passenger seat. 'One thing, they'll never be expecting you, especially at this time of day.'

'Shall we come in with you?' Jess had spotted a chapel on the left and slowed down. The village was in a narrow valley, with a river running through it and only one singletrack road. Grey houses built of local stone lined the street, with little front gardens and dogs yapping at their wrought-iron gates. These gave way to a row of shops; a bakery, a post office, a butchers. She drew to a halt at the roadside, fifty yards from the door.

'Is it all right if I go ahead by myself?' Sadie hesitated, but going alone was the best way to keep her mind concentrated on the sole object of her visit.

'We'll wait right here.' Jess pulled off her white kid gloves and folded them flat in the glove compartment. 'If you're not out in half an hour we'll come looking for you. And if you need a hand sooner than that, give us a shout.'

Almost mechanically Sadie nodded and stepped from the car. Jess's heart went out to the tall, straight figure clutching her handbag firmly under one arm, head up, making for the butcher's door.

'Mr Whittaker?' The bell jangled. Sadie's mouth was dry. She stood on the sawdust-strewn floor, looking across a marble counter at a bald man with a pink, round, hairless face, wearing a blue striped apron over a starched white coat.

He knew straight away that she wasn't a customer. Only locals got their meat from him and, since rationing, every ounce, every scrap was spoken for. He didn't answer, but put down the skewer he was using to truss up a piece of brisket, then wiped his hands on his apron.

'I'm Sadie Davidson.'

There was no click of realization in his eyes. Slowly he wiped his hands across his stomach, looking warily at her.

She quaked. Was this a bad mistake? What sort of man was this? Had she got the wrong end of the stick from Bertie's grubby letter?

'I'm Bertie and Geoff's ma.'

'Ah!' He saw the resemblance between her and the younger boy particularly. 'Mrs Davidson, you'll be a sight for sore eyes. Do they know you're coming?'

She shook her head. 'It was a last minute thing and I wanted it to be a surprise. My sister drove me in her car from Manchester.'

'Did she now? Hang on here a tick.' He untied his apron and hung it from an empty meat hook. 'Let me go and tell Mrs Whittaker. You caught us a bit on the hop, you know.'

She mumbled her apologies as he went out. So far, so good. She stood and waited in the empty shop, fascinated by a slow trickle of blood from a pig's snout onto the sawdust, its bare, smooth pink skin, the bristle inside its ears. In the background she heard a door slam, through the window she could see Jess's shiny black car.

Another door opened and a woman came from the house part of the building through into the shop. She was small and thick-set, with carefully waved, short grey hair, older than Sadie had imagined and dressed in a navy blue ribbed cardigan over a blue floral print dress. She wore an old fashioned cameo brooch at the neck, and several gold rings on her left hand. 'I'm Nancy Whittaker.'

'Sadie Davidson.' They shook hands. 'I'm sorry to drop in on you like this, only I ain't got much time. I'm due back at work on Monday.'

Nancy Whittaker seemed to be sizing her up; her voice, her dress, her intentions. 'I suppose Gordon didn't tell you?'

The woman's face was impassive. Sadie in turn tried to read the situation. 'Tell me what?'

'The boys aren't here.'

'Not here?' Dazed, she looked round the shop as if she might find them hiding between the carcasses, as in her dream.

'Not at the moment, no.'

'How long will they be?'

'I can't say for sure. Now, if you'd given us a bit of warning —'

'Yes, I'm sorry.' She trailed off. Nancy Whittaker was neither friendly nor hostile, only a bit put out that Sadie had dropped in out of the blue. 'Where did you say they were?'

'I didn't. They go out to a farm on a Saturday. Fresh air does them good.'

'And is it far, this farm?'

'Slingsbys? It's a bit out of the way, yes.'

'I think we came past it on the way in.'
She began to feel that it was like getting
blood out of a stone. If she'd been in Nancy
Whittaker's shoes, she would have moved
heaven and earth to let the boys see their
mother.

Mrs Whittaker stepped in smartly with a
suggestion. 'I'll tell you what; Gordon has
to go up there on his delivery round. Why
don't you let him collect Bertie and Geoff?
He can bring them down to see you.'

This was better. Sadie curbed her impatience. 'That'd be champion. When would
it be?'

'In about an hour.'

The words brought a flush of excitement
to her cheeks. 'Oh that's grand, Mrs Whittaker. I can hardly wait. It must mean
Geoff's feeling better, then, if he can go up
to the farm for the day.' She sensed the
butcher's wife stiffen. 'I heard he's been a
bit off-colour. I expect it was nothing
much.'

The woman walked her to the door. 'His
stomach's a bit delicate, that's all. He has
to watch what he eats.'

This was news to Sadie. 'There was nothing wrong with his appetite at home.' She
hovered on the step, more puzzled than
alarmed. After all, she was very near to

seeing them and satisfying herself one way or another.

'Growing boys.' Nancy Whittaker stood, head to one side. 'Shoot up like sticks of celery, don't they?'

'I'll go and tell my sister the latest.' Distracted, Sadie walked away from the shop.

'Well?' Jess leaned out of the open window.

'They'll be here in a little while.' She explained as she got in and sat with a sigh against the brown leather seat.

'And she never asked you in?'

'No.'

'Not to see how they lived?'

'No.'

'How did she seem?'

'Ordinary. Old. She didn't smile much.'

'Well that ain't a crime,' Jess said. They watched customers come and go.

'No, but she don't look the sort to cope with two lively boys.'

They sat for a while. 'Odd that she never asked you in. It's the least she could do.'

From the back seat Grace noticed the high top of a delivery van edge down a narrow lane onto the main road. 'There he is. Let's follow him back to the farm.'

Sadie considered it. 'I said I'd wait here.'

'But we don't have to.'

162

'They might think I'm too pushy.'

'And so would anybody be, after not seeing their kids for six months. Come on.' Jess made up her mind for Sadie and started the engine, but the van had turned in the wrong direction for Slingsby Farm and headed away from them towards the top of the valley.

'What's he up to?' Sadie wondered if she'd got her wires crossed.

'Never mind. Let's drive to the farm anyhow.' Grace grew impatient. 'He's too slow to catch cold.'

'No.' Jess's eyes narrowed. 'I think we should follow him.' Without more ado, she set off after Whittaker's van, which travelled at a fair speed, without stopping to drop off any deliveries. Instead, it braked abruptly outside a large wooden barn set back from the road at the far end of the village. They watched as the butcher jumped down and opened up the back of the van, taking a bulky sack from inside and carrying it over his shoulder to the open door of the barn. Above the door they could make out the peeling name board; 'Calvert — Fertilizers.'

'Why can't he get a move on?' Sadie whispered after five minutes had passed. 'At this rate we're never gonna get back to the farm.'

'Wait.' Jess held on to her wrist. Out of

the dark barn came the butcher, minus his sack, but accompanied by two small, scrawny figures.

'Oh!' Sadie gave a cry. Her hand flew to her mouth.

'Right!' Jess turned swiftly to Sadie. 'That's them, ain't it?'

'But I thought they were at the farm —' She was too shocked to see straight. The boys followed Whittaker to the van, feet dragging, heads bowed.

'No, he's got them working in that horrible place. It grinds bones for fertiliser.' Jess jumped from the car, quickly followed by Grace. They ran to intercept the butcher, while Sadie sat petrified.

She saw Whittaker stop, turn his back and heave the boys up into the back of the van. He had the door slammed shut before Jess and Grace could get to them. Slowly Sadie got out of the car.

'Look here,' Jess began to remonstrate. Whittaker turned, hands on hips. 'Just open up that van for me, please.' She was imperious, lording it over him to put him off his stride. 'We've come for these boys, so open the door.'

He was slow to react, but once he did, it was to stand in front of the door handle to prevent Grace from opening it. 'Don't you lay a finger on that,' he warned. 'I'll have the bobbies on you if you do.'

Grace dodged around the side of the van while her mother tackled the man.

'And I'll have the police on to you if we find you've been mistreating those boys. You told their mother a lie. You said they were up on a farm getting some fresh air, not working in a stinking bone factory.'

'Helping out,' he insisted, not in the least shamefaced. 'Not what you'd call really working —'

Sadie began to run. She flung herself at him, beating her fists against his chest. 'Where are they? Let me see them. What have you done?' She was beside herself with anger and guilt.

But clear-thinking Grace had already wrenched open the driver's door and clambered up. In the back of the van she made out Bertie and Geoff cowering on a pile of old sacks. 'This way, that's right! Climb over the seat, quick as you can.' She held out her arms to help them. Bertie scrambled towards her, then Geoff. When she lifted him to the ground he was light as a feather. 'Here they are!' She called to the others. Two men, sleeves rolled up, waistcoats hanging open, had come out of the barn to see what the racket was.

Jess pulled Sadie off Whittaker, who began to shrug and laugh it off when he saw the onlookers. 'Leave him. Grace has got them out safe. Come this way.'

'A lot of fuss about nothing.' Whittaker pulled his shirt straight and tucked it in at the waist. 'All she has to do is come knocking nicely at my door like any normal woman, instead of running at me like a raving lunatic.' He went into a huddle of self-justification with the two men.

But Sadie knew only one thing. There were Bertie and Geoff standing hand in hand with their cousin Grace. They were thin, white-faced, grimy, their eyes big as saucers beneath untidy mops of matted hair. They looked like wild boys fed on berries and nuts, but they cried out with joy when they saw her and flung themselves around her neck. Soon she was on her knees, crying, hugging them, holding their little bodies to her, wiping their smudged faces with the hem of her dress.

Up the West End on a sunny Saturday morning, Meggie found it hard to believe that there was a war on. True, the windows were all taped up, and posters everywhere pressed you to do your bit, but the spirit of Londoners wasn't in the least crushed by daily warnings and deprivations. On the contrary, life went on in a whirl of music wafting across the airwaves, with new heroes and heroines on the silver screen to show them how to dress, dance, fall in love and be brave.

She walked up Shaftesbury Avenue, past box offices advertising 'Performance Tonight As Usual', cheek by jowl with warnings to 'Wear Your Gas Mask EVERYWHERE.' Instead of clouds in the blue sky, there were silver barrage balloons, but Tommy Handley's ITMA popped up all over the place to take her mind off what they were doing there, and Arthur Askey's cheerful playmates set up rousing choruses of 'Run, Adolf, Run' through open windows and doorways.

Meggie felt cheated by the glitz and glamour of theatreland, knowing full well that her errand probably had no happy ending, that in taking up the latest clues dropped by her Uncle Rob, all she was likely to see at the end of the day was a helpless old drunk. No celebrations. No grand reunions.

Still, she was dogged. She'd set out in the middle of the morning, saying she was going to scour the shops for a pair of fashionable summer shoes. Walter had waved her off without a second thought and, at the pub,

Annie had warned her to find herself a decent pair. 'Not them peep-toed platform things that you fall off and break your ankle on.' Her gran had a thing about shoes being sensible. Meggie had said she would do her best and hurried off.

Her real mission took her away from the empty shops and into the thick of theatreland, where her pace slowed and she allowed herself to gaze starry-eyed like any young woman at the huge photographs of Lupino Lane in *Me And My Girl* and, with envy, at the diamante bodices, ostrich feathers and long legs of the Windmill girls. Down every side street, round every turning there was a new distraction; a smell of food, a queue at a box office, a pub opening its doors.

When at last she came to Bernhardt Court, she found it to be a narrow side street which cut along the side of one of the grandest theatres; an alley where the sun never shone. Yet the throng never subsided as people wove through on bicycles, news vendors called and hoardings advertised the night's performance.

Meggie stared up at the tall, dark buildings. The theatre wall ran almost the length of the court, mostly blank brick, with a small stage-door at the far end. On the opposite side of the street was a hotch-potch row of buildings — mostly restaurants and pubs — adapted for the blackout but still open for trade. She counted one, two, three, four pubs down the length of the alley. For a moment she hesitated, uncertain of her course.

'You lost?' A voice enquired from behind a high barrow of cockles and oysters.

Meggie squared her shoulders. 'No, ta. I'm looking for a pub.'

'Bit young for drowning your sorrows, ain't you?' The voice belonged to one Shankley, seller of seafood up and down Bernhardt Court for fifty years. Known only by his last name, time seemed to have pickled his skin in brine; his face was puckered, his eyes pale. He wore a long white apron down to his polished shoes and a walrus moustache. As he stepped out from behind his barrow, he came just as high as Meggie's shoulder.

'Not to drink in,' she protested, then realized she was being got at. She took off her straw hat and sighed. 'Hot, ain't it?'

'Not partickly.'

'It is if you've walked as far as I have.' She took a breather, grateful for someone to talk to.

'I bet I've walked further than you with this barrow.' He eyed her quickly. 'Keep an eye on it for me, will you, while I slip off for a quiet pint?'

She had no time to argue. Anyway, she didn't mind. Shankley, if that was who he was, and his barrow proclaimed it in red and white fairground lettering, could take as long as he liked provided she could rest her poor feet and work out what to do next. She even managed to sell half a dozen oysters and was struggling to find the change when the comical little man returned.

'You trying to ruin me?' He elbowed her to one side and dipped into his deep apron pocket. 'Good job I ain't offering you a job.'

'I already got one, ta.'

He teased her again when he heard she was a telephonist. 'La-di-dah. You should get on the wireless with a voice like that. That's it, that's the job for you.'

'No ta.' But she was flattered. She turned back to the barrowman from looking up and down the length of the Court. 'Mr Shankley, to tell you the honest truth I'm here looking for someone.'

He winked. 'Not a young man by any chance?'

'No, worse luck.'

'I was gonna say, what's he thinking of, letting a lovely young girl like you out of his sight.'

Encouraged, she took the plunge. 'As a matter of fact, it's a down-and-out. Have you seen one?'

He pitied her naivety. 'One? If I seen one I seen a hundred. What particular size and shape you looking for?'

'I'm serious. This one don't hang round here all the time; he only comes when he's in a real bad way. There's a landlady in one of these pubs keeps an eye on him.'

'Who told you this cock and bull story?' He tried to put her off. In Shankley's long experience it wasn't healthy for a young girl to go poking around in the gutter.

'I heard it off my uncle.' She looked at him with big, pleading eyes.

'And does your uncle know you're out?'

She shook her head. 'It's private. I take it you ain't seen this tramp? He's about this high.' She raised her hand just above her head. 'He's got dark hair and brown eyes.' She went by her memory of the man on the platform at Tottenham Court Road. 'They call him Richie Palmer.'

By the look in Shankley's eyes she knew he knew him.

'You've seen him, ain't you?'

'When?'

'Last night, after chucking-out time. Did he come?'

'No.' He shook his head.

'But you do know him?'

'Why, who's asking?'

'Look, Mr Shankley, if you don't want to help I can just go up and down the street asking at all the pubs; I don't mind.'

'No need.' He saw that she was determined. 'If you take my advice, you'll steer clear of his sort, or you'll get your uncle to come and look after you. Ain't you got no pa?'

'What if I have?' Her defences shot up, like bolts through iron locks.

'Well . . .' He twitched his moustache. 'Try the Bell on the corner, right. And don't say I sent you.'

She nodded. 'Who's the landlady? Who do I ask for?' Excitement shone in her eyes. One tiny part of her heart still held the hope that they were all wrong about Richie Palmer; a family grudge, past history that prevented them from seeing him clearly. She had a romantic idea that she would find him and reclaim him from the streets.

'Ask for Gertie Elliot. And mind how you go.'

'Ta!' She ran, hat in hand. Since she was brought up in a family that kept a pub, they held no mystery. She was able to push easily through the etched glass door into the public bar of the Bell.

Its walls were lined with photographs of the famous stars who'd drunk there. Dark wooden booths gave customers some privacy and the bar shone with copper, glass and bottles of spirits. A pianist tinkled at a piano by the window, a fug of cigarette smoke rose blue-grey in a shaft of sunlight over a few men sitting playing dominoes. They looked up at the bright figure of Meggie in her forget-me-not-blue dress.

The landlady approached from the other end of the bar, ready to turn down any request for a job. Meggie looked too young by far. 'What can I do for you?'

'Nothing, thanks. I'm looking for someone.' She was breathless from running.

'And can you see "someone" here?'

Meggie glanced round. 'He ain't a customer.'

'*He?*'

'This person. They say the landlady will know who I mean.'

'I am she,' Gertie Elliot said with a flourish. She could have stepped offstage herself, with her chestnut-coloured hair piled high, Rita Hayworth-style figure, daisy earrings, red nails, arched eyebrows. 'Now tell me what's up, and I'll see if I can be *h*of *h*assistance.'

A couple of men down the bar smirked. 'She's having you on.' One winked at Meggie.

'I can see that.'

'Come on, spit it out.' Gertie needed to get a move on. Back in the kitchen it was all hands on deck.

Meggie leaned closer and spoke in a low voice. 'The man I'm looking for is Richie Palmer. Do you know him?'

There was a flicker of puzzlement on Gertie's face, then a studied attempt to consider the question. 'Palmer? No, there ain't no one of that name here.'

'He didn't end up here last night? A tramp, worse the wear from drink. He nearly ended up under a cab. Someone sent him up here in a taxi.'

'A taxi?' She patted Meggie's hand. 'Now I know someone's been leading you up the garden path.'

'He didn't come to you for help?' Meggie's heart sank. 'Sure? His name might not be Palmer. Maybe he changed it.'

'No one came.' She looked long and hard. 'What's this to you?'

'Nothing. My uncle used to hang around with him.'

Meggie looked so cast down that Gertie hadn't the heart to send her on her way.

'Have a drink in any case. On the house. Strictly teetotal, mind.'

'I'm old enough to drink,' Meggie insisted. She sat dejectedly on a stool, her hat on the bar.

'And I'm Queen Mary, the Queen Mother.'

'No, honest I am.'

'And where are you from?'

'Across the water.'

'Where exactly?'

'Southwark.'

'That's a long way to come looking, ain't it?' Gertie pried kindly as Meggie took up her glass of orange juice. 'Just on the off-chance.'

'It weren't on the off-chance, least I didn't think it was.'

'A proper little Agatha Christie.' Gertie seemed sorry for Meggie. 'Tell you what, I bet you could do with a bite to eat.'

'No ta, I'm not hungry.' This was a big let-down, and it hit her hard. She'd been certain she was on the right track, but now she must think again. Rob must have made a mistake. The man he'd nearly run over couldn't have been Richie Palmer after all. It had probably been pitch dark in the blackout. How could he have been certain it was him all this long time later? After setting

175

her whole heart on finding her father, Meggie was ready to give up.

'This is a big day for us.' Unperturbed, Gertie reached for a packet of crisps and shoved them towards her. 'On the house.'

'How come?' Looking round, Meggie noticed for the first time the Union Jack bunting hung from the ceiling and a big welcome sign over the door.

'It's my boy, Ronnie, he's due home on leave.'

Meggie looked again at the landlady. She seemed too young to have a son serving his country.

'He's in the Royal Navy.'

'Never.'

'He is. He just turned twenty-one. This is his big birthday knees-up. We have to celebrate today, better late than never.' Pride lit up her face. 'Hang around if you don't believe me.'

The bar had begun to fill up with girls and young men in uniform. An older woman came out from the back, her tray laden with sandwiches and sausage rolls. 'What time's he due?' she asked.

'Half twelve.' Gertie studied her gold wristwatch.

'What time is it now?' The woman smacked the hand of a young squaddy about to help himself to a sandwich.

'Nearly twenty-past.' She stopped to look in the mirror behind the till, tweaking her hair into place and checking her make-up. By the time she was satisfied, she'd forgotten all about Meggie.

But Meggie stayed put, caught up in the excitement and warmth. She realized how drab her life had become with the endless searching, the disappointments.

Then it was too late to nip out. A cheer went up at the far side of the room, and a loud chorus of 'Happy Birthday'. The door swung open and a young man in a sailor's tunic and collar, kitbag on his shoulder, hat tilted back on his wavy dark hair, stood grinning his head off. Ronnie Elliot had arrived.

CHAPTER NINE

A stream of piano notes swept through the bar of the Bell. The pianist launched into a swing number, heavy on the bass chords, rhythmical and upbeat. Gertie rushed to embrace her son.

'Steady on, Ma.' He staggered back, embarrassed.

'Look at you!' she crowed. 'Blimey, just look at you!' She released him and stood him back at arm's length, straightening the collar that she'd skewed out of true. Her hands shook with gratitude that he was home in one piece. 'Happy birthday, son. And ain't we glad to see you.'

'Put him down,' a voice shouted from the bar.

Ronnie grinned acknowledgements to friends from the street. He shook hands with a couple of the older men.

'How about some service round here?' Another call for Gertie's attention rose above the piano tune. 'Some of us are standing here parched!'

'Hold your horses.' It was hard for her to take her eyes off Ronnie. She wanted to drink in his presence, still smoothing the edge of his collar. Then she gave him a peck on the cheek and a wink. 'Leave your stuff and come and have a nice cold pint of Guinness. We set it up for you ready and waiting.'

She let him go and he was soon swallowed up in a crowd of well-wishers. When she took up her station behind the bar she was back to her normal self, pulling pints, full of banter, ready to flirt with whoever happened to be nearby.

Meggie watched the homecoming from her corner of the bar. She picked up the fact that Ronnie Elliot had been conscripted into the Navy at the start of the year and had spent the last three months square-bashing down at Hayling Island. But he'd got a rating after completing his trade test in the dockyard. He was now a Leading Motor Mechanic, ready to be drafted onto his first ship; home on a two day leave before he joined a convoy for the war proper.

'You'd think he'd won the whole blinking show single handed,' a thirsty drinker complained.

Girls crowded round Ronnie to cadge

cigarettes and adore his filmstar-handsome face.

'And he ain't even seen action yet.' A second man recalled the hard-lying money he'd earned on a sub at the end of the first war. 'Mind you, when I say action, I mean day after day creeping along the seabed waiting for the bosun's whistle and "Up Spirits!" That's all that kept us going, I can tell you.'

'What a hero.' Gertie shoved a pint of bitter at him. 'Don't take the shine off it for him, Sparky, there's a good chap.' She glanced up, surprised to see Meggie still sitting there. 'Here, love, you look as if you could do with something a bit stronger than that orange juice.'

'No, I'd best be off, ta.' She climbed down awkwardly from her stool and picked up her hat.

'Never.' Gertie poured her a generous glass of sweet sherry. 'Down the hatch. It's the weekend, ain't it? What have you got to rush off for?'

'Nothing much.' Meggie didn't expect her mother back from Lancashire before Sunday at the earliest. She had no work today, and no enthusiasm now to carry on looking for Richie Palmer. Besides, the warm atmosphere of the pub and Gertie's brash cheerfulness drew her in. If she was straight with herself, so did Ronnie Elliot in his dashing uniform, with his clean-cut good looks.

'Well then.' Gertie watched her settle back down. 'Why not wait for things to liven up here? They'll be dancing in the aisles before too long, and you look like the sort to enjoy a good knees-up.'

She was right. The pianist ploughed on through the hubbub of greetings, the jokes, the reminiscences. Soon someone had pushed back a couple of tables and two couples took to the floor; a boy in army uniform with a blonde-haired girl, and an older man in pinstripes, his trilby tilted forwards, arm around the elderly woman who'd been serving the sandwiches. When the music turned fast and furious to a jitterbugging number, she shrieked and protested, but her partner danced on.

'Fancy a turn?' One of the drinkers at the bar sacrificed his stool and came to draw Meggie onto the floor. He was young and quite good looking, so she said she'd give it a go.

As luck would have it, he was an expert dancer. In the crowded space he was still able to twist and turn her, swaying to the beat and guiding them with tricky sidesteps and twirls. Meggie held her end up; she was naturally rhythmic and graceful, knowing not to fight against the pattern her partner set up. Their skill soon drew admiring looks.

'You done this before?' He held one arm aloft to let her spin by herself.

She nodded. Her hair flew back then swung in against her cheek, a solid, shiny mass. She felt her skirt lift above her knees.

'I'm Eddie.' He held her waist and hunched his shoulders, sliding across the floor in a series of small rocking movements.

'Meggie.'

'I ain't seen you down here before.'

'I ain't from round here, that's why.' The music, the movement exhilarated her.

'You ain't one of Ronnie's girls, then?'

'Why? Does he have lots?'

'Lucky devil. Still, you can't blame him.' Eddie spun her round and round as the number came to a close. 'These days you gotta make hay while the sun shines.'

They stopped at the edge of the dance floor. 'Ta, Eddie.'

'My pleasure.'

That was only the start of it. She had more dances throughout the afternoon with her first partner, and many others with the boys queuing up to dance with her, some with two left feet it had to be admitted, some reasonable, none as good as Eddie. The versatile piano player, a man with a ready, flashing smile, happy to play so long as they ferried drinks to him from the bar, changed his tune from jitterbug to waltz, from music hall to jazz. Meggie loved every minute.

She was at the bar with a crowd of girls, all recovering from a scrum at the end of the hokey-cokey, breathless and laughing, when Ronnie tapped her on the shoulder and asked her to dance. Her heart gave a sudden tilt; she'd been hoping and praying that he would notice her. She nodded and blushed, put down her glass of orange juice. He led her back onto the floor.

They danced a quickstep, very sedate compared to the convulsions of the jitterbug and the hokey-cokey. Ronnie led well, but she hardly noticed what they were doing, so caught up was she in the thrill of being close to the most handsome man in the room. She thought he was wonderful, his skin smooth and fresh after the tough routine of drilling, his wavy hair very smart. He had light brown eyes — she thought you would call them hazel — and dark lashes which didn't make him look feminine, for his brows were straight and thick, his jaw firm and square. He was taller than her by a good three inches, broad shouldered, her ideal man.

'You just moved into the Court?' He opened the conversation.

'No. I was passing by.'

'Glad you did?'

She nodded.

'I bet you never knew what you were walking into.'

The effort of finding something interesting to say to her was proving difficult. He cursed himself for sounding like a thickhead.

'That's true, I never.' In a panic of her own, she began to babble. 'Mind you, it was in my horoscope this morning. It said something unexpected would turn up.' Now he would think she was the sort who never did anything without reading her stars.

'In the *Picture Post*?' They collided with a table. 'Sorry.'

'That's OK. Yes, the *Picture Post*. Silly, ain't it?'

'What did it say, your star sign?'

'It said to be prepared for the unexpected. Make the most of your opportunities, something like that.' She didn't say that she'd read that the moon was in line with Venus, right for romance, or some such rubbish.

'Well, that's something.' He could hear the music drawing to a close. It was as much as he could do to ask her to stay on the floor for another dance. His head was spinning with the drink and the welcome his mother had laid on. He'd had to dare himself to approach Meggie; she seemed different from the girls he usually went out with — a cut above. Ronnie's short time in the Navy had taught him to divide women into two groups. Meggie belonged to what he called the 'decent' sort. 'Fancy another?' he said, half under his breath.

She nodded. 'Then I'll have to push off.' It was almost teatime. Walter and Annie would be wondering where she'd got to, and there might be news from Sadie.

The next number was a waltz. It emptied the floor of couples who preferred the fast dances and left space to breathe. Ronnie took the plunge and held Meggie close, ignoring the curious stares of his pals and numerous casual girlfriends. He felt his mother's beady eye on him from behind the bar.

Meggie swooned to the music and the experience of being in Ronnie Elliot's arms. She closed her eyes. Was this what it was like to fall in love? She drifted out of the present on a gentle wave of sentiment and disbelief. Was this really happening? Could it be true?

All too soon the waltz came to an end. They'd said very little, and what they had said was unsatisfactory chit-chat. But as he walked her off the floor, Ronnie wasn't ready to release her. He kept his arm around her waist, steering her to the bar.

'I have to go.' She looked round for her hat, not daring to meet his gaze.

'Here.' Gertie picked it up from a safe place by the till. 'I stashed it for you.'

'Ta.'

'What's the rush?' Ronnie aimed for the casual, off-the-cuff comment. 'Have you got a train to catch?'

Gertie looked on, evidently amused.

'Tube. But I have got to get back. I never said I'd stop out late.'

'Can't you telephone?'

She could. There was the phone in Walter's office, but she didn't want to sound too keen. So she shook her head. 'I've been here ages already.'

'Well come again, now you know where to find us.' Gertie stacked glasses into the sink. 'Mind you, we don't have a do like this every day of the week.'

'Only when I'm twenty-one.' Hands in pockets, he waited for her to gather herself

186

together. 'I'll see you out if you like.'

Meggie glanced at Gertie, whose eyebrows had risen, but who said nothing. 'Ta.' She said goodbye to the landlady and followed Ronnie through the crowd. Outside all was light, fresh and busy.

'Where to?' He turned to wait.

'Oh, no, you go back in and have a good time.' She stepped past him into the street.

'No, I don't mind.' He offered her his arm and they began to stroll. 'I need a breather in any case.'

'Where are we?' They'd come out of the Bell on to a different road.

'Heading for St Martin's. That's why the pub's called the Bell, see: it's practically in the shadow of the church bells.' Bleeding fascinating, he told himself. Absolutely bloody riveting.

'So where's the tube station?'

'Where do you have to get to?'

'Borough.'

He stopped to search in his pockets. 'Here, never mind the tube. Take a taxi.' He wanted to give her a handful of change.

'Oh, no.'

But he'd already hailed a cab. He leaned in and instructed the driver, handed over the money, told him to hang on a second.

'I don't know what they call you.' He turned back to her.

'Meggie. Meggie Davidson.'

It was now or never. The taxi driver sat with the engine idling, casting his cynical eye over them. 'Will you come out with me, Meggie?'

'When?' Her heart did another mad tilt. She clutched the brim of her hat.

'Tomorrow. Meet me. You say when.'

'Afternoon.' She would be able to fix it, she was sure. 'Where?'

'Wherever you like.'

'Here?'

'By the church. Righto.' He ran a hand across his mouth. 'Two o'clock, then. Champion.'

'You getting in this cab or not?' a weary voice cut in.

Startled, Meggie jumped. Ronnie opened the door.

'Where to?' The cabbie slid into gear.

'Ta, Ronnie. I had a lovely time.'

'Me too. See, it was in them stars.' He had one arm on the cab roof, leaning in.

'Happy birthday.' She reached out to kiss him, looking straight into his hazel eyes.

He kissed her back as the cab eased away.

'Watch out, don't fall over!'

He pretended to stagger, and she laughed

and waved. 'See you tomorrow, two o'clock!' Now he blew kisses, standing in the road.

'Ronnie, watch out!' She pulled her head in through the window and collapsed against the seat. He was mad. She was mad. She didn't care, not now she was in love.

As soon as Sadie saw the state of Bernie and Geoff outside the bone merchant's shed, she bundled them into Jess's car. Gordon Whittaker acted the injured innocent; no wonder those boys didn't know how to behave if this was how their mother carried on. What they needed was a firm hand, not mollycoddling.

'It's the luck of the draw,' commiserated one of the workers from the bone shed. 'You never know what you're getting with these evacuees.'

'Head lice and snotty noses, according to my missus,' the other chipped in. 'And she says you can't turn your back on them for a single second, thieving little devils.'

This was one blow too many for Sadie, who might simply have walked away from the Whittakers and good riddance. But overhearing this, she couldn't let it go. Asking Grace and Jess to look after the boys, she stalked across the gravel yard and had her

189

say. 'For your information, my children don't steal. And they don't tell lies.'

'Steady on,' Whittaker said, uneasy in spite of his bluff manner.

'No, I won't steady on. You're making out things that ain't true. For a start, what you call a firm hand I call downright cruel. It's not on to put a seven-year-old boy to work in this filthy place.' The stink from the barn was fit to make her retch.

'We've all got to do our bit.' He spread his hands and shrugged.

'Is that what you call it? And what about giving them a square meal once in a while? Or a hot bath, or running a comb through their hair?'

'See?' he appealed. 'Case proven.'

'You need reporting, you do.' Her blood was up. 'You never even let them see the letters we wrote, let alone making sure they wrote home, 'cos if they had we'd have found out what was going on up here and you'd have been landed in the cart straight off. Look at the state of them!' She gestured angrily towards the car. 'I hardly even knew them myself when I set eyes on them, and it's all your fault!'

'I said steady on.' He sniffed, ready to turn his back.

'No!' She grabbed his arm and wheeled

190

him round. 'I wouldn't treat a dog the way you treated my boys, and that's God's honest truth.' Her eyes blazed, full of contempt. She didn't care whether or not he retaliated. 'You tell that wife of yours she can take all their things and stick them on the fire, 'cos she won't see hide nor hair of my boys after this. And tell her I'm going straight to the billeting officer and I only hope they never let you take in no more evacuees ever again. You ain't fit to be let loose with children.'

'Lay off, will you.' He wrenched himself free.

Beside herself, she stormed away back to the car, before he regained his bullying stance, where the other four peered anxiously out.

'Feel better now?' Jess pushed open the passenger door and urged her to get in quick.

'Loads better.' Sadie took a deep breath and sank into her seat. 'Let's get out of here!'

Jess obeyed. 'Think twice before you go taking on a fourteen-stone butcher in future, will you?' She turned full circle in the yard and sped away. 'Grace and me nearly had to come out and lend a hand!'

They could laugh about it now, from a

safe distance, with Geoff and Bertie perched on the back seat of Jess's car. And they could make plans. Jess was sure she would be able to find a decent outfit for each of the boys, once they got back to Manchester. Her neighbours would help out. 'And a nice hot bath for you two,' she promised, glancing in her driver's mirror.

They made faces. 'Do I have to have a hair wash?' It was, as ever, Geoff's worst dread.

Half laughing, half crying. Sadie said he looked like a scarecrow, not fit to be seen. She told Jess that she would telephone Walter and let him know they hoped to be back late that evening.

'You sure?' Jess would have loved them to stay overnight.

'You're the best,' Sadie told her, brim-full of gratitude. 'And I love you with all my heart, but I gotta get these boys back home. I won't settle till we're all together under one roof; me, the boys, Walter and Meggie.'

So they got back to Jess's house and scrubbed the pair clean, washing off the stain of their experiences as evacuees. 'Never you mind,' Sadie told them over and over, 'we ain't going to lose sight of you ever again.' They submitted to the scouring and the soap, gradually understanding that their nightmare was over.

'I tried to look after Geoff,' Bertie stammered, 'only he got sick and I didn't know what to do.'

'You did fine. You wrote and told us like a good boy.'

'Geoff cried at night.'

'Never mind.' Sadie got them dry and let them dress in clean clothes.

'He said it was the witches. They kept coming through the wall in the dark.'

Sadie shook her head. 'I hope you told him there ain't no such things.'

'I hate it there,' was all Geoff said.

On the train back to London, Geoff wolfed down the ham sandwiches that Grace had packed.

'I thought you had a poorly stomach?' As the miles of track lengthened behind them, Sadie began to relax. The long day was drawing to a close, Walter would be there waiting on the platform at King's Cross and all would be well.

'It's better now.'

'Good.' She winked across at Bertie. 'Magic, ain't it?' Their second-hand jackets hung loose on their shoulders, their shirt collars curled at the corners, but already they looked more like their old selves. Geoff fiddled with the wrapper of his chocolate bar and shot her a look that was meant to melt her strict heart. 'Oh, go on,' she sighed, 'go ahead and eat it if it'll make you happy. There'll be none left for later, mind.'

He scoffed it there and then. Bertie, on the other hand, made a manful attempt to save his. She noticed, however, when she came back from the toilet just before they pulled into the station, that his mouth, too, was rimmed with melted chocolate. 'Lick your lips,' she told him, 'and grab hold of this suitcase for me. Look sharp, we're here.'

The train drew in with a hiss and a mighty clank of steel. Doors flew open onto the platform, which came alive with rushing feet, flapping coats, people urgently pressing through the barrier. Walter stood waiting for them. Geoff saw him first and flew at him, was gathered up and swung round and round. Bertie looked up, fighting the tears.

'Well done, son.' With Geoff still dangling under one arm, Walter ruffled Bertie's hair. 'Come on, let's get you home. Your gran's waiting with a slap-up supper, and then it's straight off to bed.'

They rode through the streets in the taxi, too tired, too happy to notice where they were. Only when they came to Duke Street did Geoff peer out.

'Nearly there,' Sadie promised.

'Is the war over?' he wanted to know.

'Not yet.' They stopped outside the Duke. 'But we'll look after you from now on.' Sadie waved at Ernie standing at the door. 'Go and say hello to your Uncle Ern.'

They stumbled upstairs to Annie's supper table, dropping asleep over the suet pudding, faces rosy from full stomachs and too much hugging. Frances and Hettie were there, ready to spoil them to death. Sadie had to take a back seat while the others fussed.

'Happy now?' Walter sat with his arm around her shoulders. Tomorrow was soon enough to hear the details. She'd got what she wanted, to have them all back together.

'I am.' It felt like a proper family again. She gazed round the room. Billy had just called in to collect Frances, George had popped up from the bar, leaving Ernie in charge. 'Where's Meggie?' she asked suddenly.

'Here.' Meggie had been busy wrapping presents at home. Now she took the stairs two at a time and burst into the room. 'Happy Christmas!' She landed the presents on the boys' laps; big square parcels, soft squashy ones, things she'd bought in an explosion of goodwill the moment she heard her brothers were on their way home.

'It ain't Christmas,' Geoff tried to explain solemnly.

'It's *better* than Christmas!' she beamed.

As the boys tore into their parcels, a Meccano set for Bertie, a toy train for Geoff, Sadie came up to her daughter. 'What got into you?' she asked.

Meggie gave a sublime smile. 'Nothing. Why?'

'You got something up your sleeve.' Her eyes were too bright, her sense of herself too jubilant to be put down to a simple homecoming. For a moment Sadie thought she might have tracked down Richie Palmer.

'Honest, Ma!' It bubbled to the surface, a secret she couldn't keep. 'I met someone at a birthday party, that's all.'

'And he swept you off your feet?' She studied the bright face, the bubbling happiness.

Meggie nodded. 'I'm seeing him tomorrow.'

With a pang of regret Sadie smiled. 'Good luck to you,' she whispered.

'You don't mind?'

'I reckon it's something I'll have to get used to.'

Meggie squeezed her hand and looked

across the room at the torn paper, the shiny new toys. 'It'll be all right, don't you worry. I got this feeling; everything's gonna work out just fine.'

PART TWO

Taking It

September 1940

CHAPTER TEN

Ring-a-ring-a roses,
Pocket full of posies,
A-tishoo, a-tishoo,
We all fall down!

Saturday was Geoff's eighth birthday, and the weather in early September was fine enough for Sadie to give a small party that soon spilled out into Paradise Court. The children played their street games and chanted their songs while the grown-ups looked on.

'I like these light evenings,' Annie told Dolly Ogden. 'I like to see the kiddies making the most of them while they can.' Soon enough the evenings would close in and their lives would be dominated by the blackout once more.

The circle of children which had collapsed onto the cobbles sprang up with a laugh and a shout, then Meggie stepped in to organize an outdoor version of blind man's bluff. She gave Geoff first turn with the blindfold, tied it tight, spun him round. 'No peeping!' she warned and launched him, arms outstretched, with faltering footsteps. These days, since she'd given up the search for her elusive father, she threw herself into playing with and appreciating her half-brothers.

'She's a sight for sore eyes,' Dolly observed. Meggie wore her hair more elaborately these days, a hidden scaffolding of pins keeping it high off her forehead. She wore a plain dove-grey dress, tailored to show off her waist, with a sweetheart neckline picked out in purple braid. Though it was a hand-me-down from Hettie, Meggie had picked out the seams and remodelled it to suit herself. The cut and the cloth were still good quality. 'What I mean is, Sadie had best keep an eye on her, or else.' Dolly pressed on in the face of Annie's silence. 'I hear Jimmie O'Hagan's sweet on her for a start.'

Geoff blundered into his big brother, Bertie, and made the right guess. It was Bertie's turn for the blindfold. More squeals, more stumbling and fumbling.

'I can't see Meggie being interested though.' Dolly ploughed on, certain of her target. 'She's known Jimmie since they were knee-high, when he was a snotty-nosed little blighter, always hopping the wag. Then, when he was at school, he was always getting into some scrape and getting six of the best. No, if you ask me, Jimmie don't stand a chance.'

'But he's grown up lately and all.' Annie pictured him, sitting this very minute at the bar in his corduroy trousers and polo-neck, in a haze of cigarette smoke, planning with Bobby which venue would give them the best chance of picking up birds that evening.

'Too fast for his own good.' Dolly considered Jimmie a bad influence on her much taller, brawnier grandson. 'He needs a firm hand, he does.'

'Well you wouldn't wish him on Meggie then.' Annie closed off this avenue of speculation. She knew for a fact that Meggie and Jimmie were pals, but that was as far as it went. She carried on with her plate of sandwiches down the Court to number 32.

Dolly frowned after her. Annie had shut up like a clam as usual, as if Dolly couldn't be trusted with any scrap of information. Whereas Dolly herself appreciated the candid response. Knowledge was power, she thought, and might allow a person to do some good. Dolly prided herself on her judgment; she'd brought up Amy to be a good wife and mother, hadn't she? Annie could certainly cast no aspersions in that direction. The ground was laid for more backbiting between the two old rivals. Dolly would go and have a good moan to Amy, Annie would warn Sadie that Dolly might well come poking her nose into Meggie's affairs.

'Where you off to?' Dolly quizzed, as Charlie came down the passage and squeezed past her onto the pavement. His hair was slicked down with Brylcreem, his chin freshly shaven. 'As if I didn't know.'

'Why bother asking then?' Charlie chucked the remark over his shoulder. 'If you're so clever.' He walked away without altering his pace.

By now Dolly was thoroughly out of humour. She experienced a rare moment of self-pity, cut off from the children's game, from expressing any interest in Meggie Davidson's love life, which she knew for a fact was the talk of the whole Court, shut out even by her own son. High and dry, left on the shelf like a bit of old rubbish; that's what happened when a person outlived her usefulness. No good to anyone. Before she knew it she'd have a house full of smelly cats and not a soul to care for her. High and bleeding dry, she thought.

'Here, Dolly, have a bite to eat.' Annie offered her a beef-paste sandwich on her return journey. 'And cheer up for God's sake. It may never happen.' She asked how she was getting on with the sugar ration, told how she'd had to save her coupons for weeks to make Geoff a nice birthday cake, reminded Dolly to get herself up to the Duke later that evening.

'We'll see.' Dolly stalled.

'Come again?' Annie stared, plate in hand. 'You never missed a Saturday night yet, so far as I know.'

As the children's voices ran through the verses of 'Oranges and Lemons' and two of them made an arch for the others to squeeze through, Dolly stood on her doorstep and sighed. Like a barrage balloon deflating, she rocked, then leaned against the door-post.

'Here comes a candle . . .'

'You ain't worried by the sirens, surely?' Annie studied her old sparring partner's lined face. 'They ain't getting you down?' For months now they'd ignored the false alarms. Few customers at the Duke even bothered to head for Nelson Gardens, though most still brought their gas masks along. Annie knew that both Walter and George came under heavy fire from the likes of Rob, who resented the ARP wardens' strict enforcement of the blackout. Rob said they were crying wolf and it was time the bloke in the street made a stand. Hitler wasn't going to launch his bombers on London, whatever people said. He was too busy in France, Holland and North Africa.

'Here comes a chopper . . .'

'No, they ain't,' Dolly said sharply.

'Well, it ain't that carry-on between your Charlie and Madam O'Hagan, is it?' Annie didn't like to see Dolly looking so down. 'You got the brass neck to put up with that surely?' She too could be candid when necessary.

Dolly shook her head. 'Easier said than done.'

'But it ain't like you to fret over what can't be helped.' The squeals of the children broke through. Annie turned to see Meggie trying to haul Geoff and a couple of other lads off Bertie, who'd vanished under a rugby scrum.

'No, but I do wish he'd break off with her though.' Dolly hated the whispering and sly nudges, and Charlie's conduct betrayed her own sense of honour.

'She's got him hooked.'

'You think so?'

'Good and proper.' Annie had often observed them.

Again Dolly sighed. 'What's he see in her?

That's what I'd like to know.'

'What's anyone see in anyone? If we could answer that we'd be millionaires.' She glanced down the street at Sadie, who stood watching the game from her own doorstep. 'You ain't alone,' she told Dolly, relaxing her own rules for once. 'Sadie spends half her time wondering what drags Meggie across town for a fleeting word from his ma about Ronnie Elliot. What's he got that's so special, she wants to know.'

Dolly nodded. 'Meggie still stuck on him then?'

'On Ronnie? Like glue. And she's only met him three or four times, whenever he comes home on leave.'

They stood watching her extricate Bertie from the scrum, then laugh and swing him round.

'Just like her ma,' Dolly said. The resemblance was more than just physical. 'No half-measures.'

'I hope not, for her sake.' Annie shook herself. 'You get yourself up the Duke tonight, you hear?'

'I might. What time is it now?'

'Half four.'

'Righto. I'll sort myself out down here, then I'll be up.'

Satisfied, they went their separate ways.

★ ★ ★

Half an hour later, all plans for the evening were interrupted by the siren sounding its long, warbling note. Take cover. The children had gone home from the party, the street was quiet.

'Not again.' Edie closed the ledger on her desk. In the dingy basement the wail of the siren was muffled but unmistakeable. Up on Duke Street the wardens began to usher ever-more reluctant civilians to the shelters. She went up to help empty the shop of its last customers, as Dorothy nipped down smartly from the flat above, gas mask slung across her shoulder, one of the first to respond to the siren's urgent call.

'Funny time,' she pointed out. 'They don't usually sound that thing till after dark.'

Edie thought so too. 'Anyone in the paint shop?' she called through to Lorna. The sight of people moving purposefully along the street, without panic but obviously intent on getting to safety, spurred her on.

'All clear in there.' Lorna came out, coat over her arm, hard on Dorothy's heels.

'Where's Tommy?'

'Out. I ain't seen him.' She didn't stop to elaborate, but left Edie to do one final check through the shop before she locked up and followed. Meanwhile, the thin siren wailed on.

'Don't rush me, Walt.' At the taxi depot Rob took his time. The siren had started just as he was about to set out on a call. Now he didn't know whether or not the punter would want the cab. He swore at Walter. 'How many times? Don't rush me!'

'Amy left word. She and Bobby are staying put at the Duke. She wants you there.' Walter passed on the message, cursing back. 'Look mate, it's up to you. I'm just telling you what she said.'

'I'm due out on a call.' Rob stubbed his cigarette in the ash tray and put on his hat.

'You're bleeding mad, you are.'

'Says you. Look, Hitler ain't gonna drop his bombs in broad daylight, is he? Even he ain't that stupid.' Rob convinced himself it was another false alarm. He stepped out of the office into the car yard, built into the railway arch at the bottom of Meredith Court.

'Please yourself.' Walter tightened the strap on his helmet. Until the siren stopped and the all-clear sounded, he must treat the warning as deadly serious. With no more time to waste, he ran out of the depot towards his ARP centre on Union Street, where he met up with George Mann who told him, among other things, that Sadie, Meggie and the boys were already safe under cover in the cellar at the Duke.

Before they went their separate ways, the two men stood in the schoolyard next to the sandbags stacked high to protect the entrance. They looked into the sky at the greyish barrage balloons shifting and rolling on their moorings, at the otherwise empty space. Still the siren whined.

'What do you think? False alarm?' Walter went by the usual pattern of events. Soon the warbling siren would die, replaced by a long, unchanging note; the all-clear.

George shook his head. 'I don't know. I don't like the feel of this one.'

They listened intently for the drone of engines, the bombers flying in formation with their deadly cargo. Every time they dreaded the worst, hoped for the best, thought of a thousand reasons why the enemy wouldn't attack.

Tight-lipped, George Mann started out on his two-hour ARP shift at the Commercial Dock. The docks would be Jerry's prime target if the warning was genuine, but no one knew how accurate their bombers would be; that was why you couldn't be too careful. George stopped to direct two strangers to the nearest shelter. Quickly the street emptied and traffic came to a halt.

Then the planes came, the heavy-bodied Heinkels with their stuttering propellers, their black crosses easily visible on each wing-tip. They came low and loud in a dreadful rumble of engines over the Isle of Dogs, discharging their bombs.

George heard the first thuds, saw the first balls of flame rise skywards. The bombs dropped singly at first, then in sticks of half a dozen, raining down on the docksides, setting fire to nearby piles of timber which soon blazed out of control. He ran to telephone HQ for a fire engine to come quickly to the woodyard. On the way he had to duck the flaming, floating skin of a barrage balloon, blown out of the sky in a roar of helium, descending in ghastly futility. Everywhere the firebombs rained down, fire engines rushed to the scene, brought to a standstill by a toppling crane, a road blocked by rubble, yet another direct hit.

As the bomb-sticks streaked out of the sky and the white exhausts of the planes streamed across the wide blue space, anti-aircraft guns sprang into action. George shuddered as the shattering rattle almost split his eardrums. He had to stop and lean against a wall, hands over his head. But he felt nothing, not even fear. This was beyond words; a total, mindless destruction. Up above, one of the white exhausts turned pitch black as the plane caught fire and spiralled down somewhere north of the river.

All around fires burned, the fire engines were overwhelmed, the stirrup-pumps of the wardens hopelessly inadequate. This was worse than anything anyone could have imagined. He ran back to the dockside to lend a hand in setting up emergency pumps, almost unaware by now that the bombs still dropped, that the planes still came over in droves, bank after bank of them. Close by, a tall crane crumpled and collapsed in a roar and shower of sparks onto the blazing woodyard. A stick of bombs landed just behind the hoses and silhouetted the figures of the fire-fighters, setting up a string of small magnesium fires in the craters they'd made. George went to put them out with buckets of earth, finding that they would flare up bright again under the heap of soil, until at last he defeated them; puny effort amidst a holocaust. He drew black smoke into his lungs, rasping and coughing as he dodged another mighty shower of sparks.

There was a cry; a fireman fell into darkness from the top of an extended ladder against a backdrop of red flames. 'Fetch a searchlight!' someone cried. More men ran, the anti-aircraft guns rattled on hopelessly, their own shrapnel raining back down on those who fought from the ground.

For a second George plunged with the plummeting man into the depths of horrified despair. This was London, his home, his people under attack. No longer the mud and barbed wire in the trenches of Flanders, no longer soldiers with guns in the firing-line, but his wife, her family, the children. He prayed they were safe as a high explosive bomb plunged into a warehouse, another direct hit, another deafening roar, a moment suspended in time before the walls fell out like a house of cards in a storm of flame and then, the awful shifting and scraping of debris in the dusty aftermath, the crashing of beams, the final collapse of a doorway, the splintering of glass.

At the end of his patrol George made his slow way in the dark to his HQ on Union Street, through a new landscape of craters and ruined buildings. If he raised his head from the dust and smoke, all he saw was a red glow over the river. At his feet a hole ten feet deep had swallowed a black cab, while the mangled front of a bus teetered on the opposite brink. He thought of Rob, then switched him out of his mind. It was as much as he could do to get himself back to base to report to his senior warden.

The siren started at five, and by ten minutes past Ernie had the boys safe in the cellar. He shot down the Court to number 32 to round them up, only to find Geoff protesting that it was his birthday and he didn't want to go down a rotten shelter. Sadie looked harassed, and Meggie was all too ready to believe that this was another false alarm. But Ernie knew the routine, he gave them no option.

'Air raid.' He burst through the front door and called down the hallway. 'Bertie, Geoff, air raid!'

Geoff scrambled to meet him. 'It's my birthday, Uncle Ern. I ain't going down no shelter.'

For answer Ernie picked him up and tucked him under one arm, legs kicking, V-necked jumper riding up from his waist as he wriggled. 'Get the bag, Bertie.'

Bertie knew not to argue. He hopped upstairs quick as a flash to collect the bag containing two sets of pyjamas, their slippers and a book each to read.

'Bring the cake,' Sadie told Meggie. 'Now

stop going on, Geoff, if you know what's good for you.'

Soon they were ready and running up the street, the siren wailing but the sky so far was clear of enemy planes. They met Amy and Bobby in the entrance to the public bar. Together they piled into the cellar with Annie and Hettie; that made nine of them, snug on the mattresses that the women had provided to make their refuge more comfortable, able to brew up on a primus stove when they felt like it, surrounded by their own things and with a degree of privacy unknown at the shelter in Nelson Gardens.

'I hope Rob makes it.' Amy's concern was shared by the rest. 'Knowing him, he'll take his time.'

'Don't worry, he can take care of himself.' Annie tried to keep everyone calm; the boys were still excited from the birthday fun; Amy on edge over Rob. 'Bobby, you light up the primus, we could all do with a cuppa. Ernie, you push that mattress up against the door, there's a good chap.' As soon as he'd done that, the sound of the siren would be deadened and they would get some peace. Fresh air filtered in down the ramp from pavement to cellar, where the beer barrels were rolled up and down. Its exit was carefully boarded and sandbagged, but still there was enough air to keep them from suffocating. Annie's bustle and organization kept them in line. Soon the tea was brewed and Bertie and Geoff, happy on their makeshift bunk, mouths full of birthday cake, heads stuck in their books.

When the bombs dropped, a distant thud that broke through the sirens, Amy's heart shot into her mouth. 'He hasn't!' she stuttered, meaning Hitler — horrid little man.

'He blinking well has.' Annie's eyes widened as she wielded a brown teapot. 'He's gone and done it!'

As they strained to listen, Sadie prayed that the bombs would drop on some other street, or harmlessly in the river. She couldn't imagine that they might emerge to a scene of destruction on their own doorstep, even though bombs thudded and fire engines raced against the background of anti-aircraft fire, so close it almost might be directly overhead along the well-worn tram-tracks of Duke Street, or down Paradise Court.

'Chin up.' Hettie sat quietly beside her. 'We could be worse off.'

'Yes, like Walter and George.' Sadie's hands shook, though she tried not to let the boys see.

'Maybe it sounds worse than it is.' Hettie

cast around for small comfort. No one knew yet how bad the Blitz might be; maybe they'd get off lightly once Jerry found out they were prepared with guns on the ground, the mighty barrage balloons and searchlights that pierced the sky and picked out enemy aircraft.

But when Rob finally made it home, after dark, when the bombs had been falling for three or four hours, his face told them the worst. 'It's bleeding murder up there,' he said, still breathless. 'It ain't gas we've got to worry about, it's fire-bombs. Hundreds of them. The whole place is alight.'

Amy had to check that he had survived unscathed. 'Trust you, Rob Parsons,' she said time and time again, flicking ash and dust from his navy-blue coat. 'You'll give me a heart attack one of these days.'

Annie handed him fresh tea, while Ernie barricaded them safe and sound with the mattress. 'I was up on Tower Bridge,' Rob said. 'I had to leave the cab there and walk back. Everywhere you look there's this dark red glow, and all the warehouses lit up like bonfire night. We're sitting ducks for them Luftwaffe pilots, believe you me.'

His bad news fell into silence. Sadie tucked Geoff up tight in his temporary bed.

'He's the only one who'll get any sleep

tonight,' Amy whispered, her nerves taut with listening. All night the bombardment continued. By dawn, when the long, single note on the siren signalled the all-clear, East Enders knew what it was to live in controlled terror, helpless under the bomb blast, coming up out of the shelters to houses blown apart like matchboxes, to homes which lay in ruins.

Tommy O'Hagan's first thought when the siren started at teatime on Saturday was for Edie. He was caught out far from his own patch, seeing about some scrap iron that he might be able to sell on to the Ministry. He had two choices; to dive down the nearest shelter at Liverpool Street, or risk an attempt to get home and check on the shop. This was how he phrased it even to himself, but the impulse to go back was prompted by concern for Edie. He knew she would have to wait behind for the shop to empty before she could lock up, which could mean her being stranded if the warning were to turn into reality. Without another thought, Tommy waved down a cab and headed for Duke Street.

But by the time he'd run the gamut of what Jerry could chuck at them, the incendiaries and heavy mortars causing the buildings to crumble, smashing mains that gushed water and gas out of raw craters, the sky was dark and the streets deserted. The low roar of planes continued but the searchlights scarcely pierced the black haze. Nothing could get through, so Tommy took to his own two feet, past wrecked and twisted tram tracks, blazing cars; one with its driver slumped against the wheel, still recognizably human but beyond all help. He hurried on, came onto Duke Street at the Meredith Court end and ran to the post office where Edie had her flat.

What he saw struck him stone cold. Instead of the neat red post office building, with its three floors of apartments, there was a shell. Not a window was left in place, much of the masonry on the bottom storey had been blasted out and, in the glare of a nearby fire, he saw the windows gape black and sooty. But in comparison with the offices next door, the post office had got off lightly. There, where people sat all day typing and answering the telephone, was a jagged gap; four storeys had imploded to the ground in a heap of bricks and plaster dust, the slope of a grey slate roof, sitting at an odd angle where it had fallen, almost whole, like a collapsing umbrella. The ends of rooms appeared in view, fireplaces and chimney breasts, a wall light, the remnants of a bookcase.

Tommy didn't stop to think whether Edie could possibly still be in the flat. He had to make doubly sure by going to look. The door of the post office had blown off its hinges, so he stepped over it and up the back stairs; the way he usually took up to her second storey flat. The staircase at least was intact, though the corridors billowed with smoke from a small incendiary bomb, still alight in a room off a first floor landing. He went in and hauled a mattress from the bed, shielding his face from the smoke, throwing the mattress on the glowing floor-boards to smother the fire. Then he ran on upstairs, calling Edie's name, all caution, all common sense gone. How could she still be here? Still, he had to find out.

'Edie!' Her door was locked. He ran at it with his shoulder, without success. It took a heavy blow from a piece of masonry, which he went down and salvaged from the street, to break the lock and burst in. The striped curtains blew wildly at the shattered window, flapping against the frame, smoke hovered in a room with the electricity cut off, the gramophone smashed by falling plaster, the walls dripped with water from fractured pipes. Tommy waded through the mess towards the bedroom then the bathroom, still calling her name.

Only when he was sure that the ruined flat was empty did he back out. Yes, she'd gone to the shelter, she hadn't risked it. Good for her. Sensible Edie. He ran downstairs, the siren filling his head, past his own shop, unmarked by the bombs, down a couple of back alleys to Nelson Gardens.

The shelter was jam-packed, Walter Davidson told him. He would have to head on to the tube station at Borough.

'Where the hell have you been, Tommy?' Walter surveyed his ruined suit, his smoke-blackened face.

'On my holidays, where do you think?' He gasped for breath, tried to peer over Walter's shoulder.

'It's all right, she's safe and sound.' Walter put a restraining arm on his shoulder. 'I'll tell her where you're heading, shall I?'

Tommy's momentary relief clouded again; he realized that Walter must mean his wife, Dorothy. 'What about the girls from the shop?'

'All here. All safe.'

'Fair enough.'

'I'll pass the message on to them all, if you like; that you're all in one piece, just about.'

Overhead the sky lit up with streaks of gunfire and the stick-like fire bombs. 'Not for much longer.' Tommy gave a wry grin. 'Right, mate, I'm on my way.' Tomorrow would be soon enough to pass on the bad news to Edie about her flat.

Tommy made it to the tube station. He had to step over people wrapped in blankets asleep on the stairs, old couples entangled in one another's arms, children clutching teddy bears, until he found a cramped space. The airlessness, the stench were almost tangible. Lighting up, he huddled under the arched, tiled roof. At last, he was cut off from the sounds above. Sheer exhaustion overtook him, and soon he slept.

Black Saturday, they called it. The sirens sounded intermittently for twelve hours, then came the all-clear. The Parsons family in their home-made shelter had spent a better night than most. But then they, who came up warm and dry, couldn't have been prepared for the devastation all around.

'No water,' Annie reported from the taps behind the bar.

'No electric.' Hettie tried the lights.

'What about gas?' They went from one appliance to the next, thankful that at least the building stood unharmed, its taped windows still in place.

Further up the street, though, the story was different. As Sadie and her family retreated to the relative calm of Paradise Court, and Amy, Rob and Bobby found to their relief that their own flat above the ironmongers had escaped major damage, the reason for the power cuts was soon discovered. Hettie took a walk with Ernie up Duke Street towards the railway bridge, to find an enormous crater in the road and, in it, a heap of twisted tram tracks, burst mains, rubble and the sign from the side of a bus advertising 'Swan Vesta, the Smoker's Match'. The wardens had tried to rope off the area and the smell of gas seeped from the wreckage. Hastily erected fire hazard warnings were everywhere, people hurried by with handkerchiefs over their mouths and noses.

Hettie slipped her hand through Ernie's arm. 'At least Tommy's place never copped it.' They passed by his shop, then the milk bar, towards the post office. 'Oh, my God!' They stopped dead. Eager workers already dug at the pile of rubble lying against the front wall. Beside the post office lay the flattened ruins of the Reliant Insurance Office.

Ernie frowned. Half a staircase led up the

raw, open side of the building, a tattered curtain flapped against a bannister. He saw the need to dig out the bricks and twisted metal, understood that the men with shovels were trying to put things right.

'Yes, you go back home for the shovel in the cellar,' Hettie told him. 'You come back and lend a hand here, there's a good chap.'

He ran back, keeping wide of the reeking crater, soon lost in the swirling dust whipped up by the wind.

Then Hettie saw Edie Morell standing by, head in hands, being comforted by Tommy O'Hagan. She went quietly to them. 'How bad is it?'

Tommy had his arm round Edie's shoulder. He shook his head. 'She can't get in till they're sure it's safe, but I took a quick look last night. It ain't a home no more, that's for sure.'

Edie sobbed. She'd put her heart and soul into making the place nice. She'd worked to turn it into a little palace, all due to her own efforts. When things got difficult with Bill, even before he signed up, it had been the flat that kept her going; a lick of paint here, a new mirror over the mantelpiece, saving up from her wages until she could afford a gramophone.

'Maybe it'll clean up all right.' Hettie offered her a hankie.

'They won't even let me in.' She blew her nose and managed to look up.

'It ain't safe,' Tommy explained, 'not until they've sorted out the gas leak.'

Men dug, shovels scraped against concrete, dust rose. Ernie had returned with his spade and was putting his back into shifting the heap of rubble

'Then there won't be no water, no light. She can't go back, not straight away.' Tommy began to get angry. 'What's she bleeding well supposed to do now? Sleep in the street?' He couldn't understand why the government hadn't thought up a system of dealing with people in Edie's position, suddenly homeless and with no one to turn to. 'Her and thousands of others, I shouldn't wonder.'

Edie was pulling round, however. 'Never mind, I dare say I can stay at the shop until they sort things out here.' She gazed up at the damaged frontage. 'When will they put the windows back in?'

'Soon as they can.' Hettie was sizing things up. Even looking on the bright side, it would be a good few weeks before the flat was fit to return to. 'Listen, I'll tell you what, you come back home with me. We've got plenty of space. Ernie there will move out of his room for a bit and make way for you.' She wouldn't brook any argument. 'We've all got to pull together, and I know you'd do the same for us, Edie.' She felt sorry for her in this predicament; a woman who never had a bad word to say about anyone, who naturally drew people to her with her cheerful warmth.

Edie turned to Tommy for advice. He thought it through. 'You'll be safe at the Duke. And it's still nice and handy for work.' Normally he would have stepped aside, but this morning, what with the shock of it and the sense of relief that the bombers had done their worst but here they all were still standing, he kept his arm firmly round her shoulder.

Hettie picked up the delicate situation. 'That's settled then. Why not wait here with Tommy till they let you in to salvage what you can? Clothes, a bit of make-up, whatever you might need. Then you come straight to the pub, you hear?'

Edie agreed, too grateful to say many words.

'And you make her stick to it,' she told Tommy. 'You're the boss, remember. And if she's not at our place by teatime I'll send Ernie up to fetch her, no messing.' She pretended to be stern, then gave Edie's hand a quick squeeze. 'Don't worry, we're all here to fight another day, ain't we?'

She sounded brighter than she felt as she left them, picking her way over bricks, past a burnt-out car. You put on a brave front, like everyone else, did your best to cope and not be overwhelmed by dread.

Hettie walked up her beloved Duke Street and stopped at the corner outside the Duke of Wellington. She waved to Dolly Ogden, out scouring her front doorstep; typical Dolly. You scrubbed and swept, ate cold food out of tins, listened in to Churchill and said no, you were not downhearted, that you would fight street by street to keep Hitler out. But deep down, you knew your world had changed utterly; every nerve strained for the sound of the Luftwaffe coming over again, droning low, drawing nearer.

At dusk you prayed. As night fell, the planes came; on Sunday, Monday, Tuesday, and on into the following week, and into October, without let-up. And through it all you kept your chin up and smiled.

CHAPTER ELEVEN

The shelter at Nelson Gardens took a direct hit one Sunday evening in late October. As Dolly said later, 'There was nothing but blood everywhere, and blackness.' The door blew in, the corrugated roof shuddered then split apart, beams crashed, earth flew, and the screams of the dying were succeeded by the moans of the injured.

'They was buried under all that rubble. All the lights went, so they had to work in the dark to get them out. I seen one young lady doctor, she looks twenty if she's a day, crawling through to get at someone trapped down in the main crater. She won't let nothing stop her. We're all pushing to get out into the open; anything's better than staying to be buried alive if the rest of the shelter caves in — as it could any second. And we pass her crawling on all fours right into the thick of it. She has to hang upside-down from a metal girder to get near enough to give this poor bloke a shot in the leg for the pain, and she's working by torchlight.' Dolly shook her head, recovering at the bar in the Duke. Annie had turned it over to the WVS, who had called in the Council Canteen and, now, an orderly queue had formed and a huge pan of parsnip soup stood steaming by the beer pumps.

'It's a good job Jerry decided to call it a day.' Annie sat for a moment, in between shifting trays of dirty dishes and spoons into the sink for Ernie to wash. The all-clear had sounded, the skies were silent.

'Yes, and that's only because he couldn't see where he was meant to be dropping his bombs.' Dolly was thoroughly rattled. She looked along the length of the queue for a sign of Charlie. 'They say it was the cloud cover that saved us.'

Amy finished serving the soup as Hettie took over. She came up to her mother's table. 'That's it, Ma. From now on you come down the cellar here with us.' She sat opposite. 'I'm not having you traipsing off to no official shelter no more, not after what happened today.' She felt guilty for not putting her foot down sooner.

'But I like the public places. I've got my pals, we have a sing-song and a laugh and a joke.' Dolly didn't want to give in straight away, though she would be secretly grateful to be bullied into changing her mind. She remembered that poor old man trapped deep in the earth, his wife already lying stone cold beside him.

'Yes and you'll be laughing on the other side of your face before too long.' Amy was determined.

'And what about Charlie? Don't I have to keep an eye on him?'

'Ma, he's a grown man!'

'And you'd never think it to look at him sometimes.' Dolly hadn't seen him since before the bomb blast. He'd been hunched in a corner with Dorothy as usual, playing gin-rummy and taking nips from a shared bottle of whisky. After the roof fell in, the table where they'd been sitting was squashed flat like a deck chair. Charlie and Dorothy were nowhere to be seen.

'You'll never get him down the cellar with us.' Amy knew he would stick with Dorothy and even Charlie must realize that the Parsons' charity didn't run to offering shelter to Dorothy O'Hagan, not now that Edie was treated like part of the family. 'Anyhow, that ain't the point. What makes most sense is for you to head straight here in future.'

'Can't make me,' Dolly grumbled.

'Says who?'

'You and whose army?'

'Don't need no army, Ma. I'll send Bobby down the Court to fetch you.'

Just as her resistance was about to crumble, Dolly spied the ostensible cause of their disagreement. Charlie swung in through the doors, alone, covered in dirt, with a crimson mark high on his left cheek. She jumped up to berate him. 'There you are, Charlie Ogden. Here's me thinking you was buried under that pile of rubble, dead as a doornail!' Her cry attracted a wide audience of refugees from the shelter, all glad of a diversion. 'And here you are large as life, with hardly a scratch on you!'

'Sorry about that, Ma.' He came across and spoke under his breath. 'Why don't I go back and make a proper job of being done in?' Hat on the table, white-faced, with a bleeding cut on his cheek, he sat down.

'Ha-ha, very funny I don't think. You know what I'm on about, leaving an old girl to get out of that hole all on her tod, not caring if I was alive or dead.'

The force of the blast had rolled Charlie back off his seat and buried him under a sheet of corrugated iron, which had, in fact, saved his life in the roof-fall that followed.

'But we all know who comes first with you, Charlie, and it ain't your poor old ma!'

It wasn't Dorothy either, though this was the implication. Charlie had enough to do to save himself back there, as the soil pelted

231

against the sheet of metal and he breathed in acrid smoke, scrabbling with his fingertips to dig free of the earth.

'See, he don't deny it.' Dolly appealed to Amy.

'Ma, calm down. We're all safe, ain't we?'

'What's the point?' Charlie rounded on his mother and spoke quietly, fiercely. 'Whatever I do or say, it ain't right, is it? I can't open my mouth without putting my foot in it, so I might as well not bother.'

Amy laid a restraining hand on his arm.

'No, I've had it up to here. You can bleeding well say what you like, but from now on I won't be around to hear it.'

'He means it,' Amy whispered. 'Say sorry, Ma!'

'Sorry — what for?' When it came to it, she meant what she said. Lately, he'd taken up with Dorothy, he'd turned hard-hearted and never given his family a second thought.

Charlie flashed Amy a look. 'See, she shows me up and she don't even see she's doing it.'

'You know what she's like. It ain't just you; Ma's the same with everyone.'

'Well, not with me, not any more.' He stood up and fixed his hat firmly over his forehead. 'From now on I ain't gonna be there when you whistle, Ma. You hear me?

I'll pack my bag and you won't see me no more. I'll be out of your hair for good.'

'He's in a state,' Amy whispered as he stormed off. 'Give him a chance to calm down.'

'*He's* in a state?' Dolly echoed. 'And what about me? I'm the one who should be in a state, having a son like him, and his father dead and buried and no one to look out for me.'

Stoically Amy stepped in to shoulder the burden. She sent for brandy, sat by and mopped up Dolly's loud tears. 'Anyhow, you'll be down with us next time that siren goes off and no arguments.'

Dolly wasn't the only one to go to pieces that night. Amy watched as Edie Morell came in, wet through from the downpour that had just begun, looking frantic. She dashed towards Hettie, who had served the glass of brandy into Dolly's shaking hand.

'No luck?' Hettie caught Edie's arm and held her to the spot.

'No, I've been all the way to the Gardens and back. No one saw him in the shelter tonight.'

Amy listened in. This must be Tommy they were talking about. She was all ears.

'Well then . . .' Hettie thought this was good news. 'That means he must have taken cover somewhere else. He's probably nice and snug down the tube station, or on his way home right this minute.'

Edie's hair dripped. She'd run from the pub without coat or hat through the rain, as soon as she heard about the direct hit at the Gardens.

'Come on, come with me.' Hettie took her upstairs out of earshot. 'It ain't good to rush out like that, not before the all-clear.' She found towels and went to Edie's room to fetch a dressing-gown. 'Now you get out of them wet things before you catch your death.'

Edie trembled by the gas fire, peeling off the wet clothes. 'I can't bear it when the siren goes off and I don't know where he is,' she confessed.

Hettie wrapped the gown round her shoulders. 'I see you can't.'

'I love him, Ett, and I don't know what to do!' It was the first time she'd come out into the open over Tommy, though these past few weeks had proved an agony. With her flat in ruins and no privacy for Tommy and her to be together, their affair had turned into a series of snatched kisses in the basement office, of staged meetings in un-friendly pubs and cruel separations when the sirens sounded and he insisted that she go with Hettie and the rest while he found what cover he could.

'And he loves you; anyone can see that.' Hettie didn't shy away from the intimate confession. She spoke kindly, from the vantage point of years.

'Can they?' Edie sounded surprised.

Hettie smiled. 'Yes, you don't think you managed to keep it a secret, did you? Not round here. Tommy's head over heels, it goes without saying.'

She bit her lip. 'Does Dorothy know?'

'I haven't asked her. Why, hasn't Tommy told her?'

'I won't let him. It don't seem fair, not with the war on.'

'What's fair got to do with it?' Hettie's Christian sense had struggled long enough over Edie's all too obvious love for her employer. Rules were being broken left, right and centre. No — worse — Commandments, and these were what Hettie had lived by since her Sally Army days. On the one hand, she could see the bitterness between man and wife; two people who seemed not to have recognized the bargain they made at the altar, whose disappointment in one another wrapped a straitjacket around their lives, so that Dorothy drenched herself in perfume and chased other men, while

Tommy soused himself in alcohol. On the other hand, there was Tommy and Edie together, blossoming into tenderness.

'It ain't right though, is it? There's Bill to think of . . .'

'Yes.' Hettie knew none of the details about Edie's own marriage.

'You don't hold with divorce, do you, Ett?' Edie knelt on the fireside rug, not able to control which way her thoughts ran.

'Not for myself. But I try not to judge.'

'And what would you do if you weren't happy?'

'How, not happy?'

Edie looked down at her upturned palms. 'If, say, your old man knocked you about a bit.'

Hettie let this sink in.

'I don't mean to say all the time, just now and then,' Edie went on quickly. 'If his temper was bad and, of course, he would regret it straight after, tell you he was sorry . . .'

Hettie knelt beside her. 'I don't know that I could put up with it, Edie, even now and then. I can only say how I would feel; every time he laid a hand on me it would shock me rigid, wondering how he could do such a thing than how much it actually hurt.'

Tears came to Edie's eyes. 'And would

you tell someone? You don't think that would be letting him down?'

Slowly Hettie shook her head. 'I couldn't keep it to myself, I know that.'

'And if the first person you told promised he would look after you, would you be tempted?'

'Anyone would.'

'But would you?' It was as if Edie judged herself through Hettie's answers.

'I'd want to be looked after,' she agreed.

Edie sighed. 'And then you'd be stuck.'

'I would?'

'Yes, 'cos your husband might get to know, even if he ain't on the spot and, knowing his temper, you'd be afraid he would take it out on the one who wanted to take care of you.'

'And take it out on me, too.' Hettie saw the point. 'And then, of course, I could be stuck another way, if this person who cares is married already.' They'd come full circle.

Edie stopped mincing words. 'That's it, bull's eye. It's a mess, ain't it?'

'Here, dry your hair.' Hettie handed her another towel. 'It probably looks worse from the inside, but you still shouldn't go charging out while the siren's going. If you get yourself blown up everyone's gonna end up

237

miserable, ain't they?'

Edie managed a smile. 'Only Tommy. He'd do anything for me. You know he's fixing up the flat with anything he can lay his hands on. He got the windows put back in last week, the first in the block.'

'Like I said, he loves you to death.'

'You don't mind me going on about it?' As she calmed down, Edie turned shy.

'Mind? Edie Morell, why should I mind? I only wish I had the answer.' She stood up and spread Edie's wet dress along the top of the fireguard.

'That'd be too much to expect.' She took a hairbrush from the table and began to sweep her dark blonde hair back over her shoulders. 'If I had a sister, Ett, she'd be just like you.'

'Well, you're family now, Edie, you remember that. We love having you here, so you stay as long as you like. And go when you're ready. Just one thing . . .'

'Yes?'

'Take your time. Don't jump. You'll find that's the best way.'

Upstairs, Hettie's soothing voice worked its magic, while downstairs the survivors from Nelson Gardens pulled themselves together on a diet of hot soup and rumours of Jerry's imminent comeuppance.

'Blimey, this is worse than the Blitz!' Bobby Parsons drew Jimmie O'Hagan to one side after he'd walked into the pub alongside Tommy, straight into Dorothy's line of fire.

'What's up, can't you take it?' Her caustic voice had sailed over the soup queue to where Tommy demanded a large whisky from George Mann.

He ignored her. It had been a close shave, dragging Jimmie down the Tilbury shelter just as the raid started. As luck would have it, the all-clear had brought them up onto Liverpool Street, smack into an unexploded bomb, still ticking away nicely. It had gone up in their faces, killing two and injuring a whole lot more. He'd taken a cut on his leg, where a piece of shrapnel had torn through his trousers. It bled long and hard before an ambulance girl got round to strapping it up. If ever he needed a drink and a rest from Dorothy's scorn, it was now.

'Oh, my God, he's limping, a real old peg-leg.' She didn't care what people thought of her, for what did she owe anybody round here? Every time she walked into this place she got the evil eye from Annie Parsons, all because she made an effort to keep up appearances and could still bring the men flocking round. And they obviously took Tommy's side over this mockery of a marriage. But they didn't know what he was like to live with; uncommunicative, always wanting his own way. He'd driven her into Charlie Ogden's arms, literally driven her. And now she got the blame. Like everyone else today, she was thrown off-balance by events. 'Don't tell me you copped it, Tommy? Or did you walk into a lamppost when you was the worse for wear?' The more he ignored her, the higher her voice rose.

'You shut your nasty mouth,' he warned. His leg hurt, the drink went straight to his head.

'Or else what?' She outstared Dolly Ogden sitting nearby, getting up to push through the queue to reach him.

'Look, if you two want to have a barney, could you go home and have it?' George looked with disgust at them both. Annie took the soup ladle and rapped it against the metal pot.

'No, come on, Tommy, what you gonna do to shut me up?' She used the mindless taunting he hated most. She would bait him, then turn round and walk away. 'I dare say there's a few round here who'd like a lesson from you on how to shut their old ladies'

240

'cake-holes.' She winked at a couple of men in the queue.

'Are they always at each other's throats like this?' Bobby asked Jimmie, who'd turned scarlet.

'This is nothing. Just you wait.' He shuffled into a corner, waiting for one or other to blow a fuse.

'Ain't it typical, all mouth and no trousers. Tells me to pipe down, then does sod-all about it,' Dorothy sneered.

'You're drunk,' he said sullenly.

'And what if I am? I just had a narrow escape at Nelson Gardens, and a fat lot you care.' She checked her make-up in the mirror behind the bar.

'Didn't smudge your lipstick, did it?'

George frowned harder. There'd be no merit in beating Dorothy at her own game.

'A lot you care about my lipstick,' she sneered. 'It ain't your colour, from what I hear.'

Tommy gritted his teeth. She'd be as well to leave Edie out of this.

'I'm surprised you ain't taken the trouble to track down that particular colour since you limped home. Velvet Rose, ain't it? Max Factor, gift-wrapped. Along with them pairs of nylons and boxes of chocolates.'

'Leave off,' Annie growled from behind

her ladle. 'I don't want no nastiness.'

But Dorothy was ready to take on the world. It was true, the blast at the shelter had shaken her up. She'd lost Charlie in the dark chaos and had to get herself out with no one to help. But in her case, sudden vulnerability turned straight to irrational anger; Tommy was her husband. He should have been there for her. 'What's nasty about that? It ain't me, it's Tommy and Edie Morell you should be having a go at.'

Annie mumbled something about the pot calling the kettle black, just as Hettie came down to investigate the raised voices. Tommy slammed down his glass.

'See, he knows I'm right. You're dying to find out if she's all right, ain't you? Your precious lady friend. Well tell him, Annie, she's right as rain, worse luck. The last I saw of her she was out looking, out of her mind because she couldn't find you. I ran slap-bang into her and told her not to worry, the booze would get to you before Jerry did.'

He rounded on her, pushing her to one side. Dorothy fell against the bar.

'You see that?' She rubbed her arm in protest. But if she was hoping for a display of violence she was disappointed. Tommy rubbed a hand across his eyes, then ducked his head as he pushed his way through the crowd of onlookers.

'Where's he off to now?' Bobby watched him disappear through the door.

'God knows. He'll probably end up at the shop, sleeping on the floor. Me too, worse luck.' To Jimmie this was all too grimly familiar.

'But it's Sunday, ain't it?' Bobby tried to make out exactly what was going on.

'Black Sunday, never mind Black Saturday.' Jimmie lit up a fag.

'In full view!' Dolly complained once things had quietened down sufficiently for her voice to be heard. It seemed likely tonight that they would all get a night in their own beds for a change. Black clouds hung over London like a thick blanket, too thick for the planes to get through. 'Showing herself up and dragging that poor girl's name through the mud.' She couldn't find a good word to say about Dorothy O'Hagan.

Hettie said she thought she was probably very unhappy and scared, like everyone else.

'Who's side are you on?' Dolly said sharply.

She refused to be drawn. 'No one's. What's the point?'

'No, I expect you'll just say a prayer in-

stead.' She didn't like Hettie to go all sanc-
timonious on her.

'I expect I will.' Hettie cleared glasses.
'For them all.'

'Include my Charlie in that, will you?'
Dolly said, suddenly repentant. Hettie was
so good and kind-hearted she didn't deserve
to be teased. Anyway, it was no laughing
matter when your son went off the rails with
a married woman, and that woman happened to be Dorothy O'Hagan.

CHAPTER TWELVE

'Every Night Something Awful!' Jimmie shared his cigarettes with Meggie and Bobby. 'Get it? ENSA; Every Night . . .'

'. . . Something Awful!' Bobby's broad face broke into a grin. They were gathered round the wireless at his place, tuned into a variety show. Jimmie was busy avoiding the inevitable showdown at his house, while Meggie had fled from another tiff with her mother over the amount of time she spent at Bernhardt Court.

'It ain't funny, Jimmie.' Meggie felt they shouldn't make light of Tommy's problems. She struggled to swallow a puff of the sharp smoke without coughing, using the cigarette as a signal that she was old enough to know her own mind. Still, she found inhaling the stuff unpleasant and difficult.

'Ain't it?' He fiddled with the tuning knob. The radio whistled and hummed. 'You gotta laugh, or you'd bleeding well cry.'

'You mean, they're at it every single night?' Every night something awful. She

245

couldn't imagine a house so full of discord. Her own parents rarely quarrelled. The boys could be rowdy at times, there would be a sharp word from Sadie, even a tap on the leg, but it was soon forgotten. That's why her disagreement with her mother over Ronnie was so hard to deal with, casting a shadow over an otherwise loving atmosphere.

'Every chance they get,' Jimmie reported. 'She riles him, he ignores her, so she goes at him again, nag-nag-nag. Why hasn't he done this? How come he finds time to do that? When was the last time he came home sober? On and on.'

'Why's he put up with it?' Bobby asked the logical, unmarried man's question.

'He keeps saying he won't for much longer.'

'And why do *you* have to?'

Another shrug.

'Where would he go, stupid?' Meggie was equally succinct.

'Anywhere.'

'Like, where for instance?' She'd thought this one through for herself. 'Hitler's bombed out half of London, in case you hadn't noticed.' There were always queues of homeless people on the steps of the War Damage Bureau as she passed by on her way to and from work. The few lucky ones managed to get themselves rehoused by billeting officers, but the majority stayed with family, or crammed into the rest centres to sleep on floors and feed at the WVS mobile canteens.

Jimmie kept quiet during the spat between the cousins. He had the feeling that he was, in fact, the only reason why Tommy tried to hold things together with Dorothy; to give him a roof over his head. 'Maybe I'll just flit anyhow,' he told them. 'Whether or not I got somewhere to go.'

'Oh don't do that!' Meggie cried. She brushed fallen ash from her navy-blue slacks.

'Why not? Would you miss me?' He winked at Bobby.

'Course we would.' She coloured up and angrily stubbed the fag out. 'It ain't funny, Bobby.'

Jimmie sprang up and pulled her to her feet, to dance her round the living room. 'We'll meet again . . .' he crooned, 'Don't know where, don't know when . . .'

Meggie thumped him on the shoulder.

'. . . But I know we'll meet again some sunny day.'

'This is it then?' Dorothy watched warily

as Tommy flung clothes into a battered suit-case.

'You've gone too far.'

'Me? What about you?'

'I don't want to talk about it, right?' He wouldn't discuss Edie. 'Let's just call it a day.'

She chain-smoked, following him from room to room. 'Just like that? Finished.' She snapped her fingers, barred his way as he made for the bathroom.

'No, not just like that. What do you think — that I'm enjoying this?'

'What I think is, you can't wait to jump into bed with that little trollop.'

'Wrong!'

Her bitterness spilled over in a distorted version that left out of account her own affair with Charlie and cast her in the role of abandoned wife. 'I reckon you can't get out of here fast enough.'

'Right.' They stood eye to eye. Dorothy flinched as he pushed past to get his shaving gear.

'Where will you go?'

No answer. He didn't know. First he would pack up, then he would go and find Jimmie.

'Will you keep the shop going?'

'I ain't about to cut off my own nose to

spite my face, am I? Course I'll keep it going.'

'I ain't moving out of here,' she warned. The picture of future events only gradually took shape. If the shop stayed open, that meant that Edie would still be working in the office. Not a nice idea to swallow.

'I never asked you to.' He glanced round the flat full of gadgets he'd fitted, furniture he'd bought. 'You're welcome to it.'

'And I want an allowance.' She flicked hard at her lighter, which refused to work. She shook it, then threw it onto a low table. When he didn't commit himself to paying over any money, she panicked. 'You owe me. You can't just leave me in the lurch!'

'Oh, can't I?' He snapped the case shut, then veered away from another battle. 'OK, you'll get money, don't worry. I'm sick of playing games with you, you hear? Sick of them.'

'I never started it.'

'Who did then?' He was looking round for the last time, picking up the case, saying goodbye to a chunk of his life.

'We both did.'

It was the first sincere thing she'd said in ages. He let the case slide flat again. 'How come.'

'You never loved me, Tommy, not really.

I knew that as soon as we got married.' Her voice edged towards tears as she sat heavily on the bed.

Wrongfooted, he didn't jump in to deny it. Maybe it was true. Maybe, before Edie, he never knew what love was.

'You thought you did, but really you never. Then you thought you'd cover it up by giving me things to keep me happy. That was your way.'

He was astonished. 'I treated you well, didn't I?' All this was a revelation. In his eyes, Dorothy had expected the presents, the trips to the cinema and the seaside. He'd always found her demanding in this direction, thought she gave him freedom to go out to the pub and the football.

'Like a princess,' she said flatly. 'But you'd have done as much for anyone; for your ma when she was alive, for Jimmie. It wasn't as if I was special.'

'I asked you to marry me, didn't I?'

'Only after I'd done all the running, in case you hadn't noticed.' She'd had to pull out all the stops; the perfume, the low-cut dresses. After all, she was years older than Tommy, a woman with an already tarnished reputation. With his thriving business, quick wit and lively personality, Tommy was seen as a good catch.

'I never,' he admitted, feeling a fool.

'No, you wouldn't.' She blew her nose. 'You never noticed nothing about me, not really.'

He began to think this was all true. Sitting there, she looked defeated, yet he'd always thought of her as tough. 'What are you saying, that all this carrying on with Charlie and the others was just to get your own back?'

'Bingo!'

'I don't believe you.'

'Why else would I latch onto Charlie Ogden?'

'Don't you like him, then?'

She shrugged and reached for another cigarette. 'Have you got a light? Charlie's Charlie, ain't he?'

'Does he know you don't like him?'

'I never said that. Anyhow, he don't like me much neither, so there's two of us.'

Tommy took a deep breath. The idea of using another person as a means of retaliation struck him as shocking. He used people to make money, it was true, but they always knew what he was up to and drove a hard bargain. But to pick up an unsuspecting bloke going through a hard time of his own was, to Tommy, something you didn't do. 'Am I the fool, or what?'

'You said it.' She inhaled deeply, her hand trembling, her face drawn.

'You talk about me not loving you, but what about the other way around? I reckon you was out to get all you could out of me, right from the start, like I was a soft touch or something.'

This time she didn't answer. Let him think that. She wouldn't admit now that she'd started out head over heels in love with him.

'Right.' He snapped his mouth shut with a short laugh. 'I learned my lesson there, then.'

'Better late than never.'

His mind flew back through the years; all the right things done for the wrong reasons, the long disillusionment. 'If you never loved me, why marry me?'

She hesitated. 'It wasn't just to get what I could out of you. I thought I could get you to love me.'

'That would have been enough?'

'Yes. I wanted to know how it felt.'

He'd planned to leave on a roll of anger, now he felt drained by sadness. 'We ain't talked enough, you know that?' It would take a huge effort to leave her sitting there red-eyed and subdued.

But she took another unexpected turn,

rejecting his pity. 'I ain't interested in *talking* to a man, Tommy. I thought you'd have realized that by now.'

And now it was easy to turn away; she'd made it easy by her typical coarseness. He never knew where that came from or what she got out of it, except that it put a man in his place; all men in fact, since it turned the tables and showed that she was the one in control. As she pronounced the word, 'talking', stressing it and raising her eyebrows, he took the implied insult on board. 'Righto, Dot. You go and do whatever it is you're interested in doing.'

He took up the case and headed for the door, slipping his hand into his jacket pocket. 'Here's my key. If I have to, I'll kip in the basement for a bit, until I get me and Jimmie sorted out.'

Damn; she'd tilted it and let it slide by not being able to resist a sly dig. She'd always said Tommy was no good in bed, not because it was true, but because it was the easiest, deepest way to hurt him. This was once too often. She sat marooned on the bed, submitting to his departure.

He slammed the door and his footsteps faded down the stairs. Quietly she went and picked up the telephone, dialled Charlie's new number. 'Hello, it's me.' She waited while he went and turned down the wireless. 'Yes, Tommy just left. I kicked him out. When can you come round?'

Meggie wrote to Ronnie at least twice a week, not knowing if her letters would get through. Her favourite writing time was in the shelter under the pub, where she could retreat to a quiet corner and scribble away as the others wrapped themselves in blankets and got their heads down for the night.

She would tell him how they'd grown used to the Blitz; these days everyone could get a good sleep in spite of the thud of bombs and rattle of guns. Bertie, for instance, could sleep through the end of the world. She had more complaints about the squeak of her pen nib across the paper as she wrote her long letters, she said. One night her Uncle George had brought down fish and chip suppers for everyone after his spell on duty, and it had put them in a good mood so that supper was followed by a sing-song and you would have thought they hadn't a care in the world.

She kept her letters cheerful, treasuring similar ones from Ronnie, who could give few details of his whereabouts because of security, and who concentrated instead on the tricks they got up to to better the petty-officers. He sent her a photo of himself in uniform, shoulders back, chin up, unbelievably handsome. She carried it everywhere and slept with it under her pillow.

'It ain't Ronnie I mind about,' Sadie told her one evening while they sat darning socks by lamplight, listening as usual for the siren, almost wishing it would start up. Then they would have Ernie knocking at the door to fetch them, and they would bundle everyone into the shelter for the night and know where they stood. 'A lovely girl like you is bound to find herself a nice young man sooner rather than later.'

'I'm sure you'll like him, Ma.' Meggie was glad at the friendly turn of the conversation. The boys were in bed and Walter was out on patrol. They had the warm kitchen to themselves.

'If I ever get to meet him.' Sadie's needle went in and out, weaving across the threadbare heel.

'Next time he comes home on leave,' she promised.

'You said that last time.'

'I know, but his ma needs him. She had to try and run the pub single-handed since they took her cellarman into the army. You know what it's like.'

'I should think she could spare him for a

couple of hours,' Sadie sniffed. 'That's all I'm saying. Everyone runs after that woman, you included.' She resented the time Meggie spent away from home; first on the futile search for her father, now due to the lure of the West End and Gertie's precious company.

'It ain't like that,' Meggie tried to explain. 'Gertie don't expect no one to run round after her.'

'What is it, then?' What made Meggie spend her weekends up there, even though Ronnie wasn't due any leave before Christmas?

'I don't know. You'd have to meet her.'

'No, ta.'

'Ma!'

'Well, I mean to say you can't expect me to be tripping over myself in the rush. From what I hear, she's got plenty of admirers.'

Meggie sighed and sewed on.

'Where's her husband anyway?'

'Dead.'

Silence, which Meggie filled.

'Shankley says he'd get hitched to her like a shot, only she says once bitten, twice shy.'

'Who's Shankley?'

'The oysterman in Bernhardt Court.' For a while Meggie succeeded in diverting attention away from Gertie by regaling her mother with tales of life in theatreland, seen through the eyes of the old Irishman.

'And he's sweet on Gertie Elliot?' Sadie swung it back round. 'Like everyone and his aunt, apparently. And what's she like?'

'She's good fun, Ma. She wears modern outfits and she's always got time for a joke. And she's been kind to me right from the start, even before me and Ronnie got together. You'd like her, you would.'

Sadie looked doubtful, as if this was a new and exotic food she'd prefer not to taste. It was the 'modern outfits' that did it. It made Sadie feel dowdy and left out. 'I expect you'll be up there tomorrow?' Saturday, a day off, building up to Christmas.

'I said I'd help out.'

'Lucky Gertie.' Sadie snipped the end off the grey wool and inspected the darn. 'At any rate it keeps you out of mischief.'

'Meaning?' Meggie ended up disgruntled as usual. There was no way she could persuade her mother that being with Gertie in the Bell brought her closer to Ronnie, even in his absence, and made her happy. Perhaps it was too much to expect.

She was only saved from an awkward conversation by the familiar wail of the siren and the action stations that followed. Not having to discuss him was the best refuge from further arguments.

With Gertie, however, she could say whatever she wanted. As soon as she stepped through the doors of the Bell the next evening she felt free and confident. There was Eddie, the Fred Astaire of Shaftesbury Avenue as Gertie called him, and the other young men who had as yet escaped enlistment. They all made a fuss of her and made her laugh with their extravagant compliments. Gertie told her to get behind the bar double-quick before someone whisked her off to the pictures and she lost a barmaid for the evening.

'Spoilsport.' Eddie looked down in the mouth.

'No, she saved my bacon.' Meggie ducked under the counter and took off her coat.

'What, you mean to say you don't want to cuddle up in the back row with me and Wormy?'

Wormy, alias Rodney Wormall, was a tall beanpole of a youth.

'No, I do not. In fact, I'd rather get dragged through a hedge backwards.' She set to, stacking clean glasses.

'That's telling you, Ready Eddie.' Gertie sidled up to poor Wormy. 'Ain't you gonna ask *me* to the flicks, Rodney? I ain't seen the latest Gary Cooper. You could take me if you like.'

The others laughed as Wormy reddened and failed to make a gallant reply. Meggie went along with it by winking at Eddie.

'You heard from Ronnie this week?' Gertie asked Meggie. She pulled pints with practiced ease. Tonight she wore a short black dress with a row of small shiny buttons, and a double row of pearls with matching earrings. Her copper-coloured hair was curled at the front and pinned high at the back.

'Just the once.'

'Lucky you.'

'Why, ain't he written to you?'

'I'm only his ma, remember.' She said this without any undertone, serving beer and striking the till keys with long carmine fingernails.

'He sends his love.'

'To you or to me?'

'To us both.' Ronnie's letters followed a pattern; stilted in the first paragraph containing general remarks; then joky in a schoolboy fashion; then suddenly tender to finish. 'I love you, my darling, and can't wait until we're together again', 'I think of you day in, day out, hoping that you're mine forever. Your loving Ronnie.' These were his ways of signing off.

'He's got it bad if you ask me,' Gertie conceded. 'To tell you the truth, I think you're the only thing he comes home for these days.'

Meggie blushed with pleasure.

'I mean it. You're the cream in his coffee.' Gertie hummed the tune.

'Shh.'

'What for? I don't mind if you don't.' She tackled another bout of thirsty customers. 'What it is to be young,' she sighed. ' "Keep young and beautiful, If you want to be loved, tra-la." Who sang that?'

'I haven't a clue,' Meggie laughed. 'Must have been before my time.'

'Don't rub it in.'

She took a breath, gazing up at the distinguished actors smiling down from their black photograph frames, enjoying the tinkling notes of the piano. It might have been her imagination, but she thought she recognized a customer who had just come in. He wore a long camelhair coat, collar up, trilby hat pulled forward. 'Wasn't he in that film about the German spy?' she whispered to Gertie, who laughed like a drain.

'No, but he'd like you to think he was.' She drew Meggie to the far end of the bar. 'You see him over there? Now he *is* a film actor over in Ealing.' She pointed to a disappointingly small, fat man with a balding head and a surprising number of female hangers-on. 'He does the comedies with George Formby.'

Meggie looked again. Maybe he wasn't as fat and bald as she'd first thought. In a way he was quite attractive. He had a wicked smile. Yes, she could guess what an older woman might see in him, she admitted to Shankley, who had just made his way into the bar carrying a flat, square basket full of best seafood.

'Rose-tinted glasses.' He set the basket down. 'I knew Roly Spence for donkeys years before he was in the flicks, when he was a fat, bald little geezer with a lisp. Now anyone would think he was Rudolph Valentino.'

'He's dead, ain't he?' Meggie served him his favourite mellow Guinness.

'So what?' Shankley wiped the froth from his top lip with a luxurious sucking noise. 'Now I know who I'd rather spend my time looking at, if you ask me!'

'Hands off, Shanks,' Eddie warned. 'Meggie's taken.'

'Only kidding.' He winked at her, then raised a forefinger and tapped it against the bar. 'That reminds me.'

'What?' Trust him, standing there looking as if he had something important to say, keeping her in suspense.

'This Richie Palmer . . .'

'What, have you seen him?' Her heart thudded at the sound of the long-forgotten name.

'Hold your horses. I only heard he was up this way.'

'You ain't seen him then?' Her face fell.

'I ain't. But he was seen earlier this week, that's definite. What's the matter? Why ain't you over the moon.'

She needed to know every detail. 'Did anyone talk to him? Where did he go?' Guilt consumed her, that she could have been so callous as to have dropped all thought of finding her poor father.

'Hang on, let's see. It must've been Tuesday. And to tell you the honest truth, he weren't fit to talk to by all accounts. He spent more time in the gutter than on his own two feet, until the coppers came and cleared him out of the road. That's what I heard.'

Meggie nodded at each scrap of information. 'The coppers? Which station?'

'Search me.' Shankley looked sorry that he'd dropped the bombshell. 'Look, they probably carted him off to some shelter for a kip, or to one of the big hostels. All I know is they wanted to tidy him off the street before the final curtain. It don't look good to have tramps cluttering the place up; bad for morale, so they say.'

She went to serve a customer, then came back. 'But you say you didn't see him yourself?'

'No. How many times? Look here, what's so bleeding fascinating about Richie Palmer? Because for the life of me I can't see why a girl like you would waste five seconds on the likes of him.'

Meggie trusted Shankley. He was like the streetlamps, the billboards; part of the furniture. He had a lilt in his voice and a light in his eye. She leaned across the bar and whispered, 'Don't say nothing, Shanks, but Richie Palmer's my pa. That's why I want to track him down. He's my pa and I ain't never seen hide nor hair of him since I was a little baby. You understand, don't you? You'd do the same if you was me.'

Jimmie insisted on staying at Bobby's place when Tommy left the flat. 'I don't want to hear her carrying on with Charlie Ogden,' he said darkly. 'It's like bleeding musical beds up there.' Charlie had moved in just as soon as Tommy had walked out.

Anyway, Dorothy had made it plain that she didn't want to catch sight of Jimmie's ugly mug as she came up and down stairs.

Meanwhile, it took Tommy a week or two to fix up Edie's flat.

'I don't want it to feel like I'm rushing you,' he told her in the bar at the Duke. He was sleeping for the time being on a sister's floor over in Lambeth. 'I ain't doing the place up just so we can live together.' If she thought things had moved too quick, he said, he was prepared to wait.

But Edie had been the one to suggest it. 'No, I want to be with you.'

'Sure?'

'Yes.' They'd even planned how to deal with the problem of Bill. 'I'll wait until I next get a letter from him,' she'd decided. 'He don't write often, but when he does it's to tell me when his next leave's due. Then he'll ring me up at work and let me know exactly what time to expect him. That's when I'll tell him.'

'On the blower?'

'Well, I'll say we have to talk.'

'Then tell him face to face?'

Neither relished the prospect, but Edie gained strength from having Tommy around. Making plans to move back into the flat, she felt confident that she could cope with Bill when the time came.

'Sure you're sure?' Tommy seemed to keep something up his sleeve as they downed their drinks.

'Yes, why?' Out of the corner of her eye Edie noticed Hettie at work behind the bar. It was Wednesday, a quiet night so far and she'd arranged to come downstairs to meet Tommy after he'd put in a spell of work at the flat. Now she recalled Hettie's well-meaning advice about not jumping into anything too quickly.

Instead of answering, Tommy stood up and held out his hand. 'Come right this way.'

They walked out onto Duke Street, past houses untouched by the bombs, past shops pock-marked by flying shrapnel, past the large crater near the post office and the demolished office building where scavengers had picked the fallen roof bare, leaving a skeleton of wooden beams on a pile of rubble. A wag had stuck a Union Jack on top in an ironic show of bravado. It fluttered in the red light cast by the warning lamps surrounding the crater, making Tommy and Edie smile. Then he led her into the flats and upstairs to the third floor.

'Close your eyes.'

Standing outside her own door, she did

as she was told. 'What's that smell?'

'Paint.' He opened it and led her in. 'Righto, now you can open them.'

It could only be that he'd finished fixing things up, she knew. Yet when she looked she wasn't prepared for the way he'd done it. 'Oh Tommy, it looks good as new!'

Everything was the same; the green striped wallpaper, the copper fender, the parchment lampshades, it was as if the bomb had never touched it.

'How did you do it?'

'Easy.'

'Get away!'

'I know a man who knows a man . . .' He led her across the room, clasping her arms round his waist from behind so she had to peer over his shoulder to see him lift the lid of the mended gramophone and set the turntable in motion. She bent with him to put the needle on the record, then wound her arms around his neck to the strains of Bing Crosby.

'Like it?' They turned slowly.

'What do you think?'

'I wanted to keep it as a surprise.'

'It is. You must have worked till all hours.'

He put on a smooth, deep voice. 'For you, my dear . . .'

'Seriously, Tommy.'

'I am. Don't you know I am? Listen,' he said, taking half a step back but without letting go of her waist. 'You don't think I did this all on my tod, do you? I got Jimmie to do all the hard work, had to pay him a week's wages and all. Bleeding daylight robbery.'

She laughed. 'You should see your face, Tommy O'Hagan.'

'And you should see yours.' He moved in and kissed her. 'You know I said a while back that I didn't want to rush you?'

'Mmm.'

'Well I changed my mind. I do.'

She opened her eyes wide. 'They'll be expecting me back down the Duke.' It was a half-hearted protest, she knew.

'They'll know where you are.'

'What if they send out a search party?'

'George with his tin hat and stirrup-pump?' He couldn't stop kissing her and inching her towards the bedroom.

'There could be a raid.' Tonight would be the first night for weeks if there wasn't.

'I'll barricade the door and we'll hide under the bed.' They stepped into the room and he closed the door so that they stood in darkness.

'Tommy, I love you.'

'I love you too.' He said the words because he knew that was what she wanted. On top of that, he meant them.

She swam through the dark with him, sinking onto the bed and letting him unbutton her dress as she lay there, waiting to be guided by him.

'Don't you want to?' He wondered at her passivity, whispered into her ear.

She nodded. 'I'm not used to you yet.'

He could see her eyes were wide open, but had to lean down to catch her voice. 'You put your arms round my neck here and hang on tight. That's right. We're gonna take our time, you hear?' As ever, Edie brought out the gentleness in him.

She'd never known what it was like to be considered, to be herself, Edie, in the act of making love. First steps took a long time to master; that he should kiss her more, that she should be able to ask for what she wanted. 'Talk to me, Tommy.'

'What for? What do you want, for me to tell you a joke?'

They rolled apart laughing. Then she raised herself on one elbow and let her hair fall onto his chest which was smooth and pale. She ran her fingers down his ribs, he caught hold of her hand and pulled her down onto him.

In the end, it was for her a perfect time

with the man she adored; passionate and funny, a journey in which she felt she'd come home. 'What did I do to deserve this?' she asked as they lay side by side.

'Hey, I thought I was the joker round here.' He had one arm under her neck, hooked over her shoulder.

'I mean it. I'm the happiest woman alive.'

'Tell me.' He turned his head sideways to look in her eyes. 'Go on, say how you feel.'

'I never knew anything till I met you, and how old am I? It's like I've just been born into a new world with everything shiny as if it's never been used.'

'You're a funny girl.' Stroking her neck, he kissed her.

When the siren sounded and the old world broke in, they were slow to dress and go downstairs. Outside a drizzle was falling, a metal shutter banged against the window of the chemist's shop opposite. Tommy took her to the door of the Duke, kissed her again and said she should take shelter as usual. She went down into the cellar as he headed for Borough, taking his time through the war-torn streets, feeling in a mad way that he was invulnerable, that nothing the Germans had thought up so far could get him, not tonight.

CHAPTER THIRTEEN

'Nice girls don't do that, that's why!' Sadie was indignant with Meggie. Walter had taken the hint and taken the boys down the park to kick a football and stay out of the way.

'Anyone would think I'd committed a murder, the way you go on.' She'd only heard late in the day that Ronnie was coming home on a spot of New Year's leave and asked her mother if she could stay at the Bell overnight. 'After all, no one felt much like celebrating Christmas this year. And Gertie don't mind.'

'You're sixteen years old!' she said bitterly.

'And what do you think we'd get up to if I stayed? It ain't what you're thinking anyhow.'

'I'm not thinking anything.' Sadie banged dishes in the sink, whisking up a froth of soap bubbles in the hot water. 'But others might. What would your gran say if she got to hear? No, Meggie, it ain't on.'

'But Ma, he's only got forty-eight hours.

We want to be together.' She felt Sadie's resistance harden and grew more desperate. 'What's the use? You ain't got a clue what it's like.'

'Oh ain't I?' Sadie knew all too well how it felt to be under a man's spell. She'd gone overboard with Richie, risked everything to win that man's love. 'You listen to me; you're chasing too hard. It don't look nice.'

'I don't care.'

'Then you're a little fool.'

For a while Meggie maintained a silence. Then she tried to conciliate. 'Look Ma, you gotta trust Ronnie and me. He's decent, not like you think.'

'Says you.' A reminder that so far Meggie hadn't seen fit to introduce them. Sadie dried her hands and turned away.

'He is. And things are different, with the war on and everything. It's only natural for us to want to be together, ain't it? We have to snatch our happiness while we can.'

'Oh?' Sadie's monosyllable carried much weight. She didn't need to say that she considered her daughter had been watching too many Hollywood films.

It bounced Meggie back into open defiance. 'Well, you can't stop me. Ronnie starts his leave tonight, and I already wrote and told him I'd be at the station to meet him.'

'Why bother asking me then?' She took out the carpet sweeper and began to push it vigorously across the living room rug. 'Since you had it all nicely arranged.'

'Righto, I won't ask. Forget I mentioned it. I must have been stupid to open my mouth in the first place.'

'Yes, and I'd like more respect from you, Miss.' Sadie's temper was up. She took it out on the carpet.

Meggie, who had followed her from the kitchen to stand, arms crossed, leaning against the doorpost, now sprang forward to snatch her coat from the back of a chair. Her mother caught hold of one sleeve and tugged it from her grasp. The coat fell on the floor between them. They were both past reason, shocked by the sudden violence of feeling.

It was Sadie who spoke out, voice strangled, rising to a shout as she cornered Meggie and slammed the door shut. 'You listen to me; I never brought you up to behave this way. I brought you up decent, didn't I? Not to chase the first bloke you can lay hands on. And don't you tell me it's the war that makes things free and easy. What kind of excuse is that? What I say is, staying the night with him ain't nice, and it'll lead you into all sorts of trouble.'

'I ain't staying the night with him!' Meggie shouted back. 'I'm staying at his Ma's.'

'It's the same thing. Do I know this Gertie Elliot? No. What's she like? For all I know she could be encouraging you two to go further than you ought.'

'That's stupid.'

'How do I know it is?'

'Because I say so.'

'And I say the opposite. Meggie, I'm telling you once and for all, you ain't old enough to know what you're letting yourself in for.'

'And I suppose *you* were?' She blurted it out, then immediately wished it unsaid.

Sadie backed off as though she'd been punched in the stomach. Meggie made as if to help her, but she warded her off. Her voice dropped to a whisper. With one arm across her middle, she held on to the back of an armchair. 'Right, while we're about it I'll tell you a thing or two. You mean me and Richie, right? Well, I was a good bit older than you for a start, and I tell you now, he was the worst mistake I ever made in my life.'

Meggie shook her head.

'He was, believe me.' Sadie's anger had melted into the pain of remembering. 'Oh, he was handsome. He was the most beautiful man I ever saw. Dark and tall, and his eyes spoke to me, though he never used words to flatter me and draw me in. But he did want me though, and I fell for him.'

'You loved him?' Meggie had always clung to this idea.

'I adored him, but I was badly let down, Meggie. We both were.'

'But all men ain't the same. Ronnie won't do what my pa did.' She cried for her mother now, who had never before spoken so openly about her past.

'Listen, I ditched everything for him. I just about broke Pa's heart. And Rob couldn't stick him neither. So there I was all alone with him, and expecting.' She put out a hand and let Meggie grasp it. 'He couldn't take it, the responsibility. By the time you came along he'd already decided he couldn't cope. He was drifting off. He never even wanted to see you after you was born, and wouldn't have come back for those few weeks, if he hadn't wanted to get his own back against Rob. Then Frances and Ett had to come along and rescue me; and Walter, of course.'

'You don't need to tell me no more. Stop now.' She hung her head.

'You see, it wasn't you he ditched. It was the idea of you. Not ready to be a pa, see?'

Sadie put both arms around her daughter. 'And it all happened because I rushed into things with Richie. I've been paying for it ever since.'

Meggie sobbed harder.

'No, not that way. Not through you. You've been the light of my life right from the start.'

'I ain't been in the way?'

'Never.' Sadie spoke softly. 'Without you I don't think I'd have pulled through. I don't say I wasn't low when Richie left us in the lurch. I was; very low. But I only had to look at you in your little crib and you would fill my empty, aching heart. You did. So don't cry.' She rocked her gently. 'I'm sorry I shouted at you, Meggie. You're the last one in the world I want to hurt.'

'Are we friends?' She wiped the tears with the back of her hand.

Sadie nodded. 'But that don't mean to say I ain't worried sick about you.'

'Is that what this is all about? You don't really think I'm a painted lady, do you?'

'It ain't that. But you're a lovely, warm-hearted girl, Meggie, and people can take advantage.'

'Not Ronnie.' She stared earnestly at her mother, hoping and praying.

In the end, Sadie had to trust her judgment. 'And you're sure you have to stay the night?' This was still the sticking-point.

'It's all above board, don't worry. Gertie's letting me share her room. She says it makes sense not to have me traipsing about town in the blackout. Ronnie's promised to take me ice-skating tomorrow.'

'Still, I wish she'd thought to ask me.' Gradually Sadie relented.

'But we ain't on the phone. How could she?'

'Still . . .' She went back into the kitchen deep in thought.

'You don't mind then?' Meggie's face was clear, bright with expectation.

'Oh, I mind. But then you'd expect that — oh, go on!'

Meggie grabbed her coat from the floor, hardly pausing to comb her hair and fix her face.

'What's the rush?'

'I'm late. Ronnie's train's due in at Victoria in half an hour.' She was ready and halfway to the door.

'Be careful.'

'I will. Thanks, Ma!' She flew back to kiss her cheek.

'We'll see you tomorrow . . .' Standing on the doorstep, watching Meggie run up the Court, she felt a heavy sadness settle on her.

As a teacher put out of work by the closure of the schools during the Blitz, it was one of Charlie Ogden's tasks to help with emergency relief. Though he struck up a cynical casualness when talking about having to take the names of the homeless at the War Damage Centre, when it came to actually issuing replacement ration books, providing food, transport and a roof over people's heads, he found a new energy to deal with the problems. He struck those he helped as cheerful and efficient.

It was a Sunday in early January. Christmas had come and gone and the whole country was digging in for another long year of fighting, listening to Churchill on the wireless and growing ever more determined to take it on the chin.

Charlie came away at teatime from a church hall on Blackfriars Road, where several families under his wing had been given temporary shelter. He'd promised to follow up a request to have a mobile laundry van sent along, and hoped to have things under way by early next morning, but he hadn't reached the street corner when the sirens went and he had to change his plan to get

277

back to Duke Street. Instead, he accepted the offer of shelter in the basement of the vicar's house attached to the church where he'd been working.

Annoyed, he took cover, impatient for the raid to be over.

But tonight the Germans really had it in for the City. Not the docks, but the old square mile itself. Hundreds of fires sprang up, fanned by the wind. Deep in the cellar, the vicar got reports on the telephone of the heart of London ablaze, of buildings which had been locked up for the Christmas week razed to the ground, of temperatures rising to 1,000 degrees centigrade, of historic churches gutted.

This was 'taking it' with a vengeance, Charlie thought, watching the distress on these religious folks' faces as they feared for the stray bomb that would set their own church alight. For three hours they were stuck in the makeshift shelter, hearing a bomb blast overhead at last, but not daring to move.

'That was close,' a woman said, staring up at the cellar roof. Following the muffled sound of the huge explosion, there was silence.

'Come on, we're going to take a look.' Two of the men could bear it no longer.

Charlie followed them out of the cellar, lured by the eerie quiet. He lost them at ground level as they were swallowed by smoke and dust. Then he lost his own way back to safety. Feeling along the side of the vicarage as best he could, he heard an ambulance, could just see the glimmer of its blue light as it crept through the wreckage.

A rotten smell overcame him; perhaps gas and sewage from fractured mains. His throat constricted and he edged forward. By the light of the fire that blazed where the church hall had been, he understood that all those whom he had helped that day were dead.

The building blazed. Its windows shattered, flames poured out through the arched frames. Burning beams crashed in on the ruined shell and the wind fanned the flames towards the church itself. He stayed until he could see that this fight, too, was hopeless. The firefighters' hoses quickly ran dry. The Thames was at low ebb, they were unable to draw water from the river and the mains had burst. Charlie stood ankle deep in a gushing, muddy stream, watching the water trickle uselessly down the street. Flames soon flickered into the church towards the altar and, at last, he heard the great bells fall from the tower in a rush of flames and deep clanging metal.

Charlie turned and made for home, to the drone of Heinkels, with the whole of the London skyline red with flames.

Charlie copped it during the night they were calling the Second Fire of London. Dolly blamed herself. She should have put her foot down and made Amy find space for him in the cellar at the Duke. Then he wouldn't have been out in the street when it happened. She sat now by his bedside holding his white hand.

'Ma, he was working. He wouldn't have got to the Duke in any case.' Amy tried to comfort her.

'What sort of job is it that leaves him stranded in the middle of nowhere?'

'I know, but someone's gotta do it.'

'What exactly is it?' Since their row over Dorothy, mother and son had ceased to be on proper speaking terms. 'Something to do with re-housing?'

'Yes, and he does a good job, Ma. You can't blame him for doing his bit.'

'No, no.' She patted his hand. 'Come on, Charlie, wake up. You ain't gonna let them Jerries chalk up another victory, son.'

A nurse passed by and smiled kindly at Amy. 'That's all right, let her talk away. He might like the sound of her voice.'

'I thought he was unconscious?'

'It can sometimes help.'

'How long will he stay like this?'

'You'd best ask the doctor.' She moved off briskly.

So Amy left Dolly to whisper and scold Charlie, and went out into the corridor in search of further information. It was here that she came across Dorothy O'Hagan, sitting on a wooden bench, crying quietly.

'Dorothy?' Amy had to look more closely. 'I never saw you there before.' She remembered seeing this figure in the corridor when Rob dropped them at the hospital and she'd rushed Dolly into Charlie's ward, but it hadn't struck her then that this was the cool and collected Dorothy. She sat huddled inside a man's grey coat, hair falling lankly over her unmade-up face.

Dorothy didn't look up. 'He ain't gonna die, is he?' She sounded drained.

'No.' Amy forced a bright reply. 'He's tough as old boots, is Charlie.'

'He did look dreadful, though, when they brought him in. He'd lost a lot of blood.'

'I know. They told us.'

'I used my jacket to stop it, pressed hard with both hands. We were there I don't know how long.'

'Until the ambulance came?'

She nodded. 'We were just coming down from my place. He came to fetch me, said I should take cover, it was worse than usual. I haven't bothered much lately.'

'Where had Charlie been?'

'Blackfriars Road. He came to me in a state, made me promise to go with him to Nelson Gardens. We didn't get far before it went off in our faces.' She looked up at Amy. 'We both got knocked flat. I got up and said to him, "Stay awake, Charlie. Don't go to sleep!" He tried but he couldn't hang on. He'd lost too much blood.'

Amy sat down beside the dazed woman. 'What about you? Were you hurt?'

'Not a scratch, see.' She opened up the coat to show a blood-soaked blouse. 'All Charlie's!'

Amy gasped. 'And has anyone given you a hot cuppa?' She didn't wait for an answer, but took Dorothy's arm, raised her to her feet and led her towards the hospital canteen, where she shovelled sugar into the hot tea and made her drink it. 'Have they let you see him?'

Dorothy shook her head. 'They said to stay outside.'

'Come on!' Amy made sure she drank to the dregs, then they were on the move again. 'He'll want you there when he comes round, so let's get a move on.' Back up the tiled corridor past squeaking trolleys and silent, starched nurses, swinging through the doors into Charlie's ward.

'Ma, here's Dorothy to see how he is.' Amy stood the poor woman at the end of the bed where her brother lay, still motionless, tubes feeding into his arm, white bandages strapped across his chest.

Dolly stiffened. She refused to look round.

'Ma, they stuck her out in the corridor.'

Still no answer.

'She has a right to see him, like the rest of us.' Dogged, Amy cut through the resistance of Dolly's stiff back. No one should have to go through what Dorothy had just gone through; the explosion, the confusion, the blood.

'She ain't family.' Dolly echoed the hospital policy.

'So what? She only went and saved his life.' She watched the news creep up on her mother, heard her sigh and give a small sob. 'She stopped him from bleeding to death, that's all.'

Amy said later that she'd never seen anyone shake as much as Dorothy did when she finally got to sit by Charlie's bed, on the opposite side to Dolly, holding his other hand. 'They're there now,' she told Rob.

'Ma on one side, Dorothy on the other, like a pair of bookends. When he finally comes round he'll think he's seeing double. Two of them crying all over him and hugging him half to death.'

'Poor geezer.' Rob thoroughly enjoyed the picture. 'They'll most likely finish him off between them; your ma and Tommy O'Hagan's ex-missus.' They'd do what Jerry couldn't, the pair of them.

'Who'd have thought that Charlie Ogden would be the first round here to cop it?' Conversation round the bar at the Duke next night had only one focus.

'He ain't copped it for good though?'

'No. Tommy says he took one across the chest, here.' Jimmie demonstrated. 'A bleeding great beam falls on top of him. He's lucky it ain't finished him off.'

'What was he up to?' Bobby had a new respect for Charlie now that he was a war hero. But he wouldn't let on. 'Didn't he have the savvy to keep his head down like the rest of us?'

'Search me. Something to do with Her Royal Highness, according to Tommy.'

'Her Royal who?'

'Dorothy. Charlie gets back from work to find her in the flat tipsy, sitting in the blackout, taking not a blind bit of notice. He'd been over on Blackfriars Road where the church got bombed out.'

'Sixty-four copped it there. The altar went up in white-hot flames, just before the six o'clock service.' Annie provided dramatic details from behind the bar.

'I still don't see why they say Dorothy's to blame for Charlie copping it.' Back at home, Amy had been in too much of a hurry to explain to Bobby.

'He ain't copped it,' Annie insisted. 'Dolly's still at the hospital. She'll send news when she can.'

'Anyhow, if Dorothy hadn't been squiffy, Charlie wouldn't have had to help her downstairs and head for Nelson Gardens right in the thick of it. He could've saved his own skin.' Jimmie broadcast his opinion. 'She slowed him right down. They was there when the Sally Army hostel on Bear Lane took a hit. The whole front blew off, smashed to smithereens. Charlie got caught, never knew what hit him.'

'What did Dorothy do?'

He shrugged. 'I bet she's sober as a judge now, though.'

CHAPTER FOURTEEN

Meggie ran along the platform at Victoria Station to meet Ronnie. Her coat flew open, she held onto her hat as she ran and the great locomotive sighed and settled against the buffers. Ronnie had hopped out of the carriage before the train had fully stopped and dumped his kitbag at his feet. He stood waiting for her, arms wide open. She felt herself lifted from her feet and swung round, enveloped in a cloud of steam which cut them off from other couples caught in a flurry of passionate reunions. Her arms were round his neck, his round her waist, their cold lips kissed.

'Did you miss me?' At last he swung his bag onto his shoulder and walked her up the platform, one arm around her waist.

'Need you ask?' To her he looked more handsome than ever in his black doeskin jacket with its gold braid.

'Just checking. 'Cos I missed you.'

'Not you. You've got a girl in every port, I bet.'

'Two in some,' he grinned. As Meggie

headed for the tube station he pulled her towards the street. 'Come on, let's take a cab.'

'You must be joking.'

'No, I can afford it. I got money to burn.' Endless weeks on duty and nothing to spend it on had given him a wallet full of cash.

'It ain't that.' They stood in the vast arched entrance to argue it out. The station, packed with uniforms, was the venue for hundreds of meetings and partings. Couples criss-crossed the marble-tiled floor; young men in khaki, navy blue, grey and black, hats set at an angle, shoulders square, boots clicking alongside the tap-tapping of their girls' high heels. Meggie gestured towards the raw, dark expanse of the streets. 'Cabs take forever these days. They get diverted because of the roadblocks,' she explained. 'Or because there's been a bomb down this street or that and they have to steer well clear. Even Uncle Rob was saying he gets lost, and he's been a cabbie Lord knows how long.'

But Ronnie was curious to see if this could possibly be true. He wanted to see how London was taking it, he said.

'No you don't, believe me.' She didn't go in for the official picture of heroic fighting on the home front, not if it meant the destruction of half of her known world; the familiar streets smashed by bombs from the dreaded Stukas and Dorniers, her friends and family in danger of being blown to bits each and every night. If this was their finest hour, she wanted none of it.

Anyway, there were no cabs in the forecourt. Ronnie stopped to light a cigarette and consider the options. 'Let's try shanks's pony.'

'Ronnie!'

'Come on, shake a leg, we'll be there in two ticks.' He picked up his bag and strode onto Buckingham Palace Road, jaunty at first, but soon taken aback by the damage: the dark side streets cordoned off, the buildings ripped open, the mountains of rubble. He stopped to stare at the sight of women queuing in a bombed-out street, each patiently holding an empty milk bottle, waiting to reach the head of the queue for the bottle to be filled by the WVS from a battered churn.

'No milk,' Meggie commented. 'No bread, no electricity, no gas. You get used to it.'

Firehoses still snaked down the middle of the street. A couple of ARP wardens stood atop a pile of smoking bricks.

'Blimey.' Ronnie imagined that dodging

torpedoes in the Med was going to be bad enough but this was worse. That's where he was due to be posted when he reported back for duty on Tuesday night.

'You were the one who wanted to take a look,' she reminded him. 'They even bombed the Palace.'

He shook his head. 'Never! And did the Queen have to queue for milk?'

'That ain't funny.' She dug him in the ribs and smiled anyway. 'You do see them round and about, though, and hear them on the news. Everyone puts on a brave face for them. I suppose it does some good.'

'You don't sound sold on the idea.' Slowly they walked on along the dusty, damaged streets, past the Albert Memorial and other grand, austere emblems of the nation's power and importance.

She shook her head. 'Now they're saying we should give Jerry what he's given us. They want to send Spitfires over there, then they can see how they like being blitzed.'

'And so we should.' Ronnie wouldn't see it any other way. 'You can't go soft on Jerry, Meggie, not when you stop to think about it.'

'But women and children . . . ?'

'And do they think of that?'

'We make ourselves as bad as them, then?'

She grew heated. She hated the simple-minded war talk, yet at the same time she recognized that Ronnie himself had signed up to save them from being overrun by Hitler. And now she seemed to be doing him down. So she clammed up and walked on in confused silence.

'Look, I know it's hard.' Ronnie put it down to female squeamishness. 'It don't do to think about it too much. Let's just get on with the job and hope the Yanks come in on our side, right?' He took her silence as acquiescence. 'And let's have a good knees-up while I'm here and try and forget the whole bleeding business.'

It seemed the best way. To walk through the ruins with her chin up, listening to stories of Ronnie's close shaves, looking forward to a warm greeting from Gertie and an evening in the pub, drinking, dancing, wallowing in his company, trying not to think a day, an hour, even a minute ahead.

'They say Tommy Handley earns over three hundred quid a week!'

'Get away!'

'He does. And what about Arthur Askey, then?' Talk at the Bell was all of theatre and wireless stars. Some people, at least, made a profit out of the war.

'I wouldn't mind jumping on his band wagon.' There was obviously money in being a cheeky chappie.

'Not a chance, Wormy, mate. You ain't good looking enough.' Eddie enjoyed goading someone in front of an audience.

'Arthur Askey ain't no oil painting.'

'Exactly. I'll tell you what though; why don't you audition to be George Formby's lamp-post?'

'Leave the poor bloke alone.' Shankley did his rounds, bringing with him the aroma of vinegar and salt. 'Here, Wormy, have these on the house, see if we can fatten you up a bit.'

'And ruin his show business career?' Eddie was relentless. He winked at Meggie. 'Now Meggie here, she could definitely be top of my bill.' He appreciated the effort she'd put into her outfit for Ronnie's homecoming: a cream woollen dress that skimmed her knees. Her thick dark hair fell to her shoulders.

But something distracted her from responding to Eddie's flattery.

'Cheer up,' Shankley said. 'You ain't run out of Guinness, have you?'

'What? Oh no.' She pulled the pint and set it before him.

'Where's Gorgeous Gert tonight?' He

slapped a coin onto the bar.

'Upstairs with Ronnie. He just got back on leave.' They'd walked through the door and Gertie had whisked him out of sight, sticking Meggie behind the bar and leaving her to cope. Luckily, trade was slow.

'What, she's hogging him to herself?'

'She's giving him a good feed.' Meggie tried not to mind; it was natural that Gertie would want some time to herself with Ronnie.

'And how is the boy? The Navy ain't ruined his good looks yet? Come to think of it, there ain't no point asking you. You think the sun shines out of him in any case.'

Shankley seemed in no hurry to move off. Business was slack for him too, he said. It was cold outside and he fancied a spell in the warmth. 'Did you track down that Richie Palmer yet?' He leaned over the bar as if for a confidential chat, keeping close to his chest the fact that he'd straight away gone and betrayed Meggie's trust by telling Gertie the vital truth. Now he broadcast his question loud and clear. Several heads turned.

'Shh, Shankley. No I ain't.' Somehow, her courage had waned. Now, when she had him almost at her fingertips, she hesitated and let other events get in the way.

He grunted. 'Just as well, maybe.'

'You sound like my ma.'

'Don't she want you to find him neither?'

'She ain't over the moon about it, no.'

'Well, then.' He drained his glass. 'Why not let sleeping dogs lie?'

No reply from Meggie, who didn't look much like a girl newly reunited with her sweetheart.

'You ain't in any trouble, are you?' He was genuinely concerned. 'Or has the course of true love turned choppy all of a sudden?'

'Nothing like that.' Her gaze drifted to the door, around the half-empty room where the piano stood silent, the film stars gazed down from the frames containing their looped and scrawled signatures.

'Come on, Ronnie, come and cheer the girl up.' Shankley spotted his entrance, newly changed into civvies, wavy hair parted and slicked back.

The moment Ronnie's smile flashed at her across the room, Meggie felt herself light up. It didn't matter that he looked on edge after his talk with Gertie, so long as he went and dragged Jacko the piano player away from the group that included Eddie and Wormy, and sat him down to play. The place would soon liven up.

'Thanks, Shankley.' Meggie nodded and smiled.

'What for?'

'Just thanks.'

Gertie followed Ronnie downstairs. Now she swept through the bar, clearing empties. 'Place looks like a rag and bone yard.' She barged past Shankley, giving him the sort of look that suggested that he was responsible for the mess.

He read the signs. 'I'm on my way.' Pulling his cap low over his forehead, he winked at Meggie. 'You have a nice time, you hear. Take her somewhere nice,' he told Ronnie. 'Take her to see *Gone With The Wind*: they like that one.'

'And who'll stay here and give me a hand?' Gertie protested.

'I will.' Eddie sprang up. He waltzed her, glasses and all, across the room. 'What's wrong? Don't you think I can keep my fingers out of the till?'

'I don't trust you as far as I could throw you, Eddie Greenwood.' She rose to the challenge and gave him a hefty jab with her elbow. 'I wasn't born yesterday.'

What with the honky-tonk music and the larking about, Meggie's spirits revived. So far this evening there'd been no siren and customers had begun to drift in, slow but sure, drawn by the cheerful sounds. Soon there was a muggy muddle of laughing voices, song, couples dancing, cigarette smoke rising. Ronnie made her come out from behind the bar to join him in a dance number; one called the 'Blackout Stroll', new even to Eddie.

'Waltz-time,' Ronnie told Jacko.

The piano struck up, one-two-three, one-two-three. He held Meggie in his arms and their jittery walk from Victoria, her confusion about the fighting, her edginess over Gertie's apparent coldness towards her, melted from her mind. The moment took over, she felt utterly happy with Ronnie's arm around her waist, his dark brown eyes gazing into hers.

'You know what I said in my letters?' His voice blurred as they danced cheek to cheek.

'What?'

'That I love you.'

She nodded imperceptibly.

'Well, it's true. I want you to wait for me, whatever happens.'

She held him tighter. 'I will.'

'And I'll come back to you when the war's over. I swear.'

Again she nodded. 'No need to worry,' she promised, 'I'll be here.'

'Sure?'

'Cross my heart and hope to die.'

They turned in time with the music, oblivious of their surroundings.

'It's all right for some.' Gertie waited until the end of the number, then called from behind the bar. 'We got a room full of thirsty customers here. Do I have to serve them all?'

Meggie blushed to be caught as the centre of attention. Reluctantly Ronnie let her go and for an hour or so she had to be content to gaze at him from a distance, watching him circulate amongst his pals, but refusing several offers to dance from girls who wanted to tempt him back onto the dance floor. She was glad about this; *she* belonged in his arms now, and no one else. At last, last orders were called and Gertie draped the towels over the pumps.

Customers drank up, buttoned their coats and stood on the step to check for any sounds of engines overhead, any signs of dog-fights in the sky.

'Run and fetch Meggie's coat,' Gertie said to Ronnie. 'It's upstairs, hanging on the hook in my room.'

Meggie thought she must have misheard.

He went up two at a time to fetch it, while Gertie turned her back and began counting up the takings. Meggie felt it like a slap in the face. This must be a misunderstanding.

'Gertie, I fixed things with my ma,' she said quietly. 'She don't expect me back. I can stay the night.'

'Dirty devils.' Gertie tutted at the confetti of cigarette butts on the floor. 'Ain't they never heard of ashtrays?'

'Did you hear? Ma says I can stay over.' Upstairs, Ronnie's footsteps creaked along the floorboards.

'You ain't mentioned it to Ronnie?' She turned at last, her face a mask of make-up, her voice cold.

Meggie shook her head. She felt her eyes begin to smart, her throat to go dry.

'Just as well, 'cos I changed my mind.'

'Why? What did I do?' She could think of no explanation. Gertie's change of heart had been obvious the moment Meggie walked in with Ronnie earlier that evening; a look like the turning off of a light switch, then blankness, coldness.

'Nothing. Can't I change my mind, then?'

'You'd like me to go home?'

'I'm telling you to, girl. Liking don't come into it.' Meggie's distress fired her own determination. She came up close to impress her with the importance of what she was about to say. 'Look, Ronnie's got in far too

297

deep with you, if you must know.'

'Have you asked him?' She rounded on Gertie.

'No, because I know you can twist him round your little finger. You get him so as he don't know what he's saying.'

'Oh, I do, do I?'

'Anyone can see it, so don't go off the deep end.' She studied Meggie's desperate face. 'It ain't the end of the world. I'm only telling you to get yourself off home like a good girl. Leave Ronnie and me to have a natter, then he can telephone you if he wants to see you again.'

This was a dead end. Meggie wouldn't get any explanation from Gertie, but she could guess that jealousy was the cause. In any case, she could hardly be the one to suggest to Ronnie that she stay the night. That would definitely give him the wrong impression. 'You did ask me,' she whispered in a last-ditch attempt.

'That was before.'

'Before what?'

'Before I had chance to think it through. It don't look good.'

'Who to?'

'What do you mean, who to? It don't look good, full stop. That's enough.'

As a rule Gertie would revel in a whiff of

scandal and play people along. So this didn't wash with Meggie. But by now, Ronnie was on his way downstairs with her coat and hat. He whistled as he came.

'I'll walk Meggie home,' he told Gertie, slipping the coat around her shoulders.

'Not all the way, surely?'

He turned sharply, but said nothing.

'What if you get caught in a raid?'

'Then I'll find a shelter.'

A frown flickered across her face. 'Righto, then.'

At the door he turned. 'You ain't worried about a raid, are you?' Something was evidently bothering her.

'No more than usual.'

He nodded. 'Let me get Meggie safely home, then I'll be back to look after my dear old ma!'

'Not so much of the old.' She blew him a kiss, but ignored Meggie as they stepped into the Court and headed for St Martin's Lane.

'What got into her?' Ronnie relaxed once they were out of sight. He slipped an arm around Meggie's waist. 'It must be the Blitz. Funny, I never thought she was the sort to let it get her down.'

'It gets us all down, Ronnie, if you did but know it.'

'You and her ain't had a barney?'

'Not that I know of.'

He looked closely at her. 'Never mind about her, Meg. She blows hot and cold. You ain't crying, are you?'

She tried not to. 'I thought she liked me!'

'She does.' He stopped and drew her into a doorway. All the neon signs were dead in the blackout, all the street lamps and shop windows. 'Don't cry.'

'I dropped in ever so often while you were away, and she's always been a brick to me until now. Why don't she like me no more?'

'What's she said?' He stroked her hair, waiting for her to stop.

'It ain't what she's said . . .'

'Take no notice. And listen, we ain't gonna let it spoil our night, are we?' He pulled her round. 'That's it. It's us that counts, you and me. I'm here, ain't I?'

'And shall we still go ice-skating tomorrow?'

He laughed. 'Is that what you want?'

She shook her head.

'What then?'

For answer she slid her arms around his neck and kissed him long and hard. He held her tight, then cradled her head between his hands. He kissed her cheeks, her eyes, her lips. These were kisses that she'd never given or received before. 'You do love me?'

He breathed deeply then went on kissing her, his lips closing over her mouth, his hands on her neck, slipping down between her coat and her soft cream dress. Her head went back against the cold stone of the door arch, she gasped and let her hands fall to her sides.

'Meggie —' He stopped and buried his face against her, his voice deep and soft. His fingers touched her breasts outside the dress, slid over them, and she let him, astonished, scared, completely given over to the sensations he aroused. 'I dream about you. I want you.'

He carried her along on a wave of intimacy. She let him undo the buttons at the neck of her dress, felt the cold air against her shoulder, though he shielded her from the street by pressing her deep into the shadowy doorway. He pulled the straps down from her shoulder, pushed the underthings from her breast. Soon he put his mouth against it and again she gave way. She was helpless to stop him.

Only, in one tiny part of her consciousness, she knew they stood in a doorway, that this was not how she wanted it to happen, that she would feel cheap, and she had been told that she, the woman, had the power to say no. She wanted him to go on, clung to his strong shoulders, then lifted his face to kiss him again. But she began to whisper, 'No, not here, not now,' until he heard and hid his face in her hair and let her cover herself. He wrapped her coat around her, saying sorry, he had lost control and now she would think badly of him.

It was her turn to stroke his head, to comfort him. 'We both did. I love you. How can I think badly of you?'

'I want us to be together,' he pleaded. 'Now more than ever. But I want it all to be above board.'

'Then we'd best wait.' Everything was clear; they loved each other and they would go one step at a time. 'You call on me tomorrow,' she suggested, stopping to kiss him in between organizing the practical things. 'Meet my ma and step-pa and little brothers.'

'Will they want to?' He was still subdued, not convinced that he hadn't overstepped the mark.

'They'll be head over heels the minute they clap eyes on you, just like me! Geoff and Bertie will drop the RAF. They'll be first in the queue for the Royal Navy when they see you in uniform!'

They planned as they walked, trying to

cram everything into his two days on shore. He would come to the house in Paradise Court to impress the boys. Then he would take her to a proper dance hall. The day after she would try for a morning off work so as to see him off back to Plymouth. Then it would be who knew how long before they could meet again.

'Don't think about that,' he whispered. They stood in the deserted street outside the Duke. On their walk across the river they'd scarcely noticed the scars of war, scarcely listened for the sirens or bothered to watch out for the nearest shelter. They had eyes and ears only for each other as they parted at last; Meggie to surprise her mother by knocking on the door at one in the morning, Ronnie to wander back across the Thames, watching its cold, black waters flow silent and swift.

The next night, while Meggie and Ronnie danced to the Big Band sound, others gathered at the Duke to discuss the merits of her new young man.

'Very nicely turned out.' Annie set her seal of approval. Ronnie had switched on the charm for her, she could see that. Still, she seemed set on seeing him in the best possible light.

'He ain't a bleeding horse,' Dolly said sourly. Charlie was making a good recovery from his injuries and she and Dorothy had patched up their differences to arrange a rota of hospital visits, but she still found the journey wearisome without a regular bus or tram service. Amy couldn't always ask Rob to give her a lift, and today had been one of the days when Dolly had struggled there and back on foot. 'You say he's nicely turned out as if he's a carthorse for the brewery.' Aside from anything else, she was annoyed at having missed this glorious specimen.

'You know what I mean, Dolly.' Annie gave no quarter, just because Dolly had a son seriously wounded in hospital. 'Ronnie Elliot is well set-up; nice manners, the lot. Ain't he, Ett?'

Hettie nodded from behind the bar.

'If I had to pick a first beau for Meggie myself, he's the very one I'd have gone for!'

'Blimey!' Dolly evidently thought this too good to be true.

'Not too pushy, not too shy. And he thinks the world of her.' Annie smiled. 'Anyone can see that. Mind you, don't bother asking Sadie about him. She's clammed up on the subject.'

'Didn't she take to him, then?'

'I never said she didn't take to him.' Annie was a scrupulous observer of the facts. 'I said she's clammed up. As soon a she set eyes on him, I could tell she was taking a back seat. She just shakes his hand and sits there very quiet, while the boys jump all over him and fire questions at him. He seemed not to notice Sadie. But I did, and Meggie did.'

'Maybe he ain't good enough?' Dolly brought up her oft-expressed notion that Sadie could be a snob. 'I once mentioned Jimmie O'Hagan's name in the same breath as Meggie's, and I swear, if looks could have killed . . .'

'Another half, Dolly?' Hettie came and cut her off. She gathered glasses from Dolly, Rob and Walter, who stood nearby. 'You two took to him straight off, didn't you?'

Rob, not much interested, said yes for a quiet life. 'How's your Charlie?' he asked Dolly.

'On the mend. He's moaning about the book I took him to read, so he must be.'

'And a little bird tells me that you and Dorothy have called a truce?' Adroitly Annie stepped in again. 'A New Year's resolution?'

While Dolly took a long drink, Rob leaned sideways to speak to Jimmie. 'Like the

305

ceasefire in the bleeding trenches,' he whispered.

'That might be putting it a bit strong,' Dolly sniffed. 'But I'm willing to admit that even Dorothy will fight on the beaches when it comes to it. You might not think it to look at her.'

'I hear you've got her to thank for Charlie living to fight another day,' Annie insisted. 'She ruined a perfectly good jacket and all.'

'Talk of the devil,' Jimmie said to Rob, loud enough for everyone to hear. All heads turned as the door swung open.

'Look what the cat dragged in!' Dorothy announced gaily. She stood holding the door open, waiting. 'I just met him on the street.'

'That makes her the cat, then.' Nothing would lessen Jimmie's loathing. Dorothy waltzed in, dressed up in her purple and black costume, fresh from visiting Charlie in his sick bed.

'Come on, Bill, come in and have a drink with the old crowd. Edie ain't gonna run away while you get a couple of drinks down your neck!' She pulled him by the arm. 'Annie, how about a nice big whisky for Bill Morell? That's your favourite tipple, ain't it?'

There was a silence. Bill came in and

nodded to Rob, cap in hand. The gold braid at his cuffs, the crisp white shirt and dark tie set off his sallow features. Although balding and heavy, he carried himself with authority. He accepted the drink with perfunctory politeness and downed it in one.

'Edie never said you had a spot of leave due.' Dorothy kept her voice raised, clinging onto the impact of their unexpected entrance.

Dolly muttered under her breath, ready to do battle on Charlie's behalf if Dorothy so much as sidled up to Morell. But Annie put a hand on her arm and warned her to listen.

'I don't suppose Edie tells you all her business.' His lack of courtesy made it plain that it was the drink, not Dorothy's company, that had waylaid him en route to the flat.

'No, but word usually gets round.' She perched on a stool next to him, crossing her legs and waiting until he produced a light for her cigarette.

'It came up; just twenty-four hours.' He remained surly, monosyllabic, but he obliged with the match.

'Hardly worth it, I would've thought.'

'That depends.' A knowing smile crossed his lips.

'So Edie don't know you're here?' She sounded amused and looked round for back-up, making sure to shoot a sharp glance at Jimmie.

'No, it's a nice surprise for her.' The smile vanished. 'Or does that depend too?'

'She'll be thrilled.' Dorothy played along. At last Jimmie had the sense to slope out of the bar. Annie stared grim-faced at Bill, while Hettie vanished quietly upstairs. Even Dolly was lost for words.

'Well, you have to grab your chance.' He accepted another drink, which Annie poured smartly, then stepped back. The second whisky went the way of the first, he reached for his hat and put it on. 'Thanks for the welcoming committee, Dorothy.'

'It's a pleasure, Bill.' They held their breath as they watched him go.

'Stone the crows!' Dolly was the first to jump in. 'Where's Tommy and Edie now, does anyone know?'

They didn't, not for sure. But it was a fair bet that since it was a cold, foggy evening, they would be sitting pretty, or worse, behind the closed doors of Edie's flat.

'I hope Jimmie gets there double-quick.' Annie shook herself back into action.

'Have a whisky yourself, Dorothy.' Rob stepped up to volunteer. 'And don't go stirring up trouble with Amy,' he warned his mother-in-law. 'This is one pal buying another a drink, that's all. And if anyone ever deserved it, it's Dot!'

CHAPTER FIFTEEN

Edie struggled for calm. She imagined she could stop the nightmare; that she could will herself to wake up and begin the whole sequence again. She would be sitting by the wireless with Tommy, Jimmie wouldn't come knocking at the door and Bill wouldn't be treading nearer with every step.

'I ain't moving a muscle!' Tommy had insisted.

Jimmie's burst of swearing had forced her into action. 'No. You go, I'll stay here and face him.'

'I ain't leaving you here by yourself.'

'You are, Tommy. It's up to me. I've got to break it to him. Jimmie, you take Tommy with you and thanks for the tip-off.'

Jimmie picked up his brother's jacket and flung it at him. 'Get a move on, for God's sake!'

'It ain't right,' Tommy had protested time and again. 'I ain't used to sneaking off. Let me stay and face the music.'

'Yes, and get your head ripped off while

you're at it,' Jimmie said. 'Come on, let's beat it.'

'Go!' Edie's panic rose as she pictured the scene. 'I know how to handle him. Leave it to me.'

'If he lays a finger on you —'

'He won't.'

'I'll be at the Duke if you need me.'

At last she'd managed to convince him. After he'd gone with Jimmie, she ran round the flat hiding all signs of his presence, amazed at her own cool eye for detail; the toothbrush in the tooth-glass, Tommy's shaving-kit. She threw his shirts into the laundry basket, moved his brand of cigarettes from the mantelpiece.

Now Bill stood outside the door. She put her hand across her mouth to stifle a whimpering cry. Could she trust herself to carry it off, to come out with the truth fair and square? *Bill, it's all over between us.*

His key turned and he stepped inside. 'Surprise!'

A cry escaped her. Her eyes widened, she backed away from the door.

'Jesus, Edie, I ain't a bleeding ghost.' He took off his hat, flung it onto a chair and stared round the room. 'Looks like you got off pretty light.'

'What?'

'You're in apple-pie order compared with some poor blighters down the corridor.'

'Yes, I am.' She tried to compose herself, taking a deep breath and smoothing the sides of her skirt with her palms. 'I never expected you, Bill.'

'I never expected me neither.' His gaze rested on her. 'My leave came up at the last minute, so I hopped on the train and here I am. Come here.'

As he moved towards her, unbuttoning his jacket, she smelt the whisky on his breath. She needed to speak up this minute, this second, but he overwhelmed her. He moved in and held her tight, looking dispassionately at the way she had her hair pinned up, smudging his thumb over her lipstick.

'You must be hungry.' She stepped back, careful to keep her eyes fixed on his face.

He refused to let go, but allowed her to keep her distance. 'You smell nice, Edie.'

She pulled away.

'And you look nice.' He appraised her white blouse with its neat Peter Pan collar, her short, slim black skirt.

'It's what I wore for work today.' She put up a hand to tidy her hair.

'No, let it down.' He moved around the back of her and circled her waist. 'Go on,

312

you know I like you with your hair down.'

Reluctantly she bent her head forward and took out the pins. She shook it loose, knowing that this was a preliminary to Bill taking her into the bedroom. She must speak out. 'Listen — let me fix you something to eat first.' She unfurled his interlocking fingers from her waist and managed to twist free. 'I got some bacon in the pantry saved from last week's ration, as it happens.'

He looked at her through narrowed eyes. 'Bacon?'

'I'll fry it up for you, shall I?'

The obscene reply, muttered through clenched teeth, made her close her eyes. Then she opened them in an effort to outstare him. 'Does that mean you don't want nothing to eat?'

'Bingo.' Instead he pulled out a crushed packet of cigarettes and lit one. 'What's up with you? Why are you acting all jumpy?'

'I'm not. I just got a bit of a shock when you walked in. I don't get many callers as a rule.' Now, she thought; now was the time to tell him about Tommy.

He sank into an easy-chair, legs sprawled, inhaling deeply. 'Is that why you ain't given me much of a welcome?'

'I wish you'd telephoned me at work.'

'Hoity-toity. Well, I didn't. Have I gone

and ruined your plans for the evening?'

'It's not that.' She gathered herself together and began to rearrange her hair. The action seemed to annoy him. He stubbed out his half-smoked cigarette. 'It's a mystery to me why they can't give you more notice when you get shore-leave.'

'What, and tell the whole bleeding U-boat fleet when the ship's due in dock?' Still he followed her with suspicious eyes.

'I suppose.' She would be normal. She would wait until her nerves had settled, then she would make a clean breast.

'Where are you off to?'

She paused in the kitchen doorway. 'To make you a cup of tea.'

'Ain't you got nothing stronger in the house?' He went to the sideboard, to the cupboard where any liquor would be kept. He found whisky, gin and port; presents from Tommy. 'Proper little distillery.' He dragged down the corners of his mouth.

'Left over from Christmas. I got it in for you in case you got home on leave.'

'But I didn't, did I?'

She shook her head, mesmerized by his actions. He moved with exaggerated fatigue, rolling his head to ease a stiff neck, pouring a refill into his glass to chase the first swig of whisky.

'Worse luck.' He drank again. 'I said, worse luck.'

'Yes.'

'Sound as if you mean it for once.' As he moved in this time, the bottle swinging from his hand, it was obvious that he didn't intend to let her go. 'I want to hear you say how much you missed me, Edie. What sort of Christmas was it, all on your ownio? No one to hang up your stocking with.' He breathed over her, pawing her with his free hand.

'Bill!'

'What?' He pushed her against the back of the sofa, making her arch away from him. Overbalancing, his weight tipped against her and they both fell over the back of the seat onto the cushions. Edie lay crushed beneath him. At first she struggled, but knew this would only make him worse. He fumbled and wrenched at the pearl buttons on her blouse.

'Careful, you'll spill the whisky!' She tried to slide sideways onto the floor, but he was too heavy.

'Have some.' He put the neck of the bottle against her lips. 'Go on, relax. Have a drink and keep me company.'

If she kept her lips closed he would have let the whisky spill and trickle down onto her chin and neck. So she took a gulp, felt it burn her throat, glad that at least he then had the sense to put the bottle to one side.

But it was only to free his hand so that he could tear at her clothes, pulling her blouse up, roughly rubbing his mouth against her skin. She was sickened by his lips, the coarse scrape of his bristled chin.

He took her without consent, without affection, as a right a husband might exercise over an unwilling wife, eyes closed and pushing towards the climax that would evade him if he once stopped to treat Edie as a person in her own right. Her distress excited him, and he answered it with brute force, leaving her with only one option; to submit in order to get it over with. She felt sick and full of loathing; this heavy man pressing down on her, the buckle of his belt scraping against her hip, not caring, and herself too cowardly to tell him the truth, that she didn't and never would want him any more. Words choked and died in her throat. She could only sob and turn her face to one side and wait.

Bill had no interest in what made her cry. Satisfied, he slumped to one side. Now she needed to judge things and make sure that he was oblivious of her before easing herself from the sofa onto the floor, helpless and undignified, scrambling to rescue her clothes. Once in the bathroom, she locked herself in, ran the water, hung over the sink and retched, feeling her hot skin turn cold and clammy. She rinsed her face, steadied herself and sobbed again. Her whole body shook, her hair was dark with perspiration. In the mirror she saw that her face was blotched, her features blurred.

'Edie!' Hours later he roused himself and came to rattle the door handle.

'I'll be out in a sec.'

'What the bleeding hell you up to?'

'I'm washing my hair.'

'Is there a clean shirt for me in the airing-cupboard?'

'I'll bring one out.'

'Get your skates on. I want to go down the Duke.'

'It's too late. They're closed.'

'So?' Servicemen could often obtain after hours drinks from a friendly landlord.

She wrapped a towel round her head, put on her dressing gown and opened the door. He stood there without his shirt, braces unhitched. 'You go by yourself, Bill. I don't feel like it.'

'I don't want to go by myself. I want you to come with me.'

She sighed.

'No use saying you're too tired. It ain't every night I get home on leave, is it? Come on, chop-chop, find something to wear. I want to catch up on what's been going on round here while I've been away. I already seen Dorothy O'Hagan on my way down here. She was a sight for sore eyes, as usual.' He talked on, trailing after her for his shirt, demanding hot water for a shave.

Edie was on tenterhooks lest he find something belonging to Tommy. Never in her worst nightmare had she imagined this. She still trembled and felt sick as she dried her hair by the fire and put on her make-up.

'About bleeding time.' Bill was back in uniform, standing by the door.

She buttoned her coat over a dark red dress.

He looked on in sarcastic amusement. 'I'd like to know what's been eating you tonight.'

'Nothing's eating me.' She brushed it off, having given up all hope of being able to confront him. Reluctantly she followed him downstairs. Then, when the air-raid siren started and the white beams of searchlights swung skywards, she nearly cried with relief. The street was suddenly full of families, elderly couples, women carrying blankets and thermos flasks, all heading for Nelson Gardens.

Bill swore heavily. 'Take no notice.' He scanned the dark sky, listened for aircraft. 'False alarm.' He wondered that there wasn't more urgency; no one ran or shouted.

'I don't think so.' Edie stopped in the middle of the street. 'Listen.'

In the distance there was a thud followed by a burst of yellow light on the skyline. Another thud. The siren wailed on.

'It's across the river,' she told him. 'But there's more coming over, listen!'

Nearer this time, an engine droned, then another. There was the whistle of a bomb as it hurtled overhead. It missed them by perhaps a mile.

'Bleeding marvellous.' Bill turned to join the band of Londoners heading for shelter. 'I come home to get away from it all and look what happens.'

They shuffled along, Edie counting her blessings. They might get blown sky-high by the Germans, but at least she wouldn't have to face going into the Duke, and all the curious, knowing looks, and a shocked Tommy propping up the bar, realizing in a split second that she'd betrayed him.

She couldn't have taken that. Silently she traipsed after her husband between the sandbagged walls at the entrance to the shelter. They and several hundred refugees from the reality of the people's war.

'Nothing but the best,' Ronnie told Meggie as he guided her through the couples dancing on the spectacular floor of the Paramount.

The dance hall was an escape from the drab, monochrome streets. The corsage of deep purple silk orchids which Ronnie had bought her matched the lilac satin of her ruched and fitted dress. Gilt wall mirrors reflected showers of coloured lights cast by many-sided silver globes hanging from the ceiling. Everywhere there was a bright, larger-than-life feel.

All this and the music. Violins soared through romantic waltzes, the brass section took over for swing sessions in seamless arrangements under the baton of a smart conductor in white dinner jacket, maroon cummerbund and matching suave dickie-bow tie.

Meggie was in seventh heaven. She was in love for the first and last time. No one but Ronnie would capture her heart. They could say what they liked; that romance soon wore out, that passionate words must be matched by a lifetime's steady deeds, but they couldn't spoil the way she felt and acted now. During the heavy beat of the drums and the roar of saxophones, she slid closer to him and almost swooned.

'Who taught you to tango?' He considered himself a good dancer, he knew the moves and led, but Meggie never put a foot wrong either. 'If you tell me you've been practicing with Eddie Greenwood I might get jealous!'

Tiny lights swirled and swept across the walls and floor. He steered her clear of a jam of other couples with a neat side-step. 'No one taught me. And I ain't been practicing,' she beamed.

'It must come natural then.'

'Runs in the family.' She told him about her Aunt Hettie's days in the music hall.

'She don't look like a dancer,' he confessed. 'Even though I did take to her. Ain't she a bit stick-in-the-mud?'

'No she ain't.' Meggie loved her aunts dearly; kind Hettie, stern Frances, her stylish Aunt Jess in Manchester.

'And your ma. I don't think she took to me though.' They danced through to the end of the number, clapped and waited to begin again.

Meggie pouted. 'Don't say that. She takes her time getting used to the idea of us walking out together, that's all.'

'Is that what you call it?' He grinned.

'It's what *she* calls it.' Meggie blushed as the band struck up a foxtrot and they took up position.

'Well, I got the feeling that she don't trust me.' Once more, earlier that evening, Sadie had greeted him with downcast eyes. The boys had run to the door at the sound of his knock, friendly as you like, and Walter had opened it with a genial smile, but Meggie's mother had kept quiet and carried on with her sewing work.

He'd been struck by her and Meggie's similarity, but it was an eerie sameness; Meggie vivacious where Sadie was subdued, laughing and excitable as opposed to sober and wary. Their faces had the same oval shape, dark brown eyes, wide, full lips. But whereas Meggie's eyes sparkled, he thought he read indifference, even dislike in her mother's.

'You can't do right for doing wrong with Ma these days. No one can.' Last night Meggie had expected her mother to let her into the house with at least a smile, despite the late hour. After all, she'd been dead set against her staying out all night. But no; she'd greeted her in silence, listened doubtfully to her explanation that Gertie had gone cold on her, offered no sympathy.

'Ain't you glad?' Meggie had cried, exasperated.

'I'd like to know what she's up to,' came the reply, brows knotted in disapproval. 'What time does she call this to turn you out into the street?'

Ronnie and Meggie might both puzzle about why their mothers seemed to have set their faces against their romance, but neither felt prepared to kowtow. Ronnie had actually stood up to his mother that teatime, when she began to complain that she'd scarcely clapped eyes on him during the whole of his leave. She wished he'd take back his word and not take Meggie dancing. It was the least he could do when he saw how hard it was for her to keep things running by herself. When he turned her down, she called him selfish.

'And you're a spoilsport, Ma. I don't know what's got into you.' She'd never objected to him having girlfriends in the past. 'I thought you liked Meggie?'

Gertie had made a sour face. 'She wants too much of her own way, that one.'

He said that was the pot calling the kettle black. 'Anyhow, Meggie goes out of her way to help around here. She don't know why you've gone off her. She's upset.'

'Aah diddums!'

'Be like that!' He'd ground his fag-end into the floor and headed off, hands thrust deep into his pockets. If she didn't like it she knew where to stick it. What did she think, that he would stay tied to her apron strings all his life?

In this spirit of rebellion to match Meggie's own, they met up and danced the night away. Maybe the tiffs at home, maybe the war hanging over everyone made them the more intense, so that tonight seemed special, perhaps never to be repeated if Hitler had his way and wiped out the whole British Navy or smashed London to smithereens. They held each other close, like all the couples whirling under the spinning lights in their shiny dresses and dark uniforms.

When the band leader put down his baton at eleven o'clock on the dot, turned and said, 'That's your lot,' it seemed like the end of a dream.

Lights dimmed, coats went on, dark streets beckoned.

'Race you,' Ronnie offered, running ahead through a drizzle of wet snow that melted the moment it landed. Meggie shrieked as he dragged her along. 'Come on, slow coach!'

Ignoring onlookers, not wanting to be beaten, she kicked off her shoes. As he stooped to pick them up, she ran ahead laughing; hair flying, dodging pillar boxes and fire hydrants until she came to the end of the street and Ronnie caught her in a breathless kiss.

'Put your shoes on, Cinders,' he said gently, dropping them to the pavement, 'before you catch your death.'

She looked down ruefully at her ruined nylons. 'I'd better not let Ma see these.'

'Never mind, I'll bring you some more.' Putting an arm round her shoulder, they walked on. 'You're round the twist, you know that?'

'It was your idea. You said "race you".' She turned her face up to the falling snow. 'When will you bring me some more stockings, Ronnie?'

'Next time.'

'When will that be?'

'When they let me out.'

'You'll come back?' Her voice floated upwards.

He stopped and drew her in. 'I said I would. Anyhow, try and stop me.'

They kissed and walked slowly on. 'I think I'll remember every single minute of tonight.'

'You better had.' His own voice cracked, he clutched her hand, dreading the turn into Duke Street which came all too soon. This was the moment when they must part.

'You take care of yourself, you hear.' She forced herself to think for a second of his life as a Navy man; the great iron destroyers, the cold, cruel sea.

'Don't you worry about me, just so long as you write.'

'Every day. And when I'm not writing I'll be thinking of you.'

'Me too. Where will you sit and write your letters? So I can picture it.'

'In the shelter at Gran's, or at home in bed.'

He nodded. 'I'll think of that. No, on second thoughts . . .'

She smiled. 'It's only a narrow little bed, Ronnie. There ain't room for two.'

'Wait, Meggie. Wait for me?'

She swore from the bottom of her heart. They came to Paradise Court.

He kissed her again and again, felt her cling to him. 'Go in,' he whispered.

'You come in with me. It looks like they're all in bed asleep.'

He shook his head sadly. 'Next time. That's a promise.'

She sighed.

'Go in,' he begged. Her hair was dusted

with snow. Flakes landed on her pale skin and melted.

One last kiss and he was gone.

Ronnie was halfway up Duke Street, heading for the railway arches when the siren started up. He passed another Royal Navy man, arguing in the street with a woman he took to be his wife. She wanted to head for shelter, the surly man preferred to ignore the warning.

'False alarm,' he said, swaying back and forth, probably drunk.

She made him listen for planes. A bomb went off on their side of the river and convinced him.

Ronnie too considered taking cover. He thought of the odds against a bomb with his name written on it falling, and decided to risk going on. Bombs dropped on houses, offices, factories, not on him. If a plane flew too close and low, that was when he would look for shelter. Like many young men used to the dangers of active service, he made the mistake of thinking that the Blitz was a homely, third division affair to be taken fairly lightly.

This time he was lucky; no wall of flame, no tumbling masonry, no crushed and burning bodies disillusioned him. As he crossed the river, he left behind the area of London chosen as the night's target; the Bankside docks and power station half a mile to the north of Meggie's house.

It was late for the alarm to sound; past midnight. Most people had reckoned it was safe to risk a night in their own beds for a change. Now they had to get up, struggle into clothes, make for the shelters bleary-eyed and grumbling. They did it automatically, children asleep in parents' arms, trudging through the wet snow.

'Come and shelter with us, Tommy!' Hettie tried to hustle him into the cellar at the Duke.

He'd hung on long after closing time, alone in the bar. No news from Edie, and no news was bad news in this case.

'No ta, I'll head for Nelson Gardens.' He could see Annie taking candles down, ready for an all-night stay. 'Edie comes to you in a raid, don't she?'

'As a rule. But there's no telling what she'll do tonight.'

'I'll make myself scarce just in case.' He paid for and pocketed a half-bottle of whisky.

'Listen, she knows what she's putting you through, so don't blame her too much.'

Hettie saw that Tommy was in a black mood over Bill Morell's return. 'Keep a cool head and make straight for the Gardens, you hear? Hear what she has to say tomorrow.'

He nodded without conviction. 'It's a bleeding mess, ain't it?' Edie evidently hadn't broken the news to Morell. He should have stayed put at the flat, not listened to Jimmie. Poor Edie shouldn't have had to face up to Bill alone. 'It's my own bleeding fault,' he said bitterly.

Bombs thudded down some way off, but the explosions only penetrated the blacked-out windows with a dull glare of yellow light.

'Go on!' Hettie was frightened that he would leave it too late. 'Or I'll get George and Walter to drag you kicking and screaming in with us.'

He went, hardly caring, but wanting to leave the coast clear for Edie. Outside it was cold and wet, a miserable snow was falling. He headed for Nelson Gardens in an angry haze, just because it was somewhere to go.

Dolly and Dorothy were there ahead of him, he noticed, already filing through the narrow entrance. It looked like another bad night; the sky already glowed with fires in all directions. Tomorrow they would emerge with grim resignation; perhaps this time it would be their house, their windows blown out by a firestorm, their brother, kid sister or father killed.

Tommy lapsed into lethargy as he stood waiting his turn, not caring now one way or the other, convinced that Edie had come face to face with her husband and changed her mind. He could see it for himself; the way her mind would work. There Bill Morell was, serving his country, relying on her being there for him. This was what kept many men going in the face of danger; the idea that they had someone waiting at home. No, she wasn't cruel or hard enough to do it. She would take pity on him, whatever he might have put her through in the past; his idle selfishness; his violence. A woman like Edie went to the altar and made her vows for life. For better, for worse.

A bomb fell two or three streets away. It whistled overhead. The crowd shoved from behind and Tommy was part of the bottleneck that was propelled through the entrance into the dank and dreary shelter.

He didn't bother to join the scramble for makeshift bunks. All he wanted was a corner where he could prop himself against the corrugated-iron sheeting and console himself with his bottle of whisky. He found one and pulled his jacket collar high around his neck, heard Dolly's voice nearby, organizing this and that. Someone stumbled against him, half-asleep. He shifted position and turned to face a different way.

The place was jam-packed with bodies stretched out under blankets and eider-downs, legs crooked, arms flung wide of the covers. Kids, it seemed, slept as soon as their heads hit the ground. Some couples didn't mind that their love-making com-manded an audience. Tommy grimaced, uncorked the bottle and drank.

His gaze rested finally on a man's broad back. He was in uniform, with a Navy great-coat, seated at a table in the tiny canteen. Beyond him was Edie, who hadn't noticed Tommy come in, apparently. She sat white-faced opposite to Bill Morell, not in fact seeing anything of what went on around her. Her husband hunched over the table; like Tommy he'd seen fit to bring a bottle.

Tommy took in the scene. Edie had changed into a different outfit since he'd left her at the flat, and her hair was newly washed. Morell ignored her and at the same time claimed her; you could tell by some-thing in his posture and her retreating into herself, not daring to raise her eyes from the table. It made him want to jump up and grab the man by the throat.

But he didn't make a move. He stayed

put amongst the sleeping bodies in the shadows, drinking steadily. Even when Morell slumped forward to sleep the night away in fits and starts and Edie sat it out wide awake, he kept to his corner unnoticed.

He was the last to leave on the all-clear next morning, for where would he go to avoid Edie, not to hear her voice pleading with him to try and understand, telling him that it was all over between them?

CHAPTER SIXTEEN

'Tommy!' Edie intercepted him on the stairs to her office. All week he'd turned his back on her. Bill had come and gone without her breaking the news about Tommy, and she'd been unable to find him to talk things through since. He hadn't been near the flat since Monday night and hardly came into work, at least when she was there. He looked grey and unkempt, unlike himself. 'You and me gotta talk.'

'What's to talk about?' He shut his ears, closed his mind.

She held her place on the stairs, refusing to let him pass. Behind her, she knew that Lorna or one of the other shop girls might pick up what was said. 'Tommy, please.'

He gave in at last and retreated into the office. Edie followed him and closed the door. 'Why won't you look at me? Just look at me for a second, Tommy.' It drove her mad that he could treat her as if she was invisible, as if nothing had ever happened between them.

He went to the desk and slammed a ledger

shut. The muscles in his jaw were clenched so tight that a nerve jumped and flicked.

'I can't bear it!'

'*You* can't?' He paced round the desk. 'That's rich.' All week he'd gone around feeling as if someone was stamping on his chest, pressing him to death. He couldn't eat; instead he drank himself part way to oblivion. Knowing that he wasn't fit company, he'd taken himself out of the way and holed up in a market pal's place behind the cathedral; a cold and draughty warehouse overlooking the docks.

'You've got to try and understand.' The sight of him, so worn and careless, made her break down. However bad she felt, Edie still made an effort to look as if she was coping. Each morning she did her hair and make-up, presented a decent front.

'Try me.' He stopped pacing and met her face to face. 'Try telling me why I'm sitting wasting my time in the Duke waiting for you to come clean with him, hanging around like a bleeding idiot, as it turns out. And all along you two are having a cosy little time, and I'm the last thing on your mind, I bet!'

'That ain't true. It wasn't like that.'

'I'm a fool, I am, letting myself get dragged in. Don't worry, I blame myself. I should've been able to see it coming a mile off.' As the days had passed, Tommy's bitterness had increased. He was back to condemning the frailty of women and his own gullibility.

'What?' She stood helpless only dimly understanding the implications of what he said.

'It happens all the time.' He was suddenly calm, shrugging it off. 'So what?'

'What are you on about? You think I did this on purpose?' She felt bad enough about her failure of nerve. Now the idea that she had coldly used Tommy and cast him aside struck home. 'Is that what you think?'

'What am I supposed to think?' He said he'd seen them together at Nelson Gardens, he'd put two and two together; her change of clothes, Morell's swaggering air. He didn't tell her that jealousy had ripped him apart worse than any gun or bomb. Edie, the woman he worshipped, had been with another man.

His eyes drilled into her. She saw what he thought of her. What could she do? Tell him what had actually happened, give a blow-by-blow account? The truth was, Bill had forced himself on her and she had given in. She hadn't resisted and so in her own mind she was guilty too. She gave a groan and hung her head.

'Go on, tell me I got it all wrong.' He raised his voice, brought his hand down flat on the desk. 'I'm listening!'

'You make it sound easy, Tommy.' One last effort to hold herself together. The room swam in front of her eyes. Tommy glared at her. 'It ain't that simple.'

'No? It looks it to me. "Bill, I've got someone else; ta-ta!" That's how it goes, see? You open your mouth and the words come out.' He'd given up his own marriage; you got it over and done with.

'He took me off-guard. I didn't have time to work up to it.'

'What do you want, a bleeding rehearsal?'

'I had to work out what I was going to say.' This was insane; trying to justify what she couldn't forgive herself for. She leaned on the desk opposite him.

He tilted his head back and frowned. 'Yes, righto. Next time, then? Or the time after that?' What sort of fool did she think he was?

There was a knock at the door. A figure stood beyond the frosted glass panel, peering in. 'It's me, Lorna. Do you want me to cash up for you? It's half five.' In reality, she had come down to spy on them.

It ruled a line under things. 'Fine, you go ahead,' he called.

'Tommy.' Edie could only repeat his name softly one last time, as Lorna retreated upstairs.

He picked up the phone. 'Listen, Edie, it never happened between us, right? Nothing. One big round nought.'

She shook her head.

'That's it, finish. From now on we're going to act as if nothing went on, OK?'

'No.' There was no fight left in her, but it would be impossible to go on treating him like an ordinary boss, if that was what he meant. 'I'll have my cards. You can find someone else.'

He shrugged and dialled a number. 'Please yourself.' He didn't enjoy being cruel. It might sound like it, but he didn't. It was the only way he could get through this.

'You left some of your things in my flat.' She reminded him about his shirts, his bathroom gear.

'Chuck 'em.'

She nodded and reached for her coat. 'You'll balance the books then?'

'I'll show Lorna. She'll soon learn.'

They dealt with mundanities as their world fell apart.

That night Edie sat alone in the flat. She took notepaper and a pen from the bureau drawer and wrote a letter to Bill. In it she told him that she had no love left for him and she didn't want them to stay married. She said that she was sorry to hurt him, that she should have told him sooner. She wished him well and hoped that he would eventually understand.

It was a cold, windy night, the dead heart of January. The politicians talked on the wireless of blood and sweat, of toil and tears. A new term had entered the language after Hitler's blitz of the Midlands. Now you were 'Coventrated' if you came up from the shelters to find your home in ruins. There was no let up in the bombing or its aftermath; a pall of dark smoke hung over shattered townscapes as workers picked their way through debris to ammunition factories and looters sifted wreckage for whatever they could sell.

Only Churchill and eye-witness proof of minor victories kept them muddling through; a Stuka shot out of the sky by a Spitfire, its plume of white smoke spiralling down. Or plucky survivors pulled out of wreckage days after a direct hit with nothing more than a scratch.

Geoff and Bertie stood with Ernie on Duke Street as Walter took part in one such rescue; a driver trapped in his train, hit that afternoon as it shunted coal across the viaduct at the top of their street. The locomotive had tipped on its side, taking the cargo with it. Bystanders said that it had rained coal onto the street below, an avalanche of precious fuel. The ARPs quickly brought cutting gear to the train driver's cab. Now sparks flew in a brilliant orange fan to the whir and whine of the blade as it sliced into the metal. The boys stood mesmerized in the road below.

Just as they pulled the driver free, an engine droned through the dark sky. It was a rogue plane that had escaped the radar and soared unseen into the heart of the city. Before anyone could shout, before the air raid siren could begin, the pilot jettisoned his deadly cargo. A searchlight pierced the sky, too late except to pick out the bomb whistling overhead. People stood transfixed, caught in the open. A thud, a flaring light as the first fire-bomb landed in a street to the south.

Ernie grabbed Geoff and Bertie. Up on the viaduct, Walter leaned over to yell instructions. 'Get them to shelter, Ernie. Quick as you can!'

'Pa!' Geoff saw him and wrenched free. He darted into the mêlée of onlookers. Bertie shouted, but they lost sight of him. He turned helplessly to Ernie.

They heard another thud. This time the glare was nearer still, the sound of splintering glass louder. Yet another. People scattered in all directions.

Walter had vanished from the top of the viaduct. Ernie kept hold of Bertie and turned this way and that. He couldn't head for shelter until he found Geoff. A bomb landed in Duke Street and the force of the blast threw him to the ground.

When the bomb went off, Tommy was sitting alone in his basement office. He heard a deafening explosion, felt a tremor shake the foundations. Ledgers and catalogues tumbled from shelves, the glass door shattered as the frame cracked and split. Using his arms to shield his head, he rolled sideways under the desk, and was plunged into darkness. The noise deafened him; the grating roar of falling masonry, the long rumble as it hit the ground. Everything above ground level caved in, sending a landslide of rubble grinding down the cellar stairs.

He knew he was trapped. Though unable to see much, he could make out that the roof of the basement had held up. The fall of rubble deadened sounds from above. Trickles of plaster dust sifted through wide cracks in the ceiling. At last the quaking roar died. Whatever had been taking place up there was complete.

Tommy eased himself out from under the desk and dusted himself down. In the gloom he saw that the door had caved in and the stairway was a solid wall of fallen rubble. He went over and felt it, his eyes slowly growing used to the dark. Tommy swore and went for the telephone. As expected, the line was dead. He took stock; before the bomb exploded he'd locked up and sent the staff home. No one to worry about there. What about the flat? As luck would have it, today was the day Dorothy had gone to fetch Charlie out of hospital. He doubted now that she would have much of a place to bring him home to. Again he tried the phone, refusing to accept that his one line of communication had been cut. But the wire must be down, the electricity gone. How would anyone know he was down here? There could be a fire up there with dozens of victims lying injured. He listened hard for ambulances and fire engines, but his office was eerily quiet. Bricks and stones separated him from the outside world; it was impossible even to guess what hell had been created up there.

Anything was better than sitting in the dark, however. He tore off his jacket and set to, dismantling the landslide of rubble in the stairwell one brick at a time. He reckoned he could soon tunnel out. But as he dislodged a section of bricks using a metal shelf bracket as a makeshift crowbar, the weight of the rubble shifted and the gap caved in. He'd worked up a sweat and scraped his hands red raw for nothing. He tried again, this time more gingerly, using his head and trying to work out what could be moved without displacing a ton of new stuff. How much was up there, he wondered?

As he worked, other grim possibilities framed themselves. For instance, was there enough air down here to see him through? He left off levering at the bricks and groped across the room, glad to find that an air vent leading from street level to a grate behind the safe seemed unobstructed. He pulled the safe clear of the wall to let the air circulate freely.

How long might it be before the rescue teams realized that he was trapped down here? Tommy had done himself no favours that week by snubbing his pals at the Duke and cutting dead all questions about where he was living. And since no one knew where to look, how would they know he was missing? He gave a grim smile as he went back to work and shifted another loose brick; one too many. His excavation grated, shifted and collapsed. Back to square one. He felt for a cigarette in his waistcoat pocket, then searched for a match. Out of luck there too. He shook the empty box and threw it down.

Walter yelled to his mates that he was heading down to street level. He vaulted the viaduct wall and scrambled down the bank, ignoring shrapnel that still showered through the air, ignoring the cries of the wounded. He couldn't leave Ernie to cope with the boys. He had to find them himself and help them to safety.

Out of the corner of one eye he saw the entire front of Tommy's shop lean outwards, sway, then swing forwards and collapse onto the street, burying several of those who fled for shelter. A hot wind gusted against him, flames lit the terrified faces of those who had escaped.

'Move!' he yelled. 'Save yourselves. You can't do anything here!'

He jumped from the bank and ran for the railway arches where he had last seen Ernie with the boys. He prayed that they'd dived for shelter; the arches were the safest place to wait while the splinters of glass, wood and metal landed. Let them be there when the clouds of dust settled, safe under an arch.

All was dark. He called into the shadows: 'Bertie, Geoff!' Women huddled and sobbed. They clutched their own children, waiting to be told what to do.

'Make for the shelter!' He hauled them out of the recesses, told them to run. The plane had stopped flying overhead, but there was fire. The wind was blowing in the wrong direction; they must get out of here quick. 'Jimmie, have you seen the boys? Or Ernie?' He caught hold of one familiar fleeing figure and demanded an answer.

'I seen Ernie. He's over there!' Jimmie struggled free. 'He ain't got the kids with him though.' Then he was running, down Meredith Court, scrambling along the railway embankment on a short cut to Nelson Gardens.

Walter went cold. Ernie had lost the boys. He was meant to hang on to them at all costs; even he knew that. Now anything could happen to them. There was all this shrapnel flying through the air, clouds of choking smoke. He saw Ernie loom out of the shadow of one of the vast arches and ran and grabbed him by both arms. 'Where are they, Ern? Have you seen them?'

Ernie couldn't take it in. One moment they'd been standing watching the sparks fly as the men cut through metal to rescue the train driver. Next thing they were thrown to the ground. He knew he had to get hold of Bertie and Geoff again, but there were people lying groaning. Some were bleeding. This was bad, very bad. He must go on looking for Bertie and Geoff. He came blundering out of the archway into Walter's path.

'Where are they?' Walter saw that Ernie's face was grazed and cut.

'I'll find them,' he promised. 'I have to get them to the shelter.'

Walter stared for a second into his uncomprehending face. 'It's all right, Ern. It's not your fault. Let's both look.' He had to calm down; the worst danger now was the fire blazing at the site of Tommy's shop, not a hundred yards down the street. Too late the sirens had begun to wail as the fire-fighters set up ladders and hoses. 'You can't get up Duke Street. If you find them, hang on tight. Shout for me as loud as you can.' He sent Ernie down Meredith Court while he scouted along Duke Street.

'Hang on tight,' Ernie gasped.

'No. Ern!' Walter called him back? 'Listen, never mind the boys. Leave them to me. You head straight for Nelson Gardens, you hear.' He didn't want any delay. He wanted to be quite sure that Ernie knew what to do. 'Got that?'

'Nelson Gardens?'

'That's it, you got it!' Walter pushed him on ahead. Then they split up, heads down, trying to shield their faces from the fierce blaze. 'Bertie! Geoff!' Walter shouted himself hoarse. He accosted anyone staggering through the thick smoke; had they seen two small boys? Which way were they heading? At last someone said, yes, there were a couple of kids hiding behind an upturned car a few yards up the road. They wouldn't budge poor things; too terrified. Walter's heart leapt. He raced across the street. It was them, his two boys. He ran and gathered them up. They sprang sobbing into his arms when they saw who it was.

'We lost Uncle Ern,' Geoff cried.

'I know. But we wouldn't go off and leave you; you know that.'

'I found Geoff.' Bertie rubbed his smudged, blackened face.

'Good boy. And you're all in one piece, both of you?' Walter checked them quickly. 'Here, grab hold of my hand. Let's get you out of here.' Relief choked him as he looked

346

up and down the street. 'Come on!'

'What about Uncle Ern?'

'He's heading for Nelson Gardens. Run, there's good boys.' He took them down the Court, away from the worst of the flames. By now the streets had emptied. An ambulance crept through the rubble, searching for survivors.

The boys shouted and yelled. They wanted to find Ernie. But the wind grew hotter in their faces, the firemen ordered them on.

'Uncle Ern's fine,' Walter told them. 'Let's go and find him at the shelter.'

'I want Ma!' Geoff cried, suddenly realizing. He pulled at Walter's sleeve as they ran.

'Ma's safe. She's at Gran's, but we can't get there right now. It ain't safe.' There was a bank of flame between them and the pub.

Walter picked Geoff up and carried him. 'We'll get you two safe and go and find Uncle Ernie. I told him to head for Nelson Gardens. That's where he is, you'll see!'

After Walter's final order to make for the public shelter, Ernie followed the stooping figures that fled from the fire down Meredith Court. Some limped, some cried out loud. In the confusion he heard an earlier voice telling him to find the boys, not Walter's last instruction to head for the Gardens. That slipped from his mind. Yes, he had to find them. Ernie coughed and wiped his face, turned towards Duke Street.

'Get back!' An ARP warden blocked his way. Ernie was heading towards the flames. 'You can't go that way.' The wind was creating a firestorm, flames sucked and roared through the ruined buildings not fifty yards away. 'You'll get burned to a cinder if you don't watch out!' he pushed and swore. 'What's the matter, are you out of your mind?'

But Ernie knew one end of Duke Street from another. His job was to find the boys, and boys knew as well as he did what to do when the siren started. They'd started now. The words 'Nelson Gardens' slipped from his mind.

'The Duke,' he said out loud. 'Geoff and Bertie. The Duke.'

'What the bleeding hell . . . ?' The warden lacked the strength to hold Ernie back.

Flames caught fresh energy from the wind and roared on. Ernie could see that the fire would stop him from running straight home to find the boys. He must duck down an alleyway, work his way around the back. The warden was right; no one could go down Duke Street. He turned and disappeared between two tall tenements, down an unlit court. The Duke of Wellington. Home. Shelter. The boys. He could hear his own footsteps, his own breath coming in choking gasps. The smoke was thicker down here. It blinded him. He ran on without seeing. A smell of smoke, another suffocating, sour smell, like gas from the cooker when it wasn't lit. The new fumes caught in his throat, he stumbled. He would have to turn back.

A fireball roared down the narrow street. It lit the escaping gas from the fractured main. The last thing Ernie knew, as a searing wind lifted him off his feet, was a sudden bright light and a wall of flame.

CHAPTER SEVENTEEN

For two nights and three days Tommy remained trapped in the dark basement. The work of rescuers at ground level was hampered by temperatures well below zero and frequent showers of snow. It settled on the blackened skeleton of his shop, falling from a grey sky, a pall provided by nature for all who had lost their lives.

Over two hundred people had been killed in Southwark alone. Thirty-six along Union Street, fifteen in the Cathedral Close, five on Duke Street and the neighbouring courts. Many more were reported missing.

Annie went with Rob to identify Ernie in his makeshift coffin.

'Let me go,' he begged. 'No need for you to come too.'

'I must.' The heart was knocked out of her when they told her the news, but she knew her duty still.

'Let her,' Frances said quietly. She held on to Annie's hand and led her out to Rob's waiting taxi. Hettie stood weeping on the doorstep, Sadie at her side. Jess was coming on the train from Manchester in spite of the danger, for no one was in any doubt that the body in the mortuary at St Guy's was Ernie.

'How can she bear it?' Sadie sobbed.

'Because she must.' Frances let Sadie bury her face against her shoulder. Their youngest sister had felt the blame fall squarely on her for their loss.

'I wish I'd never let him out of my sight!' she cried. 'I wish I'd kept them all at home, then this would never have happened.' She went over in her own mind the sequence of events: Bertie and Geoff's excitement as they heard about the train smash, Ernie's promise that he would keep an eye on them when he took them to see it. 'I should've looked after him better, poor Ern.'

He'd been discovered in the court after the flames had died down. A great force had lifted him clean off the ground and thrown him sideways. They found his body inside a burnt-out house, trapped against some cellar stairs where he had been smothered by smoke and falling stone. He had escaped the flames and was still recognizable, not even much marked, they said.

At the mortuary Annie gazed at the corpse. 'I want to bring him home,' she said.

Rob turned to the attendant, who said arrangements could be made. Then they left her alone for a few minutes, at her request.

It was hard to believe, looking at his peaceful face under the cold white mortuary lights, that they wouldn't soon have Ernie back amongst them. Shrouded to the neck, the face was still him, and in death very like Duke's, with its broad forehead, long nose, strong jaw. She stooped to draw her fingers down his cold cheek. She must touch him and say goodbye.

'It ain't too late, son. I know you can hear me, so you just listen to me. You died a brave man, thinking of others as usual. That was your way and we loved you for it, Ernie. I only hope you never suffered. Bertie and Geoff are both fine, so no need to worry there. Sadie's heartbroken. We all are.'

She sighed and stood in silence for a while. 'Why won't you wake up and come on home with us, son?' Tears fell, she bowed her head.

'He won't, Annie.' Rob had come in, and he took her arm. 'But we'll bring him back for the funeral.'

She gave Ernie one last look. 'You tell that pa of yours that we miss him too, and God bless both of you.'

Rob took her home, hollowed out by

misery, feeling how small and frail she was as she sat in the passenger seat staring straight ahead. They drove slowly through the burned and ruined streets.

'How did he look?' Frances asked him. Hettie took Annie upstairs to rest.

'Like himself.'

She nodded.

'I wish I'd looked after him, Frances.'

'You've enough to look after.'

'I should've made sure he knew what to do.' Rob refused to be comforted, slamming a table with his fist. Walter brought a stiff drink, sat him down, told Frances that he and Rob would talk while she did what she could upstairs.

Tommy knew that he might freeze to death. As the temperature dropped and still he remained sealed in the basement, he began to care less and less about surviving a first, and then a second night without food or warmth. He soon left off his early efforts to lever his way out, and after one or two failed attempts to raise help by yelling up the ventilation shaft, he came to see this as futile too. There was nothing for it but to sit it out.

Meanwhile, after the news had sunk in that the shop was razed to the ground and

Tommy missing, presumed dead, Edie came with Lorna to see what was left. Nothing remained of the building; what the explosion had left standing, the fire had soon destroyed. Oddly, in the days since the disaster, as the demolition services worked doggedly to clear the street and dismantle unsafe buildings, a milkman had been along and left his daily deliveries on whatever doorsteps he could still find.

'I've tried the shelters, I've been to the hospital and the Enquiry Bureau; no one's got any news.' Edie refused to hear what Lorna was telling her. In her own mind she still believed that Tommy could have got out before the bomb had dropped. After all, the demolition men hadn't discovered a body, he hadn't turned up on any official record. That meant there was still a chance.

'Edie?' Lorna thought she was morbid, poking at the piles of rubbish. She'd unearthed part of the sign that ran along the shop front. 'Ideal'. The rest was splintered and unreadable. 'Come and have a drink.'

Edie sat heavily on a stone ledge, part of the coping from the top storey. 'We can't. Annie's shut the Duke until after the funeral.' The day, which had hardly grown light, already began to fade. Three days since the bomb.

Lorna turned up her fur coat collar. 'When is it?'

'Tomorrow. Hettie says they're to have the coffin there overnight. They set off for the church first thing tomorrow.'

'They'll have to work hard to clear the street for the hearse to get through.' The gloom and the talk depressed Lorna. She was one of those who had to get on and live life as normal, otherwise things would get her down. Tonight, for instance, she would head up the West End and forget her troubles. She invited Edie along. 'Come on, Edie, life goes on.'

'You go. I want to stay here a bit longer.'

She didn't linger. 'You'll meet up with us later if you change your mind?'

'Yes, righto.' She promised not to stay out and freeze to death.

'Sitting there won't do any good . . .' But Lorna knew that Edie wasn't listening to a word she said. She made her way up the street alone.

Caught in a tangle of despairing thoughts, Edie didn't pay much attention to the arrival of a gang of boys who came picking through the rubble soon after Lorna had gone. They were perhaps eleven or twelve years old, five of them in boys' clothes with old men's faces; thin, shadowed and scrawny, with brutal haircuts. Scavenging their way along the burnt-out streets, they knew the value of every item they came across.

'Fire-grate!' One spotted a good find. Two others helped to pull the mangled piece of iron free. The price for scrap was good. Another of the boys found a poker. They climbed up the heap where Edie sat and turfed aside some charred, crushed tins of paint. But the site was evidently worth staying on. They ran up and down like steeple-jacks.

'Stone me!' Another good find.

'Stuff it!' This time, a disappointment.

'Over here!' They ducked out of sight as she sat on in the gathering dusk.

'Blimey, missus!' After a few seconds, one of the boys shot back over the mound. 'There's a geezer down there!'

She jumped to her feet. 'Where?' He was pointing wildly the way he'd just come. 'Tell me!' But the boy made his getaway and now she could see the others haring off in all directions. She scrambled up the heap of bricks and peered down a dark slope, where she could just make out a metal grille which they'd prised from an air vent, then abandoned in their fright. Edie slid down the slope of loose rubble and charred wood, loosening the debris underfoot. There was no light. She had to feel her way towards the vent.

'Tommy!' She knelt and put her mouth to the opening. 'Answer me if you're there!' It must be him. It wasn't a ghost, though the boy looked as though he'd seen one.

'Here!' The answer came faintly at last.

'Oh, thank God!' She worked furiously at the rubble around the hole. 'Are you all right?'

'I'm bleeding freezing.' Waking out of a torpor as a smattering of small stones trickled down the narrow shaft, he'd heard what sounded like boys' voices. He'd called hoarsely for help, but the sounds stopped and though he'd called again, no one answered. Then, a few minutes later, he picked up a woman's voice. Edie. He recognized it at once. 'You'll have to go and get help. Get me out of here!'

'I will.' Overjoyed, she lay full length and stretched her arm down the shaft. It was only a few inches wide, too narrow to crawl down. 'They said you'd copped it!'

He allowed himself a brief grin. 'Well, I haven't. But I soon will if you don't get someone quick. I can't take another night down here.'

'Just reach up for a see, Tommy, see if you can grab my hand.' She kept hers deep in the shaft, stretching her fingertips. 'Then I'll believe it's really you.'

Tommy climbed on the safe and reached out. Their hands touched. 'See.'

'I love you, Tommy, whatever happens. I want you to know.'

'Tell me when I get out.'

'I don't blame you if you hate me, only it wasn't my fault, not all of it.'

'Slow down, Edie, I hear you.'

'I'm sorry.'

'No, it was me. I went mad when I saw you with him. I never gave you a chance.' Her hand, small and warm, held fiercely to his.

'I wrote to him, did you know?' Better late than never. At least she'd done the right thing in the end. 'No, course not. How could you?'

'When?'

'The day I chucked my job. I'm getting a divorce, Tommy.'

'You never told me.' It was him clinging onto her hand now, as realization crashed down on him.

'You never gave me the chance.' In the silence and the gathering dusk, Edie had to decide what to do next.

'Listen, Tommy, I'll go for Walter and George. You stay put.' Finally she made him release her hand.

'I ain't going nowhere.' He slumped down.

Then she tore herself away, climbed over the mound and ran down the street. She hammered at the doors of the Duke, called for the men to bring shovels and pickaxes. 'He's alive, he's alive!'

'Who?' George opened up. For a second he held a glimmer of hope that Annie had made a monumental mistake in identifying Ernie.

'Tommy. He's trapped in his basement. I just spoke to him. Get Walter, come quick!'

January 25th, 1941. Royalty were to visit the stricken community. It was almost as big a boost as a tour of the blitzed streets by Churchill himself, when he would march along with his entourage. 'Are you down-hearted?' he would ask. Homes were gone, every last vestige of a lifetime's scrimping and saving. 'No!' came the rousing reply. Business as usual. Winnie would raise his hand in salute, cigar clamped between his teeth, jaunty in his homburg hat and dickie-bow. The people would run alongside to keep up, burst through the cordon of militia men and politicians, the women smiling gaily and waving at the news photographers.

But today it was a royal party, a time for compassion, for dignified endurance. Southwark had been badly affected by the great fire on Duke Street, and still the raids went on, night after night. The people needed recognition, a kindly ear for their troubles, a chance to mourn their dead. The visit was scheduled for ten o'clock, before the VIPs moved on to Kentish Town to talk to victims there.

'Are we ready?' Annie gathered the family mourners on the pavement outside the pub. Upstairs, the undertakers were standing by.

They lined each side of the door; Rob upright in his dark suit, looking older but still strong. He'd come through one war, though he'd been badly injured. He owed his life to George Mann, standing opposite him now. George had stood by him then. He'd married into the family and helped them out of other difficulties since. George was one in a million. Rob stood tall, Amy and Bobby at his side.

The women were all dressed in black. It took Ernie's funeral to bring Jess down from the North, with Maurice, Mo and Grace. The children were grown-up beyond recognition, as smart and well-to-do as anyone could wish. Frances stood with Annie, her husband, Billy Wray, quietly on her other side. Then there was Hettie with George, Sadie with Walter, Meggie, Geoff and Bertie.

Where they found their courage no one knew. Other mourners were openly in tears; Dolly, Edie and those who had known and looked out for Ernie ever since he was little, when they would give a belt around the ear to anyone found teasing or mocking him, or would set him on the right road for school. Later, they recalled Ernie on his delivery bike, working for Henshaws, taking bread, eggs and butter to doorsteps along Duke Street, Meredith Court and beyond. Never a mistake, always on time, always cheerful. And later still, as a fixture behind the bar at the Duke; methodical, reliable. When his pa grew too old and frail to do the heavy cellar work, Ernie had come into his own.

This was the boy they'd saved from the gallows after a bloody murder that had shocked and horrified the whole neighbourhood. A brutal stabbing. The police had arrested poor Ernie because they were too lazy to look for anyone else and Ernie happened to fit the bill. But no one believed it; throughout the trial and the guilty verdict, they knew that he was innocent. Ernie would never have harmed a fly. The courts had believed them at last and issued a reprieve.

And yet Hitler had got him in the end. There was no justice; the poor and helpless suffered most in this war.

They grieved for him, and for Annie especially, who had been through a lot in her long life, who had loved Ernie as her own son, a boy-man with a gentle heart.

'Ready.' Annie nodded to the undertaker's man.

The message went upstairs to the pallbearers. The mourners waiting in the snow and ice of a freezing January morning.

They carried the heavy coffin, a plain wartime one, down the stairs on Ernie's last journey from his home to the church and on to the cemetery. They brought him out into Duke Street, into the old-fashioned hearse drawn by black horses wearing plumes and fine harnesses, a splendid affair amidst the sandbags and rubble.

'He deserves the best,' Dolly whispered. Charlie was out of hospital, getting back on his feet. He'd insisted on going with her and Dorothy to the church. 'Annie will want to give him a good send-off, for Duke and the rest.' She shook her head in sorrow.

Once the coffin was safely stowed, the

hearse moved off and the procession formed behind, ready to follow on foot. Annie came at the head, flanked by Rob and George, her eyes fixed firmly on the shiny black carriage. The rest of the family came after, dry-eyed, sombre.

'You sure you can make it?' Edie asked Tommy as he fell in with the procession on the slow march to the church. They'd pulled him out the night before, just three hours after the boys' discovery. He was suffering from the after-effects of cold and hunger, but nothing worse. He shrugged off any fuss, said that all he wanted was to get back to normal. Last night they'd gone back to Edie's and made up their differences.

He nodded. 'I'm one of the lucky ones,' he reminded her.

At the top of the road, where the cortège had to turn right onto Union Street, the undertaker drew to a halt. Army personnel had put up a roadblock: they must wait for the royal visitors to pass. Word went down the procession; VIPs were to be allowed through. So they stood and waited, black figures against frosty mounds of brick and metal, the horses standing patiently, the hearse gleaming in the sharp sunlight.

The royal party approached in an open-topped car, preceded by military vehicles, accompanied by a crowd of pressmen and enthusiastic onlookers. They were set to sail past the mourners from Duke Street. But the driver received a signal to stop. The pack of cameramen grew excited as two of the visitors stepped from the car. Bulbs flashed, there was a crush along the pavement, for a moment a sense of confusion and possible disruption.

The members of the royal party approached Annie and spoke quietly to her, commiserating with her for her loss. They said they knew that kind words did little to compensate for her suffering, but they hoped she would accept their condolences. No one escaped unscathed; no family, no individual. They prayed nightly for the war to end, they would pray for her and her brave stepson. Annie shook them by the hand.

Then they returned to their car. The order was given to take down the roadblock and let the funeral cortège pass through.

It was as if the whole world had turned out to pay their last respects to Ernie. Those who never knew him stood by silently, kings and commoners alike. The hearse moved on with its solemn burden. In silence they bowed their heads. Annie and her family walked on.

PART THREE

Ashes in the Sea

June 1941

CHAPTER EIGHTEEN

'We shall get used to it,' was the grim response among East Enders. But the residents of Duke Street and Paradise Court were sadly mistaken if, after Ernie Parsons' funeral, they imagined things could not get worse.

On a single night in the middle of March 1941, seven hundred and forty Londoners had been killed in the Blitz. In mid-April a thousand more civilians were lost; on the 10th of May, almost one thousand five hundred, with eighteen hundred injured. Westminster Abbey, the Tower, the House of Commons had all been hit, and brown smoke once more blotted out the sun.

Like the Windmill Theatre, the Duke of Wellington's proud boast that it never closed held up during the worst of the bombing, though the pub felt bleak and empty without Ernie. They wondered that it could make such a difference to the place, both his loss and a general despondency as the war dragged on towards the end of its second year.

'It ain't the shortages I mind,' Dolly complained to Charlie and Dorothy, as they sat glumly in a corner of the bar. 'I can take all of that. What I can't understand is why it all has to happen on our own doorsteps. In the old days we used to send the boys off to war and we never had to worry about those that stayed home. These days we all have to kip down inside these bleeding metal cages under the stairs in case Jerry comes and blows us to smithereens, even old girls like Annie and me.' The government had recently brought out the Morrison shelters as the latest good thing.

'Put a sock in it, Ma.' Charlie didn't want to hear her moans. Back to full fitness after the nightmare explosion at the church, he nevertheless preferred to steer the talk away from daily dangers. He was determined to be upbeat, to count his blessings, which included having Dorothy come to stay in the Ogden house after her flat was demolished in January. He gave short shrift to his mother's gloomy prognostications.

'At this rate there'll be nothing left of the old East End by the end of the year.'

'A good thing too.' Dorothy sat calmly smoking. She'd learnt to deal with Dolly by being mildly provocative. 'About time they knocked these old places down; nasty rat-infested blocks of tenements, most of them.'

'You speak for yourself.' Dolly took a morose pull at her pint of stout. 'My house has never had a rat over the front doorstep, has it, Annie?'

'No self-respecting rat would dare set foot in your place, Dolly.' Annie was reminded of days before the First War, when she had lived down the end of the Court in her own little terraced house. She used to pay young Ernie a penny for every rat he caught.

'I still say give me a nice little modern semi any day,' Dorothy insisted.

'There'll be none of them left neither, if Herr Hitler gets his way.'

'Ma!'

'No, she's right, Charlie.' Dorothy didn't often agree with Dolly. The two women managed to tolerate each other within the same four walls, but they thrived on minor conflict. Dorothy took every opportunity to imply that Dolly should take more of a back seat in Charlie's life. Though he was a middle-aged man, she still poked her nose into what he ate, what he wore, whether or not he stayed out late. Dolly's only defence was that she'd poked her nose in all her life, and wasn't about to stop now.

'Blimey.' He took to his beer. 'You two ain't ganging up on me, are you?'

'I mean, if it goes on at this rate we'll none of us have a roof over our heads and that's a fact.'

'Well, as it happens, I don't think it will.' He took Dorothy up on this.

'What?'

'Go on at this rate.' He kept bang up to date with the war news. 'I heard on the wireless that Hitler's gone and invaded Russia.'

'So what?' She paid fresh interest, while Dolly vacated her seat to go and commiserate with Annie over a vanishing way of life; the old streets, people pulling together, everyone knowing everyone else.

'Russia's a big country. Have you looked at an atlas lately?'

'You reckon he's bitten off more than he can chew?'

'I'm saying he'll have his work cut out.' He didn't see how the Germans could keep on sending planes over the Channel, or at least not as many as at present. Russia's misfortune might well prove a blessed relief to the poor, battered cities of Britain.

'I only hope you're right.' She stubbed out her cigarette. 'Do you fancy coming to see a picture with me later?' These days, since settling down with Charlie, Dorothy's tastes had become more homely. She stood up, gave him a peck on the cheek and pulled on a pair of cotton gloves.

'Might do. Where are you off to now?'

'To the hairdressers. I'll see you later.'

'You will if you're lucky.'

'Cheek.'

He winked and watched her go, smart in her summer frock and white high-heeled sandals.

'Watch where you're going.' Dorothy stepped aside in the doorway as Meggie rushed downstairs. 'No need to ask where you're off to in such a hurry.'

'Sorry.' Meggie flew out of the door.

'He ain't worth it,' Dorothy called after her, guessing the reason behind her hurry.

She glanced back, grinning. 'Oh, yes, he is!'

Ronnie had telephoned Meggie to say that he had forty-eight hours. Would she meet him off the train? It was Saturday midday; a beautiful early summer's day. She wore a dress altered for her by Hettie, one with turquoise flowers on a white background, a swirling knee-length skirt and a narrow waist.

'He ain't, believe me.' Dorothy smiled wistfully after the girl, tucked her bag under her arm and set off up the street to have her hair done.

★ ★ ★

The day was special for Meggie and Ronnie. It was their first meeting since his ship had gone down in the Med two weeks earlier. They'd fished him out, one of only a dozen survivors. She'd heard the news on the wireless. A convoy attacked. Serious casualties. A day of doubt and torture, then a two-word telegram addressed to her at the Duke: 'OK — Ronnie.' She'd wept with relief when Hettie brought it down to her in the Court.

Since the early weeks of the year, their romance had been forced underground. Following Ronnie's New Year home leave, Meggie had made several attempts to visit Gertie at the Bell, but she met a firm rebuff on each occasion. Then she'd written to Ronnie to tell him that she would no longer try to stay friends with his mother. 'I don't know exactly what I did wrong, but it must have been bad. She's as good as told me to stay out of her way. Even Shankley says it ain't like her to turn against someone permanently the way she's turned against me. He says there ain't a thing I can do about it. Once Gertie makes up her mind, that's that.' It had been a difficult letter to write. She'd even offered in a half-hearted way to give him up if going on would cause a rift between him and his mother. His reply, threatening to jump ship and come to sort things out if she even so much as thought of such a thing thrilled her. Now she knew he would do anything to keep her.

So, with Gertie obviously hoping that she'd shown Meggie the door for good, and with Sadie assuming from the fall-off in trips to the West End that Meggie must be over her infatuation with the Bell, its landlady and possibly even her son, Meggie kept her emotional life deliberately secret. Her reason for not confiding in her own mother was partly altruistic, for there had been another parting in the family and Meggie wanted to avoid further upset.

After the funeral in January, Annie had called a conference over the future of Bertie and Geoff involving Jess and Maurice as well as Walter and Sadie. Walter was all for evacuating the boys again, the sooner the better. This time Jess offered them a solution. She had taken on a little house in the Lake District, where she planned to send Grace and Sadie's boys. Once again Sadie was torn; Coniston was a safe haven, but could she bear to part with them? On the other hand, she had nightmares about the fire that had killed Ernie. She knew she would never forgive herself if the boys came to harm. In the end, Bertie and Geoff spotted adventure in the move; a house in the country, a lake, boat trips — as many as they liked. They asked, would they be able to come back if they felt homesick? In Coniston, would they have to go to school?

Sadie saw that sending them with Jess was not like pushing them out into the unknown. No waving them off at the station with their name labels washed away by tears. This time they set off with smiling faces in a first-class carriage, with promises to telephone Annie regularly at the Duke. It still broke their mother's heart, but she was clear in her mind that everything had been done for the best. So she settled to life without them, enduring the Blitz, doing her factory work, looking after Walter and Meggie.

As Meggie hurried to the train station to meet Ronnie, noticing the children playing hopscotch on street corners, women gossiping in the ration queues, she felt uneasy at the idea of meeting him in secret. But what was she to do? And in any case, her spirits were soaring at the prospect of seeing him, so she raced along the pavement, her stomach full of butterflies. Before she knew it, the train drew in and Ronnie hopped off. She flew into his arms. There was nothing but joy in her heart at the sight of his tanned features, the sound of his low voice murmuring her name. He held her as if he would never let her go.

'Meggie, am I glad to see you.' He led her through the crowded station. 'I ain't been able to think of nothing else for days.'

She ran alongside, her arm around his waist. 'That's bad, Ronnie. You gotta keep your mind on your job.'

'Says you.' Hailing a taxi, he bundled her inside and told the cabbie to head for Bernhardt Court. 'Anyhow, I ain't got no ship, have I?' He sat back with a sigh. 'I'm still waiting for them to draft me. That's how I got home on leave, until they find me a new ship.'

'What happened?' Meggie had only a vague idea gleaned from newspaper reports which anyway tended to put a jingoistic gloss on things. All she knew was that Ronnie's convoy had come under U-boat attack whilst blockading the German supply route to Rommel in North Africa. According to the official version the blockade had held up, though three British ships had gone down, Ronnie's included.

'Don't ask.' He stared for a moment out of the window. They were passing through a bombed-out area of craters and rubble. Children scavenged along the ravaged streets. 'You don't want to know.'

She slipped her hand into his. 'I do, if you want to tell me.'

'Hell.' The one word said it all. He turned to look at her earnest face. 'All I remember is the klaxon for action stations. It was a U-boat, but we spotted her too late. Torpedo in the stern. We were ordered straight to the lifeboats, but it was too late for that and all. She went down, bow-up at an angle of forty-five degrees in a sheet of flame.'

'You were on fire?'

'That's what did for most of us. There was a roar, and up she went. I was at the bow-end, otherwise it would have done for me too. I took a running jump over the side and came up with the flotsam. By the time I got my bearings, she was gone, with all on board.'

Meggie sat silent.

'It was pitch-black in the water once she'd gone down. I kept bumping into bits from the wreck and bodies as well, but I took my chance and grabbed onto an upturned lifeboat with a couple of others. The worst of it was, there were men in the water who couldn't swim. No kidding. Sailors. They yelled out, but there was nothing we could do. We couldn't even see them, it was so dark.'

'How many of you got picked up?'

'Thirteen. They came to fetch us at first light. A minesweeper dropped its scrambling nets and we climbed up. She headed for Malta with us double-quick. The RAF shipped us out from there back to Portsmouth, and I've been kicking my heels ever since.' He remembered the black, oily water, the sheet of flame, the sucking, hissing, rush of the sea as it swallowed the ship.

Meggie clung to him. 'Will they send you back?'

'To the Med?' He shrugged. 'They say the Yanks are set to join us. It could be the Atlantic or the Far East.'

'But if the Yanks come in, it'll be all over, and the sooner the better.' She could only pray for a quick end and a return to normality.

'Not soon enough.' Too late for his friends on board, those who had screamed as the fire engulfed them, those who sank beneath the oily waves. Unable to offer Meggie the reassurance she craved, he lapsed into silence.

To her he seemed a lot older, more serious than before, and who could blame him? Sharing confidences, she told him quietly about the aftermath of their own tragedy; how the war had struck at the heart of her family. 'Gran took it like a hero of course, chin up all the way through the funeral, proud as anything on the day. But she's felt it since. She won't admit it, but she misses Ernie more than any of us. She keeps looking over her shoulder as if he's still there waiting to be told what to do next. Once I heard her talking to him, clear as anything.'

'How about you?'

'I miss him too. We all do. None of us can see why he didn't head for Nelson Gardens, like Walter told him.'

Ronnie could imagine all too well the chaos of the moment. Hadn't he seen with his own eyes the way well-trained men went to pieces when the jaws of hell opened before them? But he wouldn't frighten Meggie by trying to explain. 'I don't think you'll ever know the answer to that one.'

'I wish . . .' she began, then dipped her head. The taxi wove in and out between buses and pedestrians, beneath the giant theatre signs and portraits of the stars.

'What do you wish?'

'Nothing . . . I wish you didn't have to go back, Ronnie.'

He laughed at her simplicity. 'What you on about? I only just got here, didn't I?'

'All right, then. I wish we could bring

Ernie back. I wish the killing would stop.' They came to a halt at the end of Bernhardt Court.

'Blimey, you don't want much, do you?' He paid the fare.

'Only what we all want.' It seemed to her now that all they'd ever known was war. There were children growing up in the blasted streets who could hardly remember peace. She sometimes looked at their pinched, wary faces and saw suspicion, not innocence there. 'I wouldn't like to bring kids into a world like this, would you?'

'Is it as bad as that?' He followed her on her course from childlike wishing to deep-seated fear for the future.

'It is when you think about it. It ain't a safe place to bring up a family, and I wouldn't want to send the kids away like Ma had to.'

'You're too soft hearted,' he told her. 'You need me to look after you.'

'I do,' she admitted with a sudden smile.

'Well, I will.' He seized her hand. 'Ready for the lion's den?'

They marched down the Court past a news vendor and a tramp begging for coppers, past Shankley's stall. They swung through the doors of the Bell to heaven knew what greeting from Gertie.

★ ★ ★

'Open the window, Tommy,' Edie called from the bedroom, wanting to clear the cigarette smoke from the living room. She was busy combing her hair, getting ready to go out on their planned afternoon stroll up to the Embankment and over to Hyde Park. 'Let some fresh air in.'

The day was sunny and warm. She came through in her white satin slip, holding up two dresses; one with yellow and white daisies, one a plain, pale blue. 'Which one?'

'Neither.' He waltzed across and seized her. 'I like you better without.'

'You'll get me arrested, you will.' She swung the dresses out of his way and held them at arm's length while he tickled her neck with light kisses. 'I have to put something on to make me look decent.'

'What for?' He breathed in the smell of her skin, and went on covering her in kisses.

'Tommy, I thought we were going out.'

'What for?' He steered her towards the bedroom, which was flooded with warm sunshine.

'A walk. W-A-L-K. That's what we said.' She laughed at him.

'Did we? I don't remember.' That was earlier, while he sat reading the paper, before she walked in in her slip and reminded him how much he wanted her. He kissed her on the mouth to stop her talking, closed the door softly behind them.

'A walk would do us good.' Edie kept up a show of resistance. 'Careful, Tommy, you'll crease these dresses.'

He took them from her as he sat her on the bed, then went and hung them back in the wardrobe. In the sunlight her hair shone like gold, her skin took on a rosy glow. He looked at her quietly, felt her return his gaze.

'Close the curtains,' she whispered.

'All these orders,' he complained. 'Open the window, close the curtains. Anyone would think we was married.' But he did as she asked. The room fell into soft shadow, muggy in the afternoon sun.

As Tommy slowly undressed, she went on watching him. The attraction was definitely a two-way thing, and this had surprised her at first, brought up as she was to be an object of desire, but not to expect her man to arouse the same feelings in her. For years, with Bill, this had been the case. For though she had always had a strong sense of his masculinity, with his muscular arms and torso, his solid physique had not given her much pleasure. It was too thick around the waist, lacking in grace, and he never thought it necessary to present himself in a nice way. He was indifferent as to whether or not he pleased her. She had resorted to a sense of duty, been passive throughout their marriage and sometimes guilty that she wanted him so little after the first few times together. She had no idea before Tommy that she might actually enjoy love-making, but was dimly aware that there must be more to it, if only she could discover what it was. That was all she could suppose; that for some women it must be a more fulfilling thing, with admiration, desire and respect mixed into the bed experience. She had no respect for Bill, she was sad to discover. Only duty.

But with Tommy she felt entirely different. He was lean and graceful; a funny word for a man like him, brought up rough and ready in the back streets, living hand to mouth. Still, with him everything was clean and well defined, from his wide, thin-lipped mouth, straight nose and flat brow, to his long fingers and slim, smooth body. His tough upbringing combined with his Irish ancestry had given him a spare look, but not scrawny. He moved lightly, swiftly and never gave his appearance a second thought.

'What are you looking at?' He moved onto the bed and drew her to him.

'You.' She cupped his face between her

hands and kissed his lips. 'You're shame-less.'

'I'll put my clothes back on then, shall I?'

'You dare!' She reached over to stop him. He liked it when Edie made the bold move. He was half-amused, fully aroused. Soon they lay entwined, he took off her satiny slip and their bodies touched, warm, soft, curving into one another; moving, caressing, harmonizing towards a slow climax that neither was desperate to achieve, since they wanted their love-making to last. Yet when it ended, it was with a satisfaction that neither could have imagined in the days before they met.

Then there was the ritual of Tommy going into the kitchen to bring back scalding hot tea which they sipped from the same cup, propped on pillows, knees crooked under the sheets. Half an hour of luxurious talk about nothing, or about everything; them, their plans, their hopes and dreams.

'How are you feeling?' He handed her the white cup.

'Lovely.'

'I never asked you, how do you look.' He kissed her again. 'Anyhow, that'll teach you to wander around with nothing on.'

The clock on the bedside table said four

o'clock. 'There's still time for that walk if you want.'

'What happened? Did I suddenly go deaf?' He knocked the heel of his hand against his ear. 'What's that you just said?'

'Tommy!'

'Righto.' He sprang from the bed. 'Come on, I thought you said you wanted some fresh air.'

She put down the cup just in time, because he came back from flinging open the curtains and letting in the sun to tip her clean out of bed. Edie responded with a small scream of protest.

By the time she'd recovered, he was already dressed. He went to the wardrobe and brought out the pale blue dress, stood with mock impatience.

But she refused to be rushed. Time enough to get out into the sunny evening after she'd bathed and done her hair. Tommy would have to go back to his newspaper and wait. She did put on the blue dress, however. He called her a bobby-dazzler. She whisked him out of the door and down the stairs before he had a chance to get up to any more of his tricks.

They spent an hour walking across the park under the spreading leaves of the horse-chestnuts, with only the sandbagged entrances to the shelters to remind them of a grimmer reality; a sight by now so familiar that it was possible to pass them by without noticing. Edie was looking up at the pinky-cream flowers of the chestnut blossom, while Tommy kept an arm firmly round her waist and told her his plans to open up a new stall by the entrance to the covered market behind the cathedral. He wanted to sell newspapers and magazines.

'It'll be starting from scratch, I know.'

'With newspapers?' She sounded doubtful.

'Trust me,' he said. It was a commodity everyone wanted in these news-hungry days of all-out war.

Bill Morell was at the flat waiting for them when they got back. He had Edie's letter telling him that their marriage was over tucked into his top pocket, where it had stayed since he received it in the early spring. He'd read it through once; how his last visit had finally decided her, how she wasn't prepared to take any more bad behaviour on his part. Though she was sorry to hurt him, especially whilst he was away doing a dangerous job for his country, she wanted him to understand that she would never, never be a wife to him again.

The news had come as no surprise, but the tone of the letter had annoyed him. She seemed to suppose that by putting on a hoity-toity voice she could place herself above him, chuck him to one side, and sail on without so much as a backward glance. But he knew her game. No woman walked out of a marriage without someone or something else to walk into, and it didn't take a genius in this case to work out who it was. The gift of the stockings, the bottles of spirits in the cupboard; who besides Tommy O'Hagan could readily get hold of such black market goods? Though Edie never mentioned her employer, Bill's suspicious mind had fingered Tommy long before the letter had arrived.

Now he saw himself as the wronged party, as technically he was. Away at sea, he brooded on it and the wrongs assumed monstrous proportions. Edie had betrayed him for a fly-by-night street trader who'd got on through shady deals and dodgy connections; a man who'd ditched his own wife in order to start up an affair with Edie.

This was bad enough. But as for Edie, Bill had no words to describe her; or rather he had them, but none were crude enough to fit the bill. She'd sold herself for a pair of silk stockings, she was O'Hagan's tart, his fancy-piece, his whore. In this massacre of Edie's reputation to pals on board ship from whom he extracted plenty of easy sympathy, Bill's own behaviour didn't enter into the equation. She had done the unforgivable; invited another man to leap in between his sheets. Any revenge he could concoct during the dark hours on watch could never equal the crime that had provoked it.

In the event, however, Bill's return to the flat didn't bear the hallmark of careful planning. Leave had come out of the blue, as usual, and before he knew it, he was ashore and heading home on the train. No warning for Edie and her fancy-man, no time to think how best to wrench her away from Tommy and put an end to her carrying on. Brute force would enter into it, of course, since he viewed O'Hagan as a no-contest opponent, and Edie herself had always understood the language of violence. Not for a moment did Morell entertain the possibility that the marriage was truly over.

Meanwhile, he made use of the well-stocked liquor cupboard at the flat. He drank well into the evening, biding his time, sure from the signs that Edie wouldn't be gone long, equally sure that her new man had moved in lock, stock and barrel. The black certainty of a mind dulled by alcohol descended on him. Seven o'clock, then eight came and went. Outside the sky was still clear blue.

Edie came upstairs at nine in carefree mood. Tommy had stopped off at the Duke to see if he could catch Jimmie. She went on alone. There was nothing to alert or alarm her, no neighbours in residence to warn her about her unexpected visitor. But the door which she was sure she had locked opened without the key. She stood for a moment, puzzled, took a step inside and saw Bill sitting in an armchair facing her. She made as if to step back and slam the door shut, but not fast enough. He lunged to grab the handle, and with his other hand he pulled her inside the room. He locked the door and put the key in his pocket.

'Where is he?' His voice was a sneer as he went to open the window and look down onto the street.

Ignoring the question, bracing herself against the door, she spoke up at last. 'Didn't you get my letter?' He'd sent no reply, but then she'd hardly expected one.

He drew it from his pocket, unfolded it, and with his eyes directly on her, tore it to pieces.

'I mean it, Bill. We're finished.' She put

her palms flat against the door to steady herself.

'What if I say it don't work like that?' He kept his distance, but his voice was slurred, his stance unsteady. 'What if I ain't ready to let you go?'

'You have to. You can't force me to stay married to you.' But she saw plainly that he intended to try. That would be his tactic, she realised. She turned to rattle the door handle. 'You let me out of here!'

'So you can go running to Tommy O'Hagan?' His voice grew nastier, a smile appeared on his face.

'What's Tommy got to do with this?'

'Plenty if you ask me.'

'No he ain't. We were washed up long before Tommy came on the scene, and you know it.'

'So you admit he's the one? Can't keep his hands off other men's wives, dirty little bleeder.' He swayed across the room towards her.

'It's not like that.' She managed to dodge out of the way, but only into the bedroom, where she was trapped. He stood in the doorway, arms resting high on either side of the frame.

'Ain't it? Tell me how it is, then, with me tucked up in my hammock miles from anywhere, and you and him going at it hammer and tongs.'

Afraid as she was, she scorned to answer.

'Don't like that, eh? Don't like it when I call a spade a spade?' He advanced into the room.

'That ain't the point.' Somehow, the more he trapped her, the more she felt able to rise above her fear. She wasn't going to plead and make excuses. 'The point is, I want a divorce, Bill. You can do what you like, it won't make no difference.'

He swore and grabbed her by the arm, flinging her with ease into a corner. She felt his brute strength, as often before. She didn't even cry out as he moved in again, dragged her to her feet and began to hit her across the face with the palm of his heavy hand.

Tommy didn't linger long at the Duke. Jimmie wasn't there, and after a word or two with Walter, he said he thought he would turn in for an early night.

'Any news of Jerry?' he asked. Walter was ready for duty in his helmet and overalls.

'Not so far. Let's hope for a quiet night.'

'They say he's too busy with Moscow these days.'

Tommy and Walter exchanged news; the

US navy was gathering in Pearl Harbor, another good sign for the Allies. Soon though, Tommy went off to join Edie.

He sensed something was wrong as he went upstairs to the flat. The landing door was open, but it was too quiet inside. The living room was empty. A whisky bottle stood open on the mantelpiece.

'Edie!' He ran into the kitchen, then into the bedroom.

She lay on the bed. Blood trickled from a wound on her head, her face was battered, her eyes closed. Morell. Tommy saw only her poor face, the red blood soaking into her fair hair. Her dress was ripped, her body flung against the headboard, covered in cuts.

He ran over and held her. 'Open your eyes, for God's sake, Edie!' She was warm. He felt for a pulse, found one, then wrapped a sheet around her, trying not to move her in case her bones were broken. How could he have let this happen? Where was Morell now?

'Wait till I get my hands on him.' He should have been here to take and return the blows. How badly was she hurt? If Morell had killed her, if Edie should die . . .

CHAPTER NINETEEN

Morell's one-track mind ticked Edie off his list of scores to settle and came next to Tommy O'Hagan. He made for the paint and wallpaper shop on Duke Street, leaving his wife unconscious on the bed. No one could ditch him or do the dirty on him and get away with it.

The sight of the paint shop collapsed like a sandcastle into a heap of rubble threw him, however. He had to check his bearings, try to recognize some of the buildings nearby, shell-scarred and boarded-up, but still standing amongst the debris. Yes, this had been O'Hagan's shop and living quarters, now smashed to dust. Morell turned on his heel, hoping that the bombs hadn't done for him what he'd savoured doing all these last months at sea.

The Duke of Wellington was his next port of call, for news and another drink. He would go on a bender, fire himself up, then tear the bloke apart, always supposing that Hitler hadn't got there first. He swung open the doors of the pub. It was full of smoke, music, loud voices, the same old faces.

'Hello, Bill. What can I get you?' Annie stood fast behind the bar. A few heads turned as the serviceman entered. Like her, they registered trouble.

He ordered and took a whisky. 'Where's O'Hagan?'

'You mean Tommy? Not in tonight.'

'Not buried underneath his precious shop, then?' He slugged the whisky back.

'No, thank God.' The answers came slow and steady. Further along the bar, George Mann kept a wary eye on him.

It was Bill's plain intention to make his wife's lover wish that he had been killed by the bomb; the look on his face left Annie in no doubt. He shoved his glass back across the bar and nodded for a refill.

Annie poured. 'That's your lot.'

'I know. No need to tell me, there's a war on.'

He drank again. Annie annoyed him for several reasons. For instance, he didn't like the way she stood there, smart and spry, as if the whole world hadn't gone to hell and Edie wasn't making a fool of him, plain as the nose on his face. Morell knew that Annie knew.

She turned away to serve another customer. His dangerous mood had alarmed her, though she didn't show it. Tommy had only just left the pub. He'd called in minutes before, but only had the one drink, thank heavens. Now though, with Bill on the war-path, he would soon have to face the music. She wondered how to warn him, and caught George's attention by calling out: 'Can you go down and tap a new barrel of bitter?'

'I just did.' George came over, wiping his hands. He nodded at Bill. 'I hear it's bad in the Med.'

'Couldn't say. I'm in Greenock.' He stared at his empty glass, working up a fresh rage. Every other blighter in the pub was staring at him, thinking, 'Poor sap, home on leave and all alone, while his wife lets O'Hagan warm his sheets.' He felt their eyes fixed on him in quiet mockery.

'Better than the Far East at any rate.' George took over from Annie in case he was needed. 'I wouldn't fancy it out there my-self.'

'Like a nice, quiet war, do you?' Morell sneered.

'That's the ticket.'

'Tell that to Mr Hitler,' Dolly Ogden chipped in sharply, then bit her tongue. Bill Morell shouldn't be crossed. He was slur-ring his words and swaying against the bar. George and Annie were doing their best to keep a lid on things.

'Where will I find O'Hagan?'

George shrugged his broad shoulders. 'What do you think I am, his keeper?'

'I bet he was in here, though.' Bill picked up his hat which he'd thrown down on the bar. Saturday night; sooner or later everyone pitched up at the pub.

George's eyelids flickered.

'Thanks for nothing, mate.' Bill jammed the hat on. 'It don't make no difference to me. I got forty-eight hours to find the little bleeder. I ain't in a rush.' He wouldn't skulk, or run after him, he would bide his time. Let someone sneak off and warn him; he enjoyed the idea of Tommy having time to squirm before he belted him.

'What's up, Bill? Why are you looking for Tommy?' Annie took a direct line at last. After all, Bill had opened it up.

'As if you didn't know.'

'You tell me.'

He shrugged. 'Ask Edie.'

Annie didn't like this reply. The alarm bells rang louder still. They all knew how things stood with the marriage and in one small corner of her mind she did in fact afford Bill a scrap of sympathy. It couldn't be nice to come back to this; no wife, no home, no future. Being old fashioned, she also believed that Edie should have told him face-to-face. The way she did it, by letter, left too much unfinished business that was bound to catch up with her and Tommy sooner or later.

'Edie don't gossip, Bill. You should know that. She keeps her troubles to herself.'

'So my name ain't mud around here?' He scoffed at Annie. 'Do me a favour!'

'She ain't said nothing.' Reading between the lines, Annie had realized that things had been hard for Edie. You only had to look at Morell; slurred, heavy, his face glistening with sweat, to see just how hard. Her grain of sympathy dissolved. 'No need to take it out on her, is there?'

'Too late.' He turned unsteadily.

'Look here!' Annie reached over to take him by the cuff. 'You ain't done nothing silly?'

George moved in, nodding a warning to Walter and Charlie.

Morell shook Annie off. She stumbled hard against the till. 'I done what I should have done when I first clocked what they were up to, that's all. Same as any man would.'

'Watch it.' George made sure that Annie wasn't hurt, then lifted the counter, knowing that Morell would take up the challenge.

The sailor would be a difficult customer; strong and belligerent. 'No need to get nasty. Let's take it easy, shall we?' Drinkers paused to watch developments, the piano music came to a sudden halt.

Worried about Edie, Annie rang the bell behind the bar for Hettie to come down. 'Run along to Edie's flat,' she whispered. 'See how she is.'

Meanwhile, the men squared up to one another; Bill Morell versus George, with Charlie Ogden and Walter on hand if need be.

'It's like that, is it?' Morell's face suffused with anger. 'That's the line-up; three against one.'

'We're not looking for any trouble.' George's eye was steady. He wanted Morell off the premises. 'Only, no one lays a finger on Annie.'

'She laid hands on me first.'

'Yes, and you go round shoving women, do you?'

This hit home. 'Tell her she should mind her own business.' He'd noticed Hettie slide out of the door; the women had put two and two together, it seemed. Now it wouldn't be long before they discovered what state Edie was in. Even Morell didn't know how bad she was; unconscious certainly. As things began to stack up against him, he hit out.

George saw him lunge. He sidestepped, then put out an arm to stop Morell crashing against the bar. He caught him and wheeled him round, but Morell shoulder-charged him, catching George low in the midriff, winding him and sending him back against the bar instead. As George bent forward, arms across his middle, Morell got him on the chin with a double-fisted blow. Then he kicked at his ribs as he toppled and fell. It was the signal for Walter and Charlie. Everyone else sprang from their stools for a better view, as the two men piled in to grab an arm each and drag Morell clear of George who lay on the floor. George heaved himself to his feet just in time. Morell broke free, snarling and hurling himself about, head down, fists whirling. He went for George again, but this time his opponent was ready. He warded off Morell's punches and got in a couple of his own; good, solid ones that stopped him in his tracks. Charlie and Walter crouched like wrestlers, arms wide. George had his fists up, waiting for another attack.

'Go on, George, fix him!' someone yelled from the smoky back of the room.

Morell jabbed and swore, George parried.

'My, Bill, you do look queer!' came a catcall from the back.

'Just you wait, he ain't even warmed up yet.' Others had seen Bill Morell take on three, even four men and still stay standing. 'Them chuckers-out don't stand a chance!'

Dimly aware of their encouragement, he whirled round and charged at Charlie, the slightest of his opponents. He cracked his fist into Charlie's jaw and had the satisfaction of seeing him reel.

'That's enough!' George ran and seized him from behind. He locked both arms under Morell's armpits and dragged him off, hoping that Charlie would have enough sense to roll out of the way of the vicious kicks. His own strength was under a severe test as he hauled Morell off his feet and he was glad when Walter moved in to pinion the sailor's lower half. Together they carted him bodily from the pub.

'Spoilsports! Boo!' There was disappointment that the fight hadn't gone the distance. But this was only the young element at the back.

'Good riddance.' Dolly righted a couple of stools en route to Charlie, who was back on his feet, his lip cut and bleeding badly.

'That's it, show's over.' Annie grabbed a teatowel and called them to order. She attacked a stack of wet glasses. 'Anyone would think we didn't have enough to do, fighting the Jerries.' She spoke sternly, giving the impression that Morell was a minor nuisance, soon got rid of. The Duke didn't encourage rowdiness; it was a small, friendly local, a home from home.

'Annie, call a doctor!' Hettie came racing back from Edie's flat, not even bothering to ask after George and the rest. 'Edie's in a bad way. Tommy's with her. He says we need a doctor quick.'

'Morell?' Annie went straight to the phone.

Hettie nodded. 'He's beaten her up. It looks bad.'

She dialled the number, waited.

'Tommy says he'll kill him. He swears he will. You should see her, Annie. Her face is all bruised and cut. She's lying there unconscious and Tommy don't know what to do for the best. Oh quick, Annie, hurry up or it'll be too late!'

'I'm as broad-minded as the next person,' Gertie told her son, pulling pints and serving steadily. 'And I've always given you plenty of rope to hang yourself with. But this time I'm telling you loud and clear, Meggie Davidson ain't the girl for you!'

Ronnie slammed a crate of bottles onto the floor. She'd roped him in as soon as he'd set foot in the place, and now Meggie had to sit forlorn in the corner, waiting until his ma had finished finding him urgent jobs to do.

'Lay off, will you?'

'There's no point beating about the bush, is there? Straight up, I'm sick of it, Ronnie. Every time you get leave and waltz in here, there she is hanging off the end of your arm. I never see nothing of you because of her, and I'm your mother, in case you'd forgotten. You'd think she'd give me a bit of space every now and then. But no, she sticks like glue!'

'I *asked* her to meet me at the station.' The old argument was wearing him out. If Gertie didn't drop it, he would be out of the door for good.

'And she has to say yes, does she? Doesn't it occur to her to give me and you some time together?' Gertie pulled him out of sight into the narrow back kitchen. 'She's young and shallow, Ronnie. She don't know what it's like for me, managing here by myself since your pa died.'

It wasn't like her to feel sorry for herself. Again he put it down to the strains of war. 'You cope, don't you?' he said more gently,

401

taking out a cigarette and lighting it.

'I cope because I have to. And I set a lot of store by you, Ronnie. What will I do if she steals you away?'

'Is that it?' He put an arm round her shoulder. 'Is that what you've got against her?'

'I said it before; she don't think of others.'

This was plainly untrue. 'She does. Didn't she give you all the help she could? And she's always going on about her own family. And about you. She says she always wanted a ma like you, up to date and easy going.'

'She never.' Gertie sniffed. The wind had been taken out of her sails.

'She does. Meggie's ma worries a lot.'

'Me too. Only I don't show it.' She put her shoulders back and lifted her head. 'I worry about you, especially now.'

'That's natural, ain't it? Families are made that way.'

'I suppose so.' Gertie looked him in the eye. 'You sure you ain't just fallen for a pretty face?'

'What, would you like it better if I chose an ugly one?' He felt as if he might talk her round this time. It was just a matter of her learning to accept that he wouldn't be around forever. 'Look, Ma, I know Meggie's young and me being away at sea ain't perfect neither. But in a way that gives us more time to think things through. And after we've weighed it up, we find we both still feel the same way.' Ronnie hid his awkwardness behind a cloud of cigarette smoke, trying to describe his strength of feeling, but falling a long way short.

Gertie gazed at her handsome son; dashing and clean-cut. 'You know what they say, absence makes the heart grow fonder.' Perhaps it was the enforced separation that bound Meggie and him together.

'I thought it was out of sight, out of mind.'

'Yes, and you're too clever by half.' Gertie straightened her dress; a light, printed cotton one with a sweetheart neckline. She seemed to make a decision not to push him any harder over Meggie. 'But it is good to have you back safe and sound.' She patted his cheek, then kissed it.

'You ain't gone and got lipstick all over me?' He rubbed the patch of skin with his fingertips.

She laughed. 'Will it make someone jealous?'

'I wish you'd be friends with her, Ma.' He went and stood in the doorway, looking out into the bar. Meggie sat chatting with Eddie. Her face lit up when she spotted him. 'What did she do to you? That's what I'd like to know.'

'It ain't what she does. It's what she is.' Gertie's tone darkened again as she came to look over his shoulder.

He shook his head, about to give it up. 'She's been through a lot, if you did but know.'

'Meggie? She's had it easy if you ask me.'

'No.' Ronnie knew that he was breaking a confidence, but he pressed on. 'Honest. She ain't living with her real pa, you know.' His mother had taken a step backwards, begun to frown. 'It's her step-pa that runs the taxi firm. She ain't never known her real one.' It was one of the things that had softened his heart; Meggie's confession that she'd first come up to Bernhardt Court in search of Richie Palmer.

Gertie's expression changed again. She refused to show any interest. 'You call that going through a lot? I call it landing on your feet. She never goes short of nothing, does she?'

'Her real pa ran off, though. That's hard.'

'Yes, and your poor pa died queuing up for a football match, killed in the crush, never came home again —'

'I know that!'

'And stepfathers don't grow on trees

round here, so we soldiered on, right?'

He nodded. Old wounds soon opened. 'Neither do girls like Meggie,' he said.

There was an air raid that Saturday evening, but it was lighter than usual. Several German planes were brought down in dogfights and many of the fire-bombs missed their mark. It seemed true what they said, that Hitler was turning his attentions elsewhere. After a couple of hours down the shelters, the all-clear sounded and people emerged.

'Too late to open up again, thank God!' Annie looked at the big wall clock above the door in the bar. She sounded and looked tired to death. 'George, tell Hettie that it's safe to bring Edie upstairs. See if she needs any help.' The evening had left her drained; the scuffle with Morell, the discovery of poor Edie, the air raid.

Earlier they'd fetched the doctor.

'Don't worry, she'll live,' he'd told Tommy as he brought Edie round. 'No bones broken, some concussion, contusions, superficial cuts. Nothing that will cause any permanent damage.' He'd made her comfortable on her own bed, insisted that Hettie should stay to keep an eye on things. 'Keep her quiet,' he'd advised. 'And if you bring in the police, don't let them pester her until tomorrow at the earliest.'

Edie had overheard. 'No police,' she'd implored Hettie.

'We know who did it.' Tommy had escorted the doctor downstairs. 'Her old man that was.'

'It's like that, is it? Not so much *cherchez la femme* as give her a good hiding.' In his experience, it would be of little use to involve the police, then. The women never brought charges. He'd noted Tommy as the other man in the case. 'Take care; this assailant knew precisely what he was doing. He used just enough force, not too much. I expect he wanted to teach her a lesson.'

'It's the last time he'll lay a finger on her!' Tommy had vowed.

'But not the first?' The doctor had stood in the shattered street, looking up at the blue sky. Violence came in many shapes and forms. He thought he heard the distant drone of aeroplanes, then the sirens had begun to wail. 'Get her to a shelter as quick as you can.' He'd shaken hands and climbed into his car. Tonight would be no different from any other; why should it?

So Tommy and Hettie had called on Rob to bring his cab and take Edie on the short journey from her flat to the Duke, where they'd helped her straight down to the cellar, trying their best to ignore how she looked, but failing to hide their shock. Edie trembled from head to foot, her hands and arms were cut and bruised, she had marks high on her cheekbones and across her brow. One eye was swollen and closed.

'Where's Tommy?' she'd pleaded. 'Make him stay here with me.' They'd bolstered her with cushions and pillows, wrapped her in blankets.

Reluctantly he'd been brought down to the shelter. It was as if he couldn't trust himself to look at her. 'Hettie will take care of you. And Annie and Sadie. They're all here now.'

But she'd flung her arms around his neck. 'Don't go back up.' She was thinking of him and how he would ignore the sirens and scour the streets for Bill.

He'd held her tight, then unwound her arms. The others retreated to the far corners of the shelter to give them privacy. 'Edie — darling!'

'I don't care!' She'd held onto his hands. 'Leave him be, Tommy. He's only got forty-eight hours, then he'll be gone. We'll be rid of him. Please!'

'And then what?' He'd forced himself to talk it through, squashed down a burning anger that made him want to kill Morell. 'Until next time? You don't think he'll ever leave us alone, do you?'

'Not now, Tommy, I need you here.' She'd sobbed helplessly.

'I can't, Edie. I have to go.' He'd stroked her hair, her bruised, wet face. 'I have to find him.'

'Take someone with you.' She'd turned and called out to Hettie. 'Make George keep an eye on him!'

Hettie had gone and stooped over her. 'He's on duty. So's Walter.'

'They can keep a look out.'

Hettie had agreed. 'They can try.' They were already risking their necks up there this very minute, but Edie was beside herself.

At last Tommy had unfastened himself from Edie's grasp, nodded at Hettie to take over, and run from the shelter. That was the last they saw of him. The women had sat and waited for the all-clear, wondering what part of town would be bombed this time, imagining the firestorms up above, praying that it wouldn't be them.

'Take Edie upstairs to Ernie's room,' Annie told Hettie after the raid. 'Leave the lamp lit. We'll be up in a few minutes.'

They carried her there as best they could.

Walter came in from the street soon after, his face blackened, lined and weary. 'They got Sadie's factory,' he reported. 'But we got eight of their planes.'

'Any sign of Bill Morell?' Annie asked. She lifted the takings from the till and locked them safe in the strongbox, ready to carry it upstairs.

Walter shook his head. 'Looks like he went to ground.' After they'd carted him from the pub, no one had clapped eyes on him. Now, with Tommy roaming around looking, it was as if they had an unexploded bomb on their hands. 'Tommy swears he'll get even. We couldn't get him down a shelter for love nor money.'

'I ain't surprised,' Annie sighed. 'Have you seen the state of Edie?'

'How is she?'

'Sadie and Hettie are settling her down for the night. But she won't get a wink of sleep, not until Tommy comes back.'

'Sadie neither,' he confessed. 'She's worried about Meggie.' He stood, tin hat under his arm, desperately weary. It was nearly midnight and he longed for his bed.

'Tell her to stop worrying.' Annie was pleased to deliver the one good piece of news. 'Meggie just telephoned to say she was safe. Ronnie's putting her in a taxi to send her back right this minute. So Sadie can take you home and give you a nice hot cup of Horlicks, Walter Davidson. And who says you don't deserve it?'

'See them stars?' Ronnie asked. Meggie and he walked as one. The streets were empty after the air raid, the sky clear. 'It's like that at sea. I look up at the stars and I think of you.'

'Me too.'

'Then we're linked, even when we're apart, now I know you're watching them too.' The same stars, the same heart. They walked by the pale grey walls of St Martin's.

'Why does it have to be so hard?' She held both arms around his waist as they walked, leaning into him, looking up at the sky.

'It ain't. It's easy.' He knew what she meant, though. 'Forget it, Meggie. The more people say we should take things easy, the more I know I don't want to. Funny, that.' His chin rested on her soft hair, his arms folded around her. 'Listen, I've been thinking.'

An empty taxi came by. It rolled on towards Trafalgar Square. Up above, the sky was midnight blue, scattered with tiny points of white light.

'Meggie, you and me should get married.'
She clung tightly to him, kept on walking.
'You hear?'
She nodded. 'When?'
'Next time I get home on leave.'
'Without saying anything?' It was a step into space, into the unknown.
'They'd only say no.'
'Yes,' she agreed. They would summon all their old reasons.
'We can get a train to Gretna. When we come back, we'll be married.'
'And no one will be able to un-marry us!'
'We'd be legal and above board. Then they'd have to fall in with us. What do you say?'
It was breathtaking. It was an enormous step. 'You mean it?' She stopped and took him by the hand.
'I don't want to listen to them going on no more, Meg. I just want you.' He drew her in, kissed her, literally swept her off her feet. 'Do you want me?'
'Yes.'
'Will you marry me?'
They were surrounded by dangers; by torn buildings, bombs, separation. But theirs was an island that no one could invade. It was a star out there in the heavens.
'Yes.' She kissed his breath away. They

411

would put up barricades, keep out the world.

At last Meggie went home in her taxi, floating on a cloud of happiness. Duke Street was quiet, and so was Paradise Court. The blackout made the houses look dead, but silver light poured down from the sky as she slotted her key into the lock and went inside. The clock ticked on the mantelpiece beside a framed photograph of Bertie and Geoff. Her mother had left a note on the table. 'Dearest Meg, Knock on our bedroom door to let us know you're back.' Signed 'S', with a heart, her mother's unvarying mark.

The tears welled up. Meggie sat and wept with joy, head resting on the table beside her mother's note.

'What is it?'

She felt a gentle hand on her shoulder. Sadie stood in her nightgown, hair brushed back, her face washed clear of the day.

Meggie stood up to embrace her.

'What's wrong?' Sadie stroked the back of her head.

'Nothing. Ma, Ronnie and me want to get married.' She confessed it all. 'I'm so happy. I love him, Ma, and he loves me.'

CHAPTER TWENTY

Walter switched on the early morning news broadcast. Bristol had been hit hard, and Cardiff. There was a nationwide call for extra blood donors. Production of Hurricanes and Spitfires was to be stepped up yet again.

'Not in your factory, it won't.' He told Sadie about the direct hit of the night before. She was already up, looking pale and tired. Another sleepless night. 'Why not phone Jess and check on the boys?'

'I did that yesterday.' Sadie picked at her breakfast of toast and marmalade. 'I spoke to Maurice. He said Jess has gone up to Coniston for the weekend. Everyone's fine. Except Mo finally got his papers from the RAF. He'll be in uniform this time next week.'

Walter nodded. Within their own four walls they were past the stage of commenting on the rakish glamour of the boys in pilots' uniform and their heroic role. Statistics had leaked out on the number of British fliers lost in the Battle of Britain. Never was so much owed by so many to so few, maybe.

But if those few happened to be your own flesh and blood . . .

'Maurice says Jess is worried sick.'

'She ain't the only one.' He studied Sadie across the table. 'There's something eating you and all.'

Sadie pushed away her plate. She rolled her eyes at the sound of Meggie's footsteps coming downstairs. 'I'll tell you later.'

Meggie breezed in, ready to go off and spend the day with Ronnie. She wore her prettiest summer dress, a white, cap-sleeved one with a flared skirt and tucks and gathers in the bodice. Her hair shone with coppery glints, simply tied at the nape of her neck.

'Has anybody seen my little pearl ear-rings?' She felt carefully along the mantel-piece. 'I thought I left them here.'

'They're in the box on your dressing table. I moved them when I was dusting.' Sadie's voice was expressionless. She stood up and went to look out of the window onto the tiny brick back yard.

'Never mind.' Meggie stood on tiptoe to catch more of her reflection in the mirror above the mantelpiece. 'I have to meet Ron-nie at nine. I'd better dash.'

'On an empty stomach?' Sadie didn't look round. 'And you need a cardigan, just in case.'

'No, it's a lovely day.' The midnight sky had turned to eggshell blue.

'It'll be a scorcher,' Walter confirmed. 'It was on the weather forecast.'

'They could be wrong, couldn't they?' Sadie argued for the sake of it. Headstrong Meggie would go her own way.

'Where are you meeting him?' The sight of his stepdaughter so excited made Walter smile.

'Up at the bridge.'

He offered her a lift. 'Hop in, I've got the cab outside. I'll take you there.' He also wanted to tour round the neighbourhood to look at recent bomb damage.

Meggie scrambled to find her shoes and handbag while Sadie, her face still closed off, cleared the table. 'I won't be back till late, Ma. No need to wait up.'

'What's there to do till late on a Sunday?'

Meggie was bubbling, doing everything at high speed. ' "That's fine, Meggie. Have a lovely time!" ' She rebuked her mother for being a killjoy. 'It's his only full day. He goes back tomorrow dinnertime.'

And Sadie had to relent. She kissed Meggie's cheek and saw her off from the front doorstep. Meggie stepped into Walter's cab, eager to be gone. Sadie, watching them go up the court onto Duke Street, stood in the long morning shadows cast by the old houses, and came to a decision of her own.

An East Ender by birth, Sadie rarely visited the broad squares and terraces of central London, where the building lacked a human dimension. It was as if they were designed expressly to impress and intimidate and keep at bay the humble visitor who might stray across the river from the courts and alleyways of Southwark. But she made her way undeterred, a slight figure in a grey tailored two-piece, wearing a black hat with a curled brim, rehearsing the speech she would make when she arrived on Gertie Elliot's doorstep.

Approaching Shaftesbury Avenue via Piccadilly Circus, Sadie left behind the capital's monumental arches, its imperial statues, splendid galleries and museums, and entered the, to her, equally foreign world of theatreland. Sunday mornings meant empty streets, and space to notice the drabness behind the billboards and hoardings. These buildings wept soot down their carved and convoluted frontages, the pigeons showed them no respect from the crowded ledges, and the clear, bright air painted them in an unflattering light. Shattered windows had been boarded up, roadblocks erected across badly-bombed streets, dust left to lie in doorways, silting up pavements, drifting across wide streets in a flurry of summer breezes. Pages from an old newspaper lifted and blew around Sadie's ankles. Still, The Lyric, The Apollo, Queen's soldiered on.

If Sadie had been in two minds when she decided to pay a visit to the Bell earlier that morning, she had been through dozens of twists and turns since then. For one thing, how would she feel if the shoe was on the other foot and Gertie turned up unannounced in Paradise Court? For another, ought she not to have consulted Walter first? Then again, she risked denting Meggie's shining happiness by interfering. Gertie Elliot was bound to put her foot down over the harum-scarum plan to get married, and Sadie wouldn't blame her. Between them, the two mothers should form a countermovement to steady things down and make the young people behave more sensibly. It was crucial that they didn't rush into something they might later regret.

Sadie wove in and out of side streets, a frown of concentration on her face. She'd come partly because she wanted to understand what Gertie held against Meggie; was it only that she was too young for Ronnie, or that she knew something about him that

417

set her against the whole romance? Perhaps he had another girl to whom he was promised; something in his past that Meggie knew nothing about. She must go very carefully, Sadie decided. She would introduce herself and open up the general topic of Ronnie and Meggie; see how the land lay before she mentioned the bombshell news.

Bernhardt Court, squeezed between the high, blank wall of the theatre and a row of small shops and eating places, had the same ghost town feel as the rest of the West End on a summer Sunday morning. Blinds were down, windows shuttered. A disconsolate lad shouldering a ladder and wearing faded blue overalls ambled ahead of her, a woman stood in a doorway smoking a cigarette.

It was an easy matter to find the Bell by the sign over the door. The publican's daughter in Sadie approved of the newly washed leaded windows, the scrubbed doorstep, the polished brass door handles. It was a small but well-kept place, barred and bolted to the world at this time of day, but inviting looking all the same. She peered above street level at the living quarters, where the windows were open and the net curtains shifting in the breeze.

'Who do you want?' The boy in overalls had propped his ladder against a neighbouring wall. He asked out of idle curiosity, as a way of putting off whatever he had to do.

'Gertie Elliot,' she said quietly. There didn't seem to be an entrance round the side, or any way round the back. She saw that brewery deliveries were made down a shute to one side of the main door.

The boy swung the peak of his cap back from his forehead and yelled up at one of the open windows. 'Gert, you're wanted!'

Sadie took a step back from the raucous cry. It had practically split her eardrums and spoiled her carefully prepared entrance.

'She's in,' the boy assured her. 'I seen her doing the steps.'

Soon there were footsteps in the tiled hall, the sound of bolts being drawn back. Then the shiny black door opened and a grey head, a lined face with long moustaches peered out.

'Shankley, tell Gertie she's wanted, will you.' The lad spoke with the volume permanently turned up.

Reddening under the old man's scrutiny, Sadie gave the boy a few coppers to get rid of him. Meanwhile, Shankley opened the door wide, and Sadie could see beyond the man's small frame into an inner porch and a bar room lined with photographs.

'Wanted, who by?' Shankley took his time

while Gertie did her face and hair. He knew she wasn't keen on letting strangers in out of hours. As it happened, he'd called in early to lend a hand, as he sometimes did these days. According to Gertie, Ronnie was worse than useless when he came home, spending all his time with the little girl from Southwark.

'I'd like to see Mrs Elliot.' Sadie spoke firmly. She hadn't come all this way to be turned away by a go-between.

'You don't say.'

'Could you tell her, please?'

'I could if you give your name.'

'Sadie Davidson.'

Shankley chewed this over. The name meant nothing, but he was beginning to see something familiar under the smart black hat, behind the formal approach. Take them away, subtract twenty years from the age, and you had a young Meggie.

'It's all right, Shanks, ask her in.' Gertie had been eavesdropping. She came slowly downstairs and stood staring at Sadie. 'Lock the door, will you. We'll be in the bar.' Leading the way, she gestured Sadie to follow.

Though Meggie had set up an image of Gertie in her mother's mind of a woman young for her age, popular with her customers and game for a laugh, Sadie found she was still startled by coming face-to-face. It was true, her looks placed her well below what must be her real age of forty-something, but she was not so much young as ageless. To appear young she would have needed an air of vulnerability, an artlessness, which Gertie lacked. In fact, she was all art, from her rich chestnut hair piled high on her head, to her painted lips and nails, her nipped-in waist and high heels. And she was in charge. She showed no surprise, little curiosity, except to appraise Sadie's own appearance and to decide, no doubt, that she, Gertie, was wearing the better of the two.

'What will you have? Sherry?' The landlady offered Sadie a chair at a table by the window.

'Nothing, thanks. I wanted to have a talk about Meggie and Ronnie, and since they haven't seen fit to introduce us, I took things into my own hands.'

'Well, you're only young once.' Gertie took an unopened packet of cigarettes from the bar and offered one to Sadie. When she refused this too, she lit up for herself and sat cross-legged on a high stool, some distance away. 'You know what they're like.'

'I know what *I* was like at their age.'

'Exactly. No one has ever been in love before, tra-la!' Gertie's wide lips spread into a smile. 'Tell them it was the end of the world and they wouldn't take a blind bit of notice.'

'I don't know if you know it, but Ronnie is Meggie's first boyfriend.' Sadie led things forward. Gertie seemed noncommittal, waiting for her to make the moves. 'She's fallen for him in a pretty big way.'

The eyebrows flicked up. 'It'll pass, don't you worry.'

Sadie allowed herself a smile. 'Try telling Meggie that.'

'It will, though.' She'd seen it all before, she gave Sadie to understand. 'Does Meggie know you're here?'

Quickly Sadie shook her head. 'She'd wring my neck.'

'So, what do you want to know? Ronnie's taken up with your daughter. There ain't much I can do about that, is there?' Gertie held her cigarette at an elegant angle, clicking her long thumbnail against the nail of her third finger.

'And how serious is he?'

'Blimey!'

'No, I need to know.' She wouldn't be thrown off course by Gertie's scorn.

'He writes her letters, don't he? How

should I know, for God's sake?' Sadie's ear-
nestness irritated her. She reached for a
drink of the sherry that she'd offered her
visitor. 'Listen, I take it you're worried
about your girl getting in too deep? But if
you take my advice, you'll let things ride,
see if they cool down.' She wished she'd
followed this line herself with Ronnie. Instead, she'd forced his attention onto
Meggie all the more by moaning and wailing
on.

'I already tried that,' Sadie let on. 'I took
a back seat, thinking the usual things; it's
her first time, she's bound to fall hard, then
she'll pull herself together and take a good
look at what she wants out of life.'

'She will. Give her a chance.' Meggie
hadn't been the first girl to fall head over
heels for Ronnie.

'The trouble is, it's the war. It flings them
together and pulls them apart. It ain't natural.'

Gertie's determination to underplay the
strength of feeling between the young couple
began to falter. 'What are you trying to say,
that you think this is the real thing?'

Sadie shook her head. 'It don't matter
what I think. It's what they think that
counts.'

'Listen.' Gertie came down from her

stool. 'Have you tried talking some sense into her?'

Sadie sighed. 'Talking to Meggie ain't easy. She's a good girl, but she's got a mind of her own. What am I supposed to say? Ronnie Elliot ain't the one for you. I don't know that, do I? That's why we needed to have a talk.'

Gertie came and sat at the table, silent and troubled.

'Well, is he?'

Gertie stared hard. 'Is that it? You came to check up on Ronnie through me?'

'For a start.' By now Sadie wanted everything out in the open. If there were real problems to sort out, she must give Gertie the full picture.

'And then what?'

'Meggie let something slip last night, poor girl. She came home in a state, sobbing and hugging me, saying your Ronnie's asked her to marry him.'

Gertie stubbed out her cigarette with a violent twist. 'Come again?'

'He never told you, did he? I didn't think he had.' Sadie studied her. 'It was last night. She was beside herself, otherwise I'd never have got to hear. Ronnie's talking about the two of them eloping together.'

'Over my dead body.' Gertie stood up

and paced the floor. 'Has he gone out of his mind, for God's sake?' She noticed Shankley appear at the door in response to her raised voice, and went and closed it in his face. 'You're sure about this? She ain't making it up?'

'I'm cast-iron certain.' Once again Sadie was thrown. Gone was Gertie's hard shell, her tough air of knowing the ways of the world. There was panic in her eyes.

'You ain't gonna let her?' She came and leaned over the table, arms braced, eyes staring. 'She's too young, ain't she? Sixteen —'

'Seventeen, going on eighteen.'

'Seventeen. She's throwing her life away. What about her job?'

'I don't know. They haven't thought it through. All I know is what I'm telling you, they plan to get married.'

Gertie shook her head. 'Well, you'd better stop her.'

'What about you?' A new idea dawned on Sadie. She too stood up. 'Look, he ain't got a wife already, has he? It ain't nothing like that?' Something, she didn't know what, had appalled Ronnie's mother. 'What's so bad about Meggie marrying him?'

'I can't say. It ain't right, that's all. I feel it in my bones.' She pulled away as Sadie tried to take her by the arm. 'Tell her Ronnie don't mean it. His mouth ran away with him, you know how it is.'

'You mean, he only wants her to think . . . ?' It was Sadie's turn to be shocked.

'That's what men do. They make promises.'

'And don't keep them?' Sadie wanted to fly out of the door to rescue her daughter. 'Are you saying he's that sort?'

'Maybe, maybe . . . he could get himself into that sort of fix. Anyone could.' Gertie held onto this idea. It put him in a bad light, it was true, but it was possible that Ronnie was playing this game, keeping Meggie dangling on a string.

'If he's done that, I'll . . .' Sadie was speechless.

'Yes, and if your girl's been fool enough to fall for it!' Gertie's hardbitten defences were back up. She crossed the room to the door. 'Let's keep a cool head. You go home and give her a talking to when she gets back. I'll try and find out what Ronnie's up to.'

Sadie collected her hat and bag with trembling hands. She felt sick, she felt a fool. Like Meggie, she'd taken Ronnie's proposal at face value. Now his mother was exposing it as an age-old trick. Before she left, she gathered her dignity.

'It's true Meggie's only young,' she told Gertie on the doorstep. 'But she ain't a fool. If Ronnie's stringing her along, she'll see it in time, believe me. She knows lies when she hears them, and she's been brought up proper.' She fixed her hat on angrily. It was more than could be said for some, she implied.

'Then there's nothing to worry about, is there?' Gertie closed the door on Sadie. She leaned back against it, felt the blood drain from her face. She'd tried with all her might to keep Ronnie and Meggie apart, but in vain. It was time to think again, before it was too late.

Tommy waited all night in Edie's empty flat for Morell to show his face, but he was meant to stew in his own juice, it seemed. The hours crawled by. Tommy went from room to room, waiting, listening, until it grew too much to bear. He went outside into a grey dawn light and hunted for him in the streets, with the idea that Morell might have drunk himself into a stupor and was lying senseless in a doorway, or slumped at a table in an all-night speakeasy. For an hour or so he turned up no clues; Morell hadn't been seen since Walter and George had thrown him out of the Duke. Tommy

427

knew every corner, every back alley of Southwark. They were the haunts of his childhood; the railway embankments, the arches, the cathedral close.

'Take it easy, Tommy,' Walter Davidson advised, off duty but cruising round in his cab. He pulled in at the kerbside and called him over.

'How's Edie?'

'Sleeping, finally. I just called in. Hettie says she had a bad night.'

'Have you seen Morell?'

'No, and if I had I wouldn't tell you.' Walter recognized Tommy's shortening fuse. 'You'll get yourself killed if you're not careful.'

'Bleeding coward.' Tommy walked on. Walter's taxi crawled alongside. 'He batters a woman, but when it comes to a fair fight, where is he?'

'Winding you up, Tommy. Biding his time.'

'If you see the swine, tell him I'm ready and waiting. And I'll track him down like a dog if he doesn't come to me.' Already he planned to get up to Paddington in time for the departure of the Glasgow train. Morell had to be on that, come what may.

'And help you put your head in the noose?' Walter gave up trying to talk reasonably. He drove off, shaking his head, while Tommy went on scouring the streets.

By midday, his mood had set into a bitter, reckless determination. The anger died down only after Tommy had managed to eliminate from his mind the picture of Edie lying injured on the bed. He wouldn't call in to see her until all this was over. What he felt now was a cold desire to get even by using Morell's own methods. He imagined his fists thudding into that thick jaw, his feet kicking his ribs once he'd got him down.

Coming into Meredith Court at the bottom end by the factory, Tommy decided to scale the embankment for a good vantage point over the rows of terraces below. The railway line ran at roof level; once he'd scrambled up, he would be able to see much of what was going on to either side.

Come on, Morell! He lit up a cigarette and studied the streets. A couple of kids played a skipping game on one corner, a salvage man drove his horse and cart past piles of rubble. Catching sight of a dark figure nip into one of the railway arches over Duke Street, Tommy's skin crawled with the sensation of cat-and-mouse. Instinct told him the figure was Morell. Without stopping to think, he threw away the fag and raced down the bank, slipping, sliding, once losing his footing as he ran. But when he reached the spot, the arch was empty. It ran back for twenty yards, stacked with old oil drums and petrol cans, ending in a derelict workshop; perhaps a small iron works or blacksmiths. Tommy walked cautiously into the dead end, kicking aside loose bricks, rusting bits of iron and nails. The place smelt damp and disgusting, water dripped from the high arch, one of the workshop double doors hung half open.

'Morell!' Tommy's voice echoed. He'd yelled the name so often he didn't expect a response.

The door swung wide open, inviting him to enter.

'Swine!'

He picked up an iron bar from the floor of the yard and ran forward. Morell must be hiding behind the door. Tommy went for the window to one side, smashed it and leapt through. The smell hit him again, a filthy, dark smell of drains and mould. The roof of the workshop ran with dirty water which landed in a swamp of rotting wood and sludge. Tommy whirled round, looking for Morell.

'Up here.'

There was just enough light to see a ledge,

wide and high enough for Morell to stand on, reached by an eight-foot metal ladder attached to the wall. In a flash, Tommy had made it to the ladder and climbed up.

Morell waited. His idea was to stamp on Tommy's hands as he came within reach and cripple them. He raised his boot, towering overhead. But he caught only one hand, and Tommy ignored the pain. He swung himself up with his other arm to catch Morell by the ankles and topple him. Morell overbalanced, he slipped sideways, Tommy wrenched and they both fell to the sodden floor. They rolled, grabbing at one another's clothes, kicking and punching. Tommy's left hand was useless, Morell was powerful and used whatever came within reach. He seized an old sledgehammer and swung it, making Tommy dodge, and advanced slowly. It rang, metal against brick, as Morell missed. Tommy kicked at his opponent's knees and brought his legs from under him, seizing the hammer as it fell. Morell shielded his head, seeing the raised sledgehammer. He froze as Tommy pounded it down inches from one side of his face, then the other, down again, raining blows deliberately wide.

This was an unlooked-for chance, and Morell seized the reprieve. The hammer was heavy and clumsy as Tommy raised it above his head, Morell spun round in the dirt and rolled against him. They were both down again, but Morell was up first, dragging Tommy after him out into the yard, landing punches as Tommy put up his one good hand to defend himself. Morell slogged relentlessly, knowing that Tommy had let him off the hook once, determined to beat him to a pulp before he could regain the advantage.

Tommy felt the blows come thick and fast. One landed him against an oil drum, which rolled and oozed black liquid. Then the kicks from Morell's boots; semi-darkness; another kick to the head. The sounds of clashing metal cans, the smell of petrol engulfed him as Tommy tried to open his eyes. Legs astride, Morell tore off a cap from a rusty petrol can and sloshed it over him. Tommy felt it soak through his clothes, smelt the fumes, felt them catch in his throat, saw Morell back off, as he floated in and out of consciousness. Now that he'd doused Tommy in petrol, Morell intended to keep a safe distance.

He drew a lighter from his pocket. Tommy would go up like a torch; no evidence, nothing. He searched for a rag or a scrap of paper dry enough to use as a firebrand. He went back into the workshop, leaving his victim unconscious in the yard. There was a cupboard in there, tucked away behind the door. Morell wrenched it open, ignoring the fractured pipes and torn wiring which lay open to view. He found what he needed: an old pair of overalls which he tore to shreds and twisted into a rough cord. He took it to the workshop door. Tommy had come round and was slithering towards him, heaving himself along the ground with his elbows, caked in petrol-soaked mud.

Morell held out the makeshift torch, ready to light it. The silver lighter lay flat and smooth in his palm. He took it and put it to the end of the rag. When it caught light and began to blaze, he would fling it at the crawling figure. Morell's hand was steady. He pressed with his broad thumb, the flint clicked and sparked. Gas from the fractured pipe ignited all around.

Through a haze, Tommy saw a flash of blue flame turning yellow, heard the explosion, covered his head. When he looked up from behind the rolling oil drums there was no Morell, no workshop, only a fireball at the end of the arch, and the sound of glass shattering in the heat.

CHAPTER TWENTY-ONE

'Princess for a day!'

Ronnie promised Meggie anything she wanted. Was it to be Maurice Chevalier at the Tivoli, or Fred Astaire at the Regal? A touch of luxury for his girl; the chromium and gilt, the lush carpets and padded seats, the coloured flashing lights of the Wurlitzer and its booming notes to wow the audience out of its drab reality.

She *felt* like a princess; everything paid for; waited on hand and foot. Ronnie was flash with his money, and his Navy uniform inspired goodwill in the waitresses who served in the tea-room, in the cinema usherettes and in the bar staff in the pub which they visited late that evening before Ronnie finally put her in a cab and sent her home. Next day, Monday, he had half a day before he caught his train back to Plymouth.

'Meet me,' he pleaded, running alongside the taxi as it launched into the stream of traffic on Regent Street.

'Where?' She leaned out of the window to blow kisses.

'Come to the Bell.'

'What about your ma?'

'She can lump it.' He yelled and waved. A second taxi squealed its brakes and swerved as he leapt sideways out of its path. 'Say yes!'

'Yes.' She mouthed the word in case he couldn't hear, waved until he was out of sight, lost among the trams and buses, then sat back in her seat with a sigh. She would call in sick at work with a summer cold, would croak a message into the phone; what good was a telephonist without a voice? Then she would get the tube to Shaftesbury Avenue and brazen it out with Gertie. She'd given Ronnie her word.

Back home, the talk was all of Tommy O'Hagan's narrow escape. Hettie had called on Sadie with the news that Bill Morell had blown himself up in a jealous bid to finish Tommy off. The story was confused; Tommy had managed to crawl to Duke Street from one of the old archway workshops, a passer-by had found him in a terrible condition and got word to the ARPs that there was someone else inside the inferno that blazed there.

'Morell never stood a chance,' Hettie reported as Meggie came in.

'It sounds like he never gave Tommy

435

much of one neither.' Sadie was dead against Morell after what he'd done to Edie.

'Still.' Hettie's was the only charitable voice on the street. 'No one deserves to die like that.' She sat back in an easy chair, eyes closed for a few moments, until she heard Meggie arrive. 'Here's love's young dream.' She turned her head and smiled.

'Don't you go encouraging her,' Sadie warned. She was back in her everyday clothes of blouse and skirt after her morning's smart excursion. Time for reflection had convinced her that she and Meggie must have another serious talk, but not until things had calmed down after Ronnie had gone back to his ship. Meggie was still buoyed up by the thrill of his proposal; her eyes were bright, a smile played across her lips, she seemed hardly to notice what went on under her nose.

'It don't look as if she needs encouragement.' Hettie was glad that romance could still blossom, against all the odds. She'd heard that marriages were on the increase because of the war; couples were queuing up at the church doors and registry offices. Wives of twenty-four hours' standing were seeing their husbands off at railway stations up and down the country.

'You're her godmother. Talk some sense

into her.' Sadie smiled in spite of herself. 'I'll put the kettle on and make us a cuppa.' Walter would soon be in from firewatch. There'd been no siren so far this evening; perhaps for once they would get a night off.

Meanwhile, Hettie told Meggie the street news. 'Edie's in a state of shock, of course. But Annie and me can take care of her. She keeps on saying it's all her fault.'

'Has Tommy been to see her?' Meggie curled up in a chair by the hearth. She felt for Edie and Tommy, wondered what she would have done in Edie's position.

'He came in for a bit. But she's not in a fit state for much talking, poor thing. When you think of how she is as a rule, a tower of strength, it makes you want to cry along with her.'

'But she'll get better?' this sounded worse than Meggie had thought.

'The doctor says she'll mend. We'll have to wait and see. Tommy's better off, but he looks a sight too. His face is all bruised, and they think he's broken some bones in his hand. He's gone to stay with Jimmie at Rob and Amy's place, so they can look after him for a bit. Amy's threatening to feed him up. Stew and dumplings, just what the doctor ordered.'

Gradually the repercussions of Morell's

violent rampage would settle and form a new pattern. Hettie had seen enough of the world not to suppose that she could predict what this might be. It would take time for Edie to calm down and decide what she wanted to do next. Tommy had risked everything for her, but it didn't follow that they would slide smoothly into living together again in Edie's flat. Hettie suspected that Edie's conscience might play her up. Poor Tommy. She sighed, while Meggie came across, put her arms around her neck and gave her a kiss.

'What was that for?' She squeezed her niece's arm.

'Just because . . .' She hugged her back. 'No tea for me, ta,' she told Sadie, who had returned with the tray. She went up to bed, brought closer to earth by Hettie's all-embracing kindness, but still her dreams were full of Ronnie; the thrill of his touch, the sorrow of parting.

For once, Gertie wasn't displeased to see Meggie land on her doorstep early next morning. It was time to take things in hand and though she balked at the idea of destroying Ronnie's happiness, she was old enough to know that people got over the pangs of parting; that feelings however intense did die down in time. What seemed like tragedy today would turn tomorrow to odd moments of quiet regret.

Sending Ronnie off to the bank with the weekend's takings, she enlisted Meggie to help stack shelves behind the bar. It gave her the opportunity she needed, beginning with a no-nonsense manner to squeeze the emotion out of the situation. She thought she could appeal to Meggie's intelligence.

'I've been thinking . . .' She handed bottles from the crate to Meggie, who stood on a small stepladder. 'You know you put in an appearance all them months ago looking for Richie Palmer?'

Meggie's hands clenched around the bottles at the sound of his name.

'You asked Shankley about him, from what I gather?'

She nodded. Now she recalled the intensity of her search for her real pa as if it was a journey through a different lifetime. Since Ronnie had taken over her heart, she'd given Richie almost no space. There was room for only one obsession. But Gertie's reminder sent a flicker of guilt through her.

'Shankley said you should leave well alone.' Gertie pressed on with lifting bottles. A slanting summer sun threw bright shafts of light across the mahogany table tops, filtered red and green through the ornate leaded windows.

'Yes, and so did you too.' Meggie spoke not much above a whisper. The bottles clinked against one another.

'I didn't want you getting upset. And I couldn't think what a nice girl like you would want with a type like that.'

Meggie tried to guess what was coming. Shankley and Gertie had obviously put their heads together over it. She bet that he'd gone and blabbed the connection between her and Richie.

'That's right.' Gertie read her shifting expressions and helped her down from the steps. 'I can see it all; you hear a story that Richie Palmer is your pa. You're dead set on tracking him down. It's only natural. You land up here, then the trail goes cold. In the end, you have to let someone in on why you want to find him. That someone lets it drop in conversation with me. That's how I find out.'

For the first time Meggie felt some shame about her connection with the down-and-out. 'I only wanted to see him, nothing else.'

'And to let him get an eyeful of you?' Gertie took hold of Meggie's hand. 'Let him see what he missed.'

'Maybe.'

'He threw it all away, didn't he?'

Meggie was swept away on the tide of memory. 'I saw him once, ages ago, in the shelter down Tottenham Court Tube. I think he saw me!'

'And knew you?' Gertie looked doubtful. 'He never slapped eyes on you, did he?'

'Only when I was a little baby. But I look like my ma. Everyone says we're the spitting image.'

Gertie would have confirmed this, only she knew better than to include Sadie's visit in the picture.

'At any rate, it's no good. Everyone clams up when I mention him.' Meggie withdrew her hand and turned away. Why bring it up now? Ronnie would be back in a few minutes and she wanted to enjoy the day.

'Like I say, I've been thinking.' Gertie took the plunge. She wanted to make a bargain. 'I'll come clean, Meggie. It's true Richie Palmer does hang around here on and off.'

'But you said . . .'

'That was then, before Shankley filled me in. Now I see it different.'

'How?'

'Well, what right have I got to keep father and daughter apart?' Her hypocrisy shamed even her, but she went on. 'I know you better now, and I think you've the right to know.'

Gradually Meggie began to see the size of this shift. If Gertie was sincere, and could truthfully lead her to Richie Palmer, one of her life's dreams could come true. She had visions of their meeting, of Richie coming to realize what he had thrown away, of him being brought back into the fold of respectability. Part romantic, part zealot, she had nurtured the dream. Now it blossomed into reality as Gertie unfolded her plan.

'Where is he? Where does he live?' It was Meggie's turn to seize Gertie's hand.

'Steady on. I can't drop everything on the spot; it ain't that simple.'

'But you know how to find him?'

'I do.'

'Well then?'

'I want you to do something for me first.' Gertie saw the doubt creep into Meggie's shining eyes. She steeled herself. 'You don't get something for nothing in this world. You know what I want.'

Meggie hung her head. 'I don't.'

'I want your promise to back off from Ronnie.'

'No.'

'Yes. Are you listening to me, Meggie? I'll show you where your pa is if you ease off from my son. That's fair enough.'

'No, it ain't.' Meggie sprang back. 'What kind of promise is that? Where's the sense in it?'

'All the sense in the world. Ronnie thinks he's in love with you, but he ain't seeing straight.' Gertie withstood Meggie's angry onslaught. She barred her way and tried to beat her down with cold logic.

'How do you know? You ain't got a clue how he feels; I do. You're jealous, you're a wicked woman to say he don't love me.'

'And you're seeing it all through rose-coloured glasses. You're flattered because he picked you out from all the rest. You fell for the uniform, you were putty in his hands.' She resorted to cliché to make Meggie see she was no different from the crowd.

'You don't know nothing about us!' Outrage choked her.

Gertie stared back, cold-eyed. 'Take it or leave it.'

'I'll tell Ronnie,' Meggie threatened.

'What good will that do you? Ronnie knows nothing about your pa. If you go to him, you're back to square one. Think about it.' She must use all her powerful presence to knock Meggie sideways. Her face gave nothing away. She waited.

443

'You're . . . wicked!' Meggie's feelings twisted and turned, came up against a dead-end.

'Who's it to be; Ronnie or your pa? You can't have both.'

'I can't give him up. Why do I have to?' She covered her face with her hands, began to sob.

'Because I want you to let go of him. That's so he can see out the war and come back home without you pulling him this way and that.'

'He won't want me to.' Meggie fought on.

'That's why you have to be the one to do it.' She hammered it home. 'Let him down gently and get what you can out of it for yourself.'

All her life she'd longed to know her father. Everything tilted and shifted inside her. Letting Ronnie go was unthinkable. Turning away from her father, who might need her and grow to love her, was too cruel. Once more she hid her face in her hands.

'You'll think about it?'

Silence meant that she would.

Hooked but not landed. Gertie would have to let it drop for now. 'Come and see me tomorrow.' Gertie left Meggie alone in the bar, vanishing upstairs as Ronnie came back from his errand, ready to whisk Meggie into town on a last flurry of treats before his leave ran out.

'A front is what it is all right.' Charlie Ogden reckoned he could see beneath the friendly spirit of co-operation that the politicians were so keen to promote. 'This so-called London Front; what do they know?'

'Better than being down in the mouth.' Dolly still preferred the party line. East Enders had played their part in seeing off the Huns in the First War with a gritty cheerfulness. Charlie's generation might scoff, but Annie and Dolly's lot believed in keeping their chins up.

'They make us out to be fools.' His mood was bitter. The summer was slipping away and still the cinema newsreels showed the ARPs steadily shovelling sand into sandbags, while Churchill appealed on the wireless for the tools to finish the job. 'Who do they think they're kidding?'

'Don't you go getting my dander up,' his mother warned.

'No, don't do that,' Annie agreed. 'That ain't what Mr Churchill means when he says go to it!' The long summer days slipped by, she pulled pints, listened to both sides of the endless arguments.

'We'd be better off sticking our heads in the sand instead of filling bags with it, for all the good they do.' More streets in Southwark had been torn to pieces this last week. No food was coming through the docks. America still kept out of it.

'For crying out loud, Charlie!' Even Dorothy had heard enough doom and gloom for one evening. It was true, Charlie got to see more of the down side going about his job with the homeless families. He came home with tales of panic and looting that never appeared on the cinema screens. But like Dolly, she thought it shouldn't be dwelt on. 'You'll be turning conchie next.'

'Everyone's doing their bit, ain't they? You should be grateful.' Dolly followed up like a dog with a bone.

'Not everyone. That's what they want you to think.' He understood the methods and purpose of propaganda, taking an interest in the slant given to events by the official Crown Film Unit. 'The truth is, a lot are out for themselves.'

'Not round here they're not.'

'Tommy is.' Dorothy couldn't resist a sly dig at her ex, who had just walked in. He was picking himself up in a slow way after losing the shop, working from his newspaper stall by the cathedral. 'He's making money hand over fist.'

'Ha ha.' Tommy ordered a drink before he went upstairs to visit Edie. He knew that Dorothy took an interest in his income, noticing that she had less to spend on her new outfits and make-up since the shop had gone up in smoke. Well, that was up to Charlie now.

'Seriously.' How else did he ride the shortages, unless he still had his fingers in the black market? In her opinion leopards never changed their spots.

He shrugged and joined in the war talk with Charlie. Tommy had no illusions either; it was a bad business when you heard that pilots in Bomber Command had only a one in three chance of coming through a tour of duty alive.

'I don't care what they say,' Dolly insisted. 'I ain't never been one to give in and I ain't about to start now.'

The debate spread through the pub; the pros and cons of patriotism, talk which might have shocked the government into realizing how out of touch they were with the hearts and minds of the people. On balance, however, opinion went with continuing to muddle through, for what was the alternative? These days, people were not so much pro-Churchill as anti-Hitler, that despised caricature of the Low cartoons.

When it came to it, the ordinary man and woman's individual concerns far outweighed any general problems. For instance, all the time Tommy spent jousting with Dorothy and chewing things over with Charlie was time taken away from being with Edie. At her side was where he longed to be. Yet he knew that he shouldn't crowd her during these weeks when she was recovering from her injuries and Morell's horrific death. She was still staying at the Duke, laid up more with mental than physical scars. Whenever he visited, she was pleased to see him, but her stamina was poor. She tired easily. Her face, which still bore traces of bruises and fading scars, would turn pale, and he would soon leave, going back to rebuilding his own life, working hard, drinking a little too much, waiting.

He was hanging on at the bar, wondering whether to go up, when Hettie came down to fetch him.

'She knows you're here, Tommy. She'd like to see you.'

He finished his drink. 'How is she?'

'The same. A bit brighter maybe.'

Tommy went up and knocked at the living room door. There was a balance to be struck between being gentle and robust. Too much sympathy seemed to weaken Edie's resolution to stay cheerful; too little made him appear unfeeling. In truth, he wanted to lock her in his arms and spend the rest of his life looking after her.

Edie smiled as he went in. She was dressed in a warm cardigan that disguised how thin she'd become. A magazine lay open but unread on her lap.

He stooped to kiss her cheek. 'You'll never guess what I went and did earlier today.'

'No, I won't.' Her expression said that she wouldn't put anything past him. 'So I won't even try.'

'I signed up with the Home Guard.'

'Tommy, you never!' She tried to imagine him making himself useful in Dad's Army.

'I'm meant to shoot enemy parachutists and control the traffic . . . it ain't that funny.' He pretended to look disgruntled. 'A man has to do his bit.'

'Better late than never.'

'Watch it.' He settled in a chair opposite, leaning forward. 'How have you been?'

'Fine.' Her answer didn't correspond with the faded look in her eye, or with Hettie's bulletins.

'Have you been eating?'

'Yes, don't keep on.'

With her sitting there, offering the evidence of his own eyes, he couldn't keep up the cheerful presence. 'Edie, I can't help it. I wish I could do something. Tell me what.'

The tears that were always near to the surface came and pricked her eyelids. 'There ain't nothing you can do. I have to do it myself.' When the bad dreams stopped flooding the night, when she could get rid of the last pictures of Bill burning to death in a fire she seemed to have set alight, and which, try as she might, she could not put out.

'What is it?' He reached to touch her hand.

'I can't explain.' It was an aching that she couldn't point to, a bruise under her heart.

'You don't still blame yourself?' If anyone, it was him. He was the one who had let her go home from the park alone. He was the one who had pushed Morell to the limit.

'I wish I could undo it all,' she cried. 'Get back to where I was before.'

This frightened him. 'Before we got together?'

'Before it all went wrong, Tommy.' The tears streamed down. 'I would do it different.'

'How?' He wanted to know if this was

rejection. Did she wish him out of her life?

Looking up through her tears she saw how she was hurting him. She rose to stop him from turning away, stumbling as she went to him, glad to be held in his arms. 'I don't mean you and me. That would be wishing my whole life away.'

Thank God. He stood holding her. Whatever else, she didn't want to lose him.

'But I wish I'd been brave enough.'

Tommy rocked her gently. 'To tell Bill right at the start? What chance did you get? It ain't your fault, Edie.'

Eventually the crying stopped. She kept her face hidden against his shoulder. 'Don't look at me.'

'You're breaking my heart, Edie Morell, I mean that.' Having to let go of her and walk away.

'I don't mean to.' She took out a handkerchief and began to pull herself together. 'I feel better now.' She eased away.

'You don't look it.'

'I do though. I've been thinking, Tommy . . .'

He took a short, wary step back.

'I am getting stronger. Hettie and Annie look after me; they spoil me to death. But I can't stay here forever.'

Here came another crunch then. He knew what he wanted her to say; that they could move back into the flat together. But he knew just as well that this wasn't what she had in mind.

'I want to go away for a little while.'

'From Duke Street?'

'Right away.'

'Where to?' For how long? Who with? Doubtful questions peppered his brain.

'I don't know yet. Out of London. As soon as I can get back on my feet. I haven't made any plans, but I feel that's what I want to do.' There were ways of making herself useful somewhere else; they were always asking for women for the munitions factories in the Midlands, or for the Land Army; twenty-eight shillings a week and already 90,000 strong.

'Want to, or ought to?'

'Both.' She twisted her handkerchief into a tight knot. 'Does it seem like I'm running away?'

'No.' He acknowledged her reasons. She needed space. 'No, it's the right thing for you, ain't it?' Ninety per cent of him wanted to yell at her for doing this; for making him miss her every second she would be away, for leaving him in doubt. Ten per cent said he had to let her go. Fear and trust, in those proportions. God knew, the small voice had to fight hard to get through.

But Edie loved him more, if that were possible. Later she told Annie her plan. She intended to get better as soon as possible now, to put the past behind her and give herself a new start. She began to check the War Office adverts in the newspapers, to eat properly and put on weight.

She would need her strength, Annie told her. 'You ain't no good to man nor beast looking the way you do now.'

'I'm tougher than you think.' A week after her talk with Tommy, Edie had insisted on helping behind the bar. Regulars made a point of saying how glad they were to see her back.

'That's the spirit.' Annie had great faith in her own sex. It wasn't brawn that mattered, but will-power. Edie had been through it all right, and Annie sympathized. She knew about violent husbands. Without wanting to rake up the past, she let Edie know that they had that experience in common, before she'd had the good fortune to marry Duke Parsons. 'You do whatever it is you need to do. You rushed into things once already. Now do it in your own time, at your own pace. I did when I married Duke. It was the best way.'

'But will Tommy understand? Will he wait?'

Annie said she wasn't a fortune teller. 'But it don't alter the facts. We'll keep an eye on Tommy here while you're away. Write to him if it makes you feel better. But put yourself first for a change.'

During the war, a small envelope could change lives. A hand-delivered telegram was brought to Jess and Maurice's house to inform them that their son had given his life in the skies over Dover on only his fourth operation in active service. They tried to see the glory; felt only the loss.

Mo was one young man among the thousands of aircrew whose names would join the list of warriors on war memorials and church walls throughout the land. Sadie travelled to Manchester to be with Jess, then the sisters went to Coniston at Maurice's insistence. A few days with Grace, Bertie and Geoff might help heal the wound.

Then there were Edie's letters to Tommy through the autumn of 1941. She landed up in a converted manor house in Somerset, working, to start with, in the apple orchards and helping with livestock as part of the Women's Land Army. The hostel looked posh from the outside, but was basic within.

Edie had to share a room with five others, the bunks were hard, the food plain. She learned to drive a truck in which she dropped off other Land Army girls at surrounding farms. Her uniform consisted of fawn corduroy britches, knitted stockings, a green pullover and a brown velour hat. They worked alongside prisoners of war, mucking out cow barns and collecting eggs. Was this the Edie who'd worked with him in the basement office? Tommy wondered. He couldn't make out exactly how she felt about her new life, though she came across in her letters as being fit and well. Tommy tried to be glad, even though he resented what she was putting him through.

Finally, there was the letter that Gertie said Meggie must write. Her judgment that the offer she'd made over Richie Palmer would eat into the girl's consciousness proved correct; now that Meggie was within arm's length of discovering her long-lost father, the desire to see him grew daily. True, it was a slow, uneven progress. First of all, Meggie had to get over the latest separation from Ronnie; the clinging on the station platform, the undying promises. No doubt their first exchange of letters had been passionate and tender.

But Meggie had returned to the Bell on

the Tuesday evening after his departure. She'd wheedled and implored Gertie to tell her all she knew without delivering the promise that she would give Ronnie up as fair exchange. This had gone on over several weeks, with no weakening on Gertie's part. Then the visits had dropped off; possibly another lovelorn letter from Ronnie had fallen onto the mat in Paradise Court. Gertie's patience was put to the test.

At the end of September, Meggie showed up again.

'Long time, no see.' Gertie stood behind the bar, expressing no surprise or relief.

Meggie felt a flash of hatred. 'You win.' This was all she could trust herself to say.

It was the pull of the past that Gertie had banked on. 'You'll give Ronnie up?'

'I said, you win.' Meggie stood buttoned up in her white mackintosh, a red scarf around her neck. She couldn't bring herself to say the words. 'When can I see my pa?'

'Hold on.' Gertie placed the towels over the pumps. It was mid-afternoon, a Saturday. After she'd gone and bolted the doors, she sat Meggie down at a table. 'How do I know you'll keep your word?'

'I'm giving you my promise.' Everything turned to ashes, even the words in her mouth. Meggie sat stiff and upright. The

456

notion of sacrifice had meant nothing until now.

'That ain't good enough,' Gertie said calmly. 'You have to write to Ronnie first. Tell him it's all over between you.'

Hot tears trickled from Meggie's eyes. Blackmail pure and simple.

'I'll fetch a pen and paper.' Gertie left her sitting there. In any other circumstance she would have relented at the sight of the girl marooned in the empty bar, trying to hold her head up, pressing her hand to her mouth and staring into space. 'Here. Tell him you don't want to see him no more. Say you've met someone else.' She put the paper flat on the table, laid the pen across it.

As Meggie wrote, it was as if she stepped outside her own life and she was someone else signing herself Meggie; telling Ronnie that she'd been hasty in making him so many promises, that she'd since listened to advice and decided it was too early to commit herself. It was best, she thought, if they decided to call it a day. She hoped he wouldn't be too disappointed, that he would come to see it her way. No matter how much Gertie urged it, Meggie refused to write that she'd found someone else.

Gertie took the letter and told her to address an envelope. It had to be done on the

457

spot. As soon as Ronnie received this, that would be it. No matter how much he thought he loved the girl, his pride would kick into action. His mother judged that he wouldn't come begging once he'd been jilted.

Gertie collected her coat and sealed the envelope herself. 'We'll post it on the way.'

'Why, where are we going?' Meggie ran to catch her out in the windswept court.

'I thought you wanted to see Richie Palmer?'

Meggie felt another jolt, a thud against her chest. She clutched her coat around her.

'Come on then.' Gertie slid Meggie's letter into the postbox on the corner of Charing Cross Road. It was over. *You shall see your father!* The fairytale princess was in tears again. 'Let's get it over and done with.'

CHAPTER TWENTY-TWO

'This place is the Sally Army without the Bible thumping. They set it up last year, after the ARPs started turning the tramps out of the ordinary shelters. Too drunk and rowdy, I expect.' Gertie picked her way along the dirty pavement that ran down the side of Charing Cross railway station. She led Meggie past the massive arches designed to support the Hungerford Bridge on its route across the river to Waterloo on the south bank.

Meggie shrank into herself. It wasn't the raw wind, nor the rattle and roar of trains passing overhead. It was the shapes of men huddling in dank brick alcoves, or shuffling towards them, talking to nobody, or swearing at thin air. Yet she tried to keep her spirits up, for this longed-for meeting.

'It's run by officers from the last war, out of the goodness of their hearts, I suppose.' Gertie knew her way around. She ignored the drunks and the madmen. 'Don't give them none of your change,' she warned Meggie. 'They'll only spend it on meths.'

'Is this where he lives?' Meggie looked up and down the dark tunnel. Numbered arches led off to left and right, heavy traffic thundered along the main, cobbled route; trucks delivering to warehouses set up under the arches, buses loaded with grim-faced passengers.

'If you can call it living.' Gertie prepared Meggie for even more of a shock than she might expect. 'He was in a bad way when he last came up the Court.'

'When was that?'

'Last time he was sober enough to find it.' She glanced at Meggie. 'A couple of weeks ago. Look, this ain't the place where they live. It's where they come if there's an air raid, because no one else will have them. There are bunks for them to sleep on, and they can keep warm, that's about it. I've brought you here to get news of him, see? With a bit of luck we'll get enough sense out of someone to track him down in one of his usual haunts.' A drunken man in filthy rags stepped from the pavement into the road. 'Then again . . .' Gertie frowned. She stopped outside arch number 176. 'You're sure you want to go ahead?'

Meggie nodded. There was no going back, not now the letter was in the post. She'd paid a terrible price to see this man.

'Come in. Welcome to the Hungerford Club.' Gertie walked ahead into the hostel for down-and-outs.

The Club reeked of institutions, disinfectant, boiled food and human odours scarcely kept at bay. An effort had been made, however. The high arched ceiling was painted cream, the tiered bunks, empty at present, were stacked with neatly folded grey blankets. Orderlies mopped out the urinals set apart from the dormitory area, others carried scrubbed metal urns from sink to tables in the canteen.

Soon a middle-aged man in a pin-striped suit approached. He introduced himself as Captain Wallace, made it clear that visitors were both unusual and unwelcome; especially smartly dressed women whose business was difficult to determine. His clipped 'May I help?' held undertones of 'Let's deal with this swiftly before it disrupts our routine.'

Gertie nodded back. She too wanted to be quick. 'We're looking for a man named Richie Palmer. I know he comes here.'

'As you see, he's not here at present.' The veteran officer made a sweeping gesture towards the row upon row of empty bunks.

'But you know this man?'

'Not by name. But there's nothing unusual in that. The men who come here are drifters. We don't keep a record of who they are. That's not how we operate.'

'Well, I've carted him along here myself often enough.' Gertie grew impatient with the man's stonewalling. 'Or had him sent when the sirens went off. I should think you would know him.'

Meggie stood by, trying to control her growing sense of dismay. She pictured the types who inhabited the bunks; the noises, the rags, the despair.

'Give me a description.' Wallace realized that Gertie wouldn't back down unless she got some information. However, in contrast, the girl was reluctant, almost overwhelmed. 'Let me see if I can help,' he said more kindly.

As Gertie ran through Palmer's appearance; dark brown eyes, thick grey hair, over six feet tall, Meggie compared it with the Tottenham Court Road tramp who had first fired her imagination. Certain then that he was somehow familiar, that she knew him without knowing him, despite his hostility, she began to falter now. After all, there were many tall men with grey hair and brown eyes whose lives had crumbled during the Depression years, for whom the promise of houses and jobs from a grateful government after the First War had never materialized, and who slid into homelessness in the grip of memories too dreadful to be told. Meggie knew this for a fact, from Hettie's work with the Salvation Army, from the evidence of her own eyes as she rode the tubes and buses.

'Over six feet tall?' The ex-officer picked this up as unusual. 'Broad frame? Silent type?' There was such a man who was a regular here, intent on drinking himself to death.

'Richie don't say much,' Gertie agreed.

'Do you look after him?'

'On and off. What can I do? I can't turn my back on him if he turns up on my doorstep, can I?' She explained that she ran a pub off Shaftesbury Avenue, that Richie sometimes used Bernhardt Court as his pitch for begging coppers from theatregoers.

Wallace glanced at Meggie, wondering how she fitted in.

'She wants to talk to Palmer, that's all,' Gertie said quickly. 'Ain't no harm in that, is there?'

'Are you lending a hand as well?' Suspicions lingered about Gertie's motives, but Wallace evidently decided that neither she nor Meggie looked official enough to cause problems. 'Look, if I've got the right man, he is a regular here. Bunk number 85. But we're not open to visitors.' He lowered his voice. 'To tell you the honest truth, it isn't a fit place for you to be when the bunks are occupied. I wouldn't let my wife or daughter within a mile of the place, nor any decent woman. I'm sorry, but it's best to be frank.'

Gertie too was clear about not wanting to spend an air raid cooped up with a load of down-and-outs. 'I'd rather take my chances out there with Hitler's bombs,' she confessed. 'But you're my starting point, Captain Wallace. Between us, we should be able to pin down Richie Palmer for Meggie here to talk to.' She glanced at her watch. Opening time beckoned her back to the Court, but it was important to satisfy Meggie's curiosity. Without Richie, her deal with Meggie was incomplete.

The ex-army man knitted his brows. 'Wait. There's a possibility . . . yes, let me go and make enquiries.'

While he vanished into a small office and leafed through a ledger on the desk, Meggie stood numb with misery. The prospect of meeting up with her father at last now held no joy, not in a place like the Hungerford Club. She'd imagined at least that he might still be able to fend for himself, not rely on someone else being there to scoop him up with the very dregs of society.

Captain Wallace returned. He fingered his moustache as if still in doubt. 'I was right; we have Palmer down as being in need of medical aid. We keep a register of men receiving treatment from Dr Munroe in the clinic here. He's on the current list.'

Gertie nodded briskly. 'That's a start.'

'What's wrong with him?' Meggie spoke up for the first time.

'There's no record of that; only of medical requirements. Palmer needed a course of penicillin. That's all I know. However, I could take you next door. Dr Munroe will have the details.'

He ushered them across the dormitory, under the curious gaze of the orderlies, through a door into the next archway, where the space was partitioned into smaller rooms with doors marked Pharmacy, Bathhouse, Sickbay in stencilled letters. Here in an office, an introduction was made to a portly man wearing steel-rimmed spectacles and a white coat. Wallace explained their errand, and before they knew it, the doctor had confirmed that Richie Palmer was indeed on his list of patients. The man had a bad bronchial infection and had been kept in overnight. He was at this very minute in isolation in the small sickbay beyond the pharmacy.

Meggie's pulse started to race. From being stalled by the captain only five minutes before, she was on the brink of coming face to face with the man she'd built so many childhood dreams around. It was strange then how earthbound she felt. She noticed the doctor's scrubbed hands, the white crescents at the tip of each fingernail, the shininess of his bald scalp.

Dr Munroe looked up sharply from behind his desk. What did they want with his patient?

Meggie heard Gertie launch into another explanation; it wasn't her but Meggie who had an interest in Palmer. She offered to wait outside with the captain if the doctor would be kind enough to take Meggie through.

Yes, but what was the girl's business with the sick man?

For the first time Gertie hesitated. 'She can tell you that herself.' She nudged Meggie out of her daze.

Meggie took a deep breath. Falteringly she gave her name, explained her family circumstances, the tangled thread that had led her to the Hungerford Club. 'I'd like to see him, please. You see, I'm Richie Palmer's daughter.'

Richie Palmer sat in a chair in the sickbay at the Hungerford Club. The pain in his chest, the rattle of phlegm in his throat had kept him awake all through the night, though for him the days and nights merged, and life had lost all sense of shape and direction. He was washed up, finished. A lung infection on top of a bad liver, a weak heart. What did it matter? He would lay up for a couple of days here at the Club under a haze of sedatives, then drift again, drink again if he could beg the coppers, or summon the energy to look up one of his few remaining acquaintances.

He hadn't always been so low. There had been times when he'd held down a job for a few months, until he'd shown up at work with a hangover once too often and been given his marching orders again. There had been women, even in these last few years, whenever he made the effort to smarten up. Somehow he remained attractive to them. They didn't mind his surliness and his silences, since he had a masculinity that appealed in the shape of a strong, well-muscled frame before the drink did its worst. And he had features that they read things into; a full, sensual mouth, deep-set hooded eyes, a mumbling voice that slurred lazily and seemed to break down their defences. He was out of shape now, though. Muscles had gone slack, the skin on his face was lined and sagging, he rarely shaved.

A voice at his elbow slowly roused him from his daze. He looked up with a jerk. The doctor's white coat and pink face came slowly into focus.

'This is him; this is Richie Palmer.'

Meggie stood, hands clasped, a startled look on her face. She couldn't be sure that the man slumped in his chair was the one she'd seen in the Underground; his condition had gone downhill so fast. He looked up at her, slack-mouthed, unshaven, gasping for breath. Yes, it was the same man. The doctor, worn down by overwork and inadequate resources, showed little compassion. He stood by, prepared to wait only a few minutes before concluding the visit.

Though she recognized Richie as the man she was seeking, feeling his vague gaze upon her, Meggie's gorge rose. Her mother had loved her father. How could anyone have feelings other than revulsion for the broken figure opposite?

He coughed with a loose, rattling sound. His chest heaved. 'What is she, a nurse?' he asked, casting round the room to locate the doctor. 'Send her away. I don't want no nurse.'

'And you won't get one here. You're lucky to get a bed for a second night,' Munroe told him sharply. He indicated to Meggie that he would go off to fetch Richie's drugs. 'You'll be all right. He's quiet and comparatively lucid. Say what you've come to say; you have ten minutes.'

She nodded. For a few moments, as the doctor left the room, she saw Richie's eyelids droop and his head loll forward. Perhaps she would get up and leave without trying to talk. Afterwards, she would be able to tell herself that it had all been a case of mistaken identity.

'If you're not a nurse, what are you?' His eyes were still half closed. A welfare officer? A do-gooder? As he opened his eyes, his forehead creased into a frown. 'Where am I?' He struggled out of the chair, but his legs refused to support him. He fell back.

'You're in the Hungerford Club. This is the sickbay.' She didn't offer to help him.

Shaking his head, gazing round the room, at last he dragged his attention back to her face. 'Sadie?'

One word. It was like a cell door thudding

469

shut, a key turning in a lock. This then *was* her father.

'No, not Sadie. I'm your daughter, Meggie.'

Again he tried to raise himself. The small yellow room was filled with his swearing and his gasping breath. 'Sadie. It's Sadie, ain't it?'

'It's Meggie.' A dreadful calm came over her.

'I want to get out of here.'

'Shall I fetch the doctor?'

He swore again. 'Why are you here?'

He couldn't clear his head of the mad notion that he'd lost nearly twenty years and was staring into the face of the woman he'd snatched from the smug safety of her family on Duke Street, tied her to him in the face of Rob Parsons' bitter opposition, got her pregnant, then ditched her. In the corner of the room there would lurk the angry brother waiting to get his revenge.

'I ain't Sadie.' She had to repeat it over and over to calm him. 'Sadie's my mother. You saw me when I was a little baby. Don't you remember?' Meggie picked up his fear that there was someone else in the room. Despite her revulsion, she began to pity him. 'Don't worry, they don't know I came here.'

After a while the pieces fell into place;

this was many years later, time for the dark-haired, brown-eyed baby to have grown into the severe but beautiful girl sitting opposite. He got things in order. She couldn't know it, but Meggie wasn't the only child he'd fathered, then abandoned, over the years.

'Is Sadie waiting outside?' The edges of the room were blurred; he was convinced that there was another presence.

'No. She don't know!'

'How did you find me, then?'

'Through Gertie Elliot.' This was the filthy bargain; Richie Palmer for Ronnie, out of a sentimental idea that her father would clap eyes on her and instantly love her.

Gertie's name also meant something to the sick man, though he failed to make the connection between his present visitor and the landlady at the Bell. His eyelids drooped, he put a shaking hand to his temple. 'Seen enough, have you?'

'Are you very sick?' Meggie could see that he was in pain. The regulation pyjamas donated to the club gave him the look of a prisoner, known by number not by name. They'd cut his grey hair short, almost to a stubble.

'With a bit of luck, I am.'

She grimaced. 'Shall I go?' She gave up hope that he would show any interest in

471

her; he'd hardly seemed to register her presence after the initial shock.

'No. Tell me about Sadie.'

The hand shielding his face was mottled and threaded with thick veins. 'She's well, considering. We sent the boys up north because of the Blitz. She's up there with them now.'

'Boys?'

'My two brothers.'

'Who did she get hitched to?'

'Walter Davidson.' The best stepfather anyone could wish for, she reflected guiltily.

Richie coughed and turned the phlegm inside his mouth.

'You worked for him and my Uncle Rob.'

'What if I did? Are they thinking of giving me my old job back?' His laugh ended in another coughing fit. 'That's funny, if you did but know it.'

Meggie sighed. 'Ain't you ever wondered about . . . me?' She'd harboured the notion that she at least existed inside her father's head; in his thoughts and dreams, if not in his actions.

He glanced up at her from under hooded lids. 'Sometimes.'

'Won't you ask me something about myself?'

'I can see plain enough. You got your

ma's stubborn streak.'

She raised her head higher. He hadn't forgotten everything, then.

'Don't worry, you ain't got nothing of me in you.' He recognized his own worthlessness, had done for years. 'You're a Parsons through and through.' The dark brown, wavy hair, the big eyes and proud look, the slight figure. 'Will you tell her you tracked me down?'

She shook her head. This was a secret she would cling to; there was only hopelessness in it. The man was too far gone. Yet he said he had sometimes wondered about her.

'No.' He rested his head against the back of the chair.

'Shall I come again?'

It was his turn to deny her. 'I ain't got nothing to give you. You can see that.'

'I don't want anything!'

He looked her in the eye in a moment of clear, concentrated communication. 'Yes, you do,' he insisted. 'And I ain't got it to give.'

Meggie wished the visit would finish. She was glad when the doctor came back to tell her that her time with Richie Palmer was up. She would find her friend waiting outside, he said. She made a fumbled farewell, lacking the right phrase, doubtful of her future intentions as far as her father was concerned.

'You're your ma's girl,' Richie reminded her as she got up to leave.

There was one last thing; a hunger to have another question answered. She steeled herself. 'Did you see me once down Tottenham Court tube?'

Richie was falling back into confusion, or perhaps he wanted Munroe to think he was sicker than he really was. He coughed and turned away.

'Don't expect him to remember,' the doctor advised, ushering her out.

Meggie drew herself together by buttoning her white coat. She was already through the door, out in the corridor.

'I did.' Richie's reply was late, issued through the wheeze and crackle of his diseased lungs. She could hear him drumming his fingers on the arms of the chair.

Full circle.

To Meggie's surprise, the doctor offered to shake her hand. 'Don't take it too hard,' he advised.

'I don't.' She put on a brave smile and went into the street. She thought of the letter to Ronnie in the postbox on Charing Cross Road. Could she get there and retrieve it when the postman made his collection? *No,* Gertie would have planned for that too. The letter would be on its way to Plymouth.

There was no sign of Ronnie's mother in the throng of traffic that roared beneath the railway arches; the woman who must have knowingly betrayed her in this worst of all bargains. No stylish figure in fur hat and collar. Nothing.

What do I do now? Meggie asked herself. She felt tiny, lost. *Where to now?* Nowhere. *Who with?* No one.

CHAPTER TWENTY-THREE

'The Yanks are in Somerset!' Dorothy O'Hagan crowed over the newspaper spread on the bar at the Duke. 'It's true; it says here they've set up bases all over the country. They're on the verge of coming in with us.' She still loved to goad Tommy, who would go green when he heard the latest. 'That's where Edie went, ain't it? Somewhere near Taunton?'

'About time too.' Dolly headed for safer waters. It was early on a Saturday evening in autumn, the pub was crowded, but Dorothy's remark had hit home. She saw Tommy standing further along the bar, his face like thunder. 'What's the betting they come in all guns blazing, reckoning they can beat old Hitler single-handed?'

'Yes, but the Yanks!' Dorothy made cow-eyes over it. 'Don't I wish I was in Somerset right now!'

'They ain't all Clark Gable, you know. I bet there's ugly Yanks and all.' Dolly fed Dorothy all the right lines without realizing

476

it. 'Anyhow, looks ain't the important thing.'

'Ain't it?' With a voice loaded with innuendo, Dorothy continued to enthuse. 'It's them two-tone uniforms, and such nice, smooth cloth. And them fuzzy haircuts. They give you goose-bumps, just thinking about them.'

'Not me,' Dolly said.

'Me neither.' Annie slipped Tommy a sympathetic extra whisky. 'Take no notice.'

It was over a week since Edie had written. Every morning at Rob's house, Tommy was up first waiting for the post. 'I don't.' He sieved the drink through his teeth. 'In any case, Dorothy would go after anything in trousers.'

His ex-wife heard, protested loudly and looked round for support.

'Serves you right,' Dolly said, unconcerned. 'Maybe you'll pipe down in future.'

'All right?' Rob slid past Tommy, carrying drinks for Amy and himself. Tommy looked down in the dumps, cutting himself off from the general conversation. 'Don't take it to heart.'

'Would I?' Tommy said glumly.

'Not if you've got any sense, you wouldn't.' They all knew how Dorothy tried to needle him whenever she could. Usually Tommy rose well above it. Rob paused to put his drinks down on the bar. 'Look, if it's getting under your skin, I wouldn't hang around if I were you.'

Tommy drew deep on his cigarette. It wasn't Yanks that bothered him, but he couldn't explain to Rob. 'Righto.'

Rob's way of looking at it included no half-measures, as usual. He'd heard the women in the family going on about Edie needing time to get over Morell, but that was all cock and bull. Did she have to go halfway across the country to sort herself out?

'I would *not*,' he repeated. 'You wouldn't catch me waiting for a Yank or a POW to jump into my shoes.'

Tommy hunched his shoulders, glared at his glass.

Rob ploughed on. 'That's bleeding stupid, that is. I reckon she's got you just where she wants you, right under her little finger. Well, it wouldn't be any good for me. I'd be on that Bristol sleeper like a bleeding shot.'

'Easy for you to say.'

'Want to bet? I would. I'd be there keeping my beady eye on her. You ask my old lady.' Hard as it was to believe, the matronly

Amy had been a terrible flirt when they first got together.

'Edie ain't my old lady,' Tommy reminded him. He was sick of advice. What bothered him, pure and simple, was why Edie hadn't written. 'Anyhow, who'd work the news stand?' He couldn't just cut and run, even if he wanted to.

'Bobby would. And Jimmie. It'd give them something to do.' Again Rob stated what he thought was the obvious; sometimes people couldn't see the wood for the trees.

Tommy pursed his lips. He studied the wood grain on the bar. Overnight sleeper to Bristol? Then how would he get out into the sticks? By bus? He began to wonder if it was feasible.

'Stand by your beds,' Rob winked at the two boys who sat chatting up a pair of likely looking clippies from the trams. 'Looks like Tommy might need you to man his stall before too long.'

Amy chided him for poking his nose in.

'I only said the truth. Anyhow, he can't stay with us forever, can he?'

She nudged him hard, calling him heartless.

'Practical,' he insisted. 'One of us has to be.' Even from the back view, as Tommy sat hunched at the bar, it was clear he was giving serious attention to Rob's point of view.

The night train took Tommy to Bristol. Here was another silver estuary under the moonlight, another disgorging of young men in uniform into their sweethearts' arms.

Edie's billet was in a village well inland, however, at a place called Westbury Wootton, and Tommy's choice of transport, as dawn broke and he found the right road south-east out of the city, was a lift cadged from a truck driver. The open truck was loaded up with used rubber tyres from tractors and other farm vehicles, and if the driver had spotted his passenger as a handy source of cigarettes for the journey, he wasn't disappointed. Tommy kept him well supplied with fags and jokes. Neither mentioned a single word about the war.

'It's the back of beyond where you're heading,' the driver warned. His thick wrists and hands dangled inside the rim of his steering wheel, which he turned with casual ease. They'd left the city streets well behind and travelled through rolling wooded countryside. 'What do the Yanks call it — a one-horse town?'

'Have you heard of a place called Wootton Hall?'

The sun was up, but clouds gathering on the horizon.

Tommy's driver flicked a fag-end out of the window with brown stained fingers. 'The Land Army billet?' He gave a knowing look. 'I might've guessed. Does she know you're coming?'

'Call it a surprise.' Tommy kept up the banter. Inside, his stomach churned.

'Red-letter day. Well, let's hope she's thrilled!' The young driver pulled up. This was as near to the manor house as he went, he said.

Tommy hopped out and handed a full packet of cigarettes up through the window.

'Ta very much. I hope you don't mind getting wet.'

Fat drops had begun to fall. Tommy shrugged and turned up the collar of his jacket.

'How far is it?'

'A couple of miles down the lane.' The driver crunched his gears. 'Just keep right on to the end of the road. You can't miss it.'

Though your heart be weary, still carry on . . . Tommy slapped the side of the truck and watched him drive on. The tyres on the back took off a foot into the air and bounced back as he hit the worst bumps in the road.

He'd gone and landed himself in it good and proper. Damn the rain, damn the deep, muddy ruts in the track, damn his own hastiness in following Rob's advice.

Dressed in T-shirt and dungarees, Edie backed the truck out of the barn, ready to set off on the morning round of the local farms. She was due to drop the other Land Army girls at their places of work, then come back here to Wootton Hall to help prepare the traction engine for threshing. During her time in Somerset she'd discovered an aptitude for working with machinery and become a painstaking apprentice to Jurgen Scholtz, the POW fixture at the manor. A heavy rain set in as the girls filed out from the canteen, but it didn't deaden the chatter about what had gone on at the pub the night before; who went with such and such a US army corporal, what they did and didn't do. The local girls shrieked at the language of those who had come from the cities to work on the land, but Edie suspected it was the farmers' daughters who more often put their money where their mouths were. To them, having the GIs stationed in the village was manna from heaven, though it was a source of regret and bitter rivalry among the local boys. In the dormitory after lights-out, she would often overhear whispered, triumphant accounts of battles fought over girls who had hitherto thought of themselves as plain Janes; of victory going to the Yanks every time, and of the lurid spoils of that success.

Edie was careful to keep out of the fray. She tried not to be stuck-up and glum about it, but she had memories too near the surface still. To her, jealousy wasn't something to be played about with. None of the Land Army girls was married of course, but when Edie went to a weekend hop and looked at the angry faces of the Westbury boys lined up against the walls of the village institute, watching the Yanks steal their all-too-willing girls, she had to leave and walk back by herself to the hostel. She preferred the company of Jurgen; a studious type who talked constantly about his wife and child in Dresden, whose brown knee-patches signified his prisoner status, but whose calm bearing suggested a free mind, uncontaminated by the indignities of war.

Now, as she drove the truck down wooded lanes, stopped at farmyards surrounded by buildings of mellow brick and timber, and watched the girls tramp through the rain in twos and threes for a day of egg collecting and cleaning out hen-huts, or if

the weather improved of threshing, plough-
ing and apple picking, she looked forward
to getting back to the Hall.

Her own day was mapped out with span-
ners, wrenches, nuts and bolts, pistons and
gaskets, the smell of engine oil and the
satisfying chug of a well-serviced machine.
She smiled to herself as she drew up and
jumped down into the courtyard. Jurgen
came out of the barn, wiping his hands on
a rag. He waved and called out in his stilted
English, 'Edie, there is a visitor!'

Before she could register the news,
Tommy pushed his way past and came towards her. She stood in the rain, unpre-
pared.

'You never wrote.' He stopped short of
flinging his arms around her.

'I did. Last Friday.' She steadied herself
against the bonnet of the truck. Here was
Tommy in his smart brown suit, but unshaven. He was a fish out of water in his
thin-soled shoes, his fawn trilby.

'I never got it.'

'It must have got lost.' In the background
she saw Jurgen retreat tactfully into the
barn.

Tommy glanced over his shoulder. 'Who's
that?' He'd been disconcerted to find out
from the POW that Edie worked alongside

him, driving trucks and tractors, servicing the machinery.

'That's Jurgen. Come and meet him.' She offered to take his hand.

He shook his head. 'Look, I should have let you know I was coming . . .' Gone were his visions of a romantic reunion. They stood getting soaked, feeling awkward. He wasn't even sure that she was pleased to see him.

'No, that's fine.'

Since he'd refused to come into the barn, she must stand in the rain. She looked earnestly into his face, trying to work out his motives.

'Only, I wanted to see you.' He knew she needed space; that was what she'd claimed. She'd asked him to trust her and let her get over the horror of what had happened to Bill. But instead, he'd listened to gossip; to Dorothy's jibes and Rob's bad advice. His being here was a big mistake.

'You're wet through. How's your hand?'

He held it up, flexed the fingers. 'Better. How are you?'

'Better too.'

'You look it.' It was a conversation between strangers, not lovers. Here she was making a new life, tanned and healthy, without a scrap of make-up. And there was the

485

German in the barn, the sort of serious, quietly spoken bloke that Edie might go for.

'No I don't. I'm soaked through.' She tried a joke. 'If I'd known you were coming . . .'

'You'd have baked a cake. Look, Edie, I'm sorry.'

'No.' She felt his doubts and suspicions. How could she not? And it was her who'd put off his first embrace when he showed up out of nowhere. You'd think she would have been bowled over, surprised or not. 'How's the flat?'

'In apple-pie order.' He called in every now and then to check. 'No more bombs lately. We've been lucky.'

'How's everyone?'

He racked his brains. 'Still in one piece. Likewise.' To everyone on Duke Street it seemed that the Blitz had eased. The problems these days were more with siphoners stealing petrol from your tank, or the 'No Beer' signs that were appearing with increasing frequency outside the pubs. Annie and George had got to the stage where they only served regulars.

The trouble was, neither Tommy nor Edie could get a grip on the new situation, which slid further into banality with every exchange. Tommy had acted on impulse; if he had anything in mind, it was based on Rob's policing mentality that women given a free rein were bound to be up to no good. Now he felt ashamed, but at the same time vaguely vindicated. Who was this Jurgen? Had she been assigned to work with the mechanic, or had she chosen to do so? Tommy thought he'd picked up a warm, even intimate tone in the man's voice when they'd discussed Edie before her arrival.

Edie herself had been shocked by the sight of Tommy. He was lodged firmly in her heart all day, every day, and especially in her dreams at night. But in reality he was selling newspapers outside a Southwark market. What then was he doing here?

He took off his hat and shook water from the brim. 'I shouldn't have come. It was stupid.'

'Come into the canteen, out of the rain.' This time she was more insistent.

'No, you have to get back to work. I'd better make myself scarce.' His mood swung violently. Now he felt an outright fool.

'You only just got here!'

'I made a mistake. I thought it'd be a nice surprise.'

'No, you never.' She turned to argue. 'You thought you'd better come and check up on me, Tommy O'Hagan!' Suddenly it clicked, and she was angry. 'That's it. It's not to give me a nice surprise at all!'

'A good job as well.' He rammed his hat back on. ' 'Cos it weren't, were it?'

'Don't you get mad at me.' She'd asked him to trust her. 'What do you think I get up to? Look around. You think I go dancing every night?' She gestured at her soggy dungarees and dripping hair, held up her oil-stained hands. 'You don't want to believe everything you hear about Land Army girls.'

'I'm off.' Tommy turned on his heel and set off across the courtyard.

Edie watched him go through a blur of rain, splashing through puddles, heading up the cart track towards the road. She sensed Jurgen in the barn doorway, watching developments. If she let Tommy go now, there would be a rift that would be difficult to heal. She ran after him to have it out. 'You're acting like a little kid!'

He heard her run, felt her seize his arm, walked on. 'That's me; a stupid kid. You got the picture.'

'You are if you walk out on me now.'

He stopped. 'I can't cope, Edie. It's driving me mad; you stuck out here and me in town. It don't make sense.' He hung his head.

'Look at me, Tommy.'

Slowly he did as she asked.

'How do I look? Do I look how I did after Bill got killed? Am I a skeleton? Am I unhappy?' She stared at him, searching his face for a glimmer of understanding.

Gently he pushed a strand of dark blonde hair from her cheek. 'You look like a drowned rat. But one that's in good nick.' He stroked her wet face.

'There, see. *I've* been making sense of it.'

'You took your time,' he complained. But he drew her closer.

'You've gotta trust me.' What she was clawing her way out of was the guilt for Bill's death, telling herself that she was responsible only to the extent that she had been unfaithful to him, but under provocation. She accepted a time apart from Tommy as part of the price she must pay. She would punish herself as a matter of habit rather than principle, but now she was ready to bring Tommy more into account. 'Can you wait a bit longer?'

Her face was close to his, his arms around her waist. 'What if I can't?'

Edie knew he was serious. 'Wait for me, Tommy, please. We've been through a lot, haven't we? We ain't gonna give up now.'

He shook his head. 'I'm stupid again, I

know, but what the hell are we waiting for?' It meant him catching the train back by himself, slogging away to get back on his feet, with no one to go home to at night. 'Come back, Edie, for God's sake.'

She lowered her head against his shoulder, held him tight. 'I can't. I've got a job to do here.'

'That ain't the reason.'

'It is, partly. I'm learning. I want to keep on.'

'Fiddling about with engines?'

'I'm not fiddling!' This side of him made her mad. 'I do good work.'

'What else?' It wasn't the only reason she dug her heels in. 'Come on, if I'm so bleeding miserable, I gotta know why!' He began to walk her slowly up the track.

'I need a fresh start, Tommy. When we're both ready to make a move, I want it to be the right one.'

'Name it.'

'I don't know yet.' She pulled away, but held onto his hand, arms swinging as they walked.

'Let me know when you find out, will you?'

'Sarky!'

'Sorry. You could always marry me if you felt like it.'

Edie stopped dead in her tracks. 'Say that again!' They were in the middle of nowhere, it was raining cats and dogs, they were wet through and arguing, and Tommy had just proposed marriage.

'Marry me. That's a fresh start, ain't it?' There he went again, putting his mouth into action before his brain.

'You're the limit, Tommy.'

'What kind of answer is that?'

'What kind of question was it?' She walked on by herself. Her head was spinning.

'A serious one. I'll get a proper divorce, all above board. I'll get us signed up at the registry office.'

Edie went and leaned against a gate under the dripping branches of a chestnut tree. She gazed at him from a distance. 'I love you.'

As she mouthed the words, he leapt across the ditch, trapped her against the gate and kissed her. 'You ain't gone off me?' Now he couldn't get enough of her; her wet cheeks and neck, the thin T-shirt clinging to her, everything dripping wet.

She laughed at his clumsy attempts to get near. 'You be good, Tommy.'

'Not possible.' He was kissing her again, ignoring the sound of a car going past on the road, the dripping leaves, the muddy ditch.

'Yes.' She managed to catch hold of him, cupping his face between her hands. 'That's my answer. You can make an honest woman of me . . .'

'But?' he asked later that evening, after Edie had done her day's work, got changed and come to meet him in Westbury's one and only hotel. He'd signed her in as Mrs O'Hagan, the desk clerk had given her wedding ring a cursory glance, and they'd gone up to the room he'd booked for the night.

Now they lay in bed, swamped by the chinzy cosiness of flowered curtains, carpet and eiderdown. Even out here in the wild, the blackout was in force; they were reminded by the heavy blinds and the absence of lights in the street below. But it was months since the sirens had sounded within miles of this little country backwater. If Hitler came and disturbed their one and only night together, Tommy would personally volunteer to go over to Germany and do him in, he said.

'But what?' After weeks apart, the shape of his body as it lay entwined with hers, the feel and smell of his skin were achingly familiar. She turned to him in the dark.

'You'll marry me, but . . . ?' He knew Edie. He knew the sound of a condition in her soft, low voice.

'Clever you,' she whispered.

'Go on, then. Give me the bad news.'

She ran her fingers across his chest, laid her hand on his shoulder. He was so close she hardly needed to open her mouth to make him hear. 'But not in Duke Street.'

Too many bad memories, people with claims on them both, the pull of the past. 'I've learned how to be happy here, Tommy. I don't want to go back.'

Sadie grieved for Jess's Mo almost as she would have done for Bertie or Geoff. She was there in Manchester for the funeral and, afterwards, went with her sister to recuperate at the rented house in Coniston. There was the calmness of the lake in September, the golden countryside, but still the sense that all was out of joint. Sons shouldn't die before parents, young life ought not to be cut short while its begetters turned grey, their powers diminished.

Sadie would watch Jess sitting at the window looking out over the water. She felt guilty that her own sons survived. The boys were almost countrified after their months up here; they could tell her the names of trees, flowers and birds, they could row a boat, waited for the horse chestnuts to ripen and fall.

Once Jess turned at the sound of Sadie's footsteps. 'You know what I just thought?'

Sadie came in and sat beside her.

'I thought Mo could hear me. I said to him, "Righto, that's long enough. You've had your little joke, you can come home now." '

'She never breaks down,' Sadie told Walter when she got back home. 'I don't know how she does it. But Grace, poor girl, she's in tears a lot of the time. I said I'd bring the boys back with me, but Jess says no, it helps to have them around. And it still ain't safe to bring them here, I know that really.' She was weary after her journey, wrapped up in Jess's grief, far removed from the worries of Duke Street and Paradise Court.

Walter and Meggie had cleaned the house from top to bottom when they heard she was on her way. Meggie knew how she liked the cushions and antimacassars on the front room sofa, and put them just so. Walter went to meet her off the train. She acknowledged their efforts with a gentle hug, but failed to notice her daughter's pale, faded face until Walter mentioned it when they were in bed.

'No bad news, I hope?' Sadie lay back against the pillow, clasping Walter's hand. If Meggie were subdued, it could only mean a letter from Ronnie.

'What do you mean, you hope?' He knew about Sadie's visit to Gertie Elliot, ever since which Sadie had held onto the hope that the romance between the young lovers would soon fade and die. She'd come back with the conviction that something was badly amiss, but that Ronnie's mother had thought of a way of putting the dampener on things. 'I thought bad news for Meggie would be good news as far as everyone else is concerned?' Walter didn't criticize, but he disliked this female sense of duty which made mothers stand in the way of young ones. He thought Meggie and Ronnie deserved a fair chance to sort out their own problems.

Sadie sighed. 'I'm not so sure.' Jess's bereavement had given her a new perspective, closer to Walter's own.

'Well, it's no news either way,' he reported. 'Meggie goes down to wait for the post every morning. It's about the only interest she takes in anything, as a matter of fact.'

'She's going to work?'

'Yes, but otherwise she stays home. Bobby

and Jimmie come knocking and she shuts the door in their faces.'

Sadie was roused by his account. 'Walter, you don't think it could be Richie, do you? She ain't found him after all?'

'She'd have told us.' He pinned down the change in his stepdaughter's behaviour to a time after she'd come back from a trip to Bernhardt Court. Since then she didn't take her writing things down the shelter during a raid, to spend hours scribbling her love letters to Ronnie. She didn't go out. She didn't talk. She just waited for the post. 'No, it's Ronnie,' he judged. 'She's lovelorn, poor girl.'

'Sometimes I wonder why we don't just go in for these arranged marriages,' Sadie said. 'All this falling in and out of love ain't worth the candle.'

'Righto.' He turned over on his side to go to sleep.

'Except you and me, Walter. That goes without saying.'

Meggie's limbo continued until early October. She drifted through it like a ghost. It was a nothingness, an empty nightmare. Out there in the real world a letter was taken from Charing Cross Road to the sorting office, clearly addressed by name, rank and number. It sat in Plymouth waiting for Ronnie's ship to dock. Was it sunny when Ronnie received it? Did he open it at night in his hammock? She wanted to howl out loud at how Gertie had cheated her.

His handwriting on the envelope that landed on the mat one Friday in October jumped out at her. She'd waited so long that she'd schooled herself to think that he had read her letter and passively accepted her rejection. She told herself that he wouldn't reply.

Then he did. She seized the letter and ran upstairs to her room. No. Wait. This was to call her names, get his own back for the way she'd treated him. She stared at the unopened envelope, holding it in a trembling hand.

'Are you all right?' Sadie called through the door. 'Did you get a letter?'

'No.' She didn't move a muscle, waiting until her mother had gone down to make the breakfast. At last, the agony of not knowing outweighed the fear of what the letter contained. He had at least written back. She tore it open. The words swam on the page until she could focus and read the familiar sloping scrawl.

'Meggie.' Not darling, not dearest. She read on. 'This won't take long. I don't believe what you wrote in your last letter. Something's wrong, ain't it? I waited for another, but I can't wait no more. I got leave. We dock in Southampton on the fifth. Meet me at Victoria at eleven. Be there, Meggie. I'm looking at the stars. Ronnie.'

'What is it?' Sadie stood in the kitchen, unable to read her face as she ran downstairs. 'What's happened?'

The fifth was tomorrow. Her limbo world exploded like a box of fireworks. Plans sparkled and whooshed inside her head. Ronnie had forgiven her. Gertie's mean scheme had backfired. 'I got a letter!'

'From Ronnie?'

She nodded. 'I'm going to see him tomorrow.'

It was a smile lighting up at last. Sadie breathed a sigh of relief. 'Calm down,' she pleaded. 'Have something to settle your stomach. Go and get ready for work.' Methodically she laid the table with cups, plates, knives.

Somehow Meggie managed it. She went up and got dressed to go out. Back downstairs, she was glad of the hot, sweet tea, but pushed away the toast.

'Meggie!'

'I can't.' She shook her head. 'He's got leave, Ma. I can hardly wait!'

Sadie put a hand over hers. 'Go and see him,' she said gently. 'But don't go and do nothing silly.' The elopement idea still preyed on her mind. 'Sort things out with him.'

Meggie stood up. 'Don't worry, I won't run off.'

'That's it,' she agreed. 'No need to rush. Take it slow. Talk to his ma.'

'I will.' Meggie kissed her mother, took the letter and put it in her bag. 'Don't you worry, I will!'

CHAPTER TWENTY-FOUR

'Switch that off, Shankley!' Gertie was sick of the sound of the newsreaders' voices and the sonorous reports from the battle fronts. It would be more gloom and doom, no doubt.

Shankley turned the dial on the wireless set which sat behind the bar at the Bell. He twiddled and found Sandy's Half Hour instead. 'Will that do you?' He himself had become something of a fixture behind the bar. It was mid-morning on a drizzly October Saturday. Chords from the BBC Theatre organ rose and swelled through the empty room.

'They all got plums in their mouths, them wireless announcers.' She found something harmless to moan about while she wiped and dusted. Shankley went back to mopping the floor. 'And they could all do with a dose of syrup of figs by the sound of them.'

He grinned. 'Not your cup of tea, eh?' The Alvar Liddells and the Bruce Belfrages.

Gertie began to hum to the organ tunes. 'This brings it all back,' she sighed. It was a tune from the twenties; her salad days. For a brief time, before she met her husband, Sam, she'd belonged to a dance troupe that did the rounds of the East End halls.

'Them were the days.' Shankley propped his mop against the wall and lit up a Players.

'You having a go at me?' she said sharply, patting her already immaculate hair into place.

He winked. 'I bet you had the men swarming round you, Gert.' It was his way of cheering her up. She'd been low lately; grinning and bearing it was how he put it. He didn't know what was up, since Gertie wasn't the sort to share her problems. He knew, however, that she didn't get many letters from Ronnie, and this preyed on her mind. 'You still do, of course.'

She had the grace to smile back at him. 'Oh, yes? Where are they, Shanks?' She flapped her duster round the room. 'Queuing up at the door, are they?'

'Here's one!' He volunteered himself, present and correct.

She raised her eyebrows. 'Do me a favour! I'm on the shelf, Shanks, but not that hard up.' About to tell him to get a move on with the mop, she went instead to answer the phone.

'Yes, speaking.' She listened hard to a girl's voice on the crackly line. 'Is that you, Meggie?' She put a hand over the receiver to give herself time to pull herself together. Since that day at the Hungerford Club she'd tried to put Meggie Davidson firmly out of her mind.

'I thought you ought to know . . .'

The voice was high, vindictive. Gertie's knuckles went white as she grasped the phone.

'. . . it didn't work. Ronnie got that letter, but he never believed it.'

'What you on about?' Gertie had walked away, not proud of what she'd done, but satisfied that it would put an end to Ronnie and Meggie's dream. No news since then had been good news as far as she was concerned.

'He wrote to me.' Now it was triumph. Meggie couldn't resist letting Gertie know that her scheming had come to nothing. 'He still loves me. He's coming back!'

'When? What did he say?'

'Right now. I'm at the station waiting for his train, and there ain't a thing you can do to stop us!'

The phone clicked and went dead. Gertie stood for a few seconds staring at it.

Shankley wandered across. 'What's up?'

Her voice snapped into a mechanical tone. 'Nothing's up, Shanks. Open up for me and do the honours this lunchtime, will you?' She was on her way upstairs for her hat and coat.

'What about my stall?' he called after her.

She turned on the stair. 'Please?'

He frowned, then nodded. 'How long will you be?'

'As long as it takes to get to Victoria Station and back.' Flinging her coat over her arm, she headed for the door. 'Set one up for me when I get back,' she said grimly. 'I've a feeling I'm gonna need it.'

To Meggie's surprise, her phone call to the Bell hadn't made her feel better. Again and again she'd rehearsed those choice phrases, 'He still loves me. He's coming back.' She'd imagined a crushing defeat at the other end of the line to make up for the misery that Gertie had put her through. In the event, she felt shabby and cheap. Revenge wasn't sweet. It took away from the pure joy of the reunion with Ronnie. She came away from the telephone booth, glanced up at the station clock and rushed to buy a platform ticket.

'Don't panic, you ain't missed him,' the man at the ticket office grinned. He looked

503

over Meggie's white raincoat, black beret and Paisley scarf, her glossy dark hair, her nervous apprehension. 'The Southampton train's twenty minutes late.' Here was another girl waiting on tenterhooks for her sweetheart to arrive. Platform 3 was already jam-packed full of them.

Meggie thanked him and hurried anyway. She wanted to be there, peering out at the curve of steel track beyond the platform, teetering on the edge, waiting for the first hiss of steam, the clank of wheels as they braked, the sight of the mighty engine approaching the buffers. The platform clock clicked and edged forward; five minutes to go. Five minutes and she would be in Ronnie's arms, pouring out the explanations, swearing that she did love him and would never let him go.

'Meggie!' Gertie glimpsed her, got over the desire to cut and run, forced herself to go through with what she knew she must do, even though it would break her son's heart; make him ashamed of her forever. The girl was in a world of her own. She didn't hear her name being called. Gertie ran the length of the platform towards her.

The black minute hand jerked, the track remained empty. Meggie clutched her bag under her arm, imagined that she could hear a train screech. Then someone was calling her, her arm was being pulled. She turned.

'Meggie, for God's sake!' Gertie was distraught. She'd feared she would be too late, all the way on the tube, queuing for her platform ticket, until by a stroke of luck she learned that Ronnie's train was late.

Meggie wrenched her arm free. 'Go away. You can't stop us.' She half overbalanced. A nearby army corporal saved her from falling towards the track.

'Listen to me.'

She walked away, further down the platform, past the impatient sweethearts and wives.

Again Gertie took hold of her arm. 'You'll listen, like it or not.'

'Now then, girls, don't squabble.' The corporal still had an eye on them.

'Keep her off me,' Meggie pleaded.

But Gertie gave a look that warned him away. He shrugged and left them to battle things out.

'There's something you gotta know.' Keeping tight hold of Meggie, she steered her under the platform roof, against a trolley piled high with canvas mail-bags. There was no time to lose. She plunged on. 'I know what you think, but it don't matter no more. Go ahead, hate me, but at least do it for

505

the right reason this time.'

Meggie tried to twist free. 'Ronnie loves me. You can't stop that.'

'No I can't.' She let go but fixed Meggie with her stare. 'I wish to God I could. Listen to me! I'm gonna tell you something I ain't told no one for over twenty years.' With a shaking hand she delved into her pocket and drew out a paper.

'What's that?'

'Wait, I'll tell you.' Gertie prepared to unlock the secret for which she knew she would never be forgiven. 'This goes back to when Ronnie was born. Neither he nor my poor Sam ever knew. Sam went to his grave without finding out the truth.' She unfolded the paper; a simple, official document.

Meggie took the birth certificate from her.

'Sam and me was engaged. I was working the halls; that's where I met him. There was others too. Other men. But no one meant a thing to me except Sam Elliot.'

The certificate recorded the birth of a boy, Ronald Edward, and the mother's name and occupation, Gertrude Starr, dancer.

'I was young. I wasn't careful. You never think you'll get caught, but I did. I went to Sam and said he was the father. He wasn't, but I knew which side my bread was buttered. Sam would marry me and look after us, the baby and me. Not his real pa; he was already long gone.'

Meggie looked at the space for the name of the father. It was officially blank, but someone had pencilled in a name in a faint hand; Richard Palmer, motor mechanic.

Gertie watched her face, spilling out the words regardless. 'Maybe Sam knew something was up, but he gave me the benefit of the doubt. He never bothered about the certificate after Ronnie was born. He weren't one for signing things. Anyhow, he married me in the end, and we were a proper family. He weren't perfect, but he was good to us. He loved little Ronnie and Ronnie worshipped him. Why rock the boat?'

'Who wrote this in?' Meggie's hand trembled as she pointed to the pencilled name.

Gertie grimaced. 'Not Richie, believe you me. He didn't want to know. I wrote it, in case something happened to me. After I was dead and buried, I reckoned Ronnie was entitled to know the truth.' She shook her head.

'It's a trick!' For Meggie this was the only possible way out. She thrust the birth certificate back at Gertie.

'I wish it was. Richie is Ronnie's father, I swear.'

507

Above their heads, the hand on the clock jerked forward. Shared knowledge bound them together; mother and sweetheart, waiting for the train to come.

'Ask him,' Gertie whispered. 'Go to the Hungerford Club. He won't deny it.'

It was the end to a dream so sudden and painful that Meggie could only stand stunned. She clutched at the wire cage that held the mail-bags, wishing now that Ronnie's train would never come, wishing she was dead.

'Don't worry, I'll stay here and tell him. You get along home.' Gertie thought Meggie might faint. The girl had lost all urge to fight, seemed to accept the truth at last.

'Oh God!' A moan escaped, wrenched from deep inside her. She put a hand over her mouth.

'Meggie . . .' Gertie reached out to steady her.

'Don't touch me. Leave me alone.'

'I can't leave you here. You see why I had to break it to you? I didn't want to do it.' Justification ran into apology and heartfelt pity. 'Don't cry, for God's sake.'

'Don't you come near me!' She shrank back. The jolting shock of revelation ran through her again and again.

'I'm sorry. What could I do?' Gertie

forced herself to cope, since Meggie had gone to pieces. Any minute now, there would be Ronnie to deal with too. 'Do you think I wanted to do this to my own flesh and blood?' To tell him that she'd lived a lie with him, that Sam wasn't his pa. It would shatter his world. 'You gotta pull yourself together, girl. Or let me go and get some help.'

Meggie shook her head. 'I want to tell him myself.' With an effort she stood upright. She wouldn't let Gertie shunt her out of the way. Ronnie didn't have a clue what he was riding into, sitting there in that compartment, or hanging out of the window looking for her as the train reached the station.

A public announcement heralded the arrival at last of the late Southampton train. Gertie's mouth was dry. Meggie's suddenly renewed strength of mind alarmed her. The idea had been for Gertie herself to tackle Ronnie; she would be able to explain away Meggie's absence as proof that the girl didn't care, that the original goodbye letter was genuine. She still had a small hope that she could save him from the truth. 'Tell him what?' she insisted.

Meggie pushed herself clear of the wall. She directed a look of pure hatred at Gertie.

'Don't worry, I'll save your bacon.'

'You won't tell him about Richie?'

She scorned to answer. 'Ronnie means the world to me,' she said instead. The train crawled into the station spouting steam, screeching to a halt.

'To me too,' Gertie choked.

They stood watching the doors fly open. Servicemen alighted in a steady stream. Blue, khaki, grey uniforms crowded onto the platform. Girls picked out their own sailor, soldier or pilot. There were tearful reunions, smiling faces, linked arms and an ebbing away from the platform, until only half a dozen couples remained, lingering over their greetings. Solitary stragglers jumped down from the carriages with no one to meet them. Meggie and Gertie studied each one, and moving out of the shadows began to run the length of the train, looking into empty compartments.

'Where is he?' Gertie grew desperate. 'He ain't on the train.' She ran to find a guard; someone who could give them information. 'Is there another Southampton train on its way?' She yelled the question above the shunting hiss of another engine on a nearby platform.

The man shook his head. 'That's your lot. Next one's not due till tomorrow.'

Gertie's hands dropped to her side. She turned to look for Meggie. But the platform was empty. The carriage doors hung open, the big clock ticked. Ronnie wasn't on the train, and Meggie had disappeared.

Slowly she turned and walked up the long slope towards the main terminal building. She realized for the first time the full impact of what she had done.

CHAPTER TWENTY-FIVE

Meggie strode all the way up Birdcage Walk, through Parliament Square to Victoria Embankment. She was aware of walking quickly, apparently purposefully, past all the grand buildings, though in fact her mind was blank. She had no idea where she was heading.

Don't touch me. Leave me alone. These phrases recurred. If it meant walking onto one of the bridges and jumping straight into the grey old Thames, she would achieve this desire for isolation. If anyone were to come near her, she would scream her revulsion. Passers-by paid her no attention, however. Buses roared past, the wide road streamed with traffic. She was one small, anonymous figure in the swell of humanity, beneath the advertising hoardings, the autumn trees, the great dark arches of Hungerford Bridge.

What was she doing here? Meggie stared up at them, perplexed. Had she meant to come? She thought not, though there might have been some reason why she should want to find Richie Palmer again. Could it have been that she'd wanted to check Gertie's story? She tried to concentrate.

'Watch where you're going, mate!' An oldish man on a bicycle, balancing a load of firewood on the crossbar, swerved as she strayed into the road. He turned his head to watch her stumble back onto the pavement. Something must have told him to get off and go to her aid. She could have been drunk, but he didn't think so. 'Here, help me get her seen to,' he called out, as Meggie swayed and collapsed in the gutter. No one answered his plea. The girl had fainted, and he was lumbered.

Worse, a siren started up. Just what he needed. For a moment, the man thought he might leave Meggie to recover unaided. Then he noticed the down-and-outs trickling into the Hungerford Club for the duration. He helped her struggle to her feet. 'In here,' he suggested. 'I'll get someone to take a look at you.'

In spite of her daze, Meggie recognised the number 176 above the door. She seemed terrified of the place, and shook herself free. 'I'll be all right, ta.'

'There's a raid on, can't you hear?' He began to wonder if he could get home, or if he would have to shelter too. He tried to brush the mud splashes from the girl's white coat.

'Don't.' She stepped away, almost fell.

'Here, I'll get a cab.' What a state, he thought. He hailed a taxi and rattled off an instruction to the driver. 'She ain't well. How far are you going?'

'Waterloo, if I can make it.' The driver flicked a cigarette butt onto the road. 'Does she want a ride or not?'

The man waited for Meggie to nod. He picked up the bag she'd dropped in the gutter and bundled her into the taxi. The road and pavement were by now almost empty. He grabbed his bike with its load of wood, then waved the driver on. 'She ain't with it, mate, but I think she'll soon come round.'

'How do you know she's got the price of a cab on her?' But he relented when he looked in his mirror and saw Meggie's frightened white face. 'All right, all right, call it my good deed for the day.' He drove off at breakneck speed as the siren wailed in broad daylight.

'Cor, stone me, if she don't go and faint on me again!' he told his fellow drivers in the shelter at Waterloo. 'I'm out of the cab, rifling through her things to find out who the hell she is, when this copper comes up.

What a bleeding farce. We find a whole bunch of letters tied up in a ribbon in her bag. She's a Meggie Davidson of Paradise Court. I hand her over to the copper like a hot potato. Let him deal with it.' He sipped his tea and said it was the last time he was playing good Samaritan.

It was a police car that had rolled up at the Duke with Meggie in the back. George was locking up, making sure that everyone was clear before the raid got underway. The policeman stopped to ask for the Davidson's house. It was all right, George said, he was family. The girl's mother had already taken shelter in the cellar of the pub. He helped Meggie out of the car.

When she saw who it was, Hettie came rushing through the bar. Meggie stumbled into her arms. She clung to her aunt in a state of shock.

'Hush there, everything's all right.' Hettie held her tight. 'Your ma and grandma are here, we'll look after you. Come downstairs. Listen, darling, if it's Ronnie you're worried about, there's no need. We got a telephone message. He said to tell you he's fine. His leave got cancelled right at the last minute. That's why he wasn't on the train.'

Meggie stared at her, expressionless.

'There, there, he knew you'd be upset.

515

He says not to worry, he'll put in for leave again just as soon as he can. He promises to write you lots of letters. He says you gotta write too.' Gently she led Meggie down to the shelter. 'Oh, and he says to tell you he loves you, and something about the stars. What was it?'

The cellar door opened. Sadie, who had been worried stiff and had telephoned the Bell to see if Meggie was there, took one look at her and clasped her in her arms.

Tommy couldn't wait to feel solid pavement under his feet again. His excursion into the country had left him shaken. 'I ain't no local yokel,' he confided to Charlie Ogden one night soon after his return. The two men got on well, considering. He lifted a pint of Annie's best bitter and took a sip. 'I don't know how them Land Army girls stick it, and all for twenty-eight bob a week.'

'How's Edie?'

'A1, ta.'

'When's she coming home?'

'Don't ask me, mate.'

Charlie decided to mind his own business. 'How's Dad's Army treating you?'

'It's a bleeding shambles,' Tommy admitted. 'I'm a civilian volunteer despatch rider, except I ain't got a bleeding bike, have I?'

'They call it doing your bit.'

The desultory conversation drifted, until Dorothy came into the pub to collect Charlie on the way to the cinema. 'What's up, Tommy? You got a face like a wet weekend.' She had a glint in her eye as she got Charlie to order her a drink. 'How's Edie getting along?'

'I already asked him.' Charlie pushed the glass towards her with a meaningful look.

'What's the matter? She found a nice-looking Yank to take her along to the local hop?' This was more light entertainment for Dorothy. She was long past regretting the breakdown of her marriage, and although passion wasn't a large ingredient in her new relationship with Charlie, there was at least a sound understanding between them. Warts and all, she told her women friends. She had to take Charlie's gloomy fits in her stride, while his feelings for her had strengthened since his near-miss and long hospital stay. Behind the lipstick and the nail polish didn't exactly beat a heart of pure gold, but at least he knew where he was with Dorothy. 'I hear you paid Edie a visit. Is she up to her elbows in cow-muck, or what?'

'She drives a bleeding truck.' Tommy regretted giving even this much away.

'Oh God, what does she look like? Does she have to wear them nasty fawn britches like in the advert? And don't say you never noticed.' Dorothy gauged the impact of her teasing. 'You ain't been ditched for a turniphead, have you?' Why else would Edie be stopping away from home for so long?

'What if she happens to like it there, not having bombs dropped on her head every five minutes?' Charlie suggested.

'Well, I never thought of that. Maybe I should give it a go.' Dorothy sat on her stool, perky as anything.

Even Tommy smiled. 'You in a pair of dungarees? I don't think so.'

'Come on, if we're going. The picture starts at seven.' Charlie checked his watch. He helped Dorothy on with her coat and left the bar to Tommy and a couple of other customers installed at a corner table.

After they'd gone, Annie worked her way across, wiping the bar top as she came. She thought she knew what was eating Tommy. 'Cheer up, it might never happen.'

He shrugged.

'There again, maybe it already has. How long have you been coming in here, Tommy?' She put away her cloth and drew up a stool across the bar from him, an un-usual move for the ever-active landlady. 'I make you much of an age with our Ernie. He'd have been forty-four this year.'

'Don't rub it in.' He felt every day of his forty-one years.

'Ernie was never more than a boy to me, of course. Not just because of how he was. Forty don't seem any age when you get to seventy-odd.' She took her time. There was something specific she wanted to say. 'You got half your life ahead of you.' Another pause. 'How's business?'

'Picking up,' he admitted. He'd moved in on two more vacant newspaper stands, started employing Jimmie and Bobby on a full time basis.

'I knew you'd soon be back on your feet.'

'It ain't hard, Annie. Not with half the work force away fighting a war, remember.'

'Still, it takes guts to pull yourself back from the brink.'

He sipped at his beer. 'Spit it out. I know you: you're gonna give me the benefit of your advice, whether I like it or not.'

Annie sniffed. 'You always was a cheeky monkey, Tommy O'Hagan.' Still, it gave her the way in. 'Edie's making you wait, ain't she?'

He raised an eyebrow. 'Who told you?'

'No one. I worked it out for myself. As a matter of fact, it was me who told her to take her time.' She braved the impatient rap of Tommy's glass on the bar. 'No, listen. I said don't jump in until you're ready. Think about it. If she'd leaned on you straight after Bill went and did himself in, where would she be now?'

'Here with me, that's where!'

'Yes, and leaning on you for the rest of her life. That ain't Edie. It's Dorothy more like. Some women need to lean, see?'

Tommy hadn't seen his ex-wife in this light before. 'Funny, I always thought she was the boss.'

Annie shook her head. 'Dorothy's a leaner, believe me. I ain't running her down, don't think that. Some men like to be leaned on, like Charlie for instance.'

'Where's this getting us?' He was still irritated by the idea of Annie having stuck her oar in.

'Round to Edie, that's where. You say she's coping out in the sticks?'

'More than that. I'd say she's bleeding well enjoying it.' Tinkering with engines, talking to her POW. 'She only goes and tells me she don't want to come back to Duke Street!'

Even Annie was taken aback. 'What, never?'

'Not ever. She wants to give up the flat.'

'Has she chucked you?'

'She might just as well.'

'But she ain't?' Annie got this straight. She could hear more customers gathering on the pavement outside. 'What's she saying, Tommy? Is she gonna stay out in Somerset?'

'She don't bleeding well know.' They'd talked it over at the hotel, and left it that Edie needed more time to think. 'On the one hand she says she wants to marry me. On the other, she don't want to come home.'

Annie took a deep breath and eased herself off the stool. She took up her post behind the pumps. 'Well, there's only one thing for it, Tommy . . .'

'What's that?' He was damned if he could see a way out. He'd been racking his brains for days.

'*You'll* have to go to her.'

'What, and live out there?' His jaw dropped.

'No need to look like that. It can't be all bad.' Annie failed to see the advantages, she had to admit. 'Still, some people live in the country all their lives, don't they? It wouldn't be my cup of tea, mind you . . .' Finally she came up with a convincing argument. 'But if Duke had asked me to go and live in Woolbury Weston, I'd have gone with him like a shot!'

Annie and Hettie still had Meggie staying with them at the Duke. Ever since her return the previous Saturday she'd been suffering from some kind of shock. Sadie had been unable to get much out of her; only that Meggie had been to the station to meet Ronnie, and, when he failed to show up, had managed to get herself lost. She'd ended up in a state in the back of a police car. She said she didn't want to go home, she refused to speak or to eat.

When they called the doctor, he judged her to have had a complete breakdown. 'Similar in a way to shell shock. You can't pin it down to one particular event, perhaps. And, of course, you can't see any physical wound. That makes it more difficult for us to understand.'

'You're saying it's her nerves?' Sadie listened with growing dread. Meggie was staying in Ernie's old room, white as the sheets she was laid on. 'But she'll come round, won't she?'

The doctor said he'd seen many such conditions. The more the politicians advocated taking it on the chin and muddling through, the more the East End women patiently took on their shoulders; helping the war effort, coping with food shortages, worrying about their men on the front line, not to mention enduring the Blitz. Some were bound to crack under the strain. 'Give her time,' he advised. 'And plenty of peace and quiet.'

His reply had left them unnerved. Hettie redoubled her prayers, while Annie took charge of the invalid. Sadie would only fret all the more if she had Meggie at home, and Sadie herself was very near the end of her tether.

'I should've stepped in sooner,' she told Walter. 'If I'd stood up for Meggie and Ronnie, instead of letting Gertie Elliot rule the roost, Meggie would never have gone off the rails like this. Not if I'd been on her side.'

'We don't know that.' Walter felt his family begin to crumble and fall apart. Sadie's guilt didn't help, neither did the knowledge that Bertie and Geoff seemed to be getting on fine without them in Coniston. Grace sent weekly cards, and the occasional phone call from the boys revealed that they were having a whale of a time.

'I know!' Sadie pressed her lips tightly together. 'Poor Meggie's been battling all alone to find Richie and to hang onto her sweetheart. I ain't given her the help a mother should.' She sat feeling bleak and useless, going over her mistakes.

He tried to comfort her. 'She's getting help now. We're rallying round.'

Sadie nodded and looked up through her tears.

'Let Hettie and Annie look after her,' he said gently. 'And I'll look after you.' His arms were strong enough. He wouldn't let her down.

It was Hettie's habit to hum the old Sally Army tunes as she went about the sick room. They kept her spirits up and let Meggie know she was there. She had some expertise as a nurse, gained during her time at the hostel, and her stoical outlook meant that she didn't fuss over details or kill her patient with kindness. On top of this, her faith was strong that Meggie would pull through.

'Forward into ba-attle, See those banners go . . . Onward Christian so-o-o-oldiers, Marching as to-o war . . .' she sang as she brought a jug of fresh water for the bedside.

Meggie turned her head; a first weak response.

'Here, let me do your pillows.' Hettie put the tray down and offered to make her more comfortable, glad when Meggie cooperated. 'That's it.' She lowered her gently, then stroked her forehead. 'Poor Meggie, what can we do to make it better?' She saw tears roll sideways. 'Tell me, darling.'

Meggie looked up, too weak to reply. Her lips were dry, her limbs heavy. 'Aunt Ett?'

'I'm still here.'

'I found my pa.' Four simple words.

'Did you, darling?'

'He needs help. Can we take care of him?'

'We can.' Nothing could be easier. Hettie clasped Meggie's hand.

For the time being this was enough. She closed her eyes. Eventually she slept. Later she explained the circumstances and Hettie made moves for George to trace Richie Palmer through the Hungerford Club.

'George is the best man for the job,' she told Annie. 'He ain't tangled up in it the way Walter and Rob are. He can keep a cool head.'

Annie agreed. 'What if Richie Palmer don't want to be looked after?' If he was that far gone, he might not accept their help. Memories of her first husband Wiggin in a similar plight came flooding back. He had carried on drinking and causing trouble right to the bitter end.

Hettie took this into account. 'Let's try and get a roof over his head,' she decided.

'It's the least we can do.' She looked steadily at her stepmother. 'Richie is Meggie's pa, remember.'

Annie sighed. 'Let George do it,' she agreed. 'But keep Sadie out of it. She won't be able to stand it if Richie has hit rock-bottom. Believe me, I know.'

Hettie went ahead and kept Meggie informed. 'There's a hostel for the homeless off Bear Lane. Charlie Ogden knows about it. He reckons if we can get Richie back across the water he can book him in there, as long as George promises to keep an eye on him. Charlie says he can pull a few strings.'

Meggie sat up in bed. 'I don't want to visit him. Not yet.'

Hettie rolled her eyes. 'You're not going nowhere, young lady. Not until we build you up a bit.' Today had been Meggie's first attempt to take a little food. She was still weak as a kitten.

'Aunt Ett . . .'

'What now?' she teased.

'Can you find me a pen and paper?'

Hettie quickly complied. 'And here's an envelope and a stamp. Who are you writing to, Ronnie?'

Colour came into Meggie's cheeks as she ducked her head and nodded.

'She's writing him a letter,' Hettie reported to Sadie with a smile. 'That's a good sign, ain't it?'

Dear Ronnie,

I know how this letter will hurt you, and before you read it I want you to remember the good times we had. I hope that you won't forget them.

I came to meet you off the train last week to tell you that we couldn't go on. Like I said in my other letter, I thought better of us running away together, and this time I want you to believe me. Ronnie, I can't go through with it. I won't marry you.

Meggie broke off time and time again. The words lay flat on the page. What she felt was nowhere on view as the pen squeaked across the white paper. Still, she must make him believe what she wrote.

You were my first sweetheart. You were very good to me. (She crossed out this last sentence.) But you're not the husband for me. I know I'm too young to make a go of it with you, and that our lives are meant to follow different paths.

Don't think of rushing home again to try and change my mind. It won't do any good. Every word here is true. So this is goodbye, Ronnie. I want you to forget me and live a happy life. ('Without me,' she wrote, then crossed it out.) One day I hope you'll forgive me for letting you down. I'm sorry. I truly am.

Love, Meggie.

CHAPTER TWENTY-SIX

'Woolly Weston. Woody Westbury; I don't
bleeding care!' Tommy gritted his teeth and
told Edie his decision to chuck everything
and come to Somerset to join her.

'It's Westbury Wootton,' she insisted.
'And you know it!' Martyrdom didn't sit
easily on Tommy's shoulders. She pictured
him at the other end of the phone line,
hand over one ear to cut out the yells of
the market traders, the roar of traffic
trundling by. 'What are you saying, that
you'll come out here and set up home with
me?'

'If that's what it takes.' He didn't want
to sound as if he was falling over himself
with enthusiasm. He thought she should
realize the sacrifice he was prepared to
make.

'When?'

It seemed he meant it. Edie stood in the
hall of the ancient manor house, taking the
call in a public phone booth that had been
installed for the girls' use. From here she
could see into the grounds; the formal gar-

den outside the main door, the sweep of the main driveway.

'Tomorrow. Whenever you want.' He began to feel that he should have turned up on the doorstep again. As it was, giving her advance warning would give them both time to get cold feet. What if she turned him down? The trouble with Edie was that she was deep. She could always find reasons for denying herself what she most wanted. 'Are you still there?'

'Yes. You took me aback. I was just in the middle of eating my tea.'

Thrilling. She was shilly-shallying, finding ways of putting him off. 'What do you think, Edie? Can we make a go of it?' He put himself on the line for her once more.

'Come down and talk about it,' she said softly. 'I need to see you.'

So Tommy took the morning train.

'Make or break this time,' he told Rob, who dropped him at the station. 'I need a yes or a no.' His self-respect wouldn't take much more of this hanging around. 'What the bleeding hell does she expect? I've said I'll drop everything and move out there, haven't I?'

'Blimey.' Tommy in turnipland. Rob flicked cigarette ash onto the pavement. 'And the best of British, mate.' You

530

wouldn't catch him moving more than a couple of miles from Duke Street, not at his time of life.

The assignation was fixed for one o'clock at the pub in Westbury. Tommy got there in good time after another smooth lift from Bristol, his belligerence of earlier that morning having evaporated on the train journey. It had been replaced by an edgy peevishness. 'Scotch,' he ordered at the bar. He downed it in one and ordered another.

Edie had managed to wangle some time off by working overtime the night before. Tommy's offer had made her smile at first, until she realized he was serious. It had set her thinking; the two of them living together in one of these sleepy villages, perhaps setting up in a newsagents and sub-post-office, learning the ropes. She pictured them in five years time, settled and cosy. Now, the moment she walked into the pub and saw Tommy's lean figure at the bar, hat tipped back, tie and top shirt button loosened, foot up on the brass rail, the picture dissolved.

She slid up to him and put an arm around his waist, letting him sense her arrival before she said anything. She reached across for a brief kiss. When Tommy saw her smiling at him, his sense of martyrdom eased. He would do anything for this woman. He'd live on Mars, for God's sake.

'You look like . . . a million dollars!'

She was glad she'd changed out of uniform into a silky cream shirt and slacks. 'Likewise.' Accepting a drink, she noticed that he'd shaved and made himself respectable after his long journey. They went to sit in a corner, out of the landlord's gaze.

'This is it, this is the plan.' He got down to brass tacks. 'I hand over things in Southwark to Jimmie. He keeps it ticking over while we set up here. I reckon we can easily rent a place. You'll have to leave the Land Army, though. They don't have no married quarters, do they?'

'Tommy.' She put a hand over his. It was nervous energy that made him hurry. He looked worn to a shadow underneath the bravado.

He stopped, as if a switch had been flicked. Her one word cut him dead.

'Look at me, Tommy.' She waited for him to respond, moved beyond words at the sacrifice he was prepared to make. When their eyes met, she continued. 'I don't want you to do all that for me. It wouldn't work out.' Now she had to rush, to wipe out all that hurt. 'I know I said I couldn't live in Duke Street, and I can't. I still think that.

532

But it doesn't have to be so drastic, see. Think about it, we'd stick out like sore thumbs if we tried to make a go of it round here. You in your spivvy Humphrey Bogart suits, me pretending that I'd got nothing better to do with my time than make jam and knit tea-cosies.'

For a while it didn't sink in. 'You don't want us to live here?'

'In Woolly Weston, no!' She grinned. 'Let's put it this way, it's nice for a holiday and a bit of peace and quiet, but it wouldn't do long term.'

Tommy felt as if a jail sentence had been lifted. He took a deep breath, shot to his feet and went to order another round. 'Make them doubles!' He chose a cigar from the rack on the bar. 'And have one yourself!' he told the landlord, returning triumphant. 'Bleeding hell, Edie, pack your bag and let's get out of here!' He was all for heading back to the flat and consolidating the decision.

She was still firm about one thing, however. 'Hold your horses, Tommy. I can't drop everything and land them in the cart. Anyhow, I mean what I said; I won't go back to Duke Street.'

He frowned, made what was by now a minor readjustment. 'Righto, we're gonna jack in the flat? Got that. We're gonna look for somewhere new, not on the old patch.'

'But not too far away,' Edie chipped in. 'I want to keep in touch with Hettie and Annie and the others.'

He nodded. 'Do you want us to work side by side like we used to?'

'Not yet. You get your business going first.'

'What then?'

'I could dig for victory in Dolly's allotment, I suppose. Or else, they always need women in the ammunition factories.'

She didn't sound too keen. Tommy tried to envisage how Edie could make the most of her abilities. 'Got it!' Blimey, he was inspired today. 'Come back and drive an ambulance for the WVS. That'd suit you down to the ground.'

Edie smiled. 'Tommy, you're a genius!'

'The perfect job, eh?'

No problem seemed too difficult. Tommy's confidence soared. They spent the afternoon wandering hand in hand down lanes, picking late blackberries from the hedgerows, looking out over black, ploughed fields and counting the days until they could be together.

A letter from Ronnie crossed with Meggie's in the chaotic wartime postal system.

Meggie was up and about at last, trying to make herself useful at the Duke, but only able to put in an hour or two's light work. Her post office employers had promised to hold her job open; girls like her were few and far between, they let it be known. When the letter dropped on the mat at number 32, Sadie ran up to the Duke with it, her face showing she was glad to be the bearer of good news for once.

'Aren't you gonna open it?' She found Meggie sitting upstairs. 'Look who it's from. Go on, it ain't gonna blow up in your face!'

'I don't know if I can.' Meggie's hand hovered over the envelope. So far, her road back to normality hadn't included being able to admit the truth about her and Ronnie. She avoided it even in her own mind, as if by ignoring the disaster she could anaesthetize that part of her brain, and in turn numb her heart. A letter from him was in fact the last thing she wanted.

'Do you want me to read it?' Sadie offered. She thought she understood; it was the pain of separation, the disappointment over Ronnie's last cancelled leave.

'No.' She gave an exasperated cry. 'Oh, I'm sorry, Ma. I never meant to bite your head off.'

'I'll leave it here, then.' Sadie withdrew.

At the door she hesitated. 'I'm baking scones for tea. Will you come down?'

Meggie nodded. 'I'll see you later.'

The letter lay on the arm of the chair for half an hour. The clock on the mantelpiece chimed. Hettie came and went. At last Meggie picked it up. She opened it with great care, as if the envelope was both fragile and precious. Ronnie's letter, dated Sunday 6th October, was loving and tender.

He'd written it when his ship was cruising off the Portuguese coast, heading for Gibraltar. He and all his mates were mad at having their leave cancelled just like that, but in His Majesty's senior service they had come to expect it. The timing couldn't have been worse as far as he was concerned, since it had stopped him from holding her in his arms and telling her how much he still loved her.

There was more of this; much more. Ronnie's hopes and dreams were undimmed. He knew she would have been there at Victoria Station waiting for him. Whatever was bothering her could have been swept away. They would have made proper, firm plans to be married.

'Write to me soon, Meggie. I want to know how you are and how things are going with your family. Could you send me a photo? God knows where I'll be when you get this letter, but you can be sure of one thing. You'll always be my Number One girl.'

It was signed with all his love.

Meggie took the letter down the court to her mother, glad that she'd saved her from the whole truth about Richie. Sadie was won over by its sincere, boyish tone. She folded it and looked at her daughter with shining eyes.

'I wrote to him two days ago.' Meggie's voice was flat. 'I broke it off, Ma. I had to.'

October gold faded into russet browns and greys. Mornings and evenings grew misty. There was more talk in the shelters of Bomber Command setting out on retaliatory air raids over Cologne, Hamburg and Dresden. Most were on the side of Coventrating Germany and getting the whole thing over and done with, whatever the cost.

George Mann succeeded in locating Richie Palmer, who was so debilitated by drinking and a poor diet that he acquiesced to attempts to get him lodgings in the Bear Lane hostel. He turned out not to be a violent drunk, but more likely to wreck his own life and leave others out of it, dedicated to self-destruction. The dilemma of whether or not to give him funds as well as a roof over his head was an ongoing one. If they didn't give him money, he would go out and beg on the streets. On the other hand, could it be right to give him the wherewithal to bring about his final demise? Hettie, Annie and George pondered long and hard.

'One thing, we've no need to worry about him turning grateful on us,' George told them wryly. 'The air turns blue if anyone mentions the Parsons name to him.'

Annie grimaced. 'Poor Meggie.' They were all still worried about her.

'You know, Richie was the first one she mentioned when she came to her senses,' Hettie said. 'If he did but know it.'

November crept in. The days shortened. America entered the war at last after the bombing of Pearl Harbor. Flagging patriotic spirits revived.

One afternoon, on a dull, cloud-laden Wednesday, Gertie Elliot came to Paradise Court. She asked for Meggie's house and took directions from Dolly Ogden.

'That's her house, number thirty-two. But try up at the Duke first. That's where she'll be.' Dolly couldn't make out Gertie's business. She looked well set-up in her fur-collared coat and matching hat, but she was a troubled woman. She was practically shaking like a leaf as she turned back towards the pub.

Gertie stood looking at the sign above the door. The Duke was a big place compared with the Bell; built later and on a larger scale. It was well run; everything spick and span. She allowed small details to divert her; the name of the licensee; George Alfred Mann, the tulip designs in the stained-glass doorway.

Annie came out, asking if she could help. They were closed; was it a private matter?

Gertie nodded. 'Is Meggie here?'

Annie didn't ask questions. This was something important; there was a look on the woman's handsome face that wouldn't brook excuses and argument. She led her upstairs onto the landing. 'Wait here,' she said quietly. 'Who shall I say wants to see her?'

'Gertie Elliot.'

She hid her surprise, went and brought Meggie out. 'Do you want me to stay?' she asked her granddaughter.

Meggie nodded. She clasped her hands in front of her and listened attentively, like a schoolchild.

Gertie spoke calmly. 'I had to come and tell you myself. I got a telegram this morning, from the Admiralty. Ronnie's ship went

539

down. They say he's missing, presumed dead.'

Ashes. A bitterness that could only be described as the taste of ashes. Shocked to the core, Meggie took the news quietly. It was Gertie Elliot who fell into Annie's arms. The mother's grief was inconsolable.

Sadie came and gathered the news from Hettie, alerted by Dolly Ogden to the fact that a stranger had come asking for Meggie. She saw her daughter suspended in a state of disbelief, standing by and watching Gertie sob. The poor woman's heart was broken.

Slowly Meggie fitted together the pieces. In a way her own grief was bound to be less than Gertie's. After all, Ronnie was already lost to her. But she could scarcely believe that he had been robbed of his future. She needed to hear more. How fast had the ship gone down? Were all hands lost? Would it have been quick?

But, of course, they could know none of that. Ashes in the water. Meggie prayed for Ronnie, now and always the love of her life.

'What do you need?' Sadie took over from Annie and led Gertie into the living room. 'Is there anything we can do?'

'They say he's dead.' She rocked back and forth. 'He won't come home.'

'Let us help. Who can we ring?'

'No one.'

'Ring the Bell. Ask for Shankley,' Meggie suggested, out of the depths of her own despair.

After a time, Gertie grew quiet. She gripped Meggie's hand. 'God forgive me.'

'And us all,' Hettie gave the heartfelt rejoinder.

'I never meant you no harm. I pitied you when Shankley told me the truth. But I was trapped, knowing what I did. And I couldn't bear to break it to Ronnie. It would have driven him away from me for good, knowing that I'd lied to him all his life.'

'Don't talk any more,' Meggie begged. 'Ronnie loved me, and he loved you too. That's all that counts.'

The two women shared their sorrow.

Shankley came to collect Ronnie's mother. But as he led her to a taxi, Gertie pulled back and looked again for Meggie.

'Here I am.' Meggie stared at the grief-torn features, seemed to understand the unspoken question, and drew her aside. 'We won't be seeing one another no more, so listen. Richie's being cared for over this side of the water. No need to worry on that score. And I've kept your secret.'

Gertie drew a sharp breath. 'You ain't told no one?'

'Not even Ronnie.' She would take it to her own grave, in memory of him.

The women in Meggie's family knew better than to ask her about her final conversation with the landlady at the Bell. Some things were too private to speak of. Annie saw to it that Gertie went safely on her way with Shankley. She offered her deepest sympathies, took her by the hand and shared her sorrow. 'You'll find a way through,' she promised.

Gertie rode off down Duke Street. Futility was all she felt. As yet, no memories of Ronnie as a little boy, as a tall young man in Navy uniform, shone through the darkness.

Hettie and Sadie waited anxiously for the storm of grief to break over Meggie. They wondered if she had the strength of mind and faith to bear it. But for Meggie the news had thrown her beyond the orbit of customary emotions. She contemplated a death by drowning. A deeply held fear for some became an intriguing possibility; to sink through clear green water, feel the surge of bubbles rise against the skin, to become weightless, to drift on the sea bed.

'Meggie?' Sadie watched her sink to the

floor, and put out her arms to catch her.

She revived. 'Ma, can I come home?' Clinging to her mother, holding on to life, she returned to their house.

A few days later, she spoke once about Ronnie. 'Maybe he never got my last letter,' she said wistfully. She helped Sadie pack a parcel of new socks and shirts to send off to Bertie and Geoff: 'I'd like that to be the way it was.' She hoped Ronnie had died with his faith in her intact.

CHAPTER TWENTY-SEVEN

'Ten-a-penny,' was Dolly's opinion on war brides. 'Rushing to join the queue. It ain't nice.'

In spite of the war, the approach of Christmas 1941 brought celebration to the forefront amongst families in the East End. It was a time for family gatherings, when mothers prayed for holiday leave for their servicemen sons. Fathers grew gung-ho about the Tommy's gritty spirit and down-played the power of the suave Yanks who had come in late, shouting the odds.

'Edie ain't rushing nowhere,' Annie argued. They stood together on the steps of Southwark registry office waiting for the bride and groom; Annie in a dark blue wool dress, matching coat with astrakhan collar and jaunty hat. Dolly had done herself up for the occasion too, she noticed. 'She's taken her time, done things right.'

Dolly wasn't convinced. 'What's a wedding without all the trimmings? I like a white wedding, with flowers.'

'I hear she looks a treat.' Annie ignored

Dolly's grumblings and surveyed the party of guests; the men in pinstripes, with nice white collars and ties, the women got up in natty dog-tooth checks, smart velvet, big fur collars. Duke Street had gathered for the occasion, though Tommy and Edie had deserted them for a flat by the cathedral. Rob was there with Amy, trying not to look too impressed, she thought. She went down the steps to talk to her stepson.

'It's bleeding cold.' He blew into his hands. 'Can't they get a move on in there before we all freeze to death?' The couple before Edie and Tommy were taking their time. 'How long does it take to sign a bleeding piece of paper?'

Amy raised her eyebrows at the language.

'You look lovely.' Annie turned her attention to Amy's wide-shouldered, bold-checked jacket and black hat. 'Now go and cheer your ma up, for God's sake, before she puts a dampener on things.' She watched her go and take Dolly in hand.

The Parsons had arrived in force for the wedding; Hettie with George, Frances over from Walworth with Billy for the day. Even Jess, Maurice and Grace had come down from Manchester, bringing Sadie's boys home for Christmas. This made the family complete for once. Bertie and Geoff stood

545

on the steps in little tweed jackets, hair parted and brylcreemed, just like their pa's.

Annie mingled once more. She didn't feel the cold, going about with pride, keeping at bay her own sadness over Ernie, her concern for poor Meggie.

'Ma.' Jess turned to include her in their small group. 'You shouldn't be standing out here. Can't we find you a seat inside?'

Annie tutted. 'I'm fine where I am, ta.' She enjoyed being at the hub of things, asked Maurice if customers were still flocking to his cinemas despite the blackouts and the shortages.

'More like because of them,' he reported. Tall, distinguished, with his grey hair swept back from his brow, sombre in a black coat, despite the occasion. Jess and Grace were also in mourning.

'People can't get enough of the Hollywood stars,' Jess said.

'Nor the home-grown ones neither.' Business was booming. Maurice had lifted himself out of his poor beginnings through single-minded determination. He was thought of in the family as rather dour, even before the tragedy of losing Mo. Now his face had fixed into serious lines; the set of his jaw, the hollowness of his cheeks. Still, he doted on Jess, gave her plenty of space to run her own life, and looked now to Grace as the one in line to take on everything he'd worked for.

Annie chatted and moved on.

'All we need now is for the sirens to start,' Dolly moaned, looking at her watch. She looked askance at Charlie, whose head was full of Dorothy and no one but. The two of them billed and cooed in a corner. 'What's keeping that car, that's what I'd like to know.'

'Listen, Ma, why don't you come and sit in the warm in Rob's cab?' Amy suggested. She began to steer her mother down the steps, but as they reached the pavement she saw the hired wedding car approach. 'Here they come!' she called.

There was a shuffling, a rearrangement of hats, a jostling for a better view. Lorna Bennett and some of Edie's old workmates pushed to the front, as the bride and groom stepped from the car.

Edie wore a knee-length cream wool dress; slim, with wide shoulders and ruched right down the long sleeves. She had a corsage of deep red roses, and roses in her blonde hair.

'One of Hettie and Jess's creations,' Annie murmured. 'They can work wonders, even with what Edie could get on her coupons.'

She didn't care if it was blowing her own trumpet, letting people know how proud she was of all her stepchildren.

Tommy stood by the car, holding out his arm and waiting for Edie to slide her hand through. Looking up at the crowded steps and stone portico, he squared his shoulders. Getting married was something to be got through as quick as possible. He marched her up, through the door, into the registrar's room.

The plain ceremony, the solemn promises were soon over, but they cured Tommy's nerves. 'I, Thomas O'Hagan, take thee, Edith Mary Morell . . .' Now he knew why he'd put himself through the ordeal. He and Edie could put the past behind them. They were man and wife.

Edie stooped to sign the certificate, a new band of gold on the hand that held the book in place. It was more than she deserved, surrounded by friends, with her husband at her side.

The cameras clicked, the confetti flew on the registry office steps. There was to be a small reception at the Duke. The guests trooped to their cars or set off to catch cabs and buses. The next couple filed in.

Meggie stayed to watch them enter, her mind elsewhere. 'I, Margaret Davidson, take thee, Ronald Edward Elliot . . .' Weeks had gone by since the telegram. Not a scrap of further information. Missing, presumed dead.

Sadie took her hand as Walter went ahead with the boys. They waited for a moment while Meggie regained her composure.

Meggie sighed, gave a ghost of a smile.

'Lovely, wasn't it?' said Sadie. Meggie had insisted on coming, God bless her.

She nodded.

That morning a letter had arrived, addressed in her own handwriting to Able Seaman Ronnie Elliot. It was unopened. Meggie went to her room and sat with it in her lap. Every word enclosed in the dog-eared, stained envelope was etched in her mind. 'This is goodbye, Ronnie. I want you to forget me and live a happy life.' *Without me.*

An hour before Edie's wedding, Meggie had gone downstairs to the living room, knelt on the hearthrug, taken the poker and thrust the letter, still inside its grubby envelope, to the back of the fire.

If it had been summer, she would have taken flowers to the river and thrown them in, cast them adrift in Ronnie's memory. As it was, an icy wind cut through her wedding clothes as she went empty-handed and stood, looking east down the wide estuary, at the turn of the tide.

A spread was laid on at the pub, courtesy of George, Hettie and Annie.

'Like the good old days,' Dolly conceded at the height of the music from the piano; the singing and dancing. Old friends met up, had a drink together. Even Charlie and Dorothy showed their faces once things were underway.

The young ones: Bobby, Jimmie, Lorna and company, made it go with a swing.

'Say it with music!' Jimmie swirled a girl into the middle of the floor. 'Roll back the carpet and dance the night away!' His tweed jacket and silk cravat, bought on the proceeds of his share in Tommy's new business, set him up in his own mind as a star from the flicks; as a 'right pippin', according to Dolly.

Their energy and enthusiasm were catching. Soon Walter took Sadie away from her stint behind the bar to dance a slow waltz and in the next number even Maurice and Jess circulated amongst the guests.

When they were sure that the celebrations would continue without them, Tommy and Edie slipped away into the cold night air. They walked up Duke Street past Edie's old flat to the new one Tommy had rented in the close behind the cathedral. The blackout shrouded the bombed buildings in darkness and gave the inhabited ones a strangely unlived-in air. An ambulance picked its way quietly towards London Bridge. As yet, the night was free of enemy raids.

They walked as far as the river, hand in hand. Anti-aircraft guns lined Bankside, standing ready beside the fire-pump trailers. The silent current swept by, gleaming in the moonlight.

Then they turned and passed by the huge bulk of the cathedral, across its flagged court, down narrow streets to the close where they would live from now on.

We hope you have enjoyed this Large Print book. Other Thorndike Press or Chivers Press Large Print books are available at your library or directly from the publishers.

For more information about current and upcoming titles, please call or write, without obligation, to:

Thorndike Press
P.O. Box 159
Thorndike, Maine 04986 USA
Tel. (800) 257-5157

OR

Chivers Press Limited
Windsor Bridge Road
Bath BA2 3AX
England
Tel. (0225) 335336

All our Large Print titles are designed for easy reading, and all our books are made to last.